A CURTAIN

FALLS

A CURTAIN
FALLS

Stefanie Pintoff

Minotaur Books
New York

This is a work of fiction. All of the characters, organizations, and events portrayed in this novel are either products of the author's imagination or are used fictitiously.

A CURTAIN FALLS. Copyright © 2010 by Stefanie Pintoff. All rights reserved. Printed in the United States of America. For information address St. Martin's Press, 175 Fifth Avenue, New York, N.Y. 10010.

www.minotaurbooks.com

Library of Congress Cataloging-in-Publication Data

Pintoff, Stefanie.
   A curtain falls / Stefanie Pintoff—1st ed.
      p. cm.
   ISBN 978-0-312-58396-5
   1. Police—New York (State)—Fiction.   2. Girls—Crimes against—
Fiction.   3. Serial murder investigation—Fiction.   I. Title.
   PS3616.I58C87 2010
   813'.6—dc22

                                          2010008708

First Edition: May 2010

10 9 8 7 6 5 4 3 2 1

For Craig and Maddie, without whom . . .

ACKNOWLEDGMENTS

No book comes into being without the support of many people, each of whom has my sincere thanks. I owe my editor, Kelley Ragland, and her keen eye a great debt. My agent, David Hale Smith, is an invaluable source of encouragement and sound advice. Many thanks as well to so many others I've gotten to know at Minotaur: Andy Martin, Matt Martz, Hector DeJean, Anne Gardner, copy editor Fran Fisher, and all others who have played a role in bringing this book to publication.

I also owe much to Natalie Kapetanios Meir for her insightful feedback and unwavering encouragement—as well as to Karen Odden and Mark Longaker, for their exceptional attention to detail. Thanks to Alison Sheehy for things theatrical and to Luci Hansson Zahray for things poisonous. As always, the staff at

ACKNOWLEDGMENTS

the New York Public Library and Bobst Library at New York University have been wonderful.

Special thanks to Allen and Bobbi Pintoff, as well as Julie Torre; each has truly gone above and beyond. I also am grateful to James Hackett and Theresa Alvarez Hackett, Tim and Jill Vincent, April Longaker, Julie Cameron, Ed and Betty Smith, Chuck and Dotty Greenberg, and Scott and Erika Pintoff for going the extra mile in support of my career. Thanks also to all other friends and family who have done so much for me.

Most of all, thank you to Craig, my best friend and writing partner—without whom this book wouldn't be possible.

PART
ONE

Crime is terribly revealing.
Try and vary your methods as you will,
your tastes, your habits, your attitude of mind,
and your soul is revealed by your actions.
                              —Agatha Christie

Friday
March 16, 1906

CHAPTER 1

Criminal Courts Building, opposite the Tombs

Some will claim you can cut to the truth from the look in a person's eye.

I cannot. But with solid evidence, I can expose what might otherwise deceive. Usually, that is. For there are people so practiced in the art of deception that, no matter the evidence stacked against them, they persuade the most skeptical among us to believe a fairy tale. And no one had done it better than the woman who now sat at the massive wooden table opposite the judge, her thin hands pressed palm to palm as if in prayer, awaiting the jury's verdict.

For three days, I had marveled at her performance. She had dressed the part to perfection with a white lace-edged shirtwaist, a black gored skirt, button boots, and kid gloves. The effect was stylish yet conservative and sober—as befit a lady in mourning for her husband. As she answered each question on the witness stand, her manner had been shy and demure. Her voice, always tremulous, suggested she was just on the verge of tears. And throughout, she displayed a wide-eyed innocent stare, as though she could not quite believe what was happening to her. But what was truly an art was the timing with which her blue eyes watered just before she gazed through long, dark lashes toward the twelve men on the jury. Her every gesture was designed to convince them of one important truth: that she was completely incapable of the cold-blooded murder for which she stood accused.

Her defense attorneys, two oversized men wearing ill-fitting gray suits, flanked her closely. Too closely, in fact. Next to them, she appeared frail, helpless, and vulnerable. I had no doubt that was exactly her plan.

What would the jury believe: the evidence—or the story the woman had spun?

Her case should have been a simple one, open and shut. She was accused of first-degree murder. The prosecutor's argument had been persuasive, outlining how she had tired of her husband and desired her freedom. Others might have opted for divorce, but she had chosen a less conventional method—and replaced her husband's bottle of Emerson's Bromo-Seltzer with cyanide of mercury. And so, on the occasion of his last headache, he had reached into his medicine cabinet and taken poison instead of a cure. After four days of tremendous pain and violent retching, he had died.

It could not have been an easy death to witness. It should not have rested easily on her conscience.

"Gentlemen of the jury, have you reached a verdict?" The judge intoned the words the law required of him.

The woman twisted a gloved finger.

"We have, Your Honor," the foreman replied, his voice low and grave.

"Defendant, please rise," said the judge.

Her defense attorneys pulled her to her feet after she fell against the table, seemingly drained of her last ounce of strength. Her pale face beseeched the jury foreman for mercy.

He returned her gaze without self-consciousness, and I knew the verdict at once—even before the words *not guilty* sounded throughout the courtroom.

Amid gasps of surprise and murmuring voices, I turned away and quickly exited the rear of the building, eager to reach the street before the shouting crowds and hordes of news reporters swallowed me whole.

It was a bitter disappointment. I had arrested her and secured the incriminating evidence against her: the testimony of the doctor who detected the strong smell of almond; the records of the pharmacist who had sold her the poison; the words of the friend in whom she had confided her marriage troubles. The evidence was circumstantial, but solid. I had offered the truth, and her performance had refuted it. I could do no more.

My feet landed with a heavy thud on each step as I ran down the stairs toward Franklin Street. It would have been a loss, of course, no matter the verdict. Justice was imperfect, even when the verdict was guilty. No trial could restore the dead to life. Or change the fact that, in this case, a nine-year-old girl's future had been forever altered by the trial of her mother, the death of her father.

What mattered was the risk this woman posed in the months and years to come. Would she kill again? Or had she been so thoroughly scared by her close call with the executioner, and her brief imprisonment in the Tombs, that she would now abide by the law? It was possible.

But the act of shedding blood once made it easier to do twice—or so I believed. I had never taken the life of another, though I had certainly known my share of danger. It was a line I hoped never to cross.

"Detective! Detective Ziele!" The voice that called out to me was loud and self-important. A sergeant huffed behind me, his large baby face lined with beads of sweat as he tried to catch up. As I stopped to wait for him, I realized I must have been practically sprinting as I made my way toward the City Hall subway station.

"Captain Mulvaney told me you'd be finishing up at the courthouse. He sent me to give you the message that you're needed uptown."

Declan Mulvaney was the burly Irishman who had been my partner in the earliest days of my career, when I was a patrolman on the Lower East Side. He had recently been promoted to captain of the Nineteenth Precinct, which covered the Tenderloin—an area that vied with the Lower East Side for the dubious honor of being the city's most crime-ridden neighborhood. Though our careers had diverged along different paths, we had remained close. And it was unlike him to summon me in this manner.

The officer now clutched his side, out of breath. He was displeased to be executing this summons. Normally, a sergeant would have avoided this sort of errand, so there must have been no one else available.

"What's happened?" I began to walk again, forcing the sergeant to follow me.

"The captain needs you at the Garrick Theater. From the sound of it, someone put on quite a show this morning." He smirked, pleased with his own sense of humor.

"Mulvaney's waiting for me there?" I asked, determined to ignore the man's attitude.

"Yeah." His response was gruff. "There's been a murder. Some actress killed."

I stopped walking and turned abruptly to face the man. "There are murders every day, all over this city. And Mulvaney's in charge of one of the largest precincts. Why does he need me for this one?"

As captain, Mulvaney had no shortage of resources. If he had asked for my help, then it was for a specific reason. These days, I split my time between the city and the village of Dobson, fifteen miles to the north, where I had moved almost a year ago with every intention of settling into a quiet life. But my colleagues in the city—and the lack of any real work in Dobson since my last case, a tragic murder, had ended four months ago—seemed to dictate otherwise.

The sergeant looked at me in a way that made clear he was sizing me up, trying to decide what to tell me. That he knew little and was authorized to say nothing was to be expected. But rumors had certainly reached his ears, of that I was certain. And he needed my cooperation.

"My guess is the case involves someone important. The big brass are keeping news of the murder under close wraps, and they've got a man in custody already for questioning," he finally said.

It was likely that the sergeant was right. If a suspect was in custody already, then either significant evidence had been left at

the scene—or there had been pressure to arrest someone immediately for show. But neither rationale explained why Mulvaney
would want to involve me. There must be some additional complexity to the case.

Mulvaney's sergeant went his own way once I reached the
City Hall station and descended the stairs.

As I waited on the subway platform, I became aware of someone else—a man—behind me. He stared intently in my direction.

I moved several feet farther into the crowd.

But as I edged down the platform, he seemed to follow me,
drawing closer and closer. Downtown, so near the courts buildings, I could not help thinking of those I had helped to bring to
justice over the years. No doubt many harbored a grudge.

The man drew even closer.

Just then my train arrived, rushing to a stop with a great
gust of air. The doors opened, and as passengers disembarked, I
stole a backward glance and caught a glimpse of his face. Underneath a brown derby set at a jaunty angle, his sharp nose and
protruding chin were oddly familiar. Was it—?

But no. I must be mistaken. After so many years, it would
be impossible.

I stepped into the train, the doors slammed shut, and the man
remained behind. Through the window, I watched him disappear
into the crowd. But the memory of his face continued to trouble
me all the way uptown, until I reached my stop and my thoughts
returned to the crime scene awaiting me at the Garrick Theater.

CHAPTER 2

The Garrick Theater, 67 West Thirty-fifth Street

It had begun snowing and the air was thick with oversized flakes. They transformed the sky into a mass of white, but melted the moment they reached the ground, creating a slush of mud and sand. A typical March snow. I shivered as a few flakes made their way underneath my scarf to the warmth of my neck, and I became conscious of the dull ache in my right arm, aggravated as always by the cold and damp. I'd learned to anticipate the pain in such weather—ever since the day two summers ago when I'd injured my arm aboard a rescue boat taking in survivors from the *Slocum* disaster. Though the injury should have been temporary, the poor skills of the doctor who treated me had rendered it permanent.

I thrust such thoughts out of my mind as I turned onto West Thirty-fifth Street, dodging a horse and carriage that careened around the corner. It was trying to avoid a polished black auto-mobile that monopolized the center of the street, occasionally sliding on the wet road. The streets were filled with horses and cars, bicyclists and pedestrians, creating a free-for-all of sorts. It was no wonder the daily papers were filled with accident reports.

As I approached the Garrick Theater, I was immediately struck by the fact that the sergeant was right: for whatever reason, the murder inside was being kept quiet. No police officer stood outside the theater, though it would have been standard protocol to post someone by the door to keep the public at bay and deflect the questions of reporters and curious onlookers. Where I would have expected a bustle of activity, today it was as deserted as the surrounding theaters.

At this hour of the morning—it was near eleven o'clock—the theater district slept. It would be late afternoon before ticket offices opened and actors arrived for makeup and rehearsals. Only come evening would the entire neighborhood light up with the electric billboards that adorned each theater's marquee and gave Broadway its newest nickname: the Great White Way.

I entered the Garrick through its grand columned entrance into the red-velvet lobby, beyond a large, polished oak ticket booth, and went into the main house, where I finally observed small groups of policemen hard at work. The hysterical wail of a woman arose from somewhere backstage. Organization and chaos almost always existed side by side at a crime scene.

What commanded my attention, however, was the scene onstage—where a single spotlight centered on a woman. She reclined in a pose that stretched the complete length of a green-

and-gold settee, surrounded by a full set of props and scenery. Her hair, studded with glittering jewels, was piled atop her head in a mass of rich mahogany curls, some of which draped beguilingly upon a pillow above the armrest. She wore a frilled concoction of garnet satin, bordered by lace and ruby sequins that sparkled under the glare of the lights. Her face was fully made up, with rouged lips and cheeks, and she looked directly forward, not at all shy of the spotlight's glare. And when I gathered myself and walked down the center aisle toward the stage, her eyes seemed to meet my own, their bright cornflower blue framed by a dark circle of mascara. She was more stunning than I could ever have imagined and looked every bit a majestic leading lady.

Except that she was dead.

As I made my way toward Mulvaney, whose broad, six-foot frame towered above his companion's, I swallowed hard, for thick dust had caught in my throat. It always did in enclosed, windowless spaces. Today, in the spotlight's glare, I could actually see the offending particles floating in the air.

Mulvaney's voice was clear as it rose above the din of police activity, loud and determined. "Wilcox said to move nothing. So I'm moving nothing 'til he gets back."

He referred, of course, to Max Wilcox—the new coroner's physician who regularly worked cases here in the Tenderloin.

The shorter man's voice sounded angry. "Did you tell the doctor she's been here since late last night? We can't leave her like this for much longer. It's indecent. And Frohman's man will have a fit if he can't set up on schedule for tonight's performance."

"There's been murder done in this theater, by God. His schedule will adapt." Mulvaney roared the words, but the cadences of his thick Irish brogue could not help but mute the sting they might otherwise have held. He crossed his arms defiantly.

The man arguing with Mulvaney was small and dark, with a compact body and narrow black eyes. He wore a drab brown suit, which made me suspect that he was a plainclothes detective. Whoever he was, he was not particularly intimidated by Mulvaney's rank.

"Frohman's got connections, you know. You make him cancel when he doesn't want to, you'll pay a steep price."

I knew that Charles Frohman was the founder and manager of the Theater Syndicate, which ran more theaters than any company in the world. Well connected and not easily crossed, he ruled the Great White Way, which was so important to the city's burgeoning economy, with a tight control that his detractors said was actually a stranglehold.

But Mulvaney was not one to be intimidated, either—though as a new precinct captain, he would do well to avoid making powerful political enemies. When he spoke next, it was with some restraint. "The world doesn't revolve around Charles Frohman, whatever he and those who work for him may think. She stays 'til Wilcox comes. If tonight's performance is canceled as a result, then so be it."

The other man's eyes narrowed.

Backstage, the woman's hysterics rose to a high-pitched scream that made Mulvaney flinch, though he greeted me warmly as I approached.

I responded in turn before offering my hand to the man in the brown suit. Mulvaney introduced him as David Marwin, a senior detective under his command.

"I hear you've worked with Mulvaney before," Marwin

said. "Why don't *you* try to talk some sense into him?" He then excused himself to join the ongoing search backstage.

Mulvaney waited until the detective was no longer in sight. "Once you get around the fact that he's too pleased with himself, he's not a bad fellow." Then he looked at me, one eyebrow raised. "Lucky I knew you were in the city today for the Snyder case. The verdict came down, I assume?"

I nodded, my expression grim.

"She got off, then." He shook his head. "Well, juries can be a wild card. And I heard your defendant was a real looker," he added knowingly.

Another shrill cry was audible behind us.

"Who's the screamer?" I asked.

"Miss Lily Bowen, the leading lady here. I understand she is upset about her dress. *That*," Mulvaney motioned to the corpse onstage, "is her dress. We brought Miss Bowen in early today to determine if there was some connection."

At the sound of another screeching wail, Mulvaney shuddered, then recovered himself. "Not that she's been much use to us. I'm glad you came. I've got to admit, this is one of the more disturbing cases I've seen," he said.

I gazed again at the dead woman, who now loomed large above us to the left. "Who is she?"

"Name's Annie Germaine. She was a chorus girl in *The Shepherd's Daughter*, which has played here the past three weeks. Of course, as a chorus girl, she looked nothing like this. She's made up and dressed like the star."

"Any idea why?" I asked.

"Not yet." Mulvaney seemed distracted by thoughts of his own as he walked to center stage and paused, studying the

actress as though he were seeing her for the first time. "According to the stage manager—his name is Leon Iseman—everything
she is wearing belongs to Miss Bowen, even the wig and jewels.
It was all locked in Miss Bowen's wardrobe closet. The key is
missing, and there's no sign the lock was tampered with."

"The key wasn't found near the victim?"

Mulvaney indicated that it was not, then said, "Miss Germaine normally looks very different. The question is: did she
dress herself this way—or was it the work of her killer?"

I looked into her unseeing blue eyes.

"How did she die?"

"I don't have a clue." Mulvaney leaned against the edge of
the stage and ran his right hand along the shaved stubble that
surrounded his balding head. "There's not a mark on her that I
could find."

He pulled out his pocket watch to check the time. "Almost
noon. What the devil is taking Wilcox so long?"

The coroner's physician was a professional who took his cases
seriously, though his terse style of communication won him few
friends. However, it was unlike him to leave a man of Mulvaney's
rank waiting without an explanation.

"Where is he?"

Mulvaney didn't answer. Just then, a woman burst through
the curtains, crying loudly, and a man I presumed to be the
stage manager followed closely behind. He was a stout man
in his forties with thick black hair and a stern face. She was
frantic, and her words were largely unintelligible. I caught only
phrases here and there: *my dress* and something about *her own
fault.*

At this last, Mr. Iseman caught up with the woman and

forcibly grabbed her. Her long brown hair, a mass of tangles, whipped around when she stopped.

"Listen," he said, his words a sharp hiss of anger. "You've got to stop this. Imagine if word of your behavior got around!"

The rest of it was inaudible, but it had its desired effect: she immediately quieted, emitting only an occasional sob that sounded more like a hiccup.

"Do I have to speak with them now?" She looked pointedly in our direction.

Mr. Iseman's reply was careful, but there was no mistaking his implicit warning. "You wouldn't want Mr. Frohman to hear that you'd been uncooperative, now would you?"

"Miss Bowen," Mulvaney said, walking toward her. "Come over here and take a seat." He directed her offstage, just beyond the curtain, and indicated that she should sit in one of three metal chairs pushed to the side. Designed for actors awaiting their cues to go onstage, the small waiting area was cramped; Mulvaney and Miss Bowen sat with knees so close they almost touched, while the stage manager and I hovered above. But at least the dead woman onstage was no longer in view.

Lily Bowen looked at us, biting her lip.

"We won't trouble you with many questions, as we understand this is a difficult time." Mulvaney managed to inflect a note of sympathetic understanding into his voice. But he spoke fast, and I could tell he was eager to get this particular interview out of the way. "Did you know Miss Germaine well?"

A flash of annoyance crossed her face as she said, "Of course I did not! She was a chorus girl." She seemed almost indignant, but then she caught Mr. Iseman's disapproving look, swallowed hard, and reframed her answer. "Miss Germaine and I were not especially friendly, but I have known her since rehearsals began and I'm very sorry about what's happened to her."

"When did you last see her?" Mulvaney asked, moving briskly through his questions.

"Last night around eleven o'clock. She was waiting by the stage door when I left."

"Who else was in the theater?"

"I don't know. I was among the last to leave—maybe even the last." She dabbed a tissue at each puffy red eye.

"Do you know why Miss Germaine was waiting? Did she have a new beau, perhaps?"

She laughed harshly. "I can't imagine. Any more than I can imagine why she went back inside and put on my clothes and my jewelry."

"Or why she ended up dead?" I couldn't help reminding her, for I disliked the contempt she wasn't bothering to conceal.

I regretted my comment at once, however, as I watched her eyes fill with tears. She made a show of pulling a clean handkerchief out of her pocket, all the while appearing to stifle giant sobs.

After Mulvaney asked her a few more, brief questions, she retired to her dressing room.

Mr. Iseman turned to Mulvaney and spoke in a stage whisper meant to be confidential. "Mr. Frohman and I would like your men to remove Miss Germaine's body to the basement as soon as possible. I've cleared ample space where it can be housed."

Mulvaney interrupted him. "That's kind of you, but don't worry—it won't be much longer 'til we have her out of here. The coroner's wagon will be here shortly."

"Actually, that's exactly what I'm worried about," Leon Iseman said. "It's late enough in the day that she may be seen. If word spreads of her death, people will assume tonight's show is canceled. They may even be frightened and decide to stay away all this week—or even longer."

Mulvaney's ire was rising. "So what do you propose? Leaving her in your basement indefinitely? I can assure you, Mr. Iseman, that arrangement is one you'd quickly grow to dislike. Let's just say that death's odor is not something you want in your theater."

"Mr. Frohman feels strongly that publicizing Miss Germaine's death would destroy our reputation and jeopardize the future prospects for this show. We'd like to keep her corpse here, just for today, hidden in the basement. After tonight's show is over and the crowd's gone home, the coroner's men would be welcome to claim her body."

Mulvaney laughed aloud at the absurdity of it. "You want to remove her body late tonight after the show, when no one will see?"

"Exactly." Leon Iseman gave Mulvaney an icy stare.

Mulvaney set his mouth in a firm line. "I've already explained that we're following protocol on this one and taking the body downtown as soon as Dr. Wilcox clears it. It would be downright illegal to do otherwise—and the commissioner would have my job."

"Perhaps. But Mr. Frohman may have it if you don't." Mr. Iseman stalked away once he'd issued his dark warning.

Mulvaney's face set in determination.

"I know something of Charles Frohman," I said. "But what I know doesn't explain why everyone here is so . . ." I searched for the right word to characterize the odd mix of deference and fear that I had observed in both Mr. Iseman and Miss Bowen.

"Absurdly cowed by the man?" Mulvaney made an irreverent face before he grew serious again. "At least where Miss Bowen is concerned, I think I understand," Mulvaney said. "When we say Charles Frohman runs the syndicate and manages hundreds of theaters, we can't forget that means he is handpicking those actors and actresses who will play in them. He has a reputation as a star-maker. If Miss Bowen wants to become—and remain—one of his featured performers, then she'd better play by his rules."

"And Mr. Iseman?"

Mulvaney flashed a big grin. "I'd guess the man is extremely well paid."

We were interrupted by Dr. Wilcox, who was at last making his way downstage, equipment bag in hand. He was a tall, rail-thin man with a bald head and black-rimmed glasses. Always lean, he appeared to have lost weight since I had last seen him, almost a year ago.

Without preliminaries, Max Wilcox acknowledged us with a nod and set to work. It would be a precursory exam only, designed to obtain the most basic of information before Annie Germaine's body was moved. Wearing thick cotton gloves, he leaned over the corpse and gingerly raised the woman's hair to examine her neck.

"You took photographs already?" he asked.

"First thing," Mulvaney said absently. "We photographed the stage area in general, and then focused on her. We got close-ups of her neck and face."

"Good." The coroner was approving. He slowly pulled a

metal hook out of his equipment bag and used it to turn the woman's eyelid inside out. Using light from an electric lamp—a new device powered by batteries—he peered closely behind each lid, then abruptly placed the lamp on the floor and began entering information into a small notebook he pulled from his jacket.

"Hmmph. Inconclusive." He frowned in disappointment.

Then, picking up his lamp again, he shone it first upon her neck, then into her mouth, which he pried open.

"As I expected." He shook his head. "Can't do much here. Can your boys load her in the wagon without manhandling her? I don't want any bruising that's not there already."

"That's just it. There aren't any bruises. In fact, there's nothing the naked eye can see." Mulvaney stated the obvious, which earned him a stern glare.

"Bruising can take hours to appear postmortem," the coroner said, admonishing him. "And there could well be internal bruising, should this turn out to be a strangulation."

"How else could she have died?" I asked.

"She might have been smothered." He shrugged. "Poison is also possible, although most poisons leave rather unpleasant physical markers that are absent here. But from the way she's decked out, it would suggest a suicide."

"It wasn't suicide, Max," Mulvaney said. "There must be something more you can give me now. I've got nothing to go on except the certain knowledge she was murdered." His voice was soft and cajoling, but his expression made clear he would not be denied.

Wilcox inclined his head. "The *certain* knowledge? Nothing is certain until science proves it, Captain."

"In this case, your science will confirm what I already know."

There was a quiet desperation in Mulvaney's voice that suggested a deeper unease. Mulvaney was obviously aware that he risked Charles Frohman's wrath by handling matters differently than the theater magnate preferred. The consequences of that might entail repercussions beyond anything Mulvaney had ever experienced. But I didn't believe that was the whole of it.

Wilcox cleared his throat again as he grudgingly set down his bag. As he made a show of rearranging his scarf with exaggerated care, he said, "Assuming you're convinced this is murder from other evidence—evidence you're not sharing with me, that is . . ." He let his words linger pointedly before he continued. "I can tell you I believe strangulation is the most likely possibility. Carefully done, it can leave no visible sign. But I won't be able to confirm that until I autopsy her, which will show whether there's been damage done to the cartilage of her larynx or to her hyoid bone. I'll send the wagon to get her right away."

But before he left, he picked up his bag and pivoted slightly. "And until I've checked her vitals and stomach contents," he said, "I'm not supporting your murder theory. She may be a suicide yet. I'll know soon. Science doesn't lie."

Mulvaney grumbled for a few moments after Wilcox left, and my gaze was once again drawn toward the dead woman on-stage. One chorus girl out of a hundred. Why her?

"Wilcox has it right on one count. There's something important you're not telling us," I said, choosing my words carefully. "Does it have to do with why you've brought me here?"

Mulvaney was silent. He collapsed in a seat in the first row and looked up at me helplessly, his eyes filled with worry.

"You mentioned there were no physical marks on her. Why are you so certain that she's been murdered?"

"Because if she wasn't murdered, then we don't have just one suicide." He spread his hands wide apart. "We've got two."

CHAPTER 3

The Garrick Theater, 67 West Thirty-fifth Street

A second murder. So that was what he had kept from Wilcox. And it was also, I was certain, the reason he had asked me here.

"You mean there has been another death similar to hers?" I asked, watching Mulvaney carefully.

He nodded but did not look at me, focusing instead on the woman whose lifeless eyes now gazed down at us. Then, as we heard noises—the footsteps of two officers who emerged from backstage, carrying boxes of evidence—Mulvaney turned to me and spoke in a hushed whisper. "Three weeks ago at the Empire, down the block, another actress died the same way. The cleaning girls who came the next morning found her just like this one," Mulvaney said, gesturing toward the stage. "Her name was Eliza Downs. She was all dressed up, posed center stage, and there was no sign of foul play. In fact, everyone assumed she was a suicide, so there was no investigation. We weren't even called."

"Then how do you know about it?"

"Mr. Iseman," he said, admitting it frankly. "You see, the Empire is another Frohman theater and Broadway's a small community. Word of Miss Downs's death spread fast and put a damper on morale." He drew himself up straight, stretching an arm that appeared cramped. "But Mr. Iseman had no reason to think her death was anything other than a tragic suicide until early this morning, when Miss Germaine's body was found in similar circumstances."

"They were both actresses. Do we know if they were acquainted? If so, they might have talked of suicide. Or if Miss Downs's death reverberated so soundly throughout the community, Miss Germaine may have chosen to copy Miss Downs when she decided to end her own life." I knew how unlikely it was, but it was my habit of mind to consider all possibilities, even if I came to discount them later.

"No," Mulvaney said, shaking his head soberly. "I wanted to think that, too. There's more." Mulvaney looked around as though worried someone might overhear our conversation, but the auditorium was empty except for us. Satisfied, he motioned for me to walk with him to the seat in the last row where he had put his personal effects.

"We found some notes. Letters. I don't know what to call them." He fumbled for words to explain. "One was found by the body of Miss Downs at the Empire, though they disregarded it at the time. It was full of poetic nonsense about dying—and Mr. Iseman assumed it was a suicide note. But when he found this note just like it, next to Miss Germaine's body, he became suspicious."

He reached into his worn leather bag, which had anchored some papers. Using the edge of his handkerchief, he passed me a single sheet of eggshell-blue paper; I took it gingerly, being careful to touch only the cloth. The writing was in a slanted, spidery hand.

> *Once again, I have chosen a young girl lacking in natural attractions, and given her what Nature did not. Call me Pygmalion; call her Galatea, my greatest creation. Like one of the greatest poets of our English language, I say:*
> *Yet I'll not shed her blood,*
> *Nor scar that whiter skin of hers than snow,*
> *And smooth as monumental alabaster.*

Mulvaney looked at me expectantly. I cleared my throat, trying to shake off the uncomfortable sensation that had taken hold of me.

"What does it mean?" I asked. "'Call me Pygmalion.' And this business about not shedding her blood makes no sense. Is he actually trying to say he didn't kill her?"

"Thought you'd know," he said with a knowing smile. "You at least have a couple years' college under your belt." He threw up his hands in mock defeat. "I couldn't make sense of it, either. Mr. Iseman explained what I know of it, which is basically that the killer wanted her to look good in death. Annie was a plain girl, a strong dancer and able chorus member. But he claims she'd never have been a leading lady. Didn't have the looks for it."

"According to Mr. Iseman only, I presume." I shook my head as I once again surveyed the figure onstage. The dress and makeup must have radically changed her usual appearance, because whatever the woman in front of me may have lacked in talent or ability, she was certainly pleasing to the eye. Besides, plenty of actresses without conventional good looks were successful on stage. Sarah Bernhardt, for one.

"Good point," Mulvaney agreed. "She made up pretty well, once someone put the effort into her. We're going to see what the other actors and actresses have to say when they come in for rehearsal in a couple hours. But it's clear she didn't normally dress this way."

"Did you find anything in her dressing room that relates to the letter?"

"She was a chorus girl, Ziele. She didn't have a dressing room. I gather she used a common area in back. We're searching it and all the rooms backstage, of course." Mulvaney sighed in exasperation. "But so far, nothing out of the ordinary has turned up."

"Did anyone keep the note Mr. Iseman found near Eliza Downs?" I asked. Right now the letters seemed the only promising connection between the two deaths.

Mulvaney cleared his throat. "Iseman kept the note himself—though why he would keep a suicide note, I don't know. He turned it over to us early this morning when he came in to report Miss Germaine's death. It's in the evidence file at the precinct house, so I'll show you when we get back. The content is similar, right down to the wording about Pygmalion. But the poetry's different."

"If there are matching fingerprints on both letters, we'd have a solid connection," I mused aloud.

"We had it dusted—but you know *that* won't necessarily do us any good," he said, muttering the words under his breath.

He was right that it would do no good officially. Finger-printing was still a new technology that had yet to be accepted by the courts, or even by many policemen. But unofficially, many of us were beginning to rely on it.

"And these letters," I said, "are presumably why you wanted to involve me?"

"In part." He furrowed his brow as another troubling thought occurred to him. He seemed distracted as he continued. "I'd like you to talk with someone I've got in custody at the pre-cinct house. His name is Timothy Poe. He's an actor."

"From what I've seen this morning," I said, "it seems as though you've got precious little evidence to warrant taking anyone into custody."

Mulvaney jabbed his finger at the eggshell-blue paper. "You see all these references to someone called Pygmalion. According to Mr. Iseman, *Pygmalion* is a show that was revived last fall. And guess who played the starring role?"

"Had to be Poe," I deadpanned.

"Literally, he played Pygmalion to her Galatea." Mulvaney was quite pleased with himself. "Makes perfect sense, doesn't it?"

"*Too* perfect sense," I said. "If he's going to incriminate himself by leaving a message, why bother with all the fuss and poetry? He might just as well have signed his name."

Mulvaney cocked his head. "He also knew Annie Ger-maine. She even substituted in *Pygmalion* for a few weeks when another actress was laid up sick."

"As Galatea?" I asked. "That would fit nicely into your per-fect theory."

"I didn't ask," Mulvaney said, somewhat annoyed that I disagreed with him. "And there's more. Mr. Iseman is under the impression that Poe was sweet on Miss Germaine, but the lady rebuffed him."

"There must be additional evidence," I countered. "Don't tell me you're relying only on Mr. Iseman."

Mulvaney was taking our conversation in a direction I disliked. It smacked of an unwarranted rush to judgment.

Mulvaney gave me a tired look. "It's all we've got to start with. Do me a favor and talk to Timothy Poe. Just see if you can turn up some useful information, one way or the other."

Of course I agreed, though I was increasingly troubled by Mulvaney's assumptions. I could only suppose that unknown stresses weighed heavily upon him. I reached for my hat and was about to leave—when he stopped me once again.

"Wait, Ziele. There's one more thing I should tell you before you go." He took a deep breath. "*The Times* got a letter, too, just this morning. I haven't told anyone—not even Mr. Iseman, though he brought the first letters to my attention. He fears public attention as it is; he won't be happy to hear the press is involved."

I whistled softly below my breath. Mulvaney was right: that changed everything.

"What did the letter say?"

"I don't know yet. The message just arrived. I plan to go to the *Times* building shortly after I wrap up here," he said. He stood up and faced me. "I want you in on the case, Ziele."

I was silent.

He gave me a lopsided smile. "It's a good one for you. A murder with no blood."

For of course Mulvaney knew my secret. I had a weak stomach for blood—a decided liability in our chosen profession, though I liked to think I hid it well.

"So you'd like to make a formal request for my help?"

"More than that. I want you to help me lead the investigation. I daresay they can spare you in Dobson?"

"I'd say so." It was an understatement, for work there had been quiet since winter—nothing the other officer of our two-man force could not handle. Sometimes I thought of coming back to work in the city permanently. But at other times, I felt it was too soon to return.

"And you'll be all right handling this case?" He spoke casually, but his eyes were filled with a searching concern as he awaited my answer.

Mulvaney knew that the woman I had planned to marry had died aboard the *Slocum* steamship—together with more than a thousand others who were killed when it caught fire on June 15, 1904. And while my grief for Hannah and many neighbors from my former home on the Lower East Side no longer stung as sharply, I continued to find that certain areas of the city—and cases involving the violent deaths of young women—brought unwelcome reminders of all I had lost.

I set my jaw firmly but didn't acknowledge his question. Instead, I lowered my voice as a precaution, though the policemen still gathering evidence continued to work some distance from us. "You have a number of detectives under your command, not one of whom will appreciate my help. Why do you need me?"

"In part because of loyalty," he said, and he furrowed his brow with concern as he admitted it. He looked around the room, surveying those hard at work. "The men who report to me are fine officers. But they are not my own. Not yet."

"And the other part?" I asked.

Mulvaney's expression grew dark. "Because there's something at work here that's larger and more complex than the death of one—or rather, two—actresses." He clutched at the blue letter. "I feel it in my gut. I hope I'm wrong, but I fear this is just the beginning."

He took a moment to let his words sink in. Then our eyes met squarely, and he went on to say, "You're not just the only person I trust. You're the only one I know who has the skills and tenacity to help me solve this case."

And with that compliment, I was in.

CHAPTER 4

The Nineteenth Precinct, West Thirtieth Street

Mulvaney had called ahead to the precinct house, so they were expecting me when I arrived. It was a dilapidated and over-crowded building just a few blocks south of the theater, on West Thirtieth Street. While there were plans under way for a new, modern building across the street, they had been delayed for so long that it had become a running joke among the ranks. Any private space was scarce in the current building, so I did not complain about the cramped, windowless room where Timothy Poe waited for me. The air was stale with the odor of burnt coffee, but in the interest of privacy, I felt compelled to close the door behind me.

As I took the chair that was lodged behind a discolored wood and metal desk, I considered the man opposite me. He was probably about my age, thirty, but his delicate features made him appear younger. He brushed back a thin strand of dirty blond hair to get a better look at me, and I noted the creased lines of worry on his forehead and his red, puffy eyes. He met my gaze with a half-vacant expression.

"You're here to talk with me." He stated it simply.

I nodded and introduced myself. "I'm Detective Simon Ziele. I understand your name is Timothy Poe."

He nodded. "It's a stage name, actually. My real name is Tim Krautcheim."

I patronized the theater often enough to know it was common for actors and actresses to reinvent themselves with new names, especially when their given names could be considered too long or unwieldy.

"So you chose Poe," I said.

"The director of my first show asked me to choose something short and easy to pronounce." Timothy again brushed his hair out of his eyes. "Plus, I always liked his poetry."

I groaned inwardly. Comments like that would only further convince Mulvaney that Poe was the man responsible for killing two actresses and leaving strange poems as a calling card.

"You're in custody because of evidence linking you to Annie Germaine's murder." I was blunt as I drew a pencil and small notebook out of my leather bag and placed them on the table. "Where were you last night, from about ten o'clock on?"

My question was met with a blank stare.

"Start wherever you like," I said.

His long, fine-boned fingers clutched at each other, then separated, several times in rapid succession.

"I was at the theater until eleven thirty, then home sleeping until the police came for me this morning, a little after nine.

Late nights are normal at the theater, you understand." He looked at me for a moment before his gaze drifted down to the table. "They asked me questions about Annie Germaine," he said, and his voice rose barely above a whisper. "Horrible questions. Questions one should never hear asked about a friend."

"How long had you known her?"

"About eight years." He managed a halfhearted smile at the memory. "We had starring roles in a play called *The Hobby Horse.*"

"And was Miss Germaine merely a colleague, or did you form a more personal attachment?" My voice lingered on the word *personal* as I observed his reaction, but he did not flinch.

"She was an acquaintance, nothing more. We'd been in several shows together, most recently last fall." He swallowed hard, and interlocked his fingers tightly.

"How was she killed?" I did not expect a real answer; after all, I had as much idea as anybody other than Dr. Wilcox. What was important was Timothy's reaction to the question.

While he seemed uncertain and confused, I detected no sign that he was deliberately hiding relevant information when he finally stammered an answer.

"I don't know. The police have told me nothing." He paused. "You don't think they'll send me to the Tombs, do you? I won't survive it. I'm sure of it." His hands began to tremble, and he shoved them into his lap.

"I'll try to find out more from the precinct captain after we talk," I said gently. "But first I need some more information, okay?"

He nodded in agreement.

"Did you know Eliza Downs?"

"I know her name because the policeman who first questioned me mentioned it," he said.

"But you never knew her personally? Never worked with her?" I leaned across the table to look him in the eye as I pressed for specifics.

"No." His answer was immediate; he required no time to consider.

He seemed so genuinely distressed by the suspicions directed against him that I determined to back up my line of questioning. It took less than five minutes to elicit the main facts of his life. It had always been his life's ambition to work on the stage, and after beginning in vaudeville, he soon discovered that his forte lay in the dry, witty comedic parts offered on Broadway. He'd had some success, most recently in Shaw's *You Never Can Tell.* But, most important to him, he had found steady work. As he told it, he had a few close friends, but apparently neither wife nor sweetheart. His life had revolved around his all-consuming desire to work—and work regularly—on the stage.

"So you are suspected of murdering two young women, only one of whom you knew personally," I said, summing up what he had told me. "Did the police give you any indication as to why you are a suspect?"

"No." His blue eyes widened and his fingers clutched at the cuff on his sleeve. "They asked me the same sort of questions you have. Did I know these women? Had I ever formed a romantic attachment with either one?" He looked at me wistfully. "I just don't understand why they're keeping me here. I've told them all I know. I want to go home."

I looked at him with no small measure of concern. He appeared too weak in body and mind to withstand the pressures that awaited him. And yet, he had withstood Broadway's rigors so far, working in a profession that was by no means an easy one. Perhaps there was more strength in the man than I had suspected.

"Last fall, I believe you were in a revival of *Pygmalion*," I began, but he cut me off.

"You mean *Pygmalion and Galatea*? The other policeman asked me about that, too." He seemed thoroughly confused. "But the show was in October, almost six months ago. How can that have anything to do with Annie's murder?"

"We still don't know," I said, forcing a pleasant smile, "but it would help me if you could tell me something about the play." I needed Timothy's cooperation, and I had no idea how much time I would be given to speak with him.

When he remained silent, I prodded him once more. "You might start by talking about your role. . . ."

"All right." He shifted position in his chair, stretching out long legs that seemed to reach all the way across the tiny room. "I played the title role, my biggest role to date. Do you know the play?"

I indicated that I did not.

"Pygmalion is a creative man, a sculptor." As Timothy's voice grew louder and more confident, I could better imagine him onstage, transformed into the part of a vain, self-centered artist. "He is trapped in a loveless marriage and frustrated by the women around him, so he determines to create a woman. But not just any woman," his hands began to move fluidly along the curves of an invisible model only he could see, "the *perfect* woman. And when he has finished, he falls in love with her.

How could he not? She is lovely—a statue of alabaster white, pure marble perfection."

"So he creates the perfect woman . . ." I said, almost to myself.

"He prays to Venus to grant his statue life—and he is ecstatic when Venus grants his wish!" Timothy's face flushed with excitement. "He names his statue Galatea and for a brief time—so fleeting—his life is wonderful. But Galatea proves ill suited for the human world, and when he ceases to love her, she becomes a statue once more. After all, that is how Pygmalion prefers her: in marble form, fixed and unchanging."

Timothy sat in expectation of my reaction, but I could only stare at him as I tried to make sense of what he had said. Then he sank into his chair, deflated. He had apparently left behind the memory of his triumph onstage and remembered his current predicament.

I could see how Miss Germaine's killer had drawn on this story in creating her death scene. The references to Pygmalion in the letter found by Annie Germaine's body were now much clearer to me—and also more disturbing.

"And neither Annie Germaine nor Eliza Downs was involved in *Pygmalion* in any way?" It was a test, for I knew Miss Germaine had understudied a role.

He started to deny it before he remembered. "Oh—for about a week, when a handful of our small cast were ill, Annie stepped in to play a minor role—that of Myrine, Pygmalion's sister."

"How was her relationship with the regular cast members?" He shrugged. "Congenial. Professional."

We were interrupted by a knock at the door, which was notice that my time was up.

"One last thing." I pushed my pencil and notebook across the table to him. "Could you write down your name and address for me?"

"I already gave it to the officers earlier," he replied.

I repeated my request pleasantly. "All the same, would you write it down again? For me."

As he handed the notebook back to me, his hand shook, and in a voice that was barely a whisper he asked, "So what happens to me now?"

I got up and straightened my jacket. "Let me talk with the arresting officers." I pushed my chair back under the table. "I'll see what more I can find out. Chin up."

He met my efforts to reassure him with a wobbly smile.

The moment I closed the door behind me, I glanced at the lines he had written. The words were formed in a thin, tight hand. But, unlike the writing on the blue letter Mulvaney had shown me, each letter of his penmanship was tiny and rounded. There was no slanting whatsoever.

Mulvaney had returned to the station house to await further reports from his men, who would interview all employees of the Garrick as they came in for the evening's show. The door to his office was wide open, and as I entered, he spun around in a wooden chair that barely contained his bulky frame and knocked his knees into his desk. Seeing this big man—with his even larger personality—confined within four walls and responsible for a desk filled with paperwork always struck me as absurd. Today, as he leaned back and stretched his arms behind his head, he almost filled the square box that was his office.

"You met with Poe?" He regarded me soberly.

"You can't possibly think Timothy Poe is the man responsible," I said, challenging him immediately. "If you've spent even five minutes talking with him, you must realize that. And you've no hard evidence against him. You've detained him only because he was in a play that was mentioned in a crazy note left at the crime scene."

"A crazy note left by the *murderer*, Ziele. Don't forget that, before you start telling me you're certain he wouldn't hurt a fly." His brogue was thick as the cliché rolled off his tongue.

I dragged a wooden chair from the corner into the space opposite his desk and sat down.

Mulvaney mouthed an expression of disgust. "What am I to do, Ziele? I've got two dead chorus girls. I want to find their killer, but I'm getting no help at all from the people at Frohman's theaters. They'd like me to solve the murders, sure. But they're scared that a proper investigation will spread news of the killings and frighten away the audience. They're that worried about their box-office take."

"Understood," I said. "But you were explaining why you took Poe into custody. After all, you want the killer, not just a scapegoat—right?"

I eyed him warily. Mulvaney had been my friend even before we had partnered together for eight years on the Lower East Side. But he was a precinct captain now. Had new political pressures changed his typically deliberate and impartial approach to police work? While I hoped not, this leap to judgment was unlike him.

"I'll not have you think I arrested an innocent man just because he was an easy target. These letters give me valid concerns about Poe. Here, you should see the other letter." Mulvaney's thick fingers shuffled through scattered papers until he found the item he wanted, secured in a protective wrapper.

He handed it to me. "It's the original found beside Miss Downs. Take a look and then tell me you don't share my concern."

I quickly read through the letter, noting that it was written in the same light, spidery handwriting as the letter found at the Garrick.

What beauty I have given her by playing Pygmalion to her Galatea! As a wise poet has said:

> *That moment she was mine, mine, fair,*
> *Perfectly pure and good: I found*
> *A thing to do, and all her hair*
> *In one long yellow string I wound*
> *Three times her little throat around,*
> *And strangled her. No pain felt she;*
> *I am quite sure she felt no pain.*
> *As a shut bud that holds a bee,*
> *I warily ope'd her lids: again*
> *Laugh'd the blue eyes without a stain.*

Mulvaney had been right. The references to Pygmalion and Galatea were similar, but the lines of poetry differed substantially.

My old partner busied himself pouring milk and sugar into the fresh cup of coffee his assistant had just brought in. He politely offered me a mug as well, feigning shock when I accepted.

"Thought you were choosy about your coffee," he said, his tone chiding.

"You mean this swill you drink?" I said good-naturedly. Mulvaney was right: my normal taste ran toward the stronger brew offered at various coffeehouses around the city. Precinct-house coffee was a weak, watery concoction that I normally considered undrinkable. But this morning's events, which had left no time for lunch, had created a pounding in my head that I hoped the caffeine would alleviate.

After he took another gulp from his cup, he summarized his observations. "The Downs letter has the same handwriting as the one found this morning at the Garrick. It's written on the same blue paper. And we've got two references to 'playing Pygmalion.' Who else has played Pygmalion in this city other than Timothy Poe? In recent years, of course. I've confirmed that he had the title role the entirety of the play's run last fall." Pleased with his research, he then added, "All the other actors from last year's revival are out of the area. Only Mr. Poe remains here in New York."

"But look," I said, pulling out my notebook to show him where Timothy Poe had written his name and address. "Their handwriting is nothing alike. It's a dissimilar size and shape, and they make their *p*s and *y*s differently."

Mulvaney considered the lines for a moment.

"It means nothing," he decided. "He has disguised it, that's all. And in both cases, the handwriting is light, with neat, formal penmanship."

He was right about that, but I still disagreed. "There's also no slant to what Poe wrote. And his letters are tiny and curled, not elongated. That would be hard to fake for an entire letter."

Our mutual silence was unbroken for several minutes.

"To return to *Pygmalion*," I said, "how many people saw the play during its run? It must have been thousands, assuming a normal run of several weeks. There's no reason to suspect its star more than anyone else. Any member of the audience would be familiar enough with the story to write these letters and kill these women." I put it as plainly as I could, once again turning the letter on Mulvaney's desk to face him.

"'What beauty I have given her by playing Pygmalion.' What does it mean?" I flicked my fingers against the paper in frustration.

"Bloody hell if I know!" Mulvaney looked at me with indulgence. "It's early yet, Ziele. Can't expect to know everything at once. Here, take a look at the photographs of Eliza Downs, such as they are."

He flipped through yet another huge folder on his desk and handed me three pictures.

"They're not our typical postmortem photos, as you can see. Apparently the family requested them before her body was removed from the theater." His nose wrinkled in mild disgust. "Maudlin practice, isn't it, photographing the dead in their final pose? I think it's falling out of fashion, but there's still families that want it as an enduring memory." He grimaced. "I'm lucky my Bridget's not the sentimental type. Certainly wouldn't want anyone remembering me that way when I'm gone."

I agreed as I began to examine each photograph. While I knew it was not an uncommon practice, I always found it discomfiting to view death poses. Eliza Downs, at least, looked as though she had merely fallen asleep while reclining on a large, overstuffed armchair.

"Just like Annie Germaine," Mulvaney said. "She was a chorus girl, but they found her wearing the leading lady's garb. Nothing on that stage had been left to chance. Not her outfit. Not the way she was placed front and center stage. And not that letter."

He was right. The young woman pictured in the photographs was beautiful: posed in a graceful recline, she was elegantly clad in jewels and silks.

"You don't have close-ups?" I asked.

Mulvaney answered in the negative. "Like I said, these were done for the family to remember her by. At the time, no one thought her death was anything other than a tragic suicide."

I held up the last picture to the light; it offered the closest view of the woman's face and neck. While the photograph's black-and-white tones made it difficult to tell, I did not notice any bruising—an observation I mentioned at once to Mulvaney.

"Whoever he is, he wants them to die pretty, that's for sure. I should have Wilcox's autopsy report by tomorrow and I'll know more."

"You'll have to get an exhumation order for Eliza Downs," I reminded him.

He nodded mutely and placed the letter back in his files.

"And what about Timothy Poe?" I asked. "The fact that he starred in a play called *Pygmalion,* and that it's mentioned in these letters, doesn't give you enough to keep him. It doesn't give him a motive to kill; it's just a coincidence. You're missing all the elements of motive, means, and opportunity."

"What are you, his lawyer?" Mulvaney seemed amused. After a pause, he finally said, "You're right. Of course we'll let him go this afternoon, with a warning not to leave the area. But I do intend to investigate him more thoroughly."

He pushed aside his empty coffee mug, got up, and began to put on his coat and scarf. "Come with me to *The Times'* offices. I want you there when I see the new letter and talk with the reporter who received it."

But I stayed in my chair and looked up at Mulvaney. "There is one more thing."

"What?" He was halfway out the door.

"You can't make real sense of these letters. Neither can I. They seem to be all poetry and nonsense. But I agree with you that they are our first key to solving this crime."

Then I took a deep breath and said it. "I think I know the person who can help."

The thought had been in my head all afternoon, and I had become increasingly certain of both the necessity and the awkwardness of contacting him. It had been more than three months since I'd last spoken with him. And after I had made my excuses for two or three dinner invitations, further efforts on his part had ceased. Which was exactly what I had wanted.

"Out with it, lad!" Mulvaney's coat was on, and he was bursting with impatience to get to *The Times'* offices.

"Remember Alistair Sinclair?"

I watched as a medley of emotions—disbelief and surprise, then concern, and finally disapproval—played in succession across Mulvaney's face. Alistair was the law professor and criminologist who had involved himself in the murder investigation I'd led last fall. Despite our many disagreements, he had opened my eyes to new and unorthodox ways of understanding criminal behavior. In terms of learning and intellectual acumen, he had no peer. But Alistair was not without flaws, and his selfish grandstanding had nearly kept us from solving that case.

"You've got to be kidding me," Mulvaney said, his voice flat. "If you want help with the letters, why not contact a literature professor from any college in this city? An ordinary professor could help us figure out the poetry. We don't need your Professor Sinclair."

But we did.

I was certain of it, and I did my best to explain why. "This isn't just a matter of understanding a few lines of poetry. We're dealing with someone—a criminal—who is using those lines to create a dangerous message. Alistair has made it his life's work to figure out the elusive connection between criminal motivation and behavior. He believes that if you understand how the mind works, then you can better predict the behavior that follows."

We stared at each other in silence.

I took a deep breath and put the matter a different way. "Two actresses have died. And their killer has written at least three letters already that we know of: two here in our possession and one sent to *The Times*. There's simply too much at stake."

Mulvaney yielded with the grudging acceptance I had anticipated. "Well, we'd best talk with him and get it over with. Maybe he can be of help with *The Times*. Though I'll not bet on it."

He walked over to his secretary's desk. "Danny, can you check the directory and find out where a man named Alistair Sinclair lives. And call ahead, would you? See if he's home."

"No need." I cleared my throat as I wrapped my scarf tightly around my neck, bracing myself for the cold March snow, if not the confrontation to come. "In this weather on a Friday afternoon, he won't be at his office at Columbia. We'll find him at his apartment uptown, on Seventy-second Street. I know the place."

And I did. I only hoped I knew the man half as well.

CHAPTER 5

The Dakota, One West Seventy-second Street

Alistair lived in the Dakota building, at the western edge of Central Park and Seventy-second Street. It stood almost alone at the edge of the park, a Gothic structure that towered over its smaller neighbors. I'd heard the building got its name because it was so far from the heart of the city, it might as well be in the Dakotas. But Alistair insisted the Wild West motifs were responsible—for ears of corn and arrowheads adorned the walls of the brick-and-sandstone building. And I tended to think he would know, for Alistair considered it a point of pride to have been one of the building's original tenants. He had moved in nearly twenty years ago, when this area of the city was uninhabited, and Alistair's adventurous—not to mention rebellious—spirit had led him to stake his home here.

It had been almost four months since I'd last seen him. Or

Isabella. I had thought of her often, despite my resolution to see her no more. My gaze shifted uneasily to the door across the landing, opposite Alistair's. It was the apartment Alistair had procured as a wedding gift for his son Teddy following his marriage to Isabella. But Isabella had found herself widowed after only two years, when Teddy was murdered while on an archaeological expedition—the details of which I'd never learned. Now, in an unconventional arrangement, Isabella remained in the apartment, maintaining a close relationship with Alistair and assisting him with the criminological research that had become his all-consuming passion. Meanwhile, he had separated from his wife, who lived permanently abroad.

I was announced from the lobby, so even before we knocked on the door of Alistair's eighth-floor apartment, his housekeeper, Mrs. Mellown, stood ready to open the door. She greeted me with a perfunctory "Detective Ziele"—and if she remembered me from last fall, she gave no indication of it. She briskly took charge of our coats and muddy shoes before we stepped onto the plush Turkish and Indian carpets that lined the hallway to Alistair's library. Then she ushered us into a space that might have resembled a small, intimate art museum, for Alistair had traveled widely and his home was filled with artifacts from his journeys.

She led us past rooms filled with Chinese vases, European paintings, carved wooden and marble statues, and even a tapestry depicting a unicorn and its hunter. But all this was nothing compared to the library itself, filled with bookshelves that ran the expanse of all four walls. Reaching from floor to ceiling, they held leather-bound tomes and stone artifacts and were interrupted only by a marble-and-tile fireplace on the southern wall and an expansive window to the east. Today, that window offered a spectacular view of Central Park blanketed in snow. Mulvaney's breath caught sharply the moment he saw it, though he was normally not one to be impressed by such things.

Alistair faced the fireplace as we entered, and while I'm certain he heard our footsteps, he did not turn until Mulvaney discreetly cleared his throat.

At the sound, Alistair walked over to Mulvaney with a broad smile. "I don't think we've ever formally met, though I've heard much about you. I'm Alistair Sinclair."

"Declan Mulvaney" was the curt response.

They shook hands vigorously. Then Alistair turned to me with a stiff, unreadable expression. From the deep lines that ran along his face, I suspected the past few months had not been easy for him. After the conclusion of our last case together, the press had ridiculed him mercilessly, with papers sporting headlines like RENOWNED CRIMINAL LAW PROFESSOR HARBORS KILLER IN OWN RESEARCH LAB. The embarrassment had no doubt compounded the personal betrayal he had suffered.

"Ziele." He clasped my hand in a firm shake, though, as always, he was careful enough not to jostle my injured right arm.

As I greeted him in return, his eyes met my own and I was struck anew by their color and clarity. They were not a typical blue but rather a bright azure—and while they glittered with alert intelligence, their startling color also suggested an absence of warmth.

After a few more pleasantries, he came to the point. "What brings you here today, gentlemen?"

He did not invite us to sit.

"We're investigating a difficult case," I said. "We hoped you might be able to shed light on some challenging evidence we've encountered."

As Mulvaney and I continued to stand, awkwardly, Alistair moved to a side table, picked up a decanter of water, and poured himself a glass. He did not offer any to us.

Mulvaney caught my eye and signaled he was ready to abandon this meeting.

But Alistair returned to us. His intellectual curiosity appeared to overpower his desire to hold a grudge.

"What sort of case?" he asked.

"An intriguing one," I replied. "Just the sort you like best."

Alistair was quiet for a moment. Then he laughed—and it was a full-throated chuckle. He could not help himself: his eyes brightened and his face flushed with excitement.

"Come and tell me about it." With sudden enthusiasm, he motioned us to come sit with him by the roaring fire. He sprawled comfortably across a blue velvet sofa, while Mulvaney and I settled into the two paisley armchairs opposite.

I placed the two near-identical letters on the long coffee table between us. He looked at them for a moment without making any movement.

"Love letters?" He arched an eyebrow inquisitively.

"Something like that," I said, my voice rough. "Care to read?" I cleared my throat. "Obviously from the handwriting and the choice of paper, we assume each was written by the same person."

"You've sealed them." He noted their protective covering. "I take it they're evidence, not just incidental to your investigation?"

"We think so," Mulvaney said. "What can you tell us about them?"

"First, you need to tell me about your case," Alistair countered.

"Before we do, we'd like to hear your opinion about the letters," I said, doing my best to sound as though my suggestion were uncalculated.

A dark expression of stubbornness crossed his face, and I thought for a moment that he might refuse. But at last he reached toward the coffee table and in a swooping, deliberate motion, he lifted up the eggshell-blue letter marked EXHIBIT ONE. It was the letter found near Miss Downs at the Empire Theater, where she had been killed three weeks earlier.

Alistair checked the watermark, but I was one step ahead of him.

I said, "It's by Crane's, which as you know is easily obtained at almost any fine stationery store in the city. I don't think we'll be successful in tracking the writer through his choice of paper."

"The writing is more important anyhow," he said indifferently before reading aloud. "'I found a thing to do . . . and strangled her.'" He paused. "I take it this writing is regarding a person—a woman—who was strangled?"

I exchanged glances with Mulvaney. After he nodded almost imperceptibly, I said, "We think it's possible, pending the coroner's official report."

"So there were no outward signs?" Alistair was becoming more visibly excited by the moment. "No bruising around the neck? Or, what about the eyes? If they aren't visibly bulging, at least the red capillaries inside the lid may have burst from the pressure."

I shook my head as I recalled Max Wilcox's use of a buttonhole device to turn Miss Germaine's lids inside out. He had examined her capillaries yet had found nothing conclusive. I had previously heard of certain killers possessing the considerable skill required to strangle a victim and yet leave no sign of it. But such a feat could normally be accomplished only by an experienced killer—and I explained as much to Alistair.

"If she was indeed strangled, then I'll expect Wilcox to tell us her killer probably used a soft material. And to that I'll add the fact that he likely has developed some practice or expertise in the matter."

Alistair's mouth opened slightly. "Well, then. This is indeed interesting, Ziele." With renewed energy, he reached for the second letter and read it quickly. " 'Yet I'll not shed her blood, Nor scar that whiter skin of hers than snow, and smooth as monumental alabaster.' Your writer does have a way with words, though I don't think they are his own. In the first, he mentions a 'wise poet,' and here he talks of 'one of our greatest poets.' And something about the lines is familiar. . . ."

He tapped his foot as he thought, but when he came up with nothing, he rang the bell for Mrs. Mellown, his unflappable housekeeper. She soon appeared, bearing a large silver tray filled with tea and an assortment of almond butter cookies. She must have prepared it after showing us in. As we helped ourselves, Alistair asked her to check whether Isabella was at home.

"I assume you want her to come over?" Mrs. Mellown asked as she busied herself removing some dishes Alistair had left on his desk.

"Please." Alistair mumbled the word as he finished swallowing a cookie. "Of course you remember Isabella, Ziele."

How could I not?

"She loves poetry and will be familiar with these verses. I'm sure of it," Alistair said.

I took a gulp of tea to wash down the crumbs that had gone dry in my mouth. Facing Alistair again had been difficult enough. I had not expected to see Isabella as well. When we had last seen each other, she had been recovering from a gunshot wound sustained in the final moments of that murder case. I had felt it best to disentangle myself from everything associated with Alistair's world—including his widowed daughter-in-law, for whom I had developed an attraction that was as uncomfortable as it was inconvenient.

It seemed mere seconds passed before I looked up—and saw her there.

She looked thinner than in November and I could sense her reserve around us. Though her eyes still sparkled warmly, she greeted me and Mulvaney with a perfunctory smile. She had not wanted to come, I realized with disappointment.

If Alistair registered any awkwardness, however, he disregarded it. For him, any lingering resentment had disappeared. The letters had sparked his insatiable curiosity, and when he was intrigued by something, all else was irrelevant.

"Look at this," he said to Isabella, making room for her on the sofa beside him. "I've read this poem before, but I expect you will know exactly where it is from."

Smoothing her dark brown skirt as she sat, she took both letters from him; her eyes darted rapidly across the page as she read. I watched her brow crinkle as she registered their contents. "How did you come by these?" she asked.

"Each was placed near a young woman found dead, most likely strangled," I answered.

She thought for a moment. "Well, the poetry is quite simple. In your first letter, the writer is quoting from Robert Browning. His *Porphyria's Lover* contains this whole stanza."

She placed the letter on the coffee table, turning it so we might read the stanza again.

> *. . . I found*
> *A thing to do, and all her hair*
> *In one long yellow string I wound*
> *Three times her little throat around,*
> *And strangled her. No pain felt she;*
> *I am quite sure she felt no pain.*

"But the killer didn't do any of that," Mulvaney said. "She wore a wig, and she certainly wasn't strangled with her hair."

Isabella smiled. "I'll explain more in a moment. But first, look at what he did in his second letter, which is taken from Shakespeare's *Othello*."

Isabella rose from the sofa and walked to the bookshelves half a wall's distance from the fireplace. Using a small stepladder, she climbed to a midlevel shelf and pulled out a large, leather-bound volume. Returning to the coffee table, she put it down and flipped through page after page.

"Here it is," she said triumphantly. "Act five. Scene two. Line three. 'Yet I'll not shed her blood. Nor scar that whiter skin of hers than snow . . . smooth as monumental alabaster.'"

"Browning and Shakespeare." Alistair mulled it over. "I'd say your writer is an educated man. That is also supported by his general writing: he uses precise diction; his words are correctly spelled; there are no errors of usage or punctuation."

"So you think he's an upper-class gent?" Mulvaney asked.

"Not necessarily." Alistair was cautious as he explained. "Look at the handwriting: it's neat and legible. He has bought quality paper. And he has quoted from two great writers of the English language. But what that tells me is not necessarily that our man *is* of the upper class—but rather that he has put a great deal of effort into making us *think* he is."

We took a moment to consider what he had said.

"What else can you tell us about this writer, specifically from these letters?" I urged.

Alistair responded archly, "Ziele, you delight me. Am I to surmise you have come round to my way of thinking about criminal behavior?"

"No need to get carried away," I said with good humor. "I'm no convert to your theories. But in a case like this, where we've so little to go on, there's no harm in exploring all avenues of thought."

"Especially in a case like this, where your killer is actually communicating with you," Alistair said, and his voice had assumed a note of warning. "Ziele, you know I don't believe criminals are born. I've never adhered to that particular fiction perpetuated by Lombroso and his followers that locates the reason for criminal behavior in biological makeup. Biology may play a role, to be sure. But it is not *the* role. The criminal is formed through some circumstance or set of circumstances in his life. So our question becomes, what formed him? You, Ziele," he said, his eyes twinkling, "will like it better if I frame the question this way: what forms his motive? Why does he behave as he does? Why—"

"Why does he kill as he does?" I cut him off before he could finish.

"Exactly." His voice was low and grave.

We regarded each other in silent understanding.

Alistair spread the letters on the table at an angle, allowing each of us to see them. Then he continued to talk.

"First, I ask you: what do these two pieces have in common?"

And he waited. He could have told us, of course. But it was clear he wanted us to see it for ourselves.

"Uh . . . each letter talks about a dead woman," Mulvaney responded gamely.

"Exactly!" Alistair's enthusiasm was as great as if we'd just discovered something very important.

Mulvaney was dubious. "But if he didn't write the poetry, why does it matter?"

"Because he *used* it to communicate something specific," Alistair said.

"What about where he says he *played* Pygmalion at the beginning of the letter? Ziele disagrees with me, but we found the actor who played that role in *Pygmalion*'s revival last fall. I think it could refer to him. He even knows one of the murder victims." Mulvaney was insistent, even stubborn in his conviction.

Alistair answered him with infinite patience.

"Normally, I would disagree with Ziele, too. But here, I think he's right. The writer of these letters is too sophisticated. Or, to put it a different way, he's doing something far more complex than merely referring to an actual role in a play."

"Huh?" Mulvaney appeared thoroughly confused.

"What Alistair is saying is that it would be too obvious," I said.

Alistair smiled with approval. "And why are these women dead?"

"Some guy killed them. What does it matter?" Mulvaney was growing impatient and began to grumble.

"I think it matters *how* they were killed," Isabella said, sensing Mulvaney's increasing frustration. "Porphyria's lover is strangled and Shakespeare's Desdemona is smothered. But what's similar in both cases is that the woman bears no physical sign of it, so there's no visible evidence of her pain."

She paused for a moment.

"Simon, is that consistent with the actual deaths you're investigating?" She eyed me with curiosity.

I nodded yes, but it was Mulvaney who spoke up.

"Definitely. We have been saying all day that our killer wants them to die pretty."

Mulvaney's comment was music to Alistair's ears. "That's exactly my point." Alistair's broad smile revealed his perfect, white teeth. "Mark my words, once we understand more about him and why it's important to him not just to kill—but to kill in this manner—then we'll have discovered the key to understanding him."

Mulvaney and I went on to describe how each death had been staged, in the most literal sense of the word.

Alistair said, "I think it is in the staging that the figure of Pygmalion comes into play. I'm not referring to the production that Timothy Poe starred in," he cut off Mulvaney, who had opened his mouth to say something, "but to what the character of Pygmalion represents. So I'm certain he knows the legend of Pygmalion, the man who created a beautiful woman made of marble and fell in love with her. What seems important here is the act of creation."

Isabella added even more. "Yes, and look at what the lines

emphasize about her. In both cases, the man loves her. He doesn't actually wish to harm her, as the Othello quote suggests when he refuses to *shed her blood* or *scar her skin*. In the Browning passage, the poet-killer wants to preserve a perfect moment, and even when she's dead, he continues to see her features as lifelike. See the final phrase, where he says, *again laughed the blue eyes*?"

She pointed to the relevant phrases from the first letter. "He sees himself as having created something new and preserved it."

Mulvaney interrupted. "Wait just a minute. You're saying the writer of these letters killed two women because he is *preserving* something about them? That makes no sense."

Isabella was quick to respond, saying, "He's not preserving their *life*. He's preserving his idea about them—about their potential, about what they might become, if he made things a bit different."

Alistair put it a different way. "I believe what Isabella is suggesting is that for this writer, life disappoints—but perhaps art does not."

And with that comment, Alistair overreached.

"This is murder," I said heatedly, "not art."

"But perhaps not from the killer's point of view," Alistair said, making his point with renewed urgency. "His view is what matters, you recall—not your own." He held up both letters before us. "The man who writes this—and I do believe it is a man—is not governed by rational thought. But we shouldn't assume he is unintelligent or uneducated. This writer knows Shakespeare. He knows Browning. And he proceeds absolutely according to his own logic. And that is what we must—" He immediately stopped himself. "Rather, that is what *you* must remember if you are to solve these murders."

Mulvaney chuckled. "Unless we get lucky and catch him in the act."

"Well then," Alistair said pleasantly, "you will be very lucky indeed. The man you seek is a meticulous planner who is unlikely to make careless mistakes."

Isabella retreated to the corner of the room with a cup of tea. Was it my imagination, or did she seem changed? It was unlike her to take so little interest in a case that Alistair obviously found compelling.

"Don't discount luck. Sometimes it's all we've got," I said lightly.

I glanced at my watch. We needed to get to *The Times* before five o'clock.

But I had one more question for Alistair. "Why do you think he wrote these letters? I mean, why even bother? It would have been less work and less risk for him simply to kill and walk away."

Alistair shrugged. "He's not the first, you know. And he certainly won't be the last. But he is highly unusual. Most criminals do not enter into correspondence about their crimes. The fact he has done so implies we are dealing with a truly unique personality."

He picked up both letters and returned them to me.

"I'll also make a prediction: he will keep writing, and I expect you will see more of him—and less of other writers—in his future missives. He has used the work of others to demonstrate his intelligence and get our attention. Now that he has it . . ."

Alistair paused for a moment, then leaned closer to us as he continued to talk. "He wants to communicate something specific. The question is, to whom? He may be taunting you to show he's smarter than you. And we can't avoid thinking of Jack the Ripper, can we? He began by insulting the police, but when the papers published his letters—well, assuming at least some of the letters *were* his and not hoaxes—I think he fell in love with his own celebrity. I say this in order to warn you to be very careful in this case."

"Comparisons to other letters aside, Alistair, what do you really think of all this? Whom, exactly, are we looking for?" I asked.

"I don't know," he admitted frankly. "But I do know one thing. What you've seen so far is only the beginning if you cannot stop him. He put a great deal of effort into first creating a perfect crime scene and then penning a letter to make sure others would understand what he hoped to accomplish. I daresay you'll find he put similar effort into his choice of victim. He is enjoying every aspect of his handiwork. And a man who enjoys something this much will not stop—at least, not of his own accord."

After a moment's reflection, he added, "At least your man appears to be writing personally to whoever finds the body, not to the police or the papers."

Mulvaney and I exchanged guilty looks.

"Actually," Mulvaney said as he drew in a deep breath, "the man *is* writing to the papers now. I got word this morning that *The Times* received a letter. I've no idea if the other papers received one as well. If they did," his voice was grim, "they may not be so considerate as to check with us before printing it for the masses."

"We're headed to the *Times* offices now. Maybe you'd like to join us?" I asked.

Alistair's expertise would be useful, and I expected him to

be interested enough to agree. But he accepted with so much exuberance that I almost began to second-guess my decision to involve him in the matter. I had not forgotten how, during our last case together, he had withheld significant information from me because it jeopardized his own ambitions. The last thing I needed was for him to allow his own interests once again to interfere with the investigation. He would be helpful only so long as our concerns were aligned.

"Isabella?" Alistair glanced toward her, and it was plain he wanted her to accompany us.

I busied myself replacing the letters in my leather bag, and I did not look up until I heard her response.

"No, thanks, I prefer to stay home."

Her refusal had been crisp, but she came over to us and shook hands politely with Mulvaney, then me.

"It was good to see you again, Simon." She was pleasant but distant.

To think it could be otherwise would be presumptive. But once, just a few months ago, it might have been different—and that realization itself was bittersweet.

We exited the apartment into the hallway and caught the elevator waiting on Alistair's floor.

If I hadn't chanced to look back, just before I stepped into it, I wouldn't have seen the peculiar expression with which Isabella watched us leave.

But once she caught my gaze, she bit her lip, retreated into her apartment, and closed the door firmly between us.

CHAPTER 6

The City Room, Times Building, West Forty-second Street

"Those hot off the press? Bring 'em over here."

The front-desk editor, a balding man seated at the head of multiple rows of desks, barked the directions to a copyboy who was struggling to balance a stack of papers on each shoulder as he walked into the City Room of *The New York Times*. The papers the young man carried were newly printed, and their ink had marked his skin and clothing with giant black stains. He wobbled under their weight but did not drop them until he reached the editor's desk. Each pile then landed with a loud thud as the copyboy's careful efforts to ease his papers onto the desk failed, sending pencils, scissors, and notes flying.

Alistair, Mulvaney, and I surveyed this scene from the sole enclosed office on the fourteenth floor. We had been asked to wait here for the managing editor, whose office overlooked the entire room—a maze of wooden desks occupied by reporters and editors who worked amid a tremendous din, breathing air that was heavy with a mix of cigarette and cigar smoke. With the door to the office open wide, we were free to observe reporters furiously punching out their stories on new Hammond type-writers; editors working with scissors and paste pots to make corrections; and even a small group of five men, their work pre-sumably done, engaged in a raucous poker game in the back corner. Their game was punctuated only by the frequent spitting of tobacco into shiny brass spittoons that lined the room. Some-how, amid this chaos, tomorrow's paper was being produced.

"Let's check out the competition." The front-desk editor ground his cigar butt into a saucer and grabbed a copy of *The Tribune* off the top of the stack. After thumbing through it in what seemed a matter of seconds, he moved on to *The Post*. He grunted in displeasure. "We got scooped on the Tyler embezzle-ment story."

All the reporters in the room began to study whatever was on their desks with renewed interest.

"Johnny, next time you gotta work your sources on Wall Street better. Okay?"

"Sure, boss." Nervously, the reporter who answered ran both hands through his tousled mop of brown hair.

But the front-desk editor moved on to other concerns. "Frank," he said. "We got the story about the Snyder woman's acquittal in that poisoning trial, right?" He neither looked up nor ceased flip-ping pages.

"Yeah, we got it, boss." The answer came from a lean, wiry man. His voice, low with a rich timbre, came from the fifth desk down.

It was an unwelcome reminder of the verdict in my case, delivered only this morning. My stomach lurched and I felt my face burn with mortification—as though they were criticizing me, not merely discussing the jury's verdict. Of course I should not have taken it personally, but I did. If only I had found better evidence against the woman . . . evidence that might have withstood her protestations of innocence.

"What does *The Post* say about it?" This time it was the reporter asking the question.

The editor grunted again. "Just their usual bombastic drivel. But they scored an interview with her estranged mother."

Both were silent for a moment.

"Who marked up your story?" asked the editor.

"Mr. Seiden," the wiry man said, "before he left early. He does on Fridays, remember?"

Though he had not once looked up from his papers, the editor sat up straighter and seemed to focus his attention even more sharply on the article he was reviewing. Down the line of desks, every man followed suit, attending closely to the task at hand.

From the back of the room, a stout man wearing a crisp blue suit with a yellow-and-red tie strutted toward us. Ira Salzburg, the managing editor, was short and squat, but his expensive, colorful clothes enabled him to cut a distinctive figure. He knew it—and his swagger reflected it.

Without acknowledging anyone on the floor, he ambled into his office, nodded, and shut the door with a sweeping dramatic flourish.

"Gentlemen." He greeted each of us with a straightforward handshake.

After we finished our introductions, we sat in the stiff wooden chairs provided for guests while Mr. Salzburg sank into his large, cushioned chair and lit a cigar. "Welcome to Times Square."

It was Times Square, yes, but only in the mind of a *Times* employee. Nearly two years ago *The Times* had left newspaper row downtown for this new building—Manhattan's second tallest, a lone skyscraper on the small island of land created by the triple intersection of Forty-second Street, Seventh Avenue, and Broadway. The area had been named Longacre Square and more often referred to as the Main Stem. Though now it was officially renamed in the paper's honor, no one ever remembered to call it Times Square. Two years wasn't enough time to change long-held habits.

Mulvaney spoke first. "We need to talk to you about a letter you received this morning—one that may relate to police business."

Ira Salzburg regarded Mulvaney for a moment, then looked out the window to the swirling activity on the streets. The area below teemed with crowds of businessmen and tourists, chorus girls and restaurant-goers, all racing in multiple directions. Yet, up here, we sat awkwardly in silence.

Without looking away from the window, he finally put down his cigar and spoke, his voice elongating his words into a drawl. "Which letter are you specifically talking about, gentlemen?"

"The letter one of your employees contacted us about this morning," Mulvaney snapped impatiently. He didn't like it when others played games or wasted his time.

Ira Salzburg turned and concentrated his gaze again on

Mulvaney. "Oh, yes. The letter describing the murder at the Garrick Theater."

Mulvaney blanched. Although obviously we were at *The Times* because of a letter relating to today's murder, Mulvaney had hoped it contained few details.

But he forced a pleasant smile onto his face and managed to sound easygoing. "We'd like to see the letter now, Mr. Salzburg."

"You can call me Ira," he said indifferently as he swung his legs around. "Like all my men do."

The comment struck a false note. We had seen every employee on the floor treat Ira Salzburg with great deference, and it was hard to imagine even one of them addressing him as "Ira."

He swung his weight out of his chair and flung open his office door. He didn't say a word, but at his nod, the wiry man who had spoken earlier about the poisoning trial got up from his desk and came in to join us.

We learned his name was Frank Riley and he was *The Times*'s senior crime reporter. He spread before us a letter written on now-familiar blue paper in the spidery hand that arched its words in an unnatural slant. As we read the letter in haste, he lounged easily against the corner of his editor's desk.

It was Alistair's keen eye that noticed the first anomaly.

"The writer's dateline here indicates Tuesday." He pointed to the top right-hand corner. "And your own receipt stamp suggests that you received it on Tuesday." He pointed to a haphazard red-ink stamp that bore Tuesday's date, March 13. "But today is Friday the sixteenth. We were under the impression you received this letter only this morning."

"Actually," Ira admitted sheepishly, "we did receive the letter on Tuesday. But we thought it was a joke. We get lots of letters from crazy types who've got nothing better to do."

"So why bother saving this one?" Alistair asked.

Ira shrugged. "Truthfully? By accident. Frank's the one who ended up with it, and he's a saver. Never throws a thing out unless someone makes him—right, Frank?" He exchanged conspiratorial glances with his reporter.

At that moment, I trusted neither of them. They were making a show of cooperation—but in fact, they weren't helping much at all. And it was all I could do to suppress my anger when I realized that Annie Germaine's life might have been saved, had they only taken the letter more seriously.

"When a little bird told us about what you found at the Garrick this morning, Frank remembered and showed it to me," Ira was saying.

"What sort of little bird?" My eyes continued to race over the writing in front of me.

"The sort who works at the Garrick and gets a big reward for a good news tip. But I'm sure you know we always protect our sources," Frank said, smiling congenially as he demurred.

I looked at Frank sharply, trying to detect any sign of sarcasm. Not all reporters were alike, of course. But most I had known were motivated by personal opportunity rather than journalistic principle. When it suited them, they protected their sources. When it didn't, they betrayed them without hesitation. *The Times* was working hard to earn a reputation for printing serious, accurate news, but it was impossible to tell how closely Frank adhered to those ethics.

"There were no reporters at the Garrick," Mulvaney said, his voice growing louder. "I was there."

Frank inclined his head. "I might have stopped by for a moment to visit my source."

Mulvaney and I looked at each other. It was certainly possible. In an effort to keep the news as quiet as possible, Mulvaney had posted no policemen at the theater door. Of course, a resourceful reporter like Frank would have known to use the backstage entrance.

Mulvaney rose out of his chair. "You . . . you've got to know it's against the law to tamper with an active crime scene . . ." he stammered in anger.

"Simmer down, Captain." Frank made a calming motion with his hands. "I only talked to a couple janitors backstage. I didn't go anywhere near the stage where she was killed. Besides, I figured the best course of action was to contact my editor for some advice in light of that letter."

"You were there. You might have let us know and saved us some time," Mulvaney said, his voice filled with bitterness.

Frank only shrugged. "I didn't have the letter with me."

"But a girl was murdered—"

I cut Mulvaney off before his fury quashed their already half-hearted cooperation. "Let's take a closer look at the letter itself."

Mulvaney reined in his temper, and we turned our attention to the letter, addressed to the head of *The Times*.

Dear Mr. Ochs,

Here's your chance to cover the biggest story of the day. Your job? Well, you've got to recognize the opportunity I'm giving you.

I've readied a new production for the stage. I auditioned the leading lady last week, and she's perfect for the part.

Her debut will be Friday at the Garrick.
Ever gentle in my methods, she'll suffer no stage fright.
Like God, I create life in death.
Like sculptors, I forge beauty
And exquisite loveliness
Where there is none.
At last, you will behold my work of art!
In honor and
Tribute to
Sublime form.

It was signed "Yours truly." The letter was not what I had expected, and I had dozens of questions—though of course I could mention none of them in front of Ira Salzburg. I would have to wait until we were clear of him.

"You noticed the acrostic—'hell awaits'?" Alistair seemed unaware that he had spoken aloud.

"I'd say it's an allusion to Jack the Ripper, who also wrote to the papers. A couple of his letters were signed 'From Hell.'" I answered him automatically, to my immediate regret.

Ira's eyes glinted and his mouth turned up into a satisfied smirk. "So you may well be dealing with a series murderer, gentlemen."

Alistair's reproof was icy. "That's a leap of logic I wouldn't care to make—especially since there is not a single other similarity between Miss Germaine's murder this morning and that of the prostitutes in Whitechapel who were butchered almost twenty years ago."

I marveled at how well Alistair discouraged that line of thought as Ira began to hem and haw in embarrassment.

"Why would this writer—assuming he is the murderer—give advance notice of his plans to *The Times*?" Mulvaney asked.

"And specifically to Mr. Ochs," said Ira. "The writer obviously knew the name of the man in charge."

Alistair frowned. "That information is printed in the paper every day; easy enough to discover if you don't already know it. Still, the fact that he began with a personalized greeting may mean something. . . ."

"Was it delivered directly to Mr. Ochs?" I asked.

"Only to Mr. Ochs's secretary," Frank said. "When he receives mail that's not appropriate for Mr. Ochs, he passes it on. He gave it to me because he thought it was a good joke."

"And did you show it to anyone?" I was having trouble determining the chain of custody this letter had followed.

Frank eyed us with unworried detachment. "Yeah. Most of the boys on the floor and I had a good laugh. Why not? Who'd take seriously a crazy guy who thinks he's some great artist with the power of God?"

I understood his point, but still asked him to clarify it. "So at the time, you weren't troubled by the letter? You didn't think to call the police? As we now know, this letter gave you advance warning of a murder."

"Naw," Frank said with a grin. "We thought it was written by some stage-struck sap who wanted to write something highfalutin but didn't quite succeed. But when I heard today about a murder at the Garrick, I remembered it. I wasn't sure it was related." He shrugged again. "But that's your job, right?"

So they were guilty of ignoring what had turned out to be relevant evidence. But *The Times* did not—at least not yet—know about the other two letters or even the first murder. Mulvaney, for one, was eager to keep it that way, so he began to thank Ira Salzburg and Frank for their time.

"We appreciate your finally calling us. Let us know if you receive anything else." Mulvaney's voice was deliberately casual as he reached to fold and pocket the blue letter.

But Ira's thumb firmly planted itself at the letter's header near the date stamp.

"Not so fast, Captain." Though he smiled, there was no mistaking his note of warning.

We froze. No one said a word.

"I think this letter is more important than you have let on. In fact, I'd bet money on it." He laughed, and it was a grating, guttural sound. "Why not? I bet it often enough with the boys out there." He gestured toward the poker game in the main room, which was still going strong.

Then he leaned in close to Mulvaney, adding, "And I never lose."

Leaving his thumb on the blue letter, he used his other hand to open a desk drawer and pull out two pieces of paper. One was a typewritten transcript of the blue letter; the other was a photograph taken of it. Only after he had placed them on his desk did he release his hold on the original.

"You can see, Captain, that I've saved you the trouble of making a copy for me. You can have your letter. But I do have some conditions."

"This is police evidence, Mr. Salzburg. I don't need your permission to take it with me." Mulvaney remained polite, but his voice had a sharp edge.

"Of course, of course," Ira said. "But you do need my co-operation if you'd rather not see this—and more—in tomorrow morning's news. And should this writer happen to contact us again . . ."

He let the implications of his warning linger in the air.

Alistair tried to defuse Ira Salzburg's not-so-veiled threat. "You know that an actress has died at the Garrick. And you've received a letter of interest to the police. You've got nothing more than that. Unless you want to invent a tale out of thin air, doesn't sound like you have much of a story to me."

But Ira said, "I know what it means when a big-shot law professor—especially one with your history—walks into my office." His smile was greasy as he settled back into his chair, placing his feet on his desk. His black shoes, polished to a high shine, glistened in the waning sunlight that came through his window. "If you're involved in this case and taking an interest in this letter, then that tells me I've hit pay dirt on a good story."

"I'm afraid many of my interests come to nothing," Alistair said with a self-deprecating look.

Ira chortled in response. "You want this kept quiet, gentlemen?" Ira took a large puff from the end of his cigar.

"In any ongoing investigation, it's what we prefer," Mulvaney said, his voice low. "There's no need to scare the public or provide fodder for hoaxes. Especially in a case like this."

"And what sort of case is this, Captain?" The editor seemed to take a perverse delight in attempting to bait Mulvaney. He gnawed on his cigar stub. "What I want, gentlemen, is my due. We gotta trust each other. I'll give you time. But I want an exclusive story as soon as you've made sufficient progress on the case—with access to evidence that'll scoop *The Tribune* and *The World*."

"I don't like it," Mulvaney said, seething with barely repressed anger. "I don't want this story in the paper."

But Ira completely ignored Mulvaney. "To make sure I get your exclusive, I'm assigning Frank to the case, effective immediately. He's a top-notch investigative reporter."

Frank's eyes widened slightly, but he did not otherwise betray any surprise.

"That's not exactly a sign of trust, now, is it?" Mulvaney's voice dripped with sarcasm.

"Can't see how you expect us to give you any information when you are so mistrustful of us," Alistair added.

Ira Salzburg skillfully danced around the charge. "It will be a partnership between us. We have a public duty here, see? With any crime, we've got to report the straight news the public deserves to know. But we also have a duty to reassure them that criminals won't escape justice for their crimes. It's what our society needs to hear in times like these."

He leaned toward us and spoke almost confidentially. "Look here, have you considered we might actually help you by publishing the letter? Are you sure you don't want to reconsider? We could publish an exact copy of it. We might get someone who recognizes the handwriting."

"But the writer may have disguised his handwriting. And publishing a facsimile will only generate a round of hoaxes," I said.

He removed his feet from his desk and sat up straight. "Well, then. Frank will be investigating on his own, but you may make use of him if you want. I place him at your disposal. Sometimes a reporter can be more useful than a policeman in ferreting out information."

We looked at Frank, whose expression was unperturbed, as though he had been expecting Mr. Salzburg's recommendation. But after a moment, he cleared his throat. "Boss, I think I'm going to need help on this one. I want someone who knows the theater and will make people more comfortable talking with me. I know from that rash of vaudeville robberies I covered last summer, actors can be a suspicious lot. I'd like to have Jones on it."

Frank locked his gaze on Ira Salzburg, awaiting his reaction.

After another moment, he added, "He's junior, but he's been a big help to me in the past. Nobody can strike up a conversation and get information out of a stranger as well as Jones can."

Ira gazed out at the long row of desks on the floor, deep in thought. His attention seemed to center on the poker table. "Jones is good, but I've assigned him to Bronstein all next week. What about Bogarty?"

"He's a critic, not an investigator." Frank frowned in disapproval. "And he's difficult to work with. Keeps irregular hours and doesn't pull his share of the writing. Just look at him now."

I turned my head toward the poker game in the back corner, where a well-dressed young man with blond hair and a confident manner was shuffling a deck of cards.

"But he knows the theater." Ira swatted his desk with a rolled-up paper. "And theater types know him. That's what you need. He's gained their trust, so they'll open up to him nice and easy."

Frank still looked dubious. "The women will open up, they always do," he said with a smirk. "But Bogarty's not as good at schmoozing with the men, in case you haven't noticed. Not unless they've got a game on the table."

But Ira was not one to be deterred once he had made up his mind. "Frank, look. Jack Bogarty is a pretty boy who likes fancy clothes and good-looking women. I know you think he's not a serious reporter. But he is becoming a well-known critic and they'll respect that. If his charm doesn't make 'em want to talk, there's always the threat of his next review to loosen their lips. Believe me, this will work. I'll make sure he understands the deal."

Ira took a deep breath yet didn't miss a beat. "And here's how it will work." He now addressed all of us. "Every couple days, you gentlemen and Frank will check in with each other, share anything you find out. And when the case concludes, you'll grant Frank full access to each of you for an interview. And once the killer is in custody, you'll let Frank interview him—or her. He gets an exclusive. Are we agreed?"

Mulvaney looked as though someone had punched him in the gut, but he agreed. We needed the cooperation of *The Times*.

Far worse would be no deal at all—just rampant news speculation—which would be the fate of this case if the yellow sensation papers got hold of it. *The Times* at least espoused the goal of producing serious news. But should the yellow papers pick this story up, they would have a field day with it. They would embellish the truth with lies until they had riled the public into a frenzy. In short, their brand of news coverage would make it almost impossible to investigate this case.

So, after repeated mutual assurances of cooperation and confidentiality, we left the *Times* offices and returned to precinct headquarters—where Mulvaney's grim-faced secretary greeted him with the unwelcome news that the commissioner needed to see him downtown.

The commissioner, Theodore Bingham, had been in office only since January and was still a relative unknown among the ranks. But if he wanted to see Mulvaney near five o'clock on a Friday, it meant he was displeased. I suspected that Leon Iseman, the stage manager who worked for Charles Frohman, had made good on his threat to cash in his political connections and complain about Mulvaney's handling of this morning's investigation at the Garrick.

Mulvaney did not even take off his coat. On his way back out the door, he shuffled through the papers in his leather satchel.

"No need for the commissioner to see this tonight." He passed me the envelope containing the letter sent to *The Times*. "You lads may want to take a closer look. Let me know what you think."

Mulvaney was out the door even before I could agree.

Alistair started to follow him. "I've got to make a couple telephone calls before we commence our next plan of attack."

"Where are you going?" I asked, somewhat irritated. I was eager to review the *Times*'s letter with Alistair, now that Ira Salzburg no longer hovered over our shoulders.

"The question is, where *are* we going?" Alistair flashed a conspiratorial grin. "Lighten up, old boy. It's Friday night. We're about to enjoy dinner and an evening at the theater. I think we ought to see what's playing over at the Garrick."

I turned away before Alistair could see the smile I could not suppress. Even murder could not diminish Alistair's enjoyment of New York's finest entertainment and dining opportunities.

"What did you have in mind for dinner? One of the new places along Broadway?" I eventually asked. As more theaters were being built along Broadway's north end, restaurants were cropping up, too, displacing most of the clubs, brothels, and tenements that had previously anchored the neighborhood.

"Not tonight," Alistair said, in high spirits now. "Dinner at Sherry's is what I had in mind. It's a longer walk from here, but we have time. And the headwaiter knows me; he'll find us a table, even if they're busy."

More casually, he went on to say, "But I do want to make a brief telephone call. There's a colleague of mine I hope will join us."

"Who?" I raised an eyebrow, suspicious.

"A longtime acquaintance who is also an expert in handwriting analysis."

"Alistair." I sounded a note of warning. "I asked for *your* help on this case—not the help of some charlatan. I don't want to hear that a criminal's character can be determined from the size of his head or the style of his handwriting."

Alistair smiled indulgently. "You mean phrenology and graphology. It's true: those disciplines look to the circumference of a person's head or a sample of someone's penmanship and infer specific character traits." He shook his head. "Not to worry, Ziele. My colleague is well regarded as an expert in forensic analysis. He has testified numerous times in London trials on the subject of handwriting and forgery. You'll find his logic to be solid, grounded in science."

"Are you sure?" Given this morning's turn of events in the courtroom, I had no interest in pursuing evidence that would not stand up to the law.

"Yes," Alistair said emphatically. "I know you all too well, Ziele. I won't give you information you cannot present at trial."

As I reluctantly agreed, Alistair made his call, and we set off crosstown toward Sherry's and a discussion that—despite my doubts about its scientific basis—would fundamentally alter our approach to the case.

CHAPTER 7

Sherry's, Fifth Avenue and Forty-fourth Street

"He controls his players' lives more than you'd think. Would you believe he only allows his leading ladies to walk along Fifth Avenue, never Broadway?"

"What are you talking about?" I didn't follow Alistair's train of thought.

We were making our way uptown on Fifth Avenue toward Sherry's. Alistair, nonchalant as always, appeared to be surveying the storefronts we were passing, but it was clear that his mind continued to work feverishly.

"Charles Frohman, of course."

"That's preposterous," I said, scoffing at the suggestion. "How could anyone presume to control where someone walks?"

"It's only a story, of course," Alistair said easily. Then he gave me a knowing look. "But I have good reason to believe it's true. I was once acquainted with his biggest star."

He paused for effect.

"You may have seen Maude Adams onstage? Fascinating woman."

I shook my head. She was Broadway's most well-known actress, so of course I had heard of her. But I had never seen her perform.

"Well, as Miss Adams once explained it to me, Frohman believed her offstage image would directly affect her onstage reputation." His voice grew softer. "I do know his influence once led her to cut off a romance that he believed to be inappropriate."

I eyed him suspiciously but declined to comment. Whatever his personal secrets, he was entitled to keep them.

"And what does this story—assuming it's true—have to do with the murders at the Garrick and the Empire?"

"Perhaps nothing—at least not directly," Alistair said. "But it is the environment in which your investigation will take place. You should understand it."

I nodded.

"Here we are." Alistair raised his arm and pointed to the classic brownstone entrance to Sherry's, a restaurant located across the street from its chief rival, Delmonico's, in new quarters designed by Stanford White. It was one of New York's finest restaurants—a place where one went not merely to dine but to be seen. I had never been there myself, but like most New Yorkers I knew it by reputation, for its patrons' over-the-top soirees were regularly written up in the papers. And while I was not a regular reader of the society column, in recent months

I had scanned it on occasion, wondering if Isabella's name would appear.

It was a typical Friday evening and Sherry's was filled to capacity. Yet, exactly as Alistair had anticipated, the headwaiter managed to find a small table for us. Sherry's reserved exterior had not prepared me for the opulent scene indoors. Walking through the Palm Room, I gawked openly at the vaulted ceiling above, which was covered in elaborate latticework that, on each side, reached to the edge of a row of windows surrounded by a gold floral design. Numerous potted palms created a tropical effect that made me feel suddenly far removed from the icy March night outdoors.

The moment we were seated, our waiter—a stiff man in a black suit—seemed to assess the age of my worn brown suit as he placed a napkin emblazoned with Sherry's name on my lap. I looked across the table at Alistair. He had moved his napkin immediately and thus escaped our waiter's intrusive attention.

"Wine list, sir?"

This was addressed to Alistair, not to me.

"No need." Alistair instead ordered a bottle of his favorite Bordeaux—one he knew they stocked in their cellar.

Meanwhile, I counted the number of forks placed in front of me. The silverware was arranged from left to right, small to large, except for the exceptionally small fork at the top of my plate. I flipped one over to look at the engraving: TIFFANY & CO.

Putting the fork back, I reviewed the menu in haste, for there was no time to be lost if we were to make this evening's show.

Our waiter had reappeared with the requested bottle of wine. He removed the cork with a grand flourish and poured

Alistair a sample of the Bordeaux, which he tasted and approved. The waiter then poured a glass for me, accompanied by a condescending stare that I returned in kind.

"May I suggest the roast beef, sir? It comes with a delicious potato lyonnaisse and is very popular."

The menu suggestion was directed to me, and no doubt it contained a veiled insult I did not fully recognize.

"Thank you, but we're interested in your spring specials tonight, not your regular fare," Alistair said smoothly. "What does the chef recommend?"

I listened impatiently as the waiter went on to describe the spring lamb, omitting no intricate step of its preparation. In the end, I deferred to Alistair, who ordered for both of us: an oyster appetizer followed by the lamb. I had a weak constitution for oysters, and I immediately regretted delegating this task.

"I wasn't certain that I would hear from you again, Ziele," Alistair said as he swirled his glass of wine, then sniffed its aroma. "But I'm glad I did. Whether by merit or by chance, you seem to have landed a most interesting case."

But I was in no mood to entertain a heart-to-heart discussion with Alistair.

I glanced at my pocket watch. "What time did your handwriting expert say he would meet us?"

The waiter resurfaced to refill our glasses of Bordeaux, though neither of us had taken more than two or three sips.

Alistair was perturbed by my impatience. "Dr. Vollman should be here momentarily."

Another server—this one a young boy—brought over the oyster appetizer together with yet another strangely shaped fork. Alistair eagerly sampled one.

"Why not relax, enjoy the food and wine? These oysters on the half shell are delicious. Go ahead and try one."

Aware that our waiter—who was now arranging dishes to accommodate the used shells—was watching me intently, I followed Alistair's lead. It was not their briny taste that I disliked so much as their slippery, cold texture. I immediately took a large gulp of Bordeaux.

As if he sensed my lack of appreciation for what others considered a fine delicacy, the waiter frowned in disapproval. I stared back at him until he retreated once again from the table.

Alistair appeared not to notice my reaction, for he went on to say, "These are Blue Point oysters—a rare delight. The original Blue Points from the Long Island South Bay are now extinct, of course, but these transplanted ones are almost as good. They bring the oysters in from the Chesapeake and let them spend a few months in the Great South Bay before selling them." He smacked his lips. "A pure delicacy. Not like the ones you're used to in those all-you-can-eat places on Canal Street."

I was sure he was right. But I had never been a fan of the Canal Street oyster bars, either. Though many New Yorkers considered oysters everyday fare, I had never enjoyed them—never liked the look of them. While their presentation here at Sherry's was more elaborate than I'd ever seen, even so, they didn't look appetizing.

"Are you sure your expert can help us? We might have found a better use for this time, talking with some of the players at the Garrick."

Admittedly, I was second-guessing Alistair's plan already. I had never fully appreciated what I thought amounted to blind devotion to new theories. And his track record was certainly not impressive. He had been positive, based on his research and interviews, that he knew the man responsible for the brutal murder I had investigated last fall. And he had been dead wrong.

But Alistair's laugh was relaxed and easy. "The actors and actresses will be available—and likely to talk more freely—right after the show. You did ask for my help, Ziele." Alistair pointed this out with no small degree of self-satisfaction. "You can't say you need me and then reject my advice."

He refilled his glass with the Bordeaux—for I had apparently offended or frightened our too-helpful waiter—before he continued. "The art of handwriting analysis—and yes, admittedly it is an art, not a pure science—has been with us for hundreds of years. Did you know the first scientific treatise on the subject was a French work published in the early 1600s?"

Before I could respond, an elderly man, small but spry, approached us. He carried a brass cane, but as he did not appear to lean on the stick at all, I decided he employed it more for show than for need.

"Dr. Vollman." Alistair stood up.

"Professor." Dr. Vollman nodded in greeting to Alistair, even as he peered at me curiously from behind wire-rimmed glasses. "And you have a new assistant, I see?"

"This is Detective Simon Ziele, and I am assisting *him* in a new investigation," Alistair said. "Ziele, I'd like you to meet Dr. Henry Vollman, a forensic expert on handwriting—and also a professor of sociology at New York University."

"I see." Dr. Vollman smiled as he eased himself into his chair, placing his cane against the table. "So how can I help you gentlemen?"

He waved away Alistair's offer of a menu. "Perhaps just a touch of cognac. Yes, that would be nice. Something to take the chill from my bones." He leaned toward me confidentially. "You'll find as you get to be my age, that's harder and harder to do." Then he sighed dramatically as Alistair motioned to our waiter, who now came over reluctantly to take the order.

Moments later, Dr. Vollman had his drink, and Alistair and I were brought our main course. The spring lamb was served sliced over roast potatoes and accompanied by bright green asparagus. I'd had lamb many times before, but never like this. While I couldn't be sure I fully appreciated the chef's creative efforts, I knew I was eating something that was far from ordinary.

"Before we begin," Alistair said diplomatically, "it would be helpful if you would explain to Detective Ziele something of what you do."

"A novice to my branch of expertise, I presume." Dr. Vollman sighed in mock exasperation, but he actually seemed pleased to have the opportunity to talk about his occupation. "First, I should tell you my line of work arose from the proliferation of forgeries our country has seen in recent decades. As our society becomes better educated, an unfortunate few are using their newfound skills for illicit purposes. Now more than ever, the law must know if a document is forged or if it is true. And from the close observation of experts, common principles of understanding have emerged."

I interrupted him roughly, for he seemed to have digressed far afield. "But what we need to know has nothing to do with forgery."

Dr. Vollman waved me off.

"Just because this line of inquiry began with forgery doesn't mean its principles are limited only to the identification of forgers." He made a noise of impatience. "Let me show you, and then you will understand."

With a shaky, laborious movement, he pulled a notebook and pencil out of his coat and handed it to me. "Would you sign your name five times, please. Just as you normally would."

Perplexed, I obliged, making a column of my signature.

Alistair's barely repressed smile suggested he already knew the point of this exercise. Perhaps he had once been subjected to it himself.

"As you can see," Dr. Vollman said, beaming with pride, "not only is each person's handwriting unique from any other person's, but no person writes the same thing the same way twice. Consider your own five signatures. See how they differ: in each case, your Z is a different height. Your es vary in width. And even the length of your signature varies a good deal between your first and fifth attempt. Attempt number three is the longest by almost an eighth of an inch."

I examined what I had written and had to admit he was right.

Alistair said, "And you were writing your signature in a fairly controlled environment: same time, same pencil, same paper. Imagine the slight variation caused by writing on different paper, with varied instruments—sometimes a pencil, sometimes a pen, each of them a different width. Sometimes you write in a rush; other times slowly and deliberately. And your writing surface may vary from wood to a desk pad to a notebook."

"Aging influences your writing as well," Dr. Vollman said

with a rueful smile. "My writing today is a frail, shaky affair compared to what it was when I was younger, like yourself."

"Then how can analysis help us at all, if handwriting is so susceptible to environment and change?" I asked. I had begun to suspect this meeting was shaping up to be another of Alistair's frustrating exercises, a game to provide intellectual amusement but no real information.

"Ah." Dr. Vollman nodded sagely. "Because despite all these minor inconsistencies, there are things I can tell from your writing, based on close observation, that you cannot disguise however much you try."

Dr. Vollman was obviously accustomed to defending his work from skeptics. He went on to instruct us, saying, "Look at the initial *S* in your first name. It has a distinctive loop that carries throughout each of your signatures . . . despite the size variation. Your leftward slant is consistent, your writing flows firmly with a bold stroke, and your letters are somewhat crowded together with minimal lifting. But more particularly—" he broke off, and his small gray eyes bored into my own, "I suspect you have not always written with your left hand. Something happened—an injury to your right arm or hand perhaps—that caused you to change the hand with which you write. Your signature strives to be firm and bold, but it is slow. There is a wavering, a shakiness if you will, that betrays the fact your signature is newly formed, not developed from the habit of years. This trait would also be found in a man who had developed arthritis. You are no longer young, but you are not yet old enough to suffer ailments of the joints. So it follows that you were injured, and your signature bears witness to the fact, like it or not."

"Fair enough." I was impressed with his discovery, but I didn't want to show it. And what mattered was his opinion about our suspect's writing, not mine. I handed him the Downs murder letter that Mulvaney had left us, and Alistair passed him the longer missive that *The Times* had received.

"What do you make of these?"

He did not answer, though it was clear he was giving each letter close attention.

"Not that we have any real doubt," I said, summarizing, "but we assume you'll confirm they're by the same author. It's the same blue paper from Crane's and the same light, spidery handwriting. And we see similarities in how the *y*s, the *d*s, and the *w*s are formed in each letter. They are nearly identical."

Dr. Vollman grunted, then picked up the first letter found next to Eliza Downs's body. "What I tell you first about this, I suspect you already know. But to review: its content shows he is a well-educated man, familiar with poets like Browning. I see his spelling is accurate, and his word choice is formal, with no errors in usage or punctuation." But when Dr. Vollman turned to the longer letter sent to *The Times*, his eyes were full of excitement, as though he were about to impart a particularly compelling secret. "Now this letter, however, is pure gold—at least in its value to you. Why, you ask? I will explain."

He placed the letter before us so we might see, and even Alistair peered curiously as he waited to hear what Dr. Vollman would say.

Eventually he cleared his throat and spoke. "To the extent that any of this man's writing will help you to identify and find him, this letter to *The Times* will do it. Because of its length, it reveals important information about the writer's linguistic habits as well as his actual handwriting. Anyone can alter his phrasing and handwriting for a short while. But not for a longer missive. His writing is consistent throughout, so we can say with confidence that his true hand is at work."

"Why is his tone so much more casual?" I asked, quoting from the letter: "'Here's your chance to cover the biggest story of the day. Your job?'"

"He's writing for a different audience," Alistair said quietly. "By reaching out to the papers—and specifically, *The Times*—he is communicating with people who were not there. People who did not know his victim, who did not see her body. So his point is less about what he's done and more about who he is and what he wants."

So, who was he? And what did he want?

I reread the message I found so troubling—*Hell Awaits*—and I shuddered in spite of myself. It was disturbing enough to have seen this killer's victim this morning, but his writing about it struck me as even more menacing.

Dr. Vollman spoke again, drawing my attention back to the letter. "His true handwriting spacing is naturally wide, with frequent pen lifts. That movement of the pen is something ingrained in him. It would be nearly impossible for him to disguise it in any of his writing. You can compare." He gestured to the first words of each letter. "Note that he attempts a severely angled leftward slant at the beginning of each letter. But it cannot hold. So by midletter," and he showed us specifically, "he has reverted to his natural, slightly rightward slant. There is a loop to the tail of his *j* and *y* that I suspect is natural."

Dr. Vollman was pleased with himself. He went on to say, "I can also tell you with some confidence that he is a man still in the prime of his life. You may be tempted to think he is older, that he writes in a thin, frail hand."

I nodded. I thought of the style as spidery.

"But to maintain it, given his cycle of pen movements and lifts, would be extremely unlikely were he truly an elderly man. As I have shown you, age increases irregularity—whereas his pen remains consistent."

The doctor's explanation had certainly been interesting, but I remained dubious it would actually help us identify the writer of these letters—absent our having the good fortune to come into a document penned in his own name. I said as much, and, to my surprise, he agreed with me.

"There are limits to what handwriting analysis can offer, Detective." He smiled. "But what uses we have, I offer you freely."

"So you can tell me nothing about his personality from his handwriting?" I asked. I had heard of so-called handwriting experts doing so, and I admit, that was what I had anticipated of this meeting.

"That would be a whole different kind of analysis, called graphology," he responded soberly. "And while you may want to consult a graphologist to see if you learn anything of interest, be very cautious. That field is filled with charlatans who'll take your money and give you nothing for it but the ramblings of their imagination that bear no relation to scientific thought."

He pushed back his chair.

"Gentlemen." He bade us good night. "I have my own show to attend this evening. And you'd better hurry," he said, "or you, too, risk being late."

I glanced at my watch; it was half past seven.

Alistair put a few bills on the table to pay and reluctantly agreed we'd better go, but not before lamenting the fact we had not ordered dessert. "Sherry's gets fresh strawberries straight from Henry Joralemon in New Jersey. His experiments allow him to grow wonderful plants that produce every month of the year." He glanced mournfully at the table next to us, where the diners were sampling a selection of cheeses and strawberries. "It's a spectacular treat that we're missing."

Alistair had insisted on our paying two dollars each for a pair of the better seats in the house, so our tickets placed us in the center of the third row. We excused ourselves as we stepped over the knees of other patrons, managing to find our seats only minutes before the curtain rose. Then I sank deeply into the plush velvet cushion seat and allowed the darkness to envelop me, for the theater had gone pitch black and the musicians in the orchestra pit had begun their loud and brassy overture.

The first act was a series of dance and musical numbers that tried to compensate for an incomprehensible plot. Perhaps it was my imagination, but the actors and actresses seemed stiff tonight. Of course, by now they had to know that one of their own had been murdered. It was to their credit that they had put on the show at all.

The house lights had barely risen for intermission when someone tapped sharply on my shoulder.

"Are you Detective Ziele?" the usher asked in an exaggerated whisper.

I nodded.

"Then this is for you."

He handed me a folded pink note that smelled of cheap perfume. Inside, in large, childish letters, I found an invitation to meet someone—a woman named Molly Hansen—just outside the stage door after the show. "But P.S., lose the toff sitting beside you," she wrote.

I reopened my program and scanned the list of actors and actresses in tonight's performance. I was certain my sharp intake of breath was audible when I read her name toward the bottom.

MOLLY HANSEN—*Milkmaid.*

She was the actress who had replaced Annie Germaine.

After the curtain at last fell on the second act, I whispered hurried instructions to Alistair to interview the actors backstage. "I'll meet you back here in an hour," I said, knowing he wouldn't let me go easily.

His eyes narrowed in suspicion, lingering on the note in my hand. Of course, he disliked being excluded.

"Someone wants to meet me alone. Besides," I added, "it's perfect timing. I had hoped you might talk privately with Miss Bowen tonight. A leading lady of her stature is far more likely to talk with someone like you, who truly knows the theater. . . ."

Luckily, he appreciated my attempt at flattery. And the fact that Miss Lily Bowen was exceptionally pretty ended any other objections he might have had.

CHAPTER 8

West Thirty-fifth Street

I waited for her at the backstage door—growing increasingly uncomfortable when I couldn't shake the sensation that someone was watching me. I checked both the side alley and the vestibules of surrounding buildings, but saw no one. The audience had dissipated quickly, for it was a cold, unpleasant night.

I nervously checked behind me again to make sure, shivering and rubbing my aching right arm. No doubt I was reacting to the fact that Annie Germaine's killer had waited for her in this spot, mere hours before her death. Perhaps I was even sharing the same perspective: a deserted brick alley filled with garbage, a man smoking a cigarette by the newsstand across the street, and passersby moving in haste to escape the brisk March wind.

My apprehension continued to grow until Molly Hansen finally appeared, having made a poor attempt to hide herself under the thick black shawl that covered her head and shoulders.

With only a slight nod of greeting, she grabbed my arm and whisked me down the block.

"Walk faster," she commanded, casting a furtive glance behind us. "I'm going to catch it if Mr. Iseman finds out I've left the theater while still in costume. And his temper is terrible: he treats infractions like they're cardinal sins."

We hustled down the block until we arrived at The Emerald Isle, an Irish pub with which she was apparently quite familiar. It was a hole in the wall—a tiny space with dark paneled-wood walls and no more than eight tables and benches where a handful of customers sat eating and drinking. But there was a roaring fire in the grate, and the room was filled with the sweet odor of pipe tobacco, an unexpected smell for this manner of establishment.

She took a table at the back next to the bar. I followed cautiously.

"Two Bushmills," she called to the bartender.

"Aye." The bartender poured the tawny golden whiskey into two short glasses, then brought them over without a second glance toward me. "Molly, you working again?"

"Sure am," she said, taking off her coat and placing it over the empty chair between us, then pulling off a brown wig to reveal long, red curls, which she quickly whisked into a loose knot before she sat down. "I'm in a new show over at the Garrick. Come over and see me one night, why don't you?" She flashed him a broad smile that revealed even white teeth and dimpled cheeks.

She excused herself for a brief moment.

To avoid the bartender's unmistakable stare, I pulled my pocket watch out to check the time. A quarter 'til eleven.

A half hour remained until I had to meet Alistair again.

When Molly Hansen returned, she had changed into a green dress and washed her face of its greasepaint. I saw that her skin was remarkably good—clear and healthy, the color of fresh cream except for a sprinkling of light freckles around her nose. I decided she must be about ten years older than I— probably a year or so past forty—for although she was a handsome woman, I noted the telltale sprinkling of gray amid her red curls. She was also self-assured in a way that only comes to some women as they mature.

I took hold of my drink but waited to take a sip. Something about her prompted me to keep my guard up.

"So what's this about?"

She inclined her head, giving me an intent gaze. "You're not what I expected," she said finally.

"Who—or what—led you to expect anything?"

"Just people talking." She drained her Irish whiskey in one shot, flung her head back, and called out, saying, "Johnny, I'll have another."

The bartender returned with another glass, and this time he directed a worried glance to me. I gathered Molly Hansen was not normally a drinker—and he suspected I probably had something to do with her uncharacteristic indulgence tonight.

"You look familiar," he said at last. "You've been in here before?"

"Don't think so." I returned his probing gaze with a steady

look. I'd never seen him, and I'd certainly never been to this particular bar.

He walked away, shaking his head, muttering something incomprehensible.

"You were about to explain why I'm here and how you knew to contact me." I finally took a small sip of the whiskey. It was not my favorite drink, but on this bitter night I savored the slow burn as it went down.

Her entire frame tensed even as she forced a bright smile. "I thought I could help you out, Detective. I have information about Annie Germaine that you might find useful."

I waited, knowing there was more to come.

Her jaw was set in determination. "I was hoping that in return, you could help me out with a favor."

"I don't work that way, Miss Hansen," I said, leaning back. "And may I remind you that this is an official investigation. You're duty-bound to tell me anything you know. Otherwise, we have a name for it: obstruction of justice." I paused for a moment to let the words sink in.

She shook her head, smiling. "Call me Molly. And you misunderstand me, Detective. I am talking about an exchange of goodwill, nothing more."

I misunderstood nothing. But I let it pass.

"How well did you know Miss Germaine?" I asked.

She cast a furtive glance around the bar.

"We can return to the theater to talk, if you prefer. . . ."

She laughed, a low and guttural sound. "Allow me to offer my first bit of free advice to you. If you want to learn any *real* information from me or any of my colleagues, you'll need to get us in private, away from Mr. Iseman's watchful eye. No one will say a word if it's possible he may be listening."

"Why not? He doesn't sign their paychecks. He doesn't even cast them in the roles they play."

She regarded me with an indulgent look. "It's far more than that, Detective. Don't make the assumption that you understand everything about Mr. Iseman just because you know his job title. He does more than manage the theater's day-to-day operations. He not only has Charlie Frohman's ear—he also has his trust. And mark my words," her voice was suddenly sober, "you'll learn nothing of value so long as anyone thinks Mr. Iseman may hear of it."

I considered the woman in front of me. She gave every appearance of being forthright and honest. Yet I did not forget for a minute that just a moment ago she had offered me a roundabout bribe. Furthermore, she was an actress: the art of deception was her livelihood.

"Rest assured Mr. Iseman is not here now. So you've nothing to fear by talking with me," I said again.

She scanned the room once again.

"Or—" I leaned back and regarded her with a steady gaze, "does this have something to do with the favor you wanted?"

She flushed a deep red and avoided looking at me.

"I have a friend who needs help, and you're in a position to intervene." She looked down at the table, where her fingers idly played with her empty whiskey glass, tipping it first one way, then another.

"What kind of help?" My voice took on a more cautious tone.

"He needs more time to repay someone you know for losses at the table. He's good for the money, of course—he just needs a couple extra weeks." She gulped hard, watching my face anxiously for a sign of my reaction.

"And your friend's concern has become yours because . . . ?" I raised an eyebrow.

"Because he owes me money, too." Her face twisted oddly and her voice took on a desperate tone. "I'll never get it so long as he's in the hole to this sort of man. A man who'll take it from him one way or another, leaving him in no position to work."

So it wasn't a favor she wanted, it was a fool's errand. Whether she was talking about an independent bookie or the owner of one of the gambling joints downtown, she was right that I knew such men. I'd grown up among them on the Lower East Side, though after I joined the police force, I'd done my best to avoid them—at least in any professional capacity.

"And your friend owes the money to . . . ?" I asked warily. Her answer was certain to be no one I had any wish to meet.

"Let's just call him an associate of Mike Salter's."

So I had guessed right. Salter's Pelham Café in Chinatown was just like any number of saloons in the Bowery: its public restaurant area was a front for all kinds of criminal activities that happened in back behind closed doors, sanctioned by Mike Salter himself.

I made a careful reply. "Do I know this particular associate?"

She nodded, though she did not look at me, and her voice was low when she replied. "You don't need to see him or talk with him. You could just let me mention your name. It would buy us—or rather, my friend—a little more time."

I sized her up carefully. I knew it was possible there was no "friend" involved at all. It was likely she herself owed the money.

And the "associate" was as likely to be a police officer as a saloon owner like Mike Salter himself. That saloon owners colluded with the police was an open secret in the Bowery called the protection racket: money was directed to certain policemen in exchange for their turning a blind eye to illegal backroom activities. And Molly was right: I didn't want to know more.

"Let me think about it," I finally said. I made it a point never to involve myself in dealings of this sort. It would compromise my reputation and involve me in a shady transaction of which I wanted no part—and for what? To help Molly, I supposed. But it remained unclear to me whether she was worth that sort of risk.

"Tell me about Annie Germaine."

She downed her third whiskey shot.

"I've understudied her the better part of this month. Ever since I came back to town."

I took advantage of the opening. "So before then, you were . . . ?"

"In Philadelphia," she replied automatically.

But I had seen the way her eyes had flickered away from mine in that instant. Her instinctive—and evasive—response told me in no uncertain terms that there was something in her recent past she did not want me to know.

"What made you come to New York?"

Another brilliant smile. "Why does any actress come to New York?" she replied with a coy smile. "For fame and fortune." She pushed her drink aside. "I knew Mr. Iseman, actually. I looked him up when I got back into town, he vouched for me with Mr. Frohman, and I started work the next day—understudying Annie's part as well as that of the lead."

"But with no promise of a role of your own?" I asked, not unkindly. I realized how little I actually knew about the inner workings of the theater.

"No. But the show's prior three understudies each landed regular roles in other productions last month. It was a way to establish myself again in New York."

"When did you last see Annie?" I took another sip of the whiskey.

"Last night, before I went home. She was one of the last to leave."

"Was that her habit?"

"Oh, no." Though her laughter pealed, it had a hard edge. "That's what I wanted to tell you. She was meeting someone after. A man."

The words lingered between us for a moment. Then I finally said, "Which man?"

"If I knew that, I could probably solve your case for you, Detective," she said lightly. Then she leaned in close to me, so close I saw the shades of green that colored her hazel eyes. "But he was the sort of man she told no one much about—not even me. Not his name. Not how she met him. Not even the places he took her."

"Then how do you know about him at all?

"Because I've got eyes, haven't I? She was crazy about him, always getting dressed up to meet him. Had to wear her best dress, perfectly ironed, have her hair perfectly done."

"But you never saw him?"

"Never." Her voice was flat. "She called him her lucky man.

And she was convinced—" Molly Hansen drew in a deep breath and gave me a triumphant stare, "*completely* convinced—that he was gonna make her a star."

Gonna make her a star. The words resonated through my mind as we finished our conversation. The Great White Way was filled with people who wanted to be stars—and a fair number of men who were willing to create them. But only one of them had put his efforts toward murder.

As I raced back to the Garrick so as not to be late, I hoped Alistair had learned more than I had. Because, unfortunately, Molly Hansen had raised more questions for me than she had answered.

CHAPTER 9

The Garrick Theater, 67 West Thirty-fifth Street

"It's not just that Annie's dead—it's that your community has been violated." The young man looked around dramatically, pausing for effect, even though the three women in the room already hung on his every word. "Whoever killed Annie has taken something important from each of you. You've been robbed of the safety and security you should feel here in the theater, your second home."

His eyes flickered toward me as I entered the room, but almost immediately he turned and leaned in toward the lady on his left: Lily Bowen.

Behind her lace handkerchief, she half stifled a sob. "Oh, Jack, I knew you'd understand. It's simply terrible we even had to be here tonight."

The man was thin, with chiseled features and rich blond

hair perfectly coiffed in even waves. He smiled. "It's because of my father, God bless him. He worked in the theater my entire life, so I grew up among you. The theater community was my surrogate family."

Two blond women I recognized from the chorus line nodded wordlessly, their attention fixed on the young man.

A poignant expression crossed his brow. "I lived the theater life until my father died. I was just a boy of nine." His hand moved to his heart. "It affected me deeply. And still does, to this day."

I moved to the back of the green room, a simple waiting area where four dressing tables filled with jars of greasepaint were jammed along one wall, and two almost-threadbare floral sofas were placed against the rear. Alistair stood there, sullen and alone.

"Who's the dandy?" I asked quietly as I approached him.

The lines around Alistair's face tightened. "Jack Bogarty," Alistair said, his voice low. "Remember, from *The Times*? He's the theater critic who is supposedly helping us." He frowned. "From what I can see, his primary interest is making a more intimate acquaintance with Miss Bowen."

I regarded the young man more closely. A "pretty boy" who liked clothes, the *Times* editor had said. Jack Bogarty made the most of his appearance: he wore a smart brown suit accentuated by a yellow cravat and red tie. His every choice—of cut, fabric, and color—was designed to complement his boyish but handsome looks.

"How awful to lose one's father when so young." The taller blonde practically quivered.

Jack rewarded her with a broad, indulgent smile. "No one

supported me afterwards like the actors and actresses he had worked with. Each one of them came to his funeral."

The women surrounding him murmured their sympathies, which he accepted with a sheepish look.

"What about Frank Riley, the crime reporter we met this afternoon?" I whispered to Alistair.

Alistair shook his head. "No sign of him. But this one's been here the better part of the past hour, making eyes at all the women."

We watched as Jack gazed at Lily Bowen with soulful eyes. "So you see, I do understand what you're going through right now. Truly. Perhaps," he touched her arm, "you'd like to talk with me about it over drinks. Shall we go somewhere?"

"I have rooms at the Algonquin." She gave him a coy smile.

It was a fashionable hotel north of us, on Forty-fourth Street. But I knew it was dry—which no doubt explained why Jack immediately suggested an alternative.

"Let's try the Knickerbocker instead. It's right by my offices on Forty-second Street." He took Miss Bowen's hand into his own.

"Why, Jack, I adore the Knickerbocker," she cooed.

He stood. "Where is your coat, Miss Bowen?" Then he caught the eyes of the blondes to his left. "And you ladies should join us as well."

As he helped Miss Bowen into her voluminous coat, he ignored her pout.

"We didn't think you wanted us, Jack," the shorter blonde teased.

He drew back in mock surprise. "Nonsense. We should all go to the Knickerbocker; I never meant otherwise. Your hats, ladies?"

Lily Bowen was already adjusting her broad-brimmed hat in the mirror while the others quickly donned coats, hats, and scarves, chatting amiably.

"Gentlemen." With a cursory nod in our direction, Jack bade us good evening.

We discreetly waited a moment, then followed them out the backstage door. From upstairs, we heard Leon Iseman, voice raised, complaining about something in regard to the Shubert brothers—Charles Frohman's main competition.

"Should we check on him?" Alistair rolled his eyes upward.

"Not tonight." The fact was, I was simply too exhausted. Alistair immediately understood.

"Come with me, old boy," he said, clapping his arm around my shoulder as we braced ourselves for the icy March cold. "You shall have my guest room tonight, and anything else you need."

And after he easily waved off my feeble excuses, it was decided.

Despite the fog of exhaustion that muddled my thoughts, I could not sleep. Alistair's guest room, I knew, had once belonged to Teddy.

Alistair's son.

The room's every wall bore witness to his interests: a gray scabbard and chain hung to my left, bookshelves were filled with small artifacts from past digs, and an Egyptian mural hung above the headboard. I looked down and ran my fingers across the blue-and-gold coverlet on top of the bed. The fabric was thick and rich, entirely unlike the threadbare blanket atop my bed at home. Of course, nothing in my dingy flat in any way resembled this comfortable room, with its tasteful mahogany furniture. Its coordinated blue-and-gold color scheme was reflected in the wallpaper, the fabrics, and the pillows, and even the plush Turkish carpet that, I suspected, had been brought home from some Far East adventure.

I supposed that on my salary, I could afford better than the dingy flat in Dobson, north of Manhattan, that I currently called home. I had no one to support, and I'd amassed some decent savings—the result of many years of frugal living, helping my mother while saving to marry Hannah. But Hannah had been taken from me in the waters surrounding North Brother Island, and my mother had followed within the year.

Not for the first time, I wondered what it must have been like to grow up in this sort of environment. The thought was an uncomfortable one, especially knowing that Teddy Sinclair was dead—even as I lay, completely out of my element, in his room, among his belongings, determined not to think of his wife. Or rather, his widow—no doubt fast asleep in her own apartment across the hall.

All that surrounded me had been his birthright. But something in him had been unsatisfied, quieted only by the far-flung adventures he had repeatedly sought.

I stood up and pulled tight the navy-blue dressing gown—one I told myself was Alistair's, though I knew better. Then I cautiously opened the bedroom door. All was quiet.

With soft footsteps, I tiptoed down the hallway to Alistair's well-stocked kitchen, a large affair of white cabinets, black-and-white checkered floor, and a gargantuan black stove that dominated the room. The Dakota, of course, had been one of the earliest buildings to embrace electricity, so I had only to press a button to illuminate the room. The clock showed ten minutes past two in the morning. I thought momentarily of the liquor cabinet in Alistair's library—one he had invited me to sample at any point this evening.

But no drink could relieve my insomnia. Thoughts of Isabella disturbed me. Was she awake as well?

That was absurd, I decided. I'd thought of her often, always in the context of one magical evening I'd spent with her last fall. We'd had dinner and mooncakes in Chinatown, enjoyed coffee in Little Italy—and for those few, brief hours, I had forgotten the difficulties of the case I'd been investigating at the time. It had been a moment of fleeting happiness.

When I did manage to push her out of my mind, worries about this latest case came streaming in. And so, giving up on sleep, I found coffee beans in the third cabinet I opened; a grinder and French press were immediately below on the counter.

Once I had ground the beans with the hand crank, tamped them into the French press, and run steaming water through it, I was rewarded with a strong cup. I took it and sat down at the small wooden table near the kitchen window overlooking West Seventy-second Street, which was deserted at this time of night.

The coffee's aroma, as much as its comforting warmth, settled my nerves.

This particular case had gotten under my skin. Although the murder today had been disguised as suicide—bloodless and seemingly less violent—that fact actually seemed to make it more disturbing. The killer responsible was sophisticated. And that made his handiwork seem more sinister than the crude, bloody murders I usually investigated.

Moreover, tonight's display in the green room had confirmed that Jack Bogarty and his partner, Frank Riley, were
going to be hindrances to the case, not allies. Not that I'd seriously thought it would be otherwise—but the way Bogarty had
whisked away those actresses we wanted to interview seemed to
confirm it.

I could have intervened, of course. But not without including Bogarty. And I suspected that Molly's advice was solid: that
I'd have better success talking with the other actresses in private. What was even more frustrating was that Bogarty had
been so charming that he'd immediately accomplished just that.
He had elicited their trust, even though he'd just met them. I'd
not seen anyone do that so well, other than—

Well . . . other than Isabella. She'd been friendly and dis-
arming when she had spoken with so many important witnesses—
especially women—during our last case. It was a gift she had
that, just maybe, could help in this investigation.

I made myself a second cup of coffee and relaxed for the
first time that night.

I would ask her tomorrow . . . and hope that she wouldn't
refuse.

Saturday
March 17, 1906

CHAPTER 10

Central Park, near Sheep Meadow

"I remember the almond pastry is your favorite."

Isabella looked up in surprise as I took the seat beside her on the park bench, placing the white pastry box from Bernadette's Patisserie between us. She hesitated, so I helped myself to one of the warm, flaky, almond-covered croissants.

"You brought *pain aux amandes,*" she said softly.

It was a particularly fine, early-spring day, and the earthy smell of wet soil filled the air. It was mild today, and yesterday's snow had almost entirely melted except for those shady patches where towering maple trees protected the ground from the sun's warmth. March was like that: ever changeable.

"I would have thought you'd have chosen to fill your coffee mug rather than buy croissants," Isabella said, her lips curving into a half smile.

"You know me too well," I replied lightly. "I sampled the coffee while I was waiting for the pastry order. It wasn't bad." I took a bite of the croissant. "But clearly baking is Madame Bernadette's forte."

She gingerly helped herself to one of the pastries, then held it high in the air as Oban, her jubilant golden retriever, bounded over with muddy paws and a stick. Guiding his nose away from the pastry box, she passed me her croissant to hold for a moment while she stood and tossed the stick far into the field that bordered the green where, even at this early hour, a noisy game was being played by a group of boys, not far from the grazing sheep. Rumor had it that the sheep were an important part of Olmsted and Vaux's original plan for a peaceful and bucolic space within the park. They obviously hadn't taken into account how a vast green meadow would appeal to the boisterous games of men and boys alike.

And dogs. Oban retrieved the stick, but dropped it when he found another dog for a playmate—this one an energetic white terrier who wanted only to be chased.

"Shall we walk?" Isabella gestured toward the dogs.

"Of course." I picked up the white box and stepped into pace alongside her. Looking south, a few of Manhattan's tallest buildings—the kind they called skyscrapers—rose majestically into the sky. And other, similar buildings were under construction as the city continued to expand northward.

I glanced down at Isabella. She was smartly dressed in a heavy, dark blue coat, the sort women wore outdoors to protect their nicer clothing from the dirt and muck that was the reality of the city's streets. She had dressed appropriately for the weather, unlike other women I observed passing by. In small groups or accompanied by gentlemen escorts, they strolled in elaborate hats and silk dresses sure to spoil from today's mud. Isabella was the only woman within sight who walked alone—a habit that I knew concerned Alistair, despite her many assurances that Oban was escort enough.

"It's been a while, Simon. You might have called on us. I know Alistair invited you on several occasions around the holidays." Her rich brown eyes looked up at me, full of reproach.

"I had trouble making it into the city," I said, knowing the white lie would not fool her.

I had purposely avoided Alistair, politely declining some invitations while ignoring others. I had treated him unfairly and I had hurt Isabella—and that realization cost me a fresh pang of guilt. But I had believed no good could come of continuing my connection with them. While Alistair had claimed to be my partner in good faith, determined to help me catch a brutal killer in last November's murder investigation, he had in fact withheld crucial information from me. I had not once doubted his brilliance, but I had questioned his trustworthiness.

As for Isabella, we had become close during the weeks of that investigation. Uncomfortably close. No doubt it had been an affinity resulting from our mutual loss: the death of her husband, Teddy, and that of my fiancée, Hannah. The fact that my feelings for Isabella might have had something to do with my decision to keep away was a truth I was not yet prepared to acknowledge.

When I could bear her silence no longer, I added lamely, "Work has kept me busy."

She nodded. "And now work brings you here again. . . ."

It was the opening I'd hoped for. "Actually, it leads me to

ask for your help once again." I looked down at her to gauge her reaction.

"Please." She shook her head. We had caught up to Oban, and she retrieved his favorite stick from the ground. He grabbed it from her hand and trotted beside us as we followed the walking path toward the lake, where a handful of ice skaters struggled against the melting ice this Saturday morning.

"Oban," I said. "It's an unusual name. Is it from the whiskey?" I hazarded a guess.

"No, Simon, not the whiskey." She laughed, and it was the merry peal that I remembered so well. "But the whiskey—and my dog—are both from the town of Oban in Scotland. It's a small, beautiful resort town on the west coast, where I stayed for a while after Teddy died."

We were silent for some moments as an awkwardness rose again between us.

"It wasn't kind of you to treat Alistair as you did," she said slowly. "When we met you last fall, you reawakened something in him that I haven't seen since—" she took a breath, "well, since Teddy died. He felt it keenly when you ignored him these past months."

"Nonsense." My voice was rough. "Alistair has his own obligations at the law school, as well as what appears to be a full social calendar."

"Yes, but not one of his many friends or associates is like you. Most of them want something from Alistair—particularly, to take advantage of his wealth and connections. No one will stand up to him, let him know when he's wrong. As you've done, Simon. And he respects you for it."

"Maybe." I gave her a bemused smile, going on to explain to

her how things had gone last night—how Alistair and I had tried to talk with the actors and actresses backstage and been completely upstaged by the *Times* reporter. "His name's Jack Bogarty, and he's even more charming than Alistair," I added ruefully. "So last night I considered: how could we have better success? And the answer involves you."

"Me?" She seemed genuinely puzzled.

I shrugged. "People seem to trust you. I observed it last November, when you helped me interview witnesses in the Wingate investigation. Maybe it's because you're not a police detective. Or even a worldly criminologist of a certain age. I promise you will encounter no danger."

But she ignored me, unconcerned as always about personal risk.

"So you'd like me to speak with the actresses at the Garrick?" She was serious, sober.

"Yes. This afternoon, if you can."

She turned to face me. "All right, but I have one condition. I want to be fully included in the case. Meaning, I want to accompany you to the autopsy later this morning."

"How did you . . . ?" I didn't bother to finish the question. Obviously Alistair had told her when he saw her earlier this morning. He had known she was headed to Central Park, for he had told me where to find her.

"I want to be involved, Simon." Her voice was even. "If you want my help, I won't be pushed to the sidelines."

"Unless it becomes too dangerous," I said. I looked down at her with concern. "We're hunting a killer who targets young women."

"Actresses, that is," she reminded me.

"Not necessarily. Just because the two recent victims we know of . . ." I couldn't finish saying it. Luckily, I didn't have to.

"I see," she said. "You think there could be more who don't fit the pattern."

"Or—the pattern could be something larger and more complex than we think at this point. That's what worries me most."

She called Oban back to her side and, turning around, we headed back to the western edge of the park and the Dakota building. "I guess we'd better get to the autopsy then, and begin learning what we can. Things that are complicated always take time to understand," she added with a reassuring smile.

But I didn't necessarily have to understand this killer—at least, not completely.

I just had to stop him.

CHAPTER 11

City Coroner's Office

It was called the dead house. And, as coroner's physician, Max Wilcox was its guard and protector. He defended the place—and those unfortunate enough to end up there—from all interference, political or otherwise. Max had only two allegiances to speak of: the first to science and the truths it revealed, and the second to the poor souls who found themselves upon his autopsy table. A bald-headed man with lean features and a concise, soft-spoken manner, he moved with graceful agility among large soapstone tables. Each table had grooves carved into it, designed to channel all manner of fluids into the drains located strategically around the room. Three tables were stacked with equipment, including vials, sponges, jars, even scales. And there was no mistaking what lay covered under a white sheet on the room's back table: Annie Germaine's corpse.

This was the part of my job I enjoyed the least. With my aversion to blood and my weak stomach, I prepared myself for these visits by forcing my mind to detach. By focusing only on strict analysis, I usually managed to subdue my visceral reaction. Even so, I blanched in reaction to the room's overwhelming stench—a peculiar mix of bleach and bodily fluids that made my eyes tear and my breath come in short gasps.

Wilcox had just completed the postmortem examination and was ready to explain his findings. Alistair and I barely merited his attention when we entered the room, but the moment he noticed Isabella, he stared long and hard.

"You're not dressed," he said finally, his tone disapproving.

Before we had been permitted to enter the autopsy room, one of the coroner's assistants had ushered us into separate changing rooms. Alistair and I had dutifully put on the white trousers, coats, and hats that were customary to wear when entering the autopsy room. While Isabella had chosen a white coat to cover her dress, the pants would not have fit even had she chosen to remove her petticoat and skirt and wear them. And the hats we had been provided would not have begun to cover her thick hair, pulled back as it was into a loose twist.

She returned Wilcox's gaze steadily. "I'm not dressed because you've no appropriate clothing for ladies."

Wilcox seemed to consider the situation for a moment. Women were entering nursing school in greater numbers and becoming active in the medical profession. But that was not to say a man like Max Wilcox welcomed them, even as observers. He took his time sizing up Isabella.

"What you will see here is not for the timid," he warned darkly.

"Fair enough." She set her chin in determination.

"Just don't come too close to the autopsy table or my open samples. I need to protect my evidence from outside contaminants." His voice was gruff, but he seemed to suppress a smile. "But you," he gestured to Alistair and me, "should come here. I have things to show you."

We obeyed almost reluctantly, leaving Isabella toward the back of the room, next to a glass-covered cabinet that held a variety of steel utensils.

"You're seeing Mulvaney after we're done here?" Max asked me.

I nodded, adding, "Or at least telephoning him."

"Hrmmph." He made a guttural noise. "Well, you can tell him he was right. All external evidence to the contrary, this young lady is indeed a victim of murder. My internal postmortem examination leaves no doubt."

He pulled back the sheet that covered Annie Germaine to reveal her face and upper body—or what was left of it after the coroner's scalpel had done its work. My stomach lurched as I noted the start of the deep Y-shaped incision that began at her shoulders and ran down the front of her chest. He had needed access, I knew, to her major internal organs.

Alistair's intake of breath was sharp, but Max, a consummate professional, ignored our reactions and continued to explain.

"When I examined this young woman, with the aid of advanced equipment such as I did not have at the theater, I immediately noticed some very small pinpoint hemorrhages. You can see yourself if you look closely at the conjunctiva." He took his steel utensil that resembled a buttonhook and turned her eyelid inside out, just as he had done yesterday at the theater. "The tiny red marks can indicate asphyxiation."

"So this gave you your evidence of strangulation?" Alistair asked.

"On its own? No. Alone, it can neither prove nor disprove strangulation." Max closed the eyelid and put down his button-hook tool. "But taken together with other signs? Yes."

He crossed to the table next to us and returned with three jars containing what looked to be dry samples of skin and sliced muscle tissue.

"The problem confronting all of us was the entire absence of external evidence of injury. And it was important to wait until this morning before conducting the autopsy. You see, the element of time is quite often necessary for the severity of internal injury to appear.

"When I cut the Y incision and accessed her lungs, I immediately discovered that they were collapsed, with no air in them. I determined that I needed to dissect her cervical vertebrae. In other words, her neck."

He drew forth a large specimen jar filled with a pink organ of some kind and reached for a pair of steel tongs. Slowly, he pulled it from the specimen jar and we were once again overwhelmed by the smell of its formaldehyde preservative, designed to prevent shrinkage or distortion. Despite the odor, we went closer to look.

"This is her larynx, including her hyoid bone," he announced. "You will see that I left her tongue still attached." He turned the organ around for us to observe.

I swallowed hard and stole a glance at Isabella. She was

leaning forward with interest—handling the gruesome sight better than I was.

"There was no sign of fracture to the laryngeal skeleton. But look at these telltale signs of contusion hemorrhage in the deep tissue."

We observed the red marks he had indicated.

"You used the term *asphyxiation* earlier," I said. "Can you tell whether she was smothered or strangled?"

His eyes lit up as he led us to the back table, nearer where Isabella continued to stand. I glanced at her and caught her stoic expression. With another steel instrument, this one with a hooked end, he picked up a sample of what I knew to be skin.

"This," he said with a confident air, "is what tells me she was definitively strangled. As the skin dries, sometimes small contusions such as these become apparent. They are from the anterior of the neck. And notice the slight curvilinear abrasion that appears as a small set of two. That is a sign of two fingernail marks."

"Made by her killer?" Alistair leaned in eagerly.

"No." Wilcox's tone took on the indulgent note it often had when he had to explain something to an amateur. "Such marks are usually made by the victim, and these marks are no exception. I measured them against her own nails to confirm she made them herself."

"It was likely an involuntary reaction on her part, to pry off whatever—or whoever—was choking her," I added for Alistair's benefit.

"But I don't understand. How could there be no bruising on her neck if she was in fact strangled?" Alistair asked.

"Ah." Max raised a finger to his lips. "I'd say it was because her killer—whoever he or she was—formed a ligature from a very soft fabric. And when it is released at the very moment of death, it minimizes the chance of there being marks on the skin."

I looked at him sharply. "That suggests her strangulation was caused by a person with considerable skill."

"That would be your job to determine, not mine," he said dryly.

He half leaned against a tall stool near the sink. "Everything else was unremarkable," he said in conclusion. "Lungs, stomach, liver—all looked to be normal and healthy."

I glanced at the large jar containing Miss Germaine's stomach. A piece of paper underneath it indicated the organ's weight.

Dr. Wilcox was continuing to talk. "Absolutely no trace of poison anywhere. My report will indicate death by asphyxiation, specifically strangulation."

Alistair gave Wilcox a quizzical look. "You mean you have no more to tell us? You can tell us nothing about the killer himself?"

Wilcox shrugged. "Science has told us what there is to tell." He looked Alistair square in the eye. "Science doesn't elaborate or espouse hypotheses of the sort you seem to want."

"With all due respect, Doctor, I think you mean *you* will not add further detail or venture a hypothesis," Alistair said in response.

"I'm a coroner, not a criminologist, Professor. I deal in hard facts."

Alistair flashed his most charming smile. "Come, Doctor. You and I are not so very different. We both deal with crime on a regular basis, and we seek answers to the same questions: you from the secrets of the body, me from those of the mind."

He pulled over another stool and sat easily, one arm across across his knee. "I'll bet you could tell me something about the kind of person capable of strangling Miss Germaine—without conjecture, looking only to what your scientific examination has revealed."

Wilcox got up and began gathering his steel utensils for sterilization in the sink; his hands moving fluidly across the table. The action reminded me of a pianist's hands floating up and down over the keys.

I tried to reframe Alistair's question in a more diplomatic manner. "For example, was Miss Germaine's killer a man of great strength? Or could a weaker man have done it?"

Max let forth a soft guffaw. "That's one of the biggest misconceptions people have—that it requires strength to strangle somebody. Not at all. In fact," he said, as he placed the specimen jars containing Miss Germaine's organs onto a shelf near the sink, "a very small force applied to the right anatomic area will accomplish the task. Thus, a smallish woman, such as yourself," he gestured toward Isabella, who had drawn closer to us, "might actually strangle a large man such as Mulvaney." His mouth formed a slight smile, as though he found the idea amusing.

"How much knowledge—or experience—would that take?" I asked.

"To get it right?" Wilcox considered for a moment, then said, "A good deal, unless the killer simply got lucky."

I glanced at Isabella. Though she remained some distance away, she appeared unfazed by the coroner's explanation.

"Is it likely, then, that the killer has done this before?" Isabella asked.

The coroner bristled. "Science doesn't deal in *likely*." He put a scornful emphasis on the word. Then he reconsidered. "But possible, yes. I'd say it's quite possible."

He began gathering a different set of tools, and I recognized that he was preparing to sew the body back together for burial. "If her killer did not have prior experience, at the least he had done extensive preparation to know exactly where to apply force—and exactly when to release it—to avoid the telltale bruising that otherwise would result."

I briefly explained to Wilcox our suspicions regarding Eliza Downs.

"Would it strengthen our case to autopsy Miss Downs?" I frowned. "We would need to approach her family for permission to exhume her corpse."

"I'd say that's more a legal question than an investigative one." Alistair stood. "It would allow the district attorney to pursue a double-murder charge, so it may prove necessary later on. But we have enough information now to establish the killer's pattern of behavior—or modus operandi, as you would call it. I doubt a second autopsy would help us find the killer we seek any faster or more easily."

We thanked Dr. Wilcox for taking the time to explain the postmortem results to us, even before he wrote up his official report.

"What's next, Detective?" Alistair asked, in good humor again the moment we reached the street and could breathe the fresh air.

But I stopped short, frozen.

"Simon?" Isabella's brow furrowed with concern.

I stared ahead at Frank Riley and Jack Bogarty, for the two *Times* reporters were lounging against the black iron street lamp in front of us.

"Good morning, Detective." Frank took a long drag from his cigarette, then tossed it into the street, where a large puddle quickly extinguished it.

"Mr. Riley," I said coldly. "I didn't know your crime beat extended so far downtown."

His face spread into an oily grin. "No place like the dead house for a crime reporter to get his scoop. In fact, I came here looking for you. Thought we might trade some information."

"But not to print." My response was guarded.

"Not yet." He held his hand up as a pledge, the smile still in place. "You've got my word of honor." Then he removed his brown derby for a moment and pushed slickened black hair off his forehead.

"What information do you have to offer us?" Isabella spoke with self-assurance.

"I don't believe we've had the pleasure, Miss . . ." Frank Riley half bowed in greeting, giving a flourish with his hat.

"And I'm Jack Bogarty," his partner intervened, not bothering to disguise his obvious interest as he flashed his most charming smile. "Very pleased to meet you."

"My daughter-in-law, Mrs. Sinclair," Alistair said, introducing her even as he took a protective step closer to her. "You said you had information."

"Ah, yes. I understand that yesterday you interviewed a suspect named Timothy Poe." Frank directed the question to me.

I said nothing.

"Come, now—I know you did. Jack here actually got the tip."

Jack chuckled. "Even theater critics have their sources, you know."

"I spoke with Timothy Poe. So what?" I waited.

Frank scratched his chin. "Well, I think you'd do well to chat with Mr. Poe again. You'll find him at this address." He passed me a scrap of paper with a Greenwich Village address scrawled in black ink.

It read "101 MacDougal Street #5C." It was not the address Timothy Poe had given me last night as his residence.

My eyes narrowed. "What is this place?"

"Not the address he gave you, is it? You're in for a surprise. In return, I need to know if you got confirmation of murder in there." Frank nodded in the direction of the dead house.

I answered him brusquely. "We did."

"And the official cause of death?"

"Asphyxiation," I said, and hoped he would be satisfied for now. Luckily, he was.

I glanced again at the address he had given me.

"Why is Poe here?"

He gave me a knowing smile, though all he said was, "Let's just say Mr. Poe was less than forthcoming in his interview with you."

And before I could ask him any more, he and Jack disappeared into the throng of people in the street.

CHAPTER 12

The Black and Tan District

After Frank Riley's tip, it only made sense to split up. Alistair and Isabella would travel without me to West Twenty-eighth Street, where they would talk with Annie Germaine's flatmates, as originally planned. Meanwhile, I would go to 101 MacDougal Street in search of Timothy Poe—and the secrets he had apparently kept from me.

I caught the first horsecar going west on the Bleecker Street line and found myself crushed near the back of the car, pressed shoulder-to-shoulder against a half dozen other men. It wasn't until three stops later that the crowding eased and I could see through the window for the first time. Outside, pedestrians made their way along sidewalks all but blocked by pushcarts overflowing with fruits, vegetables, cheeses, breads, and sausages. People spilled from the narrow sidewalks onto the street in such numbers, it was surprising that the horsecar was able to make its way past them. It had been a long while since I was last on Bleecker Street, and I had almost forgotten how it felt to be amid its formidable crowds. It was a sensation at once strange and familiar.

A sensation not unlike seeing Isabella again this morning . . .

She had been once more as I remembered her, not the cold and distant woman I'd encountered yesterday at Alistair's apartment. And if I'd thought my time away from her these past four months had dulled my feelings for her, I couldn't have been more wrong. I'd grown accustomed to living with her memory, but reality was another matter. There was no denying the way she had taken hold of my mind and begun to monopolize my thoughts, now that I'd seen her once again. But she was Alistair's daughter-in-law, just two years a widow. And she came from a class—in fact, an entire world—that was far above my own.

If I were tempted to forget that, my destination this afternoon was a reminder. Though I'd never been there myself, I'd heard enough talk in the police precinct—and read enough in the newspapers—to recognize that I was headed into the Black and Tan district. It was a poor area, just like the block I'd grown up on in the Lower East Side. But where my neighborhood attracted predominantly Irish and German immigrants, MacDougal Street had gained a reputation as a place where different races mixed freely.

From those officers who'd worked in that part of the Village, I'd heard tales good and bad: how sober, industrious families lived side by side with more licentious-minded individuals—plus the usual array of street toughs with colorful names like Bloodthirsty or No-Toe Charley. The picture painted in the newspapers by journalists like Jacob Riis was even more scandalous, focused on those "degenerates" who frequented the Black and Tan saloons. His euphemism, of course, referred to those men who kept company with other men—and women who preferred the company of other women. And while I knew Riis focused only on those stories that would scandalize readers and sell papers, it did give me a moment's pause to think what I'd find there.

Why was Poe in this neighborhood? And what had Bogarty learned about him? Riley might have simply told me, rather than force me to travel here myself. His editor had pledged to share information freely with us. But this wild goose chase hardly seemed in keeping with the spirit of that promise. Riley had described Poe as "less than forthcoming." I'd discounted him as a suspect last night, but perhaps I'd been too hasty.

The horsecar stopped at the corner of Bleecker and MacDougal, and the moment I rounded the corner on foot, I saw a gang of six boys leaned over an iron railing at the third tenement on the right, looking intently into the sunken area beneath a large red concrete stoop. The moment I saw them, I knew they were playing a game. I knew it well—in fact, I'd played it myself at their age. The goal was to hit a particular crack in the cement with well-aimed spit. The best shot would get the penny that had been placed in the moat, which was usually traded in for candy after a couple of wins. All this assuming, of course, that the boys finished their game before a janitor or grumpy tenant interrupted them. In the tenement where I'd grown up, a widow named Mrs. Bauer on the first floor was the worst of the spoilsports; she had disliked small boys' spitting and making noise outside her window. But boys would always invent games when there was nothing to do—and Mrs. Bauer had only added an element of challenge to the game.

The smallest boy looked up, noticed me, and immediately seized a more lucrative opportunity.

"Need help finding someplace, mister?" He stopped in front of me, his left hand twisting one of the black suspenders that held up his brown knickerbocker pants. When I didn't respond right away, he eyed me anxiously. "I could help you for a penny."

He was thin and waiflike, probably about nine or ten years old, and I could see his pants were threadbare and had been patched numerous times. I had been exactly like him when I was nine: hungry.

I nodded in agreement and the boy flushed with relief.

"I'm looking for 101 MacDougal." I glanced at the sheet of paper I'd been given. "It must be one of these tenements ahead."

MacDougal Street was comprised almost entirely of tenements and saloons—and at this midday hour, the saloons were not yet open.

"It's down here. I'll show you." The boy bounded eagerly ahead of me until he came to a brown brick building. It was a nondescript structure, only five stories high. Since it was Saturday around lunchtime, it seemed to be fully occupied; in fact, I could already smell a variety of different odors from the slightly opened windows in the kitchens above.

"Which apartment are you looking for?" The boy looked at me hopefully.

"Five C, I believe. But I can find it from here." I handed the boy three coins—enough, I hoped, that he could buy his fill of treats from the pushcarts around the corner on Bleecker.

"Thanks, mister." He pocketed his treasure with a broad smile. "I think Five C is where Walter lives. Top floor."

I climbed the flight of stairs to the top floor, making my way past stairwells filled with children. Some played jacks or marbles; others, mainly the smallest boys, slid up and down the banister railings. In between floors, I glanced into hallways where more children overflowed from crowded apartments. It was a tenement, which meant that all kinds of people—of varying ages and degrees of relation—were crammed together into small living quarters. Had Alistair come with me, I'm not sure he would have comprehended it, even when he saw it.

When I knocked at apartment 5C, a large African man opened the door and regarded me with a quizzical expression. He had close-cropped hair tinged with gray and heavy lines that creased his forehead, crinkling the skin around his eyes.

I glanced at the scrap of paper Riley had given me, just to make sure I'd made no mistake.

"I was told I'd find Timothy Poe here," I finally said.

The man opposite me seemed to grow even taller and larger as he took a menacing step toward me out of his apartment. "Whoever told you that, told you a pack of lies."

I drew my identification slowly out of my coat pocket and showed it to him, deciding to use the information the boy downstairs had provided. "Are you Walter? I wasn't given your last name."

He glared at me, silent for a moment, then his voice boomed an angry, sonorous baritone that carried throughout the building. "Willie. Jim. I got uninvited company here."

I tried not to flinch as two even larger men—one who might have been Walter's brother and another who was short but solidly built, with a face framed by a red beard—seemed to emerge instantaneously from the stairwell. They came uncomfortably close on either side of me, and while they did not touch me, they clearly meant to be intimidating.

I gulped. It was working.

Only in a neighborhood like this one would anyone dare threaten a police officer.

Keeping my voice level, I said, "I'm assisting the Nineteenth Precinct in a murder investigation. Timothy Poe is part of that investigation, and I was told I'd find him here."

I drew myself up taller, attempting to appear braver than I actually felt.

"I told you already: there's no Poe here." The man I believed to be Walter glowered at me. When I made no move to leave, he drew even another step closer. "And I'm gonna give you exactly one minute to get—"

He would have said more, but for the frail, thin, pale hand that reached for his shoulder and pulled him backward into the room.

"It's all right, Walter. I know him."

Walter frowned in disapproval, but stepped back.

And from that simple interaction, I realized with a start how things stood between them. Knowing what I did about the Black and Tan area, I had come here expecting to find Timothy Poe living in quarters with a wife or girlfriend of a different race. But to find him in a relationship with an African man was a revelation I'd not been prepared for.

My instinctive response was to wonder how I could trust a man who had lied to me without hesitation when I interviewed him. If he had concealed this, then what else might he be hiding?

My other, more considered reaction was to ask myself whether my suspicions were the result of his lie—or of what I'd discovered.

"You sure, Tim?" The redheaded man on my left was dubious as he looked me up and down.

"I'm sure. But thank you." Timothy Poe came into full view in the door frame and greeted me. "Detective. Would you care to come in?"

Walter stepped aside and allowed me to enter. When he retreated, he did his best to show no reaction, but I did not miss the flash of worry that crossed his face.

It appeared to be a standard three-room flat. There was no entry hall; I immediately entered a main sitting area with floral-print wallpaper, furnished with two high-backed armchairs and a small sofa upholstered in green.

"Please sit," Timothy said. "I do apologize. My friends are only looking out for my well-being."

I couldn't help but reflect that it wasn't Timothy Poe's well-being that had been threatened.

After Walter disappeared into the kitchen, Timothy and I took seats opposite each other. He chose the sofa, and I took a chair that had a worsted-wool wrap draped over its back. It was plush and of good quality. In fact, all the furniture in the room was of high enough quality to suggest that the residents here were wealthier than I would have expected—at least relative to those in most tenement dwellings.

In front of us, the small coffee table displayed many of the more popular magazines and newspapers—*Harper's*, *The World*, *The Times*, and the weekly paper *New York Age*. Each of them was thumbed over and crinkled; in other words, thoroughly read. There was also a newsletter from the A.M.E. Zion Church—or Mother Zion, as most parishioners called it.

"I do need to ask you: who told you to find me here?" His voice quivered slightly. If possible, he seemed even more anxious than he had been yesterday at the precinct station.

I didn't want to admit it had been a *New York Times* reporter—not yet, anyway—so I merely said, "It was someone else involved in the case I'm investigating. He recommended I seek you out here for further questioning."

The thought crossed my mind: if Riley and Bogarty had known about Poe's true whereabouts, had they also known the sort of reception I might expect? If so, then they had intended to frighten and intimidate me. But that made no sense. I decided they had taken a perverse pleasure in exposing me to a situation even the most experienced police officer didn't encounter every day.

Timothy winced. "I've been so careful. How could someone have known about my relationship with Walter?" Then he sat up straight in sheer panic. "Do people at the theater know?"

"Not to my knowledge," I said gently.

He stared at me, frozen in panic.

I tried to reconcile my image of the gentle, anxious man I had met yesterday with the one in front of me today: still timid, but living in circumstances that would shock all but the least straitlaced among us. And that included me. However much I believed one should live and let live, nothing in my background had prepared me for this. Still, Timothy Poe was the same man I'd interviewed last week: eager, vulnerable, and under wrongful suspicion of murder. So I focused on questions pertaining to the case—knowing that later, I'd make better sense of it all.

Was Poe still lying? His concern about the theater seemed real, and yet . . .

More gently, I said, "I need you to tell me what you didn't yesterday."

He gave no response.

In the kitchen, Walter appeared to be ignoring us, but I suspected he in fact hung on our every word. He certainly had maneuvered himself so as to watch us as he furiously ironed a pair of black trousers and a white shirt—a task that involved rotating the three irons that currently sat on top of the black stove. As one cooled, he returned it to the stove and replaced it with another. He probably needed to dry the clothes as well as remove their wrinkles, for the weather wasn't yet nice enough to hang them outside.

I decided to try a different tack. "Walter, how long has Timothy been with you here?" I called out.

He set the iron he'd finished using back on the stove and held up the black trousers. Satisfied, he carefully draped them over a chair, then came into the living-room area, where Timothy sat, mute and unhappy.

"No offense, Detective, but how does knowing the details of our private life help your case?"

"Because right or wrong, Captain Mulvaney considers

Mr. Poe to be a potential murder suspect," I answered him. "That means *everything* about his life becomes relevant."

"Tim's just beginning to enjoy some success in the theater. Your interest here jeopardizes all that," Walter said, a low note of warning evident in his voice.

"Didn't he tell you that yesterday he was brought in for questioning on suspicion of murder?"

"But you *let him go.*" Walter enunciated the final words slowly. "You obviously cleared him of suspicion."

"Not as far as the captain is concerned," I said dryly. "Mr. Poe remains a suspect—albeit one without sufficient evidence to hold in jail. But lying to the police is damning evidence. So, if he's to be permitted his freedom, I need to know the truth."

Walter heaved a loud sigh as Timothy rubbed his forehead as though he needed to get rid of a troublesome headache. And in the briefest of words, they filled me in. They had met nearly five years ago, when Timothy was in a touring production at the Jersey shore and Walter was working there as a waiter. Walter's family was here, however; most of them still lived around the corner on Minetta Lane, though some had migrated north into Little Africa proper. "My father is an Irishman, if you can believe it, though my mother was born a slave in Virginia." He added simply, "I've lived here my whole life. And I knew that at least within the radius of these few blocks, Tim and I could establish a life together."

I cleared my throat awkwardly. "If I might add something, the theater attracts many people who don't live according to the dictates of conventional society. So why should you care if people in the theater know that you . . ." Walter and Timothy both stared at me so intently that I fumbled over my words, "well . . ."

"That I am a socratist, as Oscar Wilde liked to call himself? And that my affections are directed toward an African man?" Timothy Poe was suddenly defiant. "The ordinary people I work with might not care. But I work in a Frohman production. And he would extinguish my career in a heartbeat if he ever got wind of this."

"I've heard that his theater managers can be controlling with the leading ladies," I said, thinking of Alistair's comment the night before. "But why you? You're not—"

"A star? A leading man? No, I'm not—at least not yet. But Frohman cares, all the same. When you're associated with his shows, his theaters, then he demands a certain kind of behavior in your personal as well as professional life. And," he added bitterly, "I've seen time and again how he will blacklist any actor who doesn't comply—ensuring he never works again. Not for him. And not for Hammerstein or the Shubert brothers, either."

"But I can't imagine how your source obtained any information about us. Tim and I have always been discreet," Walter added. "And our friends here in the Village would never betray us. Most of us face similar pressures in our own lives. Myself, I'm a waiter at the Oyster Club. And I wouldn't care for my employer to know either, though I'm not quite sure what the consequence would be if he did. Speaking of which—" He then excused himself to dress for work.

His job, at least, explained their economic circumstances somewhat better. At a "good" restaurant like the Oyster Club, which was a far cry still from the level of Sherry's last night, Walter would earn a very good salary. My guess was that with tips, he easily earned over a thousand a year. That would contrast with many of his neighbors in this tenement—who more likely worked as day laborers to pull in no more than three hundred to four hundred dollars a year for backbreaking work.

"The other address—" I stopped, knowing Tim would follow my line of thought.

"If someone asks for me there, the fellows will tell them I'm not home." Tim thrust his jaw out defensively. "I pay my share of those rooms. And I do in fact stay there during the week, when I have an early rehearsal following a late show."

"Let's put that aside a moment. I'm curious to know one thing about Annie," I said. "Was there anything in her life that Frohman would have disapproved of? That she might have tried to conceal?"

"I don't know," Tim said. "But the people to talk with would be her flatmates. It's hard to keep secrets from people you spend that much time with."

That was exactly what Isabella and Alistair were doing at this moment.

"Did Annie know your secret?" I finally asked him.

"I don't think so."

But his anxious expression told me that he was unsure. Would fear of having his secret revealed have given him a motive to murder her?

We continued to talk for some minutes more, and I warned Tim, "If it is that important to conceal your life here from those in the theater, you'd better pack some things and plan to stay at your rooms uptown until this case is solved."

It was only partly my concern for him that prompted me to say it. For my own purposes, I'd rather he be in a flat of fellow actors where I could keep closer tabs on his whereabouts.

"I agree." Walter had reappeared, dressed in the uniform of

most waiters at New York's better restaurants—a black jacket and trousers paired with white shirt and bow-tie. "It won't be for long, Tim. But it's not worth the risk."

I walked out with Walter. "Are you likely to need to bother Tim again?" he asked, his voice filled with worry. "It's taken a heavy toll on him, already."

The only answer I could give, however, was the truth.

I simply did not know.

But of one thing I was certain: if I told Mulvaney any of this—and I didn't see how I could in good faith keep it from him—then he would immediately consider Timothy Poe his prime suspect.

And maybe that was not without reason, I acknowledged. Though whether my newfound suspicion was the result of logic or unwarranted prejudice, I could not say.

CHAPTER 13

Mama's Restaurant, West Thirty-fourth Street

"In light of everything we learned yesterday, I don't believe Timothy Poe to be a suspect. But what you say about him is sufficiently troubling; perhaps we ought to reconsider." Alistair was uncharacteristically reflective once I'd finished telling him and Isabella about my excursion into the Black and Tan quarter.

We were having dinner at Mama's—an "experimental" restaurant that little resembled a restaurant at all. We sat in Luisa Leone's living room, in her apartment on West Thirty-fourth Street, enjoying a fifty-cent meal with about ten other patrons. The food was exceptional, and the decor was simple but bright, with red checked tablecloths covering the five tables in the room, and long red curtains separating the eating area from the kitchen.

"Because your analysis was flawed?" Isabella asked, with a teasing lilt in her voice. "Or because Timothy's personal life is so all-important?"

A flash of discomfort crossed Alistair's face before he shook his head. "Criminological analysis can only be as good as our understanding of its subject. In this case, the subject is Timothy—and he has committed a serious lie of omission."

"I'm afraid I have to agree," I said. "If he's withheld information about this, then just imagine what else he has not told us."

I sipped my glass of Chianti from Montepulciano—one Mama herself had highly recommended from her husband's wine shop. I contemplated pouring another glass but decided against it. It was only five o'clock, and while we enjoyed an early dinner now, my night promised to be a long one.

Isabella sampled an appetizer of baked clams, a large plate of which had just been brought to the table.

"Both of you are being ridiculous," she said between bites. "So Timothy Poe lied. He's certainly not the first to do so—especially when the repercussions could easily cost him his career. It doesn't make him a murderer."

I would have preferred to avoid talking of such matters in front of Isabella, but in typical fashion, she'd had none of it when I attempted to speak with Alistair privately—reminding me I'd promised to include her fully in the case in return for her help. "Besides," she had said, "you can't think I don't read the newspapers—though I know there are those who believe them to be inappropriate for ladies. All the papers report about the trials for gross indecency. It may not be suitable for polite conversation at a ladies' luncheon. But then again, neither would most of my work with Alistair."

And she was right. I still did not understand what compelled her to spend her days helping her father-in-law with his criminological research. For her own safety, Alistair did not allow Isabella into the interview room to speak with depraved criminals. But he did involve her closely in all other aspects of his research. It had been her choice, shortly after her husband's unexpected death. But while I understood it had something to do with her grieving process, I knew that wasn't the whole of it. She was genuinely interested in criminals and their crimes, for reasons Teddy's death did not wholly explain.

But I couldn't ask her that. Instead, I asked something that puzzled me a good deal less. "Why do you defend Timothy Poe so staunchly? You've never even met him."

She drew herself up. "I should like to, then. In this particular case, I may be a better judge of character than either of you."

Alistair's face blanched. "Not until we can be positive he's not a murderer."

He was remembering, of course, the gunshot wound that had nearly killed Isabella just four months earlier. It had brought home to him the real risk of his research, and he had renewed his efforts to shield her from the more dangerous aspects of his work.

"Excuse me a moment." Alistair folded his napkin, got up, and crossed the room to greet the large, heavyset man who had just entered the restaurant. The petite woman with him barely reached his shoulder. Alistair seemed to know them both, conspicuously helping the lady out of her fur coat and hanging it on the coat rack behind them.

"That's Oscar Hammerstein and his wife," Isabella said. Her eyes flashed mischievously to the portrait of the wildly popular tenor Enrico Caruso above our table. He held that place of honor because he had been Mama's first patron—the devoted fan of her cooking who had persuaded her to open a restaurant over her own husband's objections, and then encouraged his musician friends to become regular patrons. "Let's hope it's not a night that the Metropolitan Opera singers decide to come here, too. Otherwise, we may see fireworks!"

I glanced over at the Hammersteins. "Why? They don't get along?"

She shook her head. "They're fierce competitors. Mr. Hammerstein is a huge opera aficionado, but he's been outspoken about recent disappointing Metropolitan efforts. In fact, he has begun building his own opera theater. It's under construction just down the street; you must have walked past it on your way to meet us here."

I had. But there was so much ongoing construction in this part of the city, I hadn't given it a second thought.

Alistair returned to the table with a broad smile. "Now, where were we?"

"We were about to put aside your unwarranted suspicions of Mr. Poe," Isabella said without missing a beat, "and discuss what Annie Germaine's flatmates had to share with us."

"Fair enough," I said.

But then our "waiter"—Gene, Mama's youngest son—brought out a heaping bowl of linguini topped with a spicy clam sauce. We waited until he was well out of earshot before we continued speaking.

"Annie shared a set of rooms on West Thirty-seventh Street with the same two actresses we saw briefly last night in the green room." Alistair served Isabella's plate first, his voice rough with frustration. "They went out with Jack Bogarty last night—and apparently told him everything they knew over too many drinks at the Knickerbocker bar."

I groaned inwardly as I thought of the two blondes who had hung on every word the reporter had uttered. Had one of them been the source who informed Bogarty and Riley about Poe's carefully guarded secret?

"But they spoke with you as well?"

"They did. Though who's to say they were as complete in their responses as they were with Bogarty after three bottles of champagne." He frowned. "Most of what they shared involved the mundane details of their daily life. And it's a miserable existence, by the sound of it. They barely make enough each week to subsist, much less save anything; it takes their entire paycheck to afford their weekly rent and food."

"If Annie was in a similar position," I said, thinking aloud, "then could she have owed someone money? Gotten in a spot of trouble over debts?"

Isabella shook her head. "We checked. Florence and Fannie denied it. Annie had simple tastes and normally spent little."

"Normally?" I pushed back my plate of linguini and hoped the unending supply of dishes from the kitchen was exhausted. As flavorful as each dish had been, I was not accustomed to so much food at a single meal.

"About two and a half weeks ago, everything seemed to change," she said. "New dresses found their way into her closet; new baubles decorated her wrists; there were fresh flowers every day beside her bed."

"So from the sound of it, she had acquired a new beau," I said.

"Exactly." Alistair paused a moment to order more wine, then continued talking. "Unfortunately, they never exactly made his acquaintance."

"So they didn't know him well?"

"Not at all, in fact. Annie never brought him around, even to the theater."

"But you got his name?"

Isabella and Alistair exchanged looks, then shook their heads.

"You at least learned what he looked like?" I looked at them each sharply.

Another negative reply.

"Were you able to discover anything about him at all?" My voice rose in frustration as I crumpled my napkin and shoved it aside; my appetite had vanished.

"Well—" Isabella smiled triumphantly as she reached into her deep, black leather bag and drew out a paper. "It seems Annie's new beau enjoyed sending her letters. Florence remembered that, and at our request, she checked first Annie's room, then their garbage—and she managed to recover one for us."

She held it out to me and I took it. The paper was cheap, flimsy, and perfectly square—about five inches all around. Dog-eared and crinkled, it had been stained by an oily substance.

But none of that mattered—because in the faint, unmistakable spidery lines I had come to know so well these past twenty-four hours, I read:

"'Meet me after the show. Our usual place. I'll be waiting.'"

I shuddered and caught Alistair's eye.

"Ah, you see the point." Alistair tapped his chin. "Florence and Fannie did not know anything about his identity. But *we* do."

"Now *you're* being ridiculous," I said, my words coming in a rush. "We're a long way from knowing his identity; we don't have a name or even a physical description."

"No?" Alistair's eyes lit up. "We have something that's actually better. A name could be an alias. And appearances can be disguised. But we have learned a decent amount about something that he cannot change even if he wanted: his *behavior.*"

My frustration began to get the better of me. My voice was heated, though I kept it low for the benefit of the other patrons in the room. "Please. We've learned something about his handwriting; that is all. That is not behavior. And how, exactly, will any of it help us to identify him out of all the men in this city? We could be searching for *anyone.*"

"I think," Alistair said lightly, "you are losing sight of all that we *do* know in your concern for everything that we *don't.*"

There was a long, uncomfortable moment as young Gene brought out dessert—a small plate of fried pastries. "They're called bugies," he said, helpfully. "And Mama wants to know if you enjoyed your dinner?"

"Please tell her it was wonderful, as always," Isabella said warmly, which earned her a quick smile before Gene scampered away again, promising coffee would soon arrive.

"I think I know where Alistair is headed with this," she said. "The writer of this letter," she touched it lightly with her fingers, "has wooed his victim: with dresses and baubles, flowers and dinners. He has spent time with her and gotten to know her. He has seduced her, in a way. I think we ought to speak with Eliza Downs' friends to see if we can establish a behavioral pattern."

"Exactly." Alistair launched his fork vigorously into one of the bugies. "If we are lucky, then one of them may have information you would very much like to have about his appearance or name. If not, then we still have better established his pattern of behavior. And we can use it to identify the next victim."

I could only look at Alistair wearily. "I don't pretend to know much about Broadway actresses," I said. "But it strikes me that sending notes or flowers is not beyond the bounds of normal behavior for a young man who fancies a pretty chorus girl. And remember, Molly Hansen told me that Annie's attachment to this man was driven by ambition. He'd promised to make her a star, not his sweetheart."

"Since when are the two mutually exclusive, Simon?" Isabella asked with an indulgent smile.

"And," Alistair added, "it gives a specificity to our man's behavior. He isn't simply wooing his victims. He's *improving* them in some way: how they dress, where they go, how they live. That's what we can keep our eyes open for in hopes of identifying the next victim."

"How they dress and where they go . . ." I repeated the words automatically, for they sounded familiar. And then it came to me. "That sounds exactly like what you told me about Charles Frohman last night. That he hadn't even wanted his leading ladies to walk on Broadway. It had to be Fifth Avenue, because image was everything. And Timothy Poe may have intimated something very similar this afternoon—"

Alistair looked worried. "Surely you're not suggesting . . ."

"I'm suggesting nothing except a possibility to look into." I kept my voice even. "Part of keeping our eyes open, as you said."

He nodded mutely as I accepted the hot pot of coffee Mama brought out to our table. I poured myself a large cup, though I had no appetite for the pastry Alistair had already devoured.

Because in one respect at least, I knew Alistair was right: a killer who had gone to such elaborate lengths—not just once, but twice—was not prepared to stop.

He would do it again. The only question was when.

And whether we had enough time to stop him.

CHAPTER 14

Nineteenth Precinct Station House

"Commissioner Bingham will not stand for it." Mulvaney was grim-faced and stern. He sat behind his desk, arms crossed in displeasure.

Still, I was persistent. "But you see why I need to speak with him. I'm not suggesting we bring him here for questioning. Rather, a friendly chat—at his office, or even his home."

Mulvaney practically growled at me before he responded by pounding his fist on the desk. "You're not to disturb Charles Frohman at home. You seem to misunderstand the extent of this man's connections. He is on excellent terms with the mayor, the commissioner, the whole lot of them. They like the greenbacks his shows bring to this city."

His frustration spent, he sank back in his chair. "The fact is, they'll have my job if I interfere too much where I've been told to leave well enough alone."

Mulvaney and I were virtually alone at the precinct house. It was deserted this Saturday night, except for a lone patrolman downstairs at the main desk, well out of earshot.

I started pacing back and forth in front of his desk. "You see why I need to talk with him, though. If Frohman's not involved, one of his employees may be. The murders are occurring at *his* theaters. And the control this killer exercises over his victims is not unlike how Frohman handles his actors." I spun around to face Mulvaney. "Perhaps there's a way for me to speak with Frohman informally, in a manner that leaves you out of it. Say, if I happened to cross paths with him at a party or theater event?"

The words were barely out of my mouth before he slapped his hand against the desk and burst out laughing, his exasperation momentarily forgotten. "You, Ziele? At a theater soiree? Since when have you ever been to an event like that?"

I chuckled myself, shaking my head. "You know perfectly well I haven't. But there can always be a first, right?"

Still amused at the thought, he added, "It seems more up the alley of your sidekick professor. Where is he tonight, anyway?"

"He took Isabella to the symphony."

After dinner, they had rushed up to Carnegie Hall for a performance by the New York Philharmonic. Alistair kept season tickets, and apparently tonight's program featured the Brandenburg Concerto, a favorite of Isabella's.

"Hmmph. Well, in any event, he'd be more likely than you to wangle an invitation to a theater gathering." His voice grew stern again at the end. "But I can't see it working. You've got to give up on Frohman."

"So the commissioner doesn't actually want the case solved—he will risk scapegoating the wrong man?" I pivoted to face him again.

Mulvaney looked at me with a mixture of frustration and weariness. "Come," he finally said. "Are you taking the train home? If you are, I'll walk with you. I'm headed in the direction of Grand Central myself."

I agreed, and it was only when we were outside and the glare of the streetlight illuminated his face that I noticed the deep lines of exhaustion that ran along his forehead. He reached up to button his trench coat a bit higher, though tonight's weather was much milder than we'd experienced with yesterday's brief snowfall.

We walked in silence for some blocks before he finally spoke.

"What is it they say, Ziele? Be careful what you wish for . . ." He sighed. "I've always wanted to be a precinct captain. But it can be a thankless job. Too many people with competing interests to balance."

"Are you saying I'm now another interest you need to balance? You asked for my help, remember. This was your case, not mine." I was curt as I reminded him of the fact.

"That's not what I meant. . . . The commissioner, you see—" he started to say, but fell silent before he finished.

"The challenges are greater now, I know," I said more gently. "But we've faced them at every level, you and I. Remember when we first started out? We were barely out of training and we discovered our supervising officer—"

"Was on the take?" He cut me off with a rueful expression. "I do. You almost confided in Elliott, only to find out he was involved, too."

151

I fell into step along his long strides. "And that was at the height of Roosevelt's reform efforts. He did a good deal as police commissioner to clean up corruption, but even he couldn't entirely remake the way the force did business."

Mulvaney grinned. "He put in the system that allowed you and me to join the force. That ought to count for something."

Our current president, Teddy Roosevelt, had been New York City's police commissioner in 1896, when Mulvaney and I had taken the entry exam required of all new patrolmen. We were lucky. Before Roosevelt, there had been only one route onto the force: through a patronage system that depended on bribery, recommendations from the well connected, or both.

Though no one among the passing crowds could possibly have overheard us, I lowered my voice before saying, "We decided then, you remember, that what mattered was the victims. We'd fight against any instance of corruption that interfered with their getting the justice they deserved. The rest wouldn't matter."

Mulvaney nodded sagely. "You called it a matter of picking the right battles. I remember."

I set my jaw. "Well, I'm picking this one. Because we've got two victims—Annie Germaine and Eliza Downs—whose interests are at stake."

Mulvaney pivoted to look me in the eye, and for a split second I thought he was going to erupt again. Instead, he gave me a resigned look. "Ziele, you would've made a helluva lawyer if you'd had the chance to finish college. I can't argue with you."

"So how can you justify protecting Frohman if there's a chance he—or one of his underlings—is involved in the deaths

of these two women," I said roughly. "The only acceptable answer is that you can't."

"Right now," he said, his face white, "the most I can offer
you is this: do what you must. And if you can do it while making
no waves—and without my being the wiser—then it should be
all right."

We parted on those terms at Grand Central. And as I made
my way to a bench opposite track 19, where my train was due in
ten minutes' time, I decided I'd done the right thing by not telling Mulvaney about Timothy Poe. I resolved to feel no guilt in
keeping Timothy's scandalous private life from Mulvaney for
now. Had he known, he almost certainly would have rushed to
rearrest the actor—if not from his own conviction that Poe was
guilty, then from the certain knowledge that Poe was a scapegoat to please even the toughest of higher-ups.

And that would have done no one involved any good, least
of all the two women whose deaths I was charged with investigating.

Twenty-five past nine o'clock. Knowing my train should by
now have arrived on the track, I gathered my hat, worn brown
satchel, and evening newspaper. Today's headlines focused on
various St. Patrick's Day celebrations in the city, including the
usual parade up Fifth Avenue. I was looking forward to reading
lighter fare—a welcome respite from this murder investigation
and the dark thoughts it bred.

I shoved the paper deep into my bag. I didn't notice the man
who stood just a few feet in front of me.

So his voice took me entirely by surprise when I heard it—
though some half-forgotten memory allowed me to identify its

deep, husky baritone almost immediately, long before I looked up and my eyes confirmed it.

Two words were all it took.

Hello, son.

CHAPTER 15

Grand Central Station

It had been more than ten years since I'd last seen him. There had been no goodbye. In fact, there had not been so much as a note. He'd left it to Nick Scarpetta—the owner of the gambling joint where my father had played his last hand—to inform my mother of his departure. Nicky was a gruff but good-hearted man of few words, and I'd never figured out how he'd managed to tell my mother the devastating news: not only had my father gambled away the last of their savings, but he'd left town with another woman.

Like most con artists, my father was gifted with words. And while he typically used his talent to facilitate his latest con game or extricate himself from a tough spot, I'd always thought he owed it to us to say a final goodbye. Of course, whatever he said would have been a lie. Still, words might have helped my mother to better stomach the bitter truth.

He leaned against the edge of the bench, where a lamppost illuminated his unmistakable chiseled features. He looked good, as always, a reflection of his excellent taste in clothing. So, though his shoes were worn and in need of polish, his trousers were well tailored, and his coat—a fine, dark wool—had obviously been purchased on a day when he was feeling flush. And his face was one that women considered handsome: intelligent brown eyes, strong rugged features, and a ready, charming smile. He was taller than I, with a much broader frame. But now that I was older, I recognized his face as strikingly similar to my own—albeit without the charming smile and heavy lines of age.

"What are you doing here?" I asked.

All I could manage to comprehend was how curious—how downright odd—it was to see him before me after so much time.

"Ah, Simon," he said easily, flashing a wide smile. "Not even a hint of pleasure to see your old man? Don't tell me you already knew I was back in town." He coughed, drawing his handkerchief to his mouth in seeming embarrassment.

"I didn't know," I said coldly. But in a flash, I recalled all the times in recent days that I had felt someone was watching me, following me. I now assumed it had been he.

"Of course not." He effortlessly slipped into the seat beside me and crossed his legs. Placing a finger against his chin, he seemed to be sizing me up.

"You look tired, Simon." It was a pronouncement. "You work too hard. I've been watching you."

I didn't respond for a few moments.

"Why are you back?"

"Can't a father want to see his son once in a while?" His tone was cajoling, his attention completely centered on me—and I was reminded of how, as a boy, he had always won my mother over after a night of heavy losses. Whenever he gave his complete attention to anyone, he managed to make that person feel prized, important. It could be intoxicating to the object of his attentions. But I knew it was a practiced form of flattery.

"Once in a while?" I raised a skeptical eyebrow. "Try ten years."

"Touché." He gave me a lopsided smile. "My circumstances became untenable here, you understand. I owed a great deal to some rather unsavory people. I had a large price on my head."

I leveled my gaze at him. "From my earliest memory, you were *always* indebted to loan sharks. You *always* had a price on your head. But you typically handled your problems by going to ground until you felt it was safe to come out of hiding. What was different, that last time? Was it the woman?"

Before he could answer, he was seized by a coughing fit that lasted a full minute. "Just a second, my boy. I could use some water," he said apologetically.

I dutifully got up and procured him a glass from a vendor nearby, whose stand offered most sundry items the evening's commuters might need, from mixed nuts to newspapers. By the time I returned with the water, a lady had joined our bench. She sat next to two oversized white hatboxes, studiously eating a sandwich.

After I managed to squeeze past her, by mutual agreement my father and I moved farther down the bench. He took a sip from the glass and seemed to recover himself, then he resumed our conversation exactly where we'd left off.

"No, I didn't leave New York because of a woman, Simon," he said with a strange look. "I know you won't be able to understand, but I needed a fresh start."

"And Mother . . ." My words were cold as ice.

"Your mother was a fine woman," he said firmly. "And don't think that I'm unaware that she deserved better than the likes of me."

"Well, there at least, we agree. But it didn't stop you from choosing another. Are you still with her?"

"Not her, no." He coughed.

"But you're not alone," I said sharply. He never had been.

He paused for a split second, then continued. "I heard your mother died last year." He was uncharacteristically sober. "I'm sorry."

"She was never the same after you left."

"And you lost the girl, too." He drummed his fingers together. "Beautiful young lady. What was her name?"

"Hannah." My voice was dry, stiff.

"Of course, of course." He tapped a finger against his temple and flashed another smile, assuming I'd understand. "I'm not getting younger, Simon. My mind isn't what it was."

But he had never remembered anything that didn't concern him.

He was continuing to talk. "Charming girl, she was. Would've made you a great wife." He coughed. "So many died that day. Still inconceivable to me that one burning steamship could cost so many lives. I heard about the Angers and the Felzkes—"

I cut him off. "Too many . . . far too many were lost that day." Over a thousand people had died when the *General Slocum* steamship burned and sank, many of them friends and neighbors. I'd boarded one of the police rescue boats, the moment I'd heard. We'd rescued a handful. But I'd watched as scores of desperate people leaped to their deaths—some doomed by the faulty life preservers they wore, others by the fellow passengers who jumped too closely behind, knocking them unconscious in the water. Sometimes, when my mind played its worst tricks on me, I imagined I had seen Hannah herself take the final leap to her death. But most of the time, I succeeded in telling myself I was mistaken.

He coughed. "Simon, I can't undo what's been done. But I am here to make amends if I can."

I stared at him in disbelief. "*That's* why you came back. To make things all right with me?"

"Yes, if I can." Another cough into his handkerchief. "Your mother's gone, God rest her soul. I'm too late, in her case. But I know I did you wrong too, though you're enough of a man not to berate me for it. I guess you'd have been some bigwig lawyer or banker by now if you'd been able to keep your scholarship at Columbia. As you would've done, if not for my leaving."

"It doesn't matter now." I breathed in deeply. "So what— you're here to apologize? Ten years later?"

"I suppose." But he sounded uncertain and looked at me curiously.

"All right. Is there anything more?"

He stared at me with an unreadable expression. "I suppose . . ." He waited for several moments before concluding, "There's not. That's all."

"Well, then, I should catch my train," I said, glancing at my watch and realizing I'd missed it entirely. There wouldn't be another for a half hour.

"All right. Good seeing you, son." He stood awkwardly, dropping his handkerchief as he got up.

I stooped to pick it up, but stopped short before my fingers touched it. He'd hidden it well when it was in his palm, but there was no disguising the truth laid out on the tiled floor of Grand Central Station. The white handkerchief was heavily stained with blood.

I drew back in alarm, sinking onto the bench once again. Embarrassed, he bent over and picked up the piece of cloth, shoving it into his pocket. Then he sat, too.

I'd not seen it at first. I hadn't been looking for it. But now I could see the telltale signs: the swelling around the neck, the unnatural brightness in his eyes, and the wasting away that first led people to label the disease "consumption."

"I'm guessing this is the true reason you're back." It was all I could say.

"I'm dying, Simon." He spread his hands. "I've tried all the more temperate climates the doctors recommended. Not one of them slows the progress of this disease."

"You've tried Florida? You've been down South?"

"I have. And," he added, "I've even sampled the clean air of Minnesota, which some people swear by." But he shook his head. "It's no use. Consumption's got its grip on me. It's no longer a question of if, but when. But that's true for all of us, isn't it?" He pulled a small packet of lozenges out of his pocket. "Don't know what I'd do without these. Blaudett's Cathedral Pastilles. Little brown gummies of benzoin. Whatever they're called, to me, they're pure relief." He popped one into his mouth.

"How much time do you have?" I asked awkwardly.

He shrugged. "Likely not much, though no doctor can tell me for sure. I recognize the signs, though. I cough almost continuously now. And I tire so much more easily than ever before. I'd say this is my last spring. I intend to enjoy it." His eyes glimmered—but whether that was from the disease or his irrepressible spirit, I couldn't say.

"But it needn't be a death sentence," I burst out roughly. "There are sanatoriums now, staffed with doctors to help you get better."

He made a face of disgust. "What, so I can sit in a chair and learn to knit? Play chess and take the sulfa drugs they give you? No, thank you," he said with vehemence.

"You always did like chess . . ." I said. In fact, he had loved any game where money could be won—and lost.

"Hmmph."

"You're also contagious," I warned. "There are laws about compliance. . . ."

"I'm careful to manage my contagion," he said proudly. "I always cough into my handkerchief."

"And your doctor?"

"Thinks the compliance requirements are nothing but bunk and nonsense."

Recent laws wanted the medical profession to report all cases of tuberculosis—yet, most private doctors strenuously objected and ignored the requirement, believing it to be an invasion of privacy. So I wasn't surprised. But it wasn't what I'd meant.

"What is your doctor's opinion of your prognosis?" I rephrased my question gently.

He shrugged. "Never get a clear answer out of these medical types."

That meant he'd not seen a doctor recently. He never had taken care of himself.

"You'll let me know if you need anything," I said, my words stiff and awkward.

He sidestepped the offer. "I'm fine. I stay with a friend here. A hotel there. I see what each day brings. You know me, Simon."

And I did.

I reached into my pocket and handed him my card. "You found me easily enough, but I can always be reached here."

He took it, smiled, and coughed before saying, "I'll be in touch. You'll see the last of me soon enough. But not yet."

I watched him walk away, past tracks 21 and 20—then pausing for a moment at the flower stall to buy a single yellow rose, presumably for his companion of the moment.

I would have expected any number of emotions to overtake me—anger, most likely of all. Never mind the opportunities his leaving had cost me, I'd never forgive him for the way he had hurt my mother; I was convinced he'd hastened her path to an early grave.

I didn't feel sorry for him—though I knew he had spoken the truth when he said he was dying.

This night I was conscious of one emotion only.

Emptiness.

PART

TWO

All deception in the course of life
is indeed nothing else
but a lie reduced to practice,
and falsehood passing from words into things.

—Robert South

Sunday
March 18, 1906

CHAPTER 16

Dobson, New York

"There's been another murder." Mulvaney's clipped voice was loud over the crackle of the telephone line.

I had just finished grinding my coffee beans when the jangling of the telephone—at not yet eight o'clock—sent me racing for the receiver before my landlady was disturbed. She would not appreciate being roused at this hour on a Sunday morning.

"Can you get here as soon as possible?" Now Mulvaney's voice receded to a hollow echo.

I pulled at the black cord, straining to hear. It was a new black and brass Strowger dial telephone, but the quality of its connection left much to be desired—even on its better days.

"Where?" I assumed the murder had happened at yet another theater. I leaned in close to the speaker. Chances were, he was having just as difficult a time hearing me. I switched the ear receiver to my right hand and grabbed the pencil and pad of paper that lay next to the telephone with my left.

"The Aerial Gardens."

"What's that?" I was certain I'd heard something wrong. It didn't sound like a theater.

But I hadn't. When his answer came again, it was clear. In fact, he practically shouted, assuming I had not heard his first response at all.

"The Aerial Gardens. It's the rooftop theater of the New Amsterdam on the south side of Forty-second Street off Seventh Avenue. They have shows there during the summer months. The janitor found another actress dead there this morning."

So the killer had struck again, taking only two days to target a new victim. And Alistair—who had been convinced this murderer would act again quickly—was now proven right.

"We ought to have posted a policeman at every theater until this case was solved—as we talked about. You had enough resources," I said, my bitter frustration growing. "Now another woman is dead."

There was a long moment where I heard only the rhythmic crackle of the telephone.

"Frohman actually put into place a plainclothes security man—at his own expense—to protect his theaters," Mulvaney finally said.

It was information he normally would not have kept from me. But even as I felt a flash of anger that he had not told me earlier, I was also keenly aware of my guilt in keeping secrets from him: I had not told him about Timothy Poe.

"Frohman's solution didn't work," I said flatly.

Mulvaney made a noise of displeasure. "You're still stuck on the idea that Charles Frohman is somehow involved in this, aren't you? Well, the New Amsterdam isn't even a Frohman theater."

He paused, then grudgingly went on to admit, "Though my sources tell me it's run by Klaw and Erlanger. And they're part of Frohman's syndicate."

Part of Frohman's syndicate . . . Mulvaney's words seemed to echo long after I had rung off the telephone.

Eliza Downs . . . killed at the Empire.

Annie Germaine . . . killed at the Garrick.

Now a third victim, killed at the New Amsterdam. The coincidence was too striking. If their killer wasn't Frohman himself, then he was somehow related to the syndicate. He could be someone from within the organization. Or perhaps he was a competitor from outside. But either way, the killer we sought knew Frohman's business and knew it well.

The theaters.

The actresses.

And exactly where to strike.

After profusely apologizing to my landlady for the early-morning call, I had just enough time to gather my things and catch the 8:32 train into the city. It was almost empty this Sunday morning, so I took a seat by the window and settled in with my thoughts.

The Hudson branch of the New York Central and Hudson train line ran less frequently than other lines, but it was by far the most scenic. Normally I appreciated the sweeping views of the Hudson River and Palisades that marked the beginning of my half-hour journey to the city from the quiet town of Dobson. But today, everything out my window was dull and colorless—the spiky trees, murky water, even the gray skyscrapers of Manhattan, ghostlike in the distance. The landscape had been thoroughly ravaged by winter.

Perhaps it was my mood more than the actual scenery. The shock of seeing my father last night and learning of his illness had worn off, but one thing remained unchanged: I still felt empty. Ten years since I had seen him, and I was struck by how little he had changed. Then again, most things didn't—so why should he?

The city never changed. The violent crimes and murders continued, unrelenting in their pace, despite our best efforts. No, not the private resources of Frohman, or the legwork done by the men whom Mulvaney commanded; not Alistair's learning or even my own well-intentioned efforts to help. It all seemed futile—especially in the aftermath of another woman's death.

I turned my attention to the interview reports Mulvaney had given me last night to review, hoping his officers had uncovered some lead to move this investigation forward. His senior detectives had spoken extensively with the families of both Eliza Downs and Annie Germaine and met with numerous people associated with both the Garrick and the Empire—from janitors to ticket takers to ushers. They had analyzed the fingerprint evidence gathered and even telephoned *The Times* to clear up their remaining questions. But by the time I finished reading, it became clear: each avenue they'd explored had failed to pan out.

It was half past ten by the time I made it to the New Amsterdam. Unlike last time, there was a police officer by the front door to check my name against his list, as was customary before permitting anyone to enter what was now a crime scene. This was not Leon Iseman's theater: the manager here was eager to accommodate police protocol.

A wizened, frail man who seemed to disappear behind his thick black-rimmed glasses met me just inside the lobby and introduced himself as Al Straus. "I've worked in the theater business for most of my sixty years," he said, adding with pride, "and I've worked for Mr. Erlanger in some capacity for over fifteen years." He shook his head sadly. "I've never seen anything like this."

"Who was she?" I asked, accepting his offer to take my hat and coat.

He beckoned with one finger. "Come. You'll see soon enough."

I had no choice but to follow him, passing through one of the larger and more luxurious theaters I'd ever seen, though there was no time to register more than a quick impression of its art nouveau opulence. I made my way to the two small elevators on the eastern side of a long, dark corridor, almost tripping over a black cat who raced across my path in a panic. Al Straus explained that the cat had been given a permanent home there in exchange for his services controlling the vermin population. In fact, I detected an unpleasant musky odor that was likely the product of several cats—or decomposing rodents—or both.

Al turned the elevator crank once the door closed, and we ascended to the rooftop, which was actually a theater enclosed within a wall of windows. It overlooked the gardens that gave the space its name—and looking upward, I saw how the roof was designed to retract in warm weather. In the brutal heat of a New York summer, I could see how the space would lend itself to a comfortable evening of entertainment.

"You go," Al said, easing himself into a chair near the eleva-tor. "I don't want to see her again." He nodded toward the stage, which now swarmed with men in blue and brown. I recognized Mulvaney's tall frame immediately, as well as that of the senior detective he'd introduced me to at the Garrick Theater. David Marwin stretched out his hand in greeting, and several others nodded to me as I approached.

Mulvaney was squatting down, examining a black mark on the floor. "Not important," he said. He stood up with a look of relief. "I'm glad you're here. You made good time coming in."

Around me, I saw a dozen or so officers milling about the stage, but one person was conspicuously absent: the victim.

"Has the coroner already taken her?" I asked, puzzled.

Mulvaney shook his head somberly.

Marwin pointed to the stage curtains. "We haven't even managed to get her down yet."

I followed his direction, looking up to the very top of the curtains.

There, so high up it was no wonder that I hadn't noticed her, was a macabre figure.

More doll-like than human, she stared down at us with glassy eyes, clad in a mass of cascading sequined fabric and feather boas, all in emerald green. She swung to and fro—a movement that was at once slow and horrifying. Had he actu-ally hanged her this time, not strangled her?

"Maybe letting the curtain down would release her?" a young officer piped up in an earnest voice.

"That's ridi—" Mulvaney started to cut him off with a brusque reply, then caught himself. "Of course. There's no lad-der or elaborate staging gear nearby. There wouldn't be, during wintertime. He simply hoisted her up with the curtain." He gave the young officer an approving nod. "Good thinking."

"How did you find her?" I asked. "I wouldn't think anyone came up here this time of year."

Mulvaney's reply was bitter. "They don't. We'd never have learned about her death if he hadn't wanted us to."

"He?"

Mulvaney's eyes were somber. "The killer left us another love note of sorts." He turned, picked up a twelve-by-eighteen-inch poster of the kind usually displayed in theater lobbies, and presented it to me.

I reached for it, then hesitated. "It's been dusted for prints already?"

Mulvaney indicated that it had been, adding, "Not that it will do us any good. It's covered in them. Seems half of New York has been touching this poster. Still . . ." He handed me a pair of cotton gloves like the ones he already wore.

I donned them quickly, then held the poster up to the light. Against a black background, a woman in a form-fitting dress with a large feather boa leaned into a man wearing a tux as though they were dancing. In bold yellow lettering, the play's title read PYGMALION. Beneath the figures, I read two names. The woman's name was emblazoned in red on the lower right: EMMA-LINE BILLINGS.

"Is that her name?" I glanced at the woman still suspended high above us. The morning sun caught the sequins in its light, and they glittered madly—just like in the playbill poster.

"We're pretty sure," Marwin said. "We're checking to find out whether she's missing. I'm confident we'll be able to make a positive identification as soon as we bring her down."

"What about this other name listed? Walter Howe?"

"He appears to be another repertory actor who is performing in several of this theater's productions—*The Merchant of Venice* and *Richard III* among them," Marwin said dryly. "I've sent an officer to find and interview him right away."

But I remained confused. "Please walk me through what happened. I still don't understand how *this* poster," I tapped the playbill with my left forefinger, "led you to *this* murder victim." I glanced upward once again.

Marwin sighed. "Mulvaney told you that the New Amsterdam was a syndicate theater, right? At the moment, what's playing downstairs is a rotation of about six repertory productions, from several Shakespearean plays to a revival of *Beau Brummel*. What is *not* playing is a production of *Pygmalion* on the roof at the Aerial Gardens, like you see advertised here." Marwin pointed to the relevant area of the poster.

Mulvaney picked up Marwin's train of thought. "The janitor cleaning the building this morning in preparation for today's matinee noticed this poster was a fake—but an unusual one. He recognized the advertised leading actor's name as real. So he took an elevator ride upstairs to investigate and make sure no monkey business was going on." He drew in his breath. "That's when he found her. He called Mr. Straus, who promptly informed us."

We all stared at the woman's lifeless form as someone found the rope pulley and began orchestrating the curtain's slow descent. The levers squealed in protest after so many months of disuse.

As she came down, the curtains seemed to envelop her like a cocoon.

I glanced back at Mr. Straus. He was not watching; his head was burrowed in his hands.

"Was there a letter left on the stage?" I asked Mulvaney.

"Not that we've found," he replied.

"Have you checked whether *The Times* got a letter?"

Mulvaney swore softly under his breath and I realized he'd not thought to do so.

"Don't worry—I'll check with them myself after we finish here," I said.

It took two full minutes until the curtain was lowered and she was before us, regarding us with dull, lifeless green eyes that matched her dress.

"Her face looks just like the others'," I whispered as she was hoisted down to stage level at last.

Like Eliza Downs and Annie Germaine before her, she was impeccably made up, with full rouge and eye shadow.

Her arms were covered in long, white kid gloves, and the green feather boa she wore seemed to move in the breeze, though it was really just the aftereffect of her descent.

"Why is she standing?" Marwin whispered.

It was unsettling, the way she slumped against the fabric yet managed to stand. A death pose meant to mimic the appearance of life.

My voice caught in my throat. "Looks like he made her cooperate while he attached her to the curtain. He killed her afterwards—else he'd never have been able to secure her."

From somewhere behind the curtain, a policeman called out, "Hey, you won't believe this! He literally sewed her on here."

Mulvaney, Marwin, and I lifted the far-left edge of the heavy velvet curtain and ducked under it.

Several dozen long needles—along with a series of long green stitches made with thick embroidery thread—pinned her clothing tightly to the red velvet curtain.

"Well, unless we plan to undress her to remove her body, I'd guess we'd better undo this threading," Marwin said.

"Wait," I stopped him. "Evidence, remember?"

I gestured to the officer assisting us to hand me the black No. 2 Bulls-Eye Kodak camera and took several pictures of the odd threading. When I finished, I returned the camera to the officer.

"Can't we just cut the curtain around her body?" the young officer piped up.

The man to his left shook his head. "The material's much too heavy. And he's got her pinned so high up, it'd be hard to cut."

"Give me some scissors," Marwin commanded. "I'll just cut away some of the threads so we can get the needles out."

It fell to me to bring Al Straus back to the stage area to identify Miss Billings. He halted halfway there, clutched my arm, and rasped the two words we needed to hear: "It's her." He held up his hand and turned away again, his voice breaking as he said, "Please."

Despite the fact that I had dozens of questions about who Emmaline Billings was and how she might have found herself in this deserted theater in the wee hours of a Sunday morning, I decided to give Mr. Straus a few moments to recover himself. Then I heard Marwin cry out in pain, and I pivoted sharply.

"What the hell?" Mulvaney was livid as he rushed over to Marwin, who was doubled over in agony.

"Something stabbed me," he said through clenched teeth, clutching his hand. "And it stings."

"Where is it?" Mulvaney pulled the curtain out, but there were at least twenty sewing needles still pinned through the curtains.

Writhing from the pain, Marwin nonetheless forced himself to gesture to the area where he had been working. "I'll be fine. I just wasn't expecting it. And the thing was damn sharp."

"All right." Mulvaney set his jaw squarely. "Let's get on with this and get her down. Dr. Wilcox will be here any moment, and he can't begin to examine her when she's still strung up on the curtains. But be careful, all of you, with those needles. There may be another one hidden."

"And when you find whichever one stabbed Detective Marwin," I added, "be sure to set it aside for fingerprint evidence. It will be set at an angle; else it couldn't have pricked him."

I observed his hand, which now had a raw, angry mark just above his wrist. It was starting to look nasty. But when I mentioned it, he brushed off the injury and rejoined the two other officers, who set about methodically, but gingerly, taking out the stitching.

I ducked under the curtain once again and surveyed the woman now identified as Miss Emmaline Billings. She was petite, very slightly built. She could be no more than five foot one, I was certain. And she looked very young—under twenty, if I had to hazard a guess. Her natural jet-black hair had been pulled back and supplemented with a black wig that did not perfectly match, but did allow for multiple ringlets of curls to run down her back. I looked in the folds of her feather boa, even just under the edges of her white gloves. But I saw nothing resembling a letter of the sort I had half expected to see—certainly given the pattern established by the murders of Eliza Downs and Annie Germaine.

I was once again startled by a cry, followed by the awful sound of a person vomiting.

I was on the other side of the curtain in an instant.

It could not have been five minutes since I had seen Marwin draw himself up, claiming he felt fine.

But now I watched him collapse onto the floor with a soft thud, his face sickly and blue.

The officers who had been helping him now looked on as Mulvaney dropped to the floor beside Marwin. Even Al Straus rushed back onto the stage.

"Don't just stand there," Mulvaney said roughly. "Go get some help!"

That sent Mr. Straus back to the elevator with more energy than I had thought the theater manager was capable of. I went to the curtain and scanned the mess of threads and needles that pinned Miss Billings to the curtain. We now needed the needle that had stabbed Detective Marwin more than ever.

It took me some moments to find it, for it was well hidden and sharply angled. I swore softly under my breath as I took my knife and pried it away from its embroidered cocoon. It was a hypodermic needle. And it had been sewn—or, as we now knew, booby-trapped—in such a way as to stab whoever tried to remove the needles and thread immediately above it. I took one of the cotton gloves I always carried with me and tucked the needle—now important evidence—inside. I placed it carefully within the front pocket of my brown leather satchel.

I regarded Marwin, who looked ghastly ill. "We've got to get him to a hospital."

"Dr. Wilcox should have been here already," Mulvaney muttered as he checked his pocket watch. "Let's get Marwin downstairs."

"All right. On the count of three, we'll lift," I said. The man was now thoroughly incapacitated, so I knew he would be a deadweight. It was an unfortunate term—and the more closely I looked at him, the more concerned I became.

"Wilcox will be here any minute," Mulvaney said, to reassure himself as much as the rest of us.

We struggled to make it downstairs. Finally, we maneuvered him onto the floor in the lounge and, in relief, I silently blessed Mulvaney's brawny heft.

We had just made him comfortable when the coroner's physician, Max Wilcox, came through the door. It took him only seconds to assess the situation. I explained the bizarre positioning of the corpse upstairs and how Detective Marwin had been stabbed by a needle. "It was a hypodermic needle strategically placed among sewing needles so as to injure him, you understand."

The doctor listened intently, all the while checking the detective's pulse and clammy forehead. He grabbed a vial of ammonia from his medical bag and held it to the man's nose, then administered artificial respiration.

Nothing had any effect.

"Let me see that needle."

I complied with his demand.

He squeezed the small syringe while holding on to the glove and tasted the tiny droplet that emerged.

A look of surprise followed by horror passed over his face. His two words told us all we needed to know.

Bitter almonds.

Mulvaney and I exchanged stricken looks; we knew exactly what that meant. The taste of bitter almond was a sure indicator of cyanide. And there was no poison more deadly.

"Bring in the gurney. We've got to get this man moved." Wilcox's directions to his assistant were curt.

"What about the dead woman upstairs?" his assistant asked, confused.

"She can wait. She's beyond my help." Wilcox stood and mopped his brow. "But with this man, I think there's still a chance." He considered his patient once again. David Marwin appeared to be conscious, but just barely. "Where can we move him?"

"You don't want the nearest hospital?" Mulvaney asked.

The doctor made a snap decision.

"No hospital. There's no time. I need the closest bed where I can attend to him and make him comfortable."

Mr. Straus, who had been hovering behind us, suggested, "There's a ladies' lounge with sofas right off the lobby."

"Good. Now, I need hot water. Brandy. And plenty of buckets."

Wilcox looked up in amazement when no one moved.

"You've got to make haste, all of you." He gave us a meaningful look. "Time, you see, is of the absolute essence."

CHAPTER 17

The City Room, Times Building—Forty-second Street

It fell to me to check whether *The Times* had received another letter from this killer. To be honest, I was happy to have something to occupy myself. The *Times* building was just around the corner from the New Amsterdam Theater—and I was of no use to Marwin just pacing in the lobby.

Entering the City Room at *The Times* for the second time this week, I was struck that the atmosphere was only slightly less frenzied this Sunday afternoon than it had been Friday evening. Reporters still furiously typed at their desks, trying to meet the day's deadline as editors barked orders. There were simply fewer of them on the job today. And without Ira Salzburg's presence, the mood was noticeably lighter.

"Gibson—you almost done with that piece about probating

Susan B. Anthony's will?" yelled out a voice from the first row of desks in the City Room of *The New York Times*.

"Almost, boss," a young man at the desk nearest the door answered, pushing his glasses up from where they had slipped down his nose.

"How long's it take you to pull together a few sentences saying she left a fortune to women's suffrage?" the voice grumbled.

I scanned the room in search of Frank Riley or Jack Bogarty, figuring either of the reporters assigned to our investigation would be more helpful—or at least more discreet—than someone new. Riley was nowhere in sight, but I soon noticed Bogarty sitting alone at the poker table.

"How'd you finish so quick, Jack? Let me guess—you wrote a short article about the circus elephants now in residence at the Garden?" A short man with a nasal-sounding voice began to laugh good-naturedly.

I recalled seeing the posters advertising that Barnum & Bailey's Circus was back at Madison Square Garden, where it came every spring.

Jack grinned. "Nah. Elephants are entertainment, not art. Not even Salzburg's gonna make me write about hippos and circus tricks."

"You wanna bet?" A man with a cigar hanging from his mouth spoke this time. "You'll do what Salzburg wants. You always do, for all your talk."

Jack laughed as he picked up a deck of cards, shuffling it expertly. "I do it for the free opera tickets."

"Enough already; we got work to do," the man with the nasal voice complained.

Another shrug. "For what it's worth, my piece was a retrospective on this year's opera season, which ended last night. I'd written most of it already, just had to add a bit today about last night's performance."

A man I couldn't see grumbled something about Jack having it too easy.

"Don't knock it. I got coverage on half of page three with multiple pictures," Jack said, then brightened. "So who's in for a quick poker game before I go home?"

"No chance after you stole all my winnings, last game," the cigar-wielding man said.

Jack's face spread into another easy laugh that stiffened only slightly when he saw me. "Ah, Detective Ziele," he said, putting the deck of cards away, "what brings you here today?"

"Just a simple question—but we need some privacy to discuss it," I said, glancing at the other reporters. I realized it was likely that they all knew about the theater murders and the letter of warning *The Times* had received last week. But that didn't mean I wanted to discuss it in front of everybody.

"Sure," Jack said easily. "We can use the boss's office; he's not here today anyway. I take it you got Frank's message?"

I shook my head. "There was no message—not for Captain Mulvaney, and certainly not for me. When did he leave it?"

"This morning around ten o'clock, I assume with the Nineteenth Precinct house. No matter. You're here now."

I closed the door behind us as Jack took Ira Salzburg's chair, spinning it around. I sat in the guest chair and regarded him steadily. "What was the message?"

"Another letter turned up. I assumed that was why you came."

"When?" I demanded.

A languid shrug of the shoulders. "We found it early this morning."

And by this morning, Emmaline Billings was already dead. But what if it had been ignored, just like the earlier letter?

I moved my chair closer to the desk. "I'd like to see it."

Jack opened the top drawer of Mr. Salzburg's desk. "Frank put it here for safekeeping," he explained. He handed it to me. It was the same spidery writing—on the same blue stationery.

Dear Mr. Ochs,

Your fate seems to be one of missed opportunity. I'm giving you one last chance to preview my gala night performance. Its setting: the theater under the stars. Its subject: the tragedy of man. Its hero: me.

Yours truly,

A theater lover

"What do you make of it, Detective?"

I answered his question with two of my own. "Who exactly found this? And where?"

Jack leaned back in Mr. Salzburg's chair, running his thumbs along his suspenders. "Frank and I came in early this morning and found it with the rest of the post, mixed among all the letters and bills. But it was addressed to Mr. Ochs, and of course Frank and I recognized the handwriting and stationery. All our mail is delivered there." He pointed to the front desk I had passed earlier, next to where the young man with thick black glasses sat.

"Who delivers it?"

"A man who's been with us the last ten years. His name is Arnie."

"Could Arnie—?" I ventured.

That earned a loud guffaw from Jack. "Arnie couldn't *see* a fly, much less hurt one—if that's where you're headed. Talk to him yourself, and you'll see."

I resolved to do just that.

"I don't see a postmark," I said, examining the envelope.

He answered without hesitation. "That's my point by saying 'mixed in.' Someone had to deliver it personally—and stick it in with the rest of the postal-delivery mail." He paused for a moment. "Our secretary who handles the mail during the week might have noticed something. But he doesn't come in on weekends."

"And you receive no mail on Sundays, either," I said, my tone sharp. "That means you're talking about Saturday's mail."

"Look, Detective. Frank and I asked around this morning. No one noticed anybody odd in the building overnight. And no one noticed anyone dropping off this letter this morning. It just appeared. Plain and simple. And now it's yours if you want it. We're *trying* to cooperate with you, see?" He leaned back in his chair and smiled, his tone easy. "And speaking of cooperation, Detective, what have you got for us? Haven't heard much from you of late."

"I'd say our cooperative efforts are on par with yours," I said evenly.

Jack moved forward, putting his elbows on the desk. "Let's start with the obvious. You didn't get our message—and yet here you are. That tells me the murder this 'theater lover' warns of here," he tapped his forefinger against the letter, "has already taken place."

He waited for a moment to let his words sink in. Then, with an easy smile, he continued. "So tell me, Detective. No need to be shy; we're acting as partners here, right?"

It was a partnership born of necessity only—since, given the choice, I would never want to work with anyone from *The Times*. I trusted no one here. But I couldn't very well avoid telling him what he already knew.

"There was another murder," I said slowly. "An actress at the Aerial Gardens rooftop theater—presumably, the 'theater under the stars' that he mentions here." I gestured toward the letter that lay between us. "And we just might have prevented her murder, if only . . ."

I paused for a moment from sheer frustration.

Jack regarded me with sympathy in his eyes. "Honestly, I can't see how anyone could have noticed the letter earlier, Detective. It was mixed with Saturday's mail—which is delivered so late in the afternoon that we rarely see it before Sunday morning. This letter writer couldn't have known that we wouldn't see it earlier, of course. But as a practical matter, I don't see how any of us could have stopped this murder. So rest easy, Detective, your conscience is clear."

"No, Mr. Bogarty. I'm afraid I can never rest easy. Not until these murders stop—and the killer is behind bars."

"I think you really ought to reconsider letting us publish these letters. A reader just might recognize something."

"Nice try," I answered with good humor, "but no publication until the case is closed. I expect you to honor our agreement."

A competitive edge crept into his voice. "All right. But we won't be scooped. The other papers—*The Herald, The World,* and *The Tribune*—have each run small blurbs about Annie Germaine's death. So far, they are only of the 'a twenty-two-year-old female victim has lost her life' variety. But it's only a matter of time before they discover a pattern—and the larger story behind it. And it's pure luck that they're not getting letters, too."

I took the letter. "I'll ask the reporters outside a few questions, if you don't mind. And if anything else comes up . . ."

"Don't worry, Detective. We'll call."

"And one more thing, Mr. Bogarty. If you see any other letters—or learn anything else important about this case—please try your best to reach me directly." I scribbled down several numbers in addition to Mulvaney's precinct-house number. I even included Alistair's number, knowing that any important message given to Alistair would waste no time getting to me.

I spoke with all the reporters in the City Room, but they echoed exactly what Jack had just said: the blue letter had appeared in the City Room apparently unnoticed by anyone. At least—anyone willing to admit it.

But I had the letter in hand. And if I had learned nothing else, I now knew one thing: this killer was still advertising his moves, literally daring us to stop him.

CHAPTER 18

The Ladies' Boudoir, The New Amsterdam Theater

"His change in method is what troubles me most," Alistair said, pacing the length of the sitting-room area.

He and Isabella had joined me soon after I got word to them of the latest developments. I was back at the New Amsterdam, in the ladies' boudoir, where Dr. Wilcox had set up temporary care for Detective Marwin. It was a pink lounge with a rose motif that ran along the carpets, wallpaper, and even the cushions of the satinwood furniture that filled the room. But as a large room with two distinct sections, designed to hold ladies as they attended to their elaborate, fashionable dress, its size easily accommodated the sofa and all manner of supplies brought in for Marwin's treatment. The doctor had tried to make his barely conscious patient comfortable at the rear of the room, where a velvet rose curtain was drawn for greater privacy.

"You mean because the killer didn't leave a letter at the crime scene, as he's done before?" I asked Alistair to clarify.

"Not in and of itself." Alistair spun to face me. "What disturbs me is that he's become indiscriminate. He posted notice of his victim in an advertisement—a playbill poster—for anyone to see. It was a passive method for getting his message across, whereas his prior attempts—the letters to the police, the letter to *The Times*—were specifically targeted."

"But he still wrote this letter to *The Times*," I said, pointing to the eggshell-blue letter that lay on the table in front of us. "He still gave us advance warning of his plans."

"Did he?" Alistair raised an eyebrow. "*The Times* didn't ignore it this time; in fact, they called as soon as they found it. And that was still too late to save Emmaline Billings."

"All right. The timing's in question. But the wording is meant to give advance warning—this 'theater under the stars' obviously refers to the Aerial Gardens rooftop."

Isabella ventured a guess. "What if the killer didn't leave a letter with Miss Billings's body because he was interrupted—or simply ran out of time before the janitor was expected to arrive Sunday morning?" With a slight shudder, she added, "To position her corpse as he did, he obviously took much more time than with the others."

"You might also argue," I said, thinking aloud, "that he is exercising more creativity. With the murders of Eliza Downs and Annie Germaine, he dressed them for a part before he killed them. And when their bodies were discovered, they were posed in a dramatic way. Maybe he's just becoming more theatrical about the entire death scene he creates."

Alistair became more animated once he'd heard my idea.

"Ziele, you may just be onto something. It's possible he is putting more effort into creating not just a scene, but an entire dramatic production—complete with the rescuer, whoever he or she may be, entering the drama itself." He continued to talk, his hands gesticulating with excitement. "This theory would actually give us an explanation for why he randomly planted the cyanide poison. It wasn't enough, this time, simply to kill Emmaline Billings. He also set a trap to kill whoever would untie her—literally weaponizing his first victim to target his second one."

"And that victim could have been anyone," Isabella whispered.

"Exactly. He had no way of knowing who that person would be." He gestured toward the part of the room where David Marwin was fighting for his life. "It could have been you in there," he said to me. "Or Mulvaney. Or the janitor who found her—had he decided to try to free her, rather than call for the police."

I shook my head. "But it doesn't explain one aspect of it all that seems unlike him. His crime scenes are carefully planned and orchestrated. But these last elements leave a good deal to chance."

"They incorporate the element of surprise, if you will," Alistair said with a bemused smile. "Whoever this man is, his mind works in odd ways indeed."

Beyond the curtain, Dr. Wilcox continued to work on his patient, and we overheard his sporadic commands for more hot compresses and different stimulants, including whiskey and sulfate of strychnine.

Mulvaney emerged from the makeshift sickroom, closing the curtain tightly behind.

"Are you all right?" I asked. His complexion had turned slightly green.

"They're going to inject him with a saline solution to flush his bloodstream." Mulvaney collapsed onto the sofa opposite me. "How his mother can take this, I don't know. I surely can't."

Marwin's mother, a stiff, gray-haired lady with a face of stone, had arrived within minutes of receiving Mulvaney's message and immediately set to work as the doctor's assistant.

"How is he doing?" Isabella asked.

"He's still with us," Mulvaney said. "It's enough for now." He paused for a moment. "What I can't figure out is why this murderer also wanted to kill Detective Marwin."

Alistair shook his head. "As I was saying, he didn't specifically target Detective Marwin. He was indiscriminate, intending to hurt whoever came to her aid."

"And that's very different behavior from someone who specifically targets young female actresses," I said flatly. "Should we consider that it may be someone else? A copycat, if you will? It's not as though we're unfamiliar with that sort of crime."

Alistair gave me a steady look. "I'd say the coroner holds the key to answering that question. What we learned from Miss Germaine's autopsy was that few killers possess sufficient skill to snuff out a life without leaving so much as a single mark on the body. If Miss Billings follows that pattern, then we can feel confident that this is a single killer who has simply chosen to vary his methods. Otherwise, yes, we'll have to consider the possibility of a copycat."

"Would any of you like a glass of water?" I got up and went to the pitcher on the side bar to help myself to a glass. To accommodate the doctor's request for liquids, the officers had brought in water, brandy, and other liquors they'd found in the wooden bar outside the lounge.

"I would," Isabella said.

"How about something stronger?" Alistair cast a hopeful glance toward the brandy and scotch.

"No need to use their supplies. I've got something right here." Mulvaney tapped his jacket pocket before pulling out a small bottle of Clonmel single-malt Irish whiskey. "Bring over a couple extra glasses, would you?"

After I obliged, he poured a dram of the whiskey into each of the two glasses. "Ireland's finest. There's no better."

I knew Alistair's taste ran to Scottish varieties, but to his credit, he refrained from mentioning it.

"Ziele?" Mulvaney offered to pour a third.

"No, thanks," I said dryly. "Too early for me."

And it was. The clock had just chimed two o'clock.

"So why does it matter that the killer varied his methods?" Mulvaney asked. "With this murder, I grant you that he became more diabolical. And smarter, I'd say; he picked an out-of-the-way venue where he wouldn't be interrupted. So what? It still looks to me like the exact same guy who killed the other chorus girls."

"But *why*?" Alistair said. "Three deaths, very nearly four, depending on whether Detective Marwin pulls through, and we're no closer to understanding what motivates this killer than we were a few days ago."

"Why do we need to understand him?" Mulvaney asked as he refilled his glass. "Some violence is just senseless, and some people are evil, pure and simple. In the end, isn't our ability to stop them all that matters?"

"And how will you stop them if you can't understand the nature of who or what you're trying to stop? *Mens rea*. Mental state. A guilty mind. It's the foundation of criminal law, and the essence of what we must understand to know the criminal impulse," Alistair countered. "To say that senseless violence by its nature is too difficult to understand is ridiculous. Of course, it may never make sense to reasonable minds. But it has its own logic. And *that's* what we must figure out."

Mulvaney shot Alistair a dubious look. "I don't know. . . ."

Isabella jumped in to smooth things over. "What do you have to lose by asking the questions Alistair is raising? Three women are dead, and a man's life remains in jeopardy. If asking these questions enables us to stay just one step ahead . . . to save just one life . . . then why not?"

We were all silent for a moment, thinking.

"Okay," I said, for the sake of argument. "Let's assume it is the same killer. What bothers me is not the fact that he became 'indiscriminate,' as you mentioned before, in planting a poison that might have injured anyone. Why use the poison at all? Why escalate the attack in this manner? And why write all these damn letters—to us, to *The Times*, almost to anyone who will listen," I continued. "What does he gain by doing that?"

Alistair's response was automatic. "An audience. He wants others to see and appreciate what he's doing. He is making a star—albeit of a different kind than Charles Frohman and his syndicate create. Or maybe he wants to be one himself; I'm not sure."

"Then how does his attempt on Marwin's life figure into it? With the two prior murders, it was all about the women: he dressed them up, made them pretty. He played Pygmalion, right?" I leaned against a rose-patterned sofa. "What's he playing this time? We talked earlier about how he made this crime scene even more theatrical. He dressed her up and killed her onstage; so far, he fits into your star-making theory. But then he sets a cyanide trap for her eventual rescuer. What does that accomplish for him?"

"Even more attention?" Isabella ventured.

"Not the right sort," Mulvaney groused.

But something about the comment caught Alistair's imagination. "Or was it? Look at us. Normally, each of us would be outside, pursuing other leads. Instead he's got us stonewalled, sitting at a detective's bedside, praying for his recovery."

I turned to face Alistair. "But what if he had died, then and there? The poison entered his bloodstream through injection. A deep prick . . . just a little more of the poison injected . . . he would already be dead."

"And it would have stalled our investigation all the same, albeit in a different way. He's one of your own. You'd have had department protocol to follow." Alistair addressed Mulvaney directly.

"Yes, that's true."

"But what," I interjected, "if it was the janitor? It could have been *anyone,* as you said earlier."

"Anyone who might obscure the clear focus we might otherwise have had on Emmaline Billings," Alistair said in conclusion. "I think there is something to the idea we talked about at first: he wanted to make the crime scene as theatrical and shocking as possible. And part of that involves scaring us in a tangible way."

"And how does knowing that help?" I asked.

But before Alistair could answer, there was a knock at the door. Alistair crossed the room in large strides, opening the door to admit two officers who were among the dozen I had seen earlier at the Aerial Gardens. We had not formally met, so Mulvaney introduced us now: Ben Schneider was a stocky, older man in his fifties, and Paul Arnow was his lanky, freckled assistant.

"Captain." They greeted Mulvaney formally, then nodded to me, Alistair, and Isabella.

Mulvaney motioned for them to sit. "What's the update, lads?"

Paul, though he appeared to be the junior officer, spoke first. "We finished processing the crime scene, sir. And the victim— Miss Billings—was taken downtown to the morgue. She's all set for Dr. Wilcox when he's done here."

Mulvaney nodded. "Were you able to confirm how long Miss Billings had been missing?"

"Yes, sir," Ben answered. "We found where she lived, and talked a good deal with her flatmates. They last saw her right before she left for the theater last night."

"Which show?" Mulvaney asked.

"*Beau Brummel.* It's one of the repertory shows here at the New Amsterdam. She played a bit part." He exchanged looks with Paul.

They both nodded, then Ben said, "There was apparently a gentleman she'd been seeing. He escorted her to the show last night, and she planned to be out late with him. That's why her friends didn't worry when they went to bed last night. But they worried the moment they woke up and she hadn't come home."

"Had they met him?" I asked.

"Very briefly," Paul answered. "They disagree on his age. One said he was in his late twenties to midthirties, had light brown hair, and was quite handsome. The other claimed he was much older, probably in his midforties, with blond hair. In other words, nothing to help us identify him—compared to all the other men in this city who take a fancy to Broadway actresses."

Mulvaney nodded. "Anything else important?"

He was concerned only with major details now; minor points could wait until he received their report and reviewed everything in light of Dr. Wilcox's autopsy.

Paul cleared his throat. "Just one thing, sir. This same suitor had been causing her trouble at work. She was on the verge of being fired, they thought."

"He caused her performance issues? Like being late?" I asked.

"Not exactly. Apparently the manager—he's part of Frohman's syndicate, of course—had got wind of an infraction that Frohman doesn't tolerate. At least, that's what her flatmates said."

"And they wouldn't say more than that?"

Ben looked me straight in the eye. "Only that it involved the attentions of this same man, sir."

"All right. We'll check it out," Mulvaney said.

Ben nodded. "With your permission, Captain, after we finish our initial report." He turned to go, then pivoted back, brow furrowed. "One more thing," he said. "How is Detective Marwin?"

"He's seriously ill, but he's young and has a strong constitution. I'll keep everyone informed as I learn more." Mulvaney's reply was stiff.

The moment they were out of the room, with the door closed behind them, I spoke. "A police detective is critically ill and another actress is dead. There's no question about it now. One of us must pay an official visit to Charles Frohman. Three actresses associated with his syndicate are now dead."

I watched Mulvaney closely for his reaction, but this time he offered no objection. "The gentleman suitor worries me just as much, if not more."

"So you focus your efforts there, and I'll talk with Frohman," I said.

"Be careful." His comment seemed a formality; he was already preoccupied with other thoughts. "You'd best do it sooner rather than later."

"If you want to be discreet, there's a theater gala this Saturday night, I know—" Alistair started to say.

"We can't wait until Saturday—not with three murders to solve," I said.

"His employees will know his home address," Mulvaney said.

"Then take Isabella," Alistair said curtly. "I trust you to look out for her. And from everything I know about Charles Frohman," he added, "your meeting with him will go far more smoothly if you approach him with a pretty lady on your arm."

It was good advice, but a pretty lady might not be enough— at least, not in this instance.

Because of Miss Billings's murder and Detective Marwin's continued treatment here at the New Amsterdam, performances of *Beau Brummel* and other repertory productions had been canceled by police order until further notice. From everything I'd heard about Charles Frohman and his ambitions for his theater syndicate, I could not imagine this news would sit well.

And for this intensely private man to be questioned, on top of so much catastrophe at his theater today?

No, even with Isabella beside me, this was not going to be an easy conversation.

CHAPTER 19

The Knickerbocker Hotel, 1466 Broadway

It took several hours and some investigative persistence—
specifically numerous phone calls and Alistair's discreet tip to
a low-level Theater Syndicate employee—before we elicited any
information about the reclusive Frohman. And when we finally
found him, he was right next door—specifically, at the Knickerbocker Hotel. That was only a block from the New Amsterdam,
where Detective Marwin continued to fight for his life.

Frohman's primary residence was his well-appointed house
in White Plains, north of the city, but whenever one of his plays
demanded more of his time, he stayed at his regular home away
from home, in the heart of the theater district—the penthouse
suite at the Knickerbocker. We timed our visit for dinnertime,
when he was certain to make his usual room-service order, for
he was apparently a creature of habit. A connoisseur of fine

cuisine, Frohman also was something of a recluse; as a result, he seldom dined in public. And, Alistair's source told us, we had little chance of being admitted unannounced.

At precisely a quarter past six, the elevator doors opened and a waiter dressed all in white wheeled out a tray of covered silver dishes and a bottle of French chardonnay.

"Is that for Mr. Frohman?" I asked, stepping in front of him.

He stammered in reply, "Afraid . . . I'm afraid I can't really say, sir."

"You don't need to. I'll take it from here." I flashed my police badge, then quickly passed him a few coins. His eyes widened in surprise.

I put my fingers to my lips. "And not a word to anyone."

His face tightened with concern, but he retreated all the same, pressing the button to call the service elevator without a backward glance.

Once he had departed, I rapped on the knocker, calling out, "Room service." The young maid who answered didn't give me a second look, but did a double take when she saw Isabella—who, by her gray silk dress and lace scarf, was obviously a lady, not a fellow servant.

"Should I announce . . . ?" she asked.

I interceded before Isabella could reply. "Yes, please. You may tell him Mrs. Sinclair is calling, accompanied by a Mr. Ziele."

"And has he previously made your acquaintance, sir?"

I gave her my most charming smile. "I've never had the pleasure, but he is on good terms with Mrs. Sinclair's extended family."

It was true. No family in New York was a bigger patron of the arts than the Sinclairs.

The housemaid appeared dubious, but nonetheless ushered us into a small parlor and promised to announce us. "You won't keep Mr. Frohman from his dinner, will you? He's particular about his meals."

"Not at all," I said amiably. "We're happy to speak with him while he eats, if he prefers."

Her face took on a horrified expression. "Oh no, sir. He always eats in private."

But as we continued to wait in the small parlor room with blue miniature sofas and rococo rose wallpaper, it became clear that Charles Frohman was not spending his Sunday evening alone. We heard a man's voice: a rich tenor, with mellow undertones. It had to be Frohman. I got up and slightly cracked the adjacent pocket door separating our parlor from a larger sitting-room area.

"Helen, my dear," we heard him say. "There is no reason to be intimidated by the bard. The language is different, to be sure. But at heart, it's just a story—a simple one, about a girl who loves a boy deeply, passionately, and with all her soul."

Isabella and I stole a glance through the crack. We saw him sitting cross-legged in a chair, an odd position for a grown man. But Charles Frohman was obviously not a typical man. He was of medium build with a full, pleasant face and dark hair, and this evening he wore a blue pinstripe shirt and black trousers. He sat at an angle from us, but I still observed that his eyes crinkled when he broke into a jovial smile, meant to encourage his companion. She faced our door, so we saw her quite clearly.

A young ingenue with dark hair that was nearly black, vivid blue eyes, and a shy smile, she held papers in her hand that, presumably, were part of her script.

"You make it sound so easy, Charles. But maybe not simple enough for me." She rewarded him with a sad smile.

"Nonsense." He brushed off her concern with a huge wave of his hand as he got up. He was a larger man than I'd first thought when he was sitting.

"I wouldn't have cast you as Juliet if you couldn't do it. Now come, let's try again. And *this* time," he paused dramatically, "I want you to think of it a different way. No more being intimidated because Shakespeare is the greatest playwright who ever lived. No more regarding Juliet as the greatest tragic role of your career. Got it?" He began to circle around her, and even I found myself almost hypnotized by his voice. "Now this play, see, was written by a man who loved the theater—just like you and me. He lived for the stage, and put the greatest emotions of the human heart into the plays he created for his beloved Globe Theatre." His voice grew soft, like silk. "All you need to remember is that it's just a play about a girl and a boy—and how they fall madly in love with each other. It's really that simple."

He folded his arms and regarded her. Gamely she drew herself up and tried her lines again.

> *So Romeo would, were he not Romeo call'd,*
> *Retain that dear perfection which he owes*
> *Without that title.*

Her lips parted softly, and she looked rapturously toward an imagined suitor at the rear of the room.

"'Romeo, doff they name, and for thy name, which is no part of thee . . . '"

She paused, and her final words were spoken with breathless abandon:

"'Take all myself.'"

Isabella drew back and I followed. We could hear Charles Frohman's comments, which amounted to copious praise and further encouragement.

"I feel awful having eavesdropped," Isabella said, blushing, "but I think we learned a bit more about how he transforms his actresses into sensational stars."

I nodded my head in agreement, but all I could think of was Molly Hansen's words about Annie Germaine. She'd said that Annie had met a new fellow—someone who was going to make her a star. And certainly Frohman had the literary chops to have written the letters that accompanied the first two murder victims.

Yet he spoke so pleasantly and gave every appearance of being especially good-humored. I didn't know what I expected our killer to be like, but it wasn't like this.

Still, time and again, I'd learned never to trust my preconceptions. Was it possible that Frohman was the man we sought?

We heard the housemaid's voice, low and soft, presumably announcing our visit—and perhaps also the arrival of his dinner.

After more mumbled discussion, we heard Frohman again. "Eat, eat. No reason you shouldn't start without me. I'll deal with them quickly, darling, and be right back."

"Do you suppose he treats all his actresses this way?" Isabella asked in a stage whisper.

Another few moments passed, then the maid returned to announce that Frohman would see us now. She led us to still another sitting area, this one stocked with cigars, liquor, and wide, leather nail-studded chairs.

As we entered the room, he gave us the same jovial smile I'd witnessed earlier—and immediately focused his attention on Isabella.

"I'm told we've met before, Mrs. Sinclair." He bowed slightly.

"It was two years ago, Mr. Frohman," she said, holding out her hand. "I believe my cousin by marriage, Mrs. Henry Sinclair, hosted a gala benefit you attended."

"Of course, of course." His expression was unchanged, and if he had no memory of the occasion—as I suspected he did not—he refused to let on.

"Detective Simon Ziele," I said, introducing myself. "I'm assisting the Nineteenth Precinct with a special investigation."

His smile froze. "You mean you're assisting with the investigation of the Germaine girl's death at the Garrick. I believe my people have already spoken to you. Several times."

"Yes." I pulled out my small notebook from my pocket. "Your *people* have spoken with us about Miss Germaine, as well as about Miss Downs. You'll recall she was found dead in markedly similar circumstances at the Empire. But now we need to talk with *you*." I watched him carefully. "Just this morning, another actress—a Miss Billings—was found murdered at the Aerial Gardens theater."

"Wh . . . ?" He didn't even finish the word before he sank into one of the deep leather chairs. Isabella followed his example and sat directly across from him, but I remained standing for now.

"You didn't know about her?"

"Of . . . of course not." He pulled out a handkerchief and mopped his brow, which was gathering beads of sweat. "It's Sunday," he added, as though that ought to explain the fact his employees had not informed him of a new murder at another of his theaters.

The truth, I believed, was that those few who knew had been instructed to keep quiet. But whether they'd followed those instructions, I didn't know. Frohman certainly appeared surprised. He was growing agitated, but I could not tell whether it was the agitation of a guilty man—or whether he was worried about the murder of yet another syndicate actress and its potential impact on his business.

"So no one told you that the New Amsterdam is temporarily shut down by police order?"

He mumbled words that were incomprehensible.

"Emmaline Billings played smaller roles in several of the repertory productions at the New Amsterdam," I said smoothly. "She was a syndicate actress—" I paused, "one of yours, just like the other two."

He grew increasingly red in the face as he began to bluster. "I don't like your tone or what you're implying. I assure you the fact that three syndicate actresses have been murdered is a coincidence." He fixed me with a hard stare. "*Nothing* but a coincidence."

"And I'm sure you understand that, from my perspective, I see three women murdered—at their place of work—which, in each case, happens to be *your* theater." I paused only for a second. "One victim is a coincidence. Three form a pattern."

"We find patterns where we want to," he said, and there was more than a hint of anger underneath the smooth tone he managed to maintain. "I assure you there's nothing to find in any of my theaters. All you and your fellow officers will accomplish is to interfere with the important artistic work we do there. If your investigation becomes public, news of it will scare away theater-goers. So you can see, Detective, I do not welcome your interest in my theater. Especially when I can assure you that neither I—nor anyone who works for me—had anything to do with these actresses' deaths."

"Then you should welcome the opportunity to speak with me," I said evenly. "At the moment, I find no connection among these three tragic deaths—except that each victim worked for you. If you and the others in the syndicate are truly not involved, then talk to me, and give me some information to work with to find their killer elsewhere."

"And if I refuse?" He raised an eyebrow.

I should no longer have been shocked. In the last ten years, I'd seen every reaction to murder I thought possible. But such callousness and indifference in the wake of three lives cut short never ceased to upset me. Even when, as here, I understood that it was pure self-interest that caused it.

"Does it mean nothing to you that three young women—actresses you knew and employed—have been murdered?" My voice cracked with emotion.

Embarrassed, he looked down toward the heavy gold ring on his right hand.

And I decided: if he was truly so self-absorbed, then perhaps I would have more success by appealing to his self-interest. I bluffed with every ounce of confidence I could muster.

"You put your entire organization at risk of being shut down by being uncooperative. And I don't care what reassurances Mayor McClellan or Police Commissioner Bingham gave you earlier. They spoke to you at a time when only one victim was positively known. Now there are three . . . and these killings aren't stopping. Finding this murderer is far more important," I took a deep breath, "than your personal need for privacy or your misguided desire to keep your theater organization out of the public spotlight. The victims worked for you. They were murdered in your theaters. That involves you—whether you like it or not."

Fuming, he got up, walked toward me, and simply stared. At less than three feet away, it was obvious he was a much larger man. I held my ground, even as I heard Isabella's quick noise of surprise.

Finally, he sputtered, "No one talks to me like this."

"Mr. Frohman," Isabella said sweetly, "we didn't come to fight with you. We need your help."

He turned to her and I noticed that his face somewhat softened as his anger defused.

"Come, sit again." Isabella indicated the empty chair beside her. "We know how devoted you are to your work, and how frustrating our interference in it must be. But Detective Ziele is right. We need your help," she repeated, "if we're to catch the person responsible for these killings. No one knows how your Theater Syndicate operates better than you do."

"Hmmph." He sat. "The syndicate succeeds because no one knows my *actors* better than I do. They're what make me a success."

"We know you have been rehearsing a scene with one of your actresses, even tonight. Is that typical? It strikes me as a huge investment of your personal time," I said.

"Of course." He looked at us in amazement, not quite understanding what we were asking.

"And how do you choose them?" Isabella asked. "You obviously can't give your undivided attention to all of them."

He shook his head. "No, I choose the men and women who have talent—in addition to great ambition and love for the theater. It takes no less to reach the greatest heights in this profession. But if they have what it takes, then I find the roles that will allow them to shine." He looked at us curiously. "Both of you mention 'actresses' only. It's true that my latest find was Maude Adams—and I have great hopes for the young lady working on 'Juliet' in my living room. But have you never heard of John Drew? Or William Gillette? They are major stars I created." He beamed with pride.

Their names were familiar to me, though I knew nothing of their career trajectories or how long they'd been with Frohman. That was easy enough to check, however.

"Eliza Downs was the first victim, so let's begin by discussing her. Did she ever merit your personal attention?" I asked.

He brought his fingers together slowly. "How to put this? She was a sweet girl. And she did her part well enough. But she was a short-timer."

"What does that mean?"

He looked at Isabella and me as though trying to size up whether we'd understand what he was about to say. "There are two kinds of women in the theater—men too, of course, but I see it less frequently. One kind is motivated by nothing other than love for the stage. They would follow each production, attend every play, even if they never had a chance to act themselves. But when given the chance—assuming they've some natural talent—their ambition knows no bounds. They aren't driven by the desire for fame or fortune. They're driven by the need for artistic perfection—or as close as any of us can come to it. The woman in my living room is like that. The incomparable Maude Adams is like that. But Miss Downs and her ilk?" He shook his head sadly. "They're in it because they hope to become famous, or maybe they're attracted to the glamour of it all—until they find out how much work is truly involved. And maybe one or two with that attitude will become famous, despite their attitude. They may offer a particular look that appeals. Or pure chance may land them a role perfectly suited to their abilities, such as they are. But most," he emphasized the word, "won't last for long. A few years' interlude, maybe, before they make a different sort of life for themselves."

"And how did you know all this about Miss Downs? You can't have been well acquainted with her. After all, there are hundreds of actors in your syndicate, no?"

Frohman looked me hard in the eye. "I screen every actor I hire personally. No exceptions. I look into their background. And I entrust my managers to oversee their progress and assess their commitment and ambitions. You've met Leon Iseman. He's my right-hand man and helps me with all my hiring decisions."

"And no manager is ever mistaken?" I eyed him suspiciously.

But he only shrugged. "It's a simple enough judgment to make. I have rules I ask all my players to abide by. Either the actor in question has the discipline to do what I ask—or they don't. It's pretty simple. It's all a matter of commitment and how much they want a life in the theater."

"What kind of rules?"

"Simple ones." He held up his fingers and began ticking them off, one by one. "Actors should always be prepared to perform, having learned their lines and musical numbers. They should never be late—for performance or rehearsal. They're not permitted to stay out past midnight when they've a show the next day. And they must understand," he said, putting his words carefully, "how important their personal reputation is to their success. Any offstage gossip can affect an actor's onstage reputation, so I'm insistent upon sterling behavior in every area of their lives. I tolerate no loose comportment with members of the opposite sex. And naturally, it's better if my greatest stars have no serious personal attachments that might interfere with their devotion to their art—or their fans' ability to worship them. To work in the theater is to manage the dreams and imaginations of the public—in every way possible, onstage and off."

I thought briefly of Alistair's comment about what had sounded like a brief flirtation with Maude Adams—and how quickly she had terminated it. Perhaps I now understood why.

"What about those who are not stars, but simply reliable actors playing smaller roles?" I asked.

"Other players may form personal attachments, so long as they are suitable and practiced with discretion."

"So I gather Miss Downs was not one of your more-committed actresses?"

His response was short. "No."

"And how is that viewed within the syndicate?"

Now his eyes narrowed. "What do you mean?"

"Is there room for a casual player like Miss Downs? Or was she at risk of being let go?"

For a long time he would not look at me. I watched him closely: he was a difficult man to read. On the surface, Frohman appeared to be a simple yet intensely ambitious man—devoted to his work and all that surrounded it. But how far did that driving ambition lead him to go? And this time, could it have led him—or someone within his organization—to murder?

Finally, in a low voice, he admitted it. "She was about to be fired." When his eyes met my own, they seemed to plead for understanding. "It's a hard business I'm in, Detective. The money I earn, I immediately reinvest in my productions. I want to make a real difference in the theater, but competitors are always trying to undercut me, everywhere I turn. The Shuberts, in particular." His voice turned bitter. "Miss Downs was fine enough, but she wasn't committed. And if there weren't a dozen actresses in this town ready and willing to take her place, then she might have drifted along for years before I let her go. But there *are* dozens willing to take her role. I'd rather take a chance on one of them than stay with an actress who's not working to fulfill her potential. My shows can only achieve greatness through the efforts of the very best people."

"Did Miss Downs know?" Isabella asked softly.

"We planned to tell her at the end of the month."

"But those in your organization knew?" I asked.

"Leon Iseman, my most trusted associate. All the stage managers, the clerks in payroll, and my organization associates. Basically, everyone except the players themselves. Although it should not have been a surprise to Miss Downs. She had been late to rehearsal eight times this month. And my actors and actresses know that tardiness is never tolerated."

"What about Annie Germaine and Emmaline Billings?"

A quizzical expression passed over his face. "You mean, did they know Miss Downs was to be fired? Or did they know they were about to lose their own jobs?"

"The latter."

"No formal decision had been made yet for Miss Billings, but yes, she was struggling. She was slow to learn her lines—and in repertory work, it's an important skill to memorize quickly." He drew a breath and let it out slowly. "Miss Germaine was on the verge of being let go as well."

"Why? Also attendance issues?"

He shook his head. "In her case, we simply found someone better, with experience within my organization, who was ready to play the role. We delayed firing Miss Germaine to allow her replacement time to understudy and learn the part."

I realized with a start that he meant Molly Hansen. I was matter-of-fact. "The bottom line is: three actresses in your theater syndicate have been killed. Other than working for you—and not being particularly successful in their work—is there any link you can think of to connect them?"

"I don't know." He set his jaw stubbornly. "Isn't that your job to find out?"

"Do you have any enemies, Mr. Frohman?"

"I have my share. But I'm sure you already know that."

"Perhaps more to the point," Isabella suggested, "did these three actresses have any enemies?"

"I have no idea."

"One of them, Miss Germaine, apparently had a new suitor. Her roommates report that he took her out most nights in recent weeks," I said. "And Miss Billings as well. In fact, her flatmates believe she was on the verge of losing her job because of the young man's attentions—not because she had trouble with her lines."

"I wouldn't know about that."

"Given your 'rules,' I can't see how you would not have

known—or how those working for you, like Mr. Iseman, didn't know."

"If anyone did, they didn't tell me." His reply was like steel.

"Yes, Mr. Frohman," I said lightly, "but you make it your business to know *everything* about your employees. So you'll understand if I now have trouble believing these are things you don't know. Unless there's someone you feel the need to protect?"

He bristled. "So now you're suspecting one of my employees was involved."

I was noncommittal in my reply. "Right now, it's my job to suspect everyone. And no doubt you know the expression, 'where there's smoke, there's fire.' "

I stood, and Isabella followed suit. "I'm sorry, Mr. Frohman, but your theater organization is filled with smoke. I'm afraid tomorrow morning, we'll need to have some officers look more closely into the syndicate's operations."

"That's utter hogwash," he sputtered. "I assure you not one of my people is involved in this. Why, this last murder—of Miss Billings—was at a deserted theater. My employees don't use the Aerial Gardens Theater before summertime."

"Exactly," I said. "That's what made it the perfect setting. No one is up there, not this time of year. And the killer knew that."

"But no one . . ." he tried to finish, but stopped himself.

"No one you know would do such a thing? I'm afraid that's what we must reconsider, Mr. Frohman. A couple of detectives from the precinct will be by your offices at the Empire first thing tomorrow to examine your records and speak with your employees."

"Over my dead body."

"A poor choice of words, I'm afraid. Good evening, Mr. Frohman. We'll see ourselves out."

And so we left him fuming, sputtering, and no doubt displeased about eating a cold dinner.

And we were left to decide: was he a man wrongly placed under suspicion by circumstantial evidence? Or was he himself the murderer we sought? If he was, he wouldn't be the first man whose driving ambition had led to terrible things.

"I don't think you made a friend of Charles Frohman, Simon," Isabella said soberly. "That may have been unwise."

"Be that as it may, I needed to see what the man was like. He's certainly protective enough of his theater empire that he will go to great lengths to preserve it. The question is: do those lengths include murder?"

"True. But it's hard to see how three minor actresses could possibly have threatened his success. After all, it seemed he could terminate their arrangements easily enough by firing them. Why would he—or anyone working for him—resort to murder?"

"Good point." I smiled at her. "But these murders are unique in the ways they have been staged. The killer responsible makes a statement with each victim, perhaps hoping to interest the press. . . ."

"But Charles Frohman seems a private man. I can't see him tolerating—much less doing—anything that would attract the wrong sort of publicity for his shows."

"And there are some, you know, who say all publicity is good. If the press covers these murders, numerous articles will

comment on each of these plays—not to mention Charles Frohman's name. Even if the main topic is murder, it amounts to free
advertising for syndicate productions."

"Hmm." She wrinkled her forehead as she thought. "And
one other thing—why didn't you mention Detective Marwin's
injuries or the hypodermic needle found at today's murder
scene?"

"Because tomorrow, a set of officers will search his home
and offices. I don't want him—or his associates—to hide anything."

She turned to me abruptly. "I don't think it's Charles
Frohman, Simon."

I looked at her with some amusement. "You sound convinced. Why?"

She shrugged. "Part instinct. But I just don't think he'd do
anything to jeopardize his theaters. And if these murders continue . . ."

She didn't have to finish saying it. We both knew, based on
what we'd seen this morning, that these killings showed no
signs of stopping. In fact, this morning's murder had escalated
matters in a way that was quite disturbing.

I didn't say anything to Isabella, but our conversation just
now made me think more seriously about Leon Iseman as well. I
would ask Alistair and Mulvaney for their thoughts, but the more
I considered Iseman as a potential suspect, the more troubled I
became.

He had the same knowledge of the different theaters and
actresses as had Frohman himself.

He was someone each actress would have trusted implicitly.

And one question disturbed me most: why had he had kept

the note found near Eliza Downs, the first victim? Everyone had assumed it was a suicide note.

It was a small fact. But I'd learned time and again that in a murder investigation, such details are often what matter most.

CHAPTER 20

The Knickerbocker Hotel, 1466 Broadway

Mulvaney found me in the lobby of the Knickerbocker after I had seen Isabella safely into a cab home. He was so agitated that I feared David Marwin had taken a turn for the worst.

"Marwin . . . ?" I paused, with bated breath.

"He's holding his own. But something new has come up." As Mulvaney hustled me out the door, he looked at me oddly. "Turns out the killer left a note for us after all."

I stopped short. "We searched up and down when we were at the Aerial Gardens. How did we miss it?" My voice was hoarse with frustration. We had examined the crime scene thoroughly—or so I had thought.

I took a seat in a waiting horse cab and Mulvaney clambered in beside me.

"I suppose we were distracted when Marwin was hurt. We didn't even manage to move Miss Billings from her position onstage, pinned to the curtain," I said, trying to rationalize how we had missed such a critical piece of evidence.

He leaned forward to address the driver. "The dead house."

The driver circled his horses around, directing our wagon downtown along Broadway.

"Why not deliver the note to the precinct?" I grabbed at my satchel, for the uneven jostling of the cart threatened to toss it and all its contents onto the muddy floor below. "It seems a waste of time to travel downtown when Dr. Wilcox can't possibly have completed the autopsy yet."

Mulvaney gave me the same strange look. "Wilcox plans to do the examination late tonight, when Detective Marwin is stabilized. And Wilcox's assistant had begun the usual preparations when he noticed the letter."

"Too bad he couldn't find a messenger to deliver it," I said, grumbling. "Is it just like the others?"

"Sort of. It's definitely his style—a poetic rhyme that makes little sense."

"Well, what's different about it?" It wasn't like him to be less than forthcoming, even if he was describing something unlike what we'd seen before.

He looked me in the eye, and I knew what he had to say was going to be very bad.

I tried again, hoping to ease him into it. "Where was the letter found?"

Then he answered, and I realized he was simply having trouble finding the words to explain what he did not yet understand.

"The letter was on her back," he finally said.

"You mean tucked beneath her shirtwaist?" It made perfect sense. Pinned as she was to the stage curtain, we'd been unable to examine her body closely.

"No," he said, "It was actually *on* her back. Permanently."

He looked me full in the eye. "He tattooed it in blue ink."

I am not a believer in the supernatural, but I prefer to visit the dead house in the daylight, when the sun's warmth manages to dispel some of the gloom that lurks in dark corners and ill-lit hallways. Tonight, I felt the dark rather than saw it—and its chill permeated my bones in a way that was deeply uncomfortable. And though the autopsy room was lit with no fewer than six electric lights, it did little to dispel my uneasiness.

Splayed out on the soapstone countertop—in the same room where we had learned the details of Annie Germaine's autopsy just two days ago—was Emmaline Billings. She lay facedown, her head and lower body obscured by thick white coverings that seemed to accentuate the spidery blue markings we could see on the only exposed portion of her body.

Dr. Wilcox's assistant, a small man with a Hungarian name that I could never pronounce, came over to greet us.

"I sent word as soon as I saw," he said in soft, accented tones.

Mulvaney circled to view the writing from a different angle. "Can we get more light over here?"

"Certainly, sir," the assistant said. He brought over an electric lantern and held it high above Miss Billings's corpse.

The lantern cast eerie, half-lit shadows all around us, but brightly illuminated the writing in question. It was done in blue ink, but the skin around it was irritated and inflamed such that, in the light, each letter seemed bathed in a red glow.

"The ink looks to be a standard blue henna injected beneath the skin," the doctor's assistant said.

Mulvaney shook his head sadly. "This is sloppy work. Do you see how uneven the lines are? Given that—as well as what we know about the Aerial Gardens, where she was killed—I think this was done by hand."

I saw the smudged lines that drew some alphabet letters closer together, kept others farther apart; they were thick in places, thin in others. The man who had done this work had taken little care, possessed poor skills—or both.

"No doubt you're right," I said. "It's too sloppy to be otherwise. Even an electric tattoo machine in the hands of an amateur would produce better work than this."

Mulvaney nodded. "Plus, he would have attracted attention carting a machine that large into the theater—or so I'd like to think."

We stared at the writing once more.

"Who would still have access to an old hand machine?" I asked. The new tattoo parlors around Chatham Square—in addition to those tattoo artists practicing in the backs of saloons and even barbershops—had more or less switched to electric machines within the last ten years. And with faster, better methods, tattoos had become more popular, at least among certain groups: sailors, gang members, and the rebellious young men of the privileged classes.

"Do you think he did this before he killed her—or after?" I asked.

"I can't say, sir. Perhaps Dr. Wilcox will have an opinion."

I hoped, for this victim's sake, that the answer would be the latter. If she had been alive—and the tattoo had been done by hand—then Emmaline Billings had been subjected to the tortuous process of having dye injected, one needle prick at a time, until the two lines of verse were written.

That would indicate a measure of cruelty that we had not seen in the two prior killings. It didn't mean that he wasn't capable of it, however. After all, I didn't pretend to understand what kind of person we were dealing with. His blue lettering mocked us, sending chills down my spine, as I tried to imagine why he had left his message this way.

I steeled myself to the task at hand and focused on the words.

Lo! 'tis a gala night
. . . its hero the Conqueror Worm

I could only stare.

"What the hell is this?" I finally said. "'Gala night' mimics the phrasing in this killer's letter to *The Times*—but 'Conqueror Worm'?" I knew I was missing something important.

"Your professor will no doubt have plenty to say about it." Mulvaney looked away, asking the assistant, "Do you have a camera for some photographs?" He made a face of apology to me. "I left ours at the station, unfortunately, in the rush to get downtown."

The assistant nodded, left us, then returned just moments later with a No. 2 Bulls-Eye Kodak just like the one at Mulvaney's precinct. I took it and snapped several photographs—some close-ups to focus on specific letters, others far away to capture the two lines together.

I removed the film and returned the camera to Dr. Wilcox's assistant, thanking him.

"Based on his opinion of the murder scene—even before we discovered this tattooed letter—I can guess something of what Alistair will say," I said the moment Mulvaney and I were once more alone. "He will likely point to the theatrical nature of it. It isn't writing that merely communicates; it makes a point visually . . . and viscerally." I shuddered. "He has marked her body for the first time."

"But the tattoo didn't kill her," Mulvaney reminded me. "It appears he strangled her, just like the others."

"True. But it's still a change in his behavior that may mean something," I said. And I went on to explain all that I had learned during my interview with Charles Frohman—including how in addition to the theater magnate himself, I felt his closest adviser, Leon Iseman, was a suspect worth serious consideration. "Odd coincidence, isn't it, that this message surfaces on Miss Billings's corpse—the week Frohman is rehearsing his next premiere—or 'gala night'?"

I found the fact extremely unsettling, but Mulvaney grunted in disagreement. "Actually, there's one more thing I've got to tell you."

I groaned inwardly—for after this day's revelations, I was hoping to hear no more discouraging news.

He looked at me steadily. "We took the fingerprints off the syringe on the hypodermic needle that pricked Detective Marwin."

"And?"

"Timothy Poe was the first guy I had them run the comparison against. They're a perfect match to the set of prints we took from him when he was at the precinct station following Annie Germaine's murder."

"How can that be?" I asked incredulously.

An amused look crossed his face. "You can't be hypocritical now, Ziele. You've always been a big advocate of fingerprinting, saying our department needs to do more to embrace new technology. So you can't discount what it tells you, just because you don't like the results."

He was right. But the fingerprint match went against every instinct I had. Poe had been duplicitous and less than straightforward, yet I did not believe him to be a killer. He made no sense as a suspect given the behavioral profile we sought, and I told Mulvaney so—knowing as I did that I sounded just like Alistair.

"And," I added, "you'll need evidence other than just fingerprints—unless you've got ten pristine prints on that syringe, your fingerprints won't be admitted into court."

Fingerprint evidence had achieved partial acceptance in New York as a marker of identification in one case only: where the prints were clean and complete. The prisons, for example, already used fingerprints to identify and keep track of all inmates, because they could obtain ten quality prints from each inmate in a controlled setting. But in real life, prints were incomplete and smudged. And no one yet had fully trusted a partial print as evidence.

Mulvaney regarded me indulgently. "There's always a first time, Ziele. Besides, we'll have more evidence shortly. While we were down here, I sent my men to Poe's flat with a warrant to search his rooms and arrest him. He'll be waiting for us at the precinct station."

But Mulvaney was wrong on at least that one count. When we returned, Poe was not at the precinct house. In fact, he was absolutely nowhere to be found.

Mulvaney's men were harried and exhausted when we met them. Ben Schneider and Paul Arnow had begun to show the strain of the day's events—and they remained concerned about Marwin.

"Poe wasn't at home, Captain," said Ben. "And his room-mates claim they haven't seen him the past two days."

"Days?" Mulvaney looked at them in amazement. "But they must have some idea where he's gone?"

Paul shook his head wearily. "They claim they do not. Poe apparently even missed his performance last night, which is un-usual for him."

It was an infraction that Frohman's stage manager would never tolerate—and the information I was now duty-bound to make public would doom his career in any event. But Poe was facing arrest on three charges of murder. He had larger worries now.

"We ran to ground all leads, right? The places he frequents. The people he associates with." Mulvaney cited the checklist of protocol almost by rote. "We'll find him and bring him in—and secure the evidence that will close this case."

Despite the fact that I'd never known fingerprints to lie, I could not accept Mulvaney's unwavering belief in Poe's guilt. Still, I owed it to him to share what I knew about Poe's where-abouts.

I cleared my throat uncomfortably. "I've got another ad-dress for him you can try. It's a flat down on MacDougal

Street. Number 101. Apartment Five C. I've visited him there before."

Mulvaney stared at me for a split second, then ordered his officers to check it out. Once they had left, he pulled me into his office and closed the door. I expected him to be angry, for his temper could be fierce. But instead, he sat perfectly still.

Eventually he spoke, his voice unnaturally quiet. "How did you know that Poe had a second address—and more to the point, why didn't you tell me?"

Reluctantly, I filled him in—telling him all about how Riley and Bogarty had given me the tip, how I had visited Poe there, what I'd learned, and how neither Alistair nor I truly believed Poe was culpable, despite his duplicity.

"I repeat: why didn't you tell me about it?" Mulvaney remained stone-faced.

"Because with all the political pressure bearing down on you, I feared it would provide you with an easy—but incorrect—solution," I said.

"In other words, you didn't trust me to get it right? To understand the basics of evidence?"

"As a matter of fact, no—I did not. You've been prejudiced against Poe from the beginning, prone to believe him guilty before any factual evidence proved it so. How much more inclined would you be to assume his guilt, once you knew he had lied to us? That his lifestyle is an unusual one, sure to prejudice any jury against him?" I stopped for a moment to catch my breath. "And because the public would denounce him based on that fact alone, I had the man's very career in my hands, to ruin—or not—as I saw fit. And I didn't see fit. I didn't believe him to be guilty, so I felt it was my duty to protect his interests."

"Your duty . . ." Mulvaney shook his head in disappointment. "We've found solid evidence connecting him to today's crime."

"Which is why I have told you his whereabouts now."

But Mulvaney said, "We might have had solid evidence earlier, if you'd been more forthcoming. Your sense of duty to Poe may have cost another young woman—not to mention Detective Marwin—their very lives."

"If that's the case," I said, nearly collapsing into my chair, "do you think I won't remember it every day for the rest of my life?"

Stung by whatever he had heard in my words, he immediately retracted his charge. "You know I didn't mean that, Ziele. We make the best decisions we can, based on what we know at the time. It's all we can do."

He was right. With limited knowledge, it was our only choice.

But that was something we would learn to live with—eventually. It neither corrected the mistake nor altered the terrible consequences resulting from it.

Had I missed seeing the truth about Poe? And were my instincts wrong—when they had always served me so well in the past?

I did not sleep that night, but in my tossing and turning, I decided I was right about Poe. Whatever his failings, he was not the man I sought—the one whose monstrous words and deeds tormented me mercilessly, deep into the night.

Monday
March 19, 1906

CHAPTER 21

The Nineteenth Precinct House

Timothy Poe was not at 101 MacDougal Street, but a vast array of drug paraphernalia was. Unfortunately for him, it was more than enough to raise the eyebrows of even the most jaded of Mulvaney's men: a stash of opium, a bottle of Bayer's heroin, some cocaine toothache drops, and a dozen hypodermic needles of the type that had pricked Detective Marwin. Though it was not illegal to possess any of these items, it was frowned upon by polite society—and their discovery would do Poe little good.

The presence of similar hypodermic needles was purely circumstantial, of course. But taken together with the fingerprints that damned him—not to mention the jury of his peers who would no doubt take a dim view of his lifestyle—the case against Poe appeared strong. The prosecution would have little trouble painting Poe as an unsympathetic, amoral man. So it was unlikely that his personal testimony would trump the circumstantial evidence stacked against him, as I had witnessed firsthand in the poisoning trial where Mrs. Snyder had been acquitted. It seemed a lifetime ago, but it had been only a week.

Mulvaney's men had eventually located Poe—and by Monday morning, when I met with Mulvaney at the precinct house, Poe was under arrest. I reviewed the evidence against him myself. It was solid—and should have satisfied me on an intellectual level.

But the nagging sensation in my gut was another matter. I was convinced of Poe's innocence, despite the persuasive evidence now presented to me. I simply didn't believe him capable of committing these particular murders.

"Even the best of us make mistakes." Mulvaney clapped a sympathetic hand on my shoulder. "I've certainly made my share over the years. Luckily, your mistake didn't cost us too much time in finding our man."

I looked at him sharply. "Where was Poe hiding?"

"I sent my men down into the Bowery to talk with some of the drug suppliers we use as informants. And they got lucky: they found Poe, semiconscious, in the back hall of an opium den on Mott." He looked up, distracted by a sudden commotion outside. "Speak of the devil."

We both looked through Mulvaney's doorway just in time to observe Timothy Poe being brought out, sullen and catatonic, as two policemen dragged him from the holding room, down the hall, to the waiting police cart outside.

He caught sight of me and lunged in my direction. "I didn't do it." Wild with panic, he beseeched me, saying, "I swear it. You've got to believe me." He looked me in the eye as he reached a long, thin arm toward me, grabbing on to my leather bag as though for dear life. I noticed his once-white sleeve was now dirty and mottled with yellow and green stains, and I detected the stench of vomit.

"Sorry, sir," the policeman apologized to me before he shoved Poe away. "Tell it to the judge." He pushed Poe forward. But Poe continued to protest all the way down the hallway, as if seeing me had awakened a sudden desire to talk.

"We held him here overnight 'til he sobered up; now that we've interviewed him, we'll book him at the Tombs," Mulvaney said. "We hope to get a confession now that he knows how much we've got on him. We even found his prints in the elevator leading to the Aerial Gardens theater."

"You're certain?"

"The thumbprint was a perfect match."

I was silent for a few moments. "But he's said nothing so far?"

"Nothing important. He claims he's innocent. But during the past twenty-four hours he's been missing, he can't remember a thing. According to our Mott Street informant, he'd been at the opium den since yesterday morning. In other words, since shortly after Miss Billings' murder," he added significantly.

"Did you bring in Walter as well?" I asked, remembering the tall African man with whom Timothy Poe shared his quarters on MacDougal Street.

Mulvaney made a noise of frustration. "We've heard about Willie from the neighbors, but there's been no sign of him—and I daresay there won't be, as long as he knows we're looking. Apparently someone tipped him off we were coming."

I knew that any reply I made would sound hollow. I shoved

my hands deep into my pockets and leaned against Mulvaney's desk. "What do you need help with now?"

"Nothing."

Mulvaney's sharp tone caught me off guard, and I regarded him quizzically. "Not even a report summarizing my work for you? Doesn't the liaison department usually want that for accounting purposes?"

He shook his head. "Even if I wanted your help . . . even if the case wasn't all wrapped up . . . well." He paused, then finally said, "Charles Frohman was displeased with your visit yesterday. He telephoned Mayor McClellan, who telephoned Commissioner Bingham, and . . ."

"Ah," I said with a rueful smile. "So that's how it is."

"It is." His face was grim, and I knew from the expression in his eyes that his new responsibilities and their political pressures had begun to take their toll. "We're set here."

I would say that we left each other on good terms, but that wasn't quite the case. Or that I returned to Dobson with some measure of relief, but that wasn't true, either. This case troubled me deeply.

If Poe was truly guilty, then I was wrong—something I would accept. But if he was innocent, then not only was the wrong man sitting in the Tombs, but the cost of our mistake would be exacted by the blood of the next victim.

That afternoon, I stopped by Alistair's offices at Columbia University, in Morningside Heights, to let him know that our services were no longer needed. He was not alone: the two *Times* reporters, Frank Riley and Jack Bogarty, were huddled around his desk.

"Ziele, come join us." He got up with alacrity and pulled another chair closer to his desk. "You remember our friends from
The Times."

I returned their greeting reluctantly, not moving from the
door. Then I declined Alistair's offer as politely as I could. "I'll
wait outside until you're finished," I said. "My own business is
a private matter."

Riley stood. "We were just leaving anyhow, right, Jack?"
He pumped Alistair's hand vigorously. "Thank you for all your
help today. And we're looking forward to dinner tomorrow
night."

"And we promise we'll give you a good mention in the article," Jack said. "You too, Detective," he added as he passed me
on the way out.

"Dinner?" I asked Alistair as I took the seat Riley had just
vacated. "I didn't even know you were in contact with them."

"Of course. It's an arrangement that works well, Ziele. I
share a little information with them, they share a little with me."
He shrugged. "Jack has given me tickets to a couple of Broadway shows, and Frank plans to take me to a baseball game to
see Christy Mathewson play for the Giants. But don't worry—I
would never say anything to compromise your investigation."

"It doesn't matter anymore," I said flatly. And I told him
how all evidence pointed to Timothy Poe as the man responsible
for these three horrific murders.

"I know science doesn't lie," he had said, shaking his head in
disbelief, "but it goes against everything I had thought we understood about these killings. What do they believe to be his
motive?"

They didn't have an exact motive, of course. But given all

that had been discovered about Poe's lifestyle, they didn't require anything specific. "General depravity" would suffice.

We talked for some time, both of us uncomfortable with the way this had wrapped up. Alistair seemed even more unsettled than I was. The evidence against Poe was solid. And yet we were in agreement: Poe as the murderer went against what both my experience and Alistair's learning had taught us. Unfortunately, we were now observers looking in at the case that had once been ours. And even if I'd been armed with more than the conviction of my beliefs, my efforts would have been unsanctioned, nothing more than those of a Good Samaritan. But I had nothing else.

Before I returned to Dobson, I made my way to a small coffeehouse two blocks south of Grand Central. Sitting there, enjoying the strong aroma of the coffee and its reassuring warmth, I was not in the mood for company—especially not that of my father.

I was aware of his presence moments before he took a seat in the chair opposite me.

"You've been following me again."

He flexed his thin fingers, then said, "Got to keep the skills sharp, old boy. And I've good enough reason for it lately. My creditors have resurfaced to cause me trouble."

A ten-year absence, and absolutely nothing had changed.

He continued to talk, saying, "I've actually found some information that may help you with your theater case. I brought someone . . ."

Before I could interrupt him to say it didn't matter anymore, a woman entered as if on cue. And I found myself staring yet again into a face marked by green eyes and surrounded by red curly ringlets: that of Molly Hansen.

"You know my father?" I looked at her in consternation.

They exchanged a guilty look that told me more than I wanted to know, even before my father colorfully described her as his "boon companion of late."

He stepped away, succumbing to a coughing fit. Molly cast a worried glance after him, but didn't follow.

"I'm sorry I didn't tell you when we talked earlier, Simon," she said sheepishly. "I was afraid if you knew, you wouldn't help me."

"Actually," I said delicately, "I didn't help you."

She flashed a brilliant smile. "Oh yes, you did—though you didn't know it. All you had to do was walk with me into that bar, and those watching me, wanting their money, knew I'd made your acquaintance. So when I told them a small white lie or two the next day, they were inclined to believe me. Besides," she added, rather too gaily, "you wouldn't want a sick man like your father to suffer at the hands of his creditors."

So my good name had been bandied about in backdoor dealings to secure my father more time to repay the debts he'd incurred as naturally and inevitably as other men breathed. Any other day, I would have been furious. But today, I had far worse things on my mind.

"Well," she took a deep breath, "I asked your father to bring me to you because I have some information that may help with your case."

I am not quite sure why I responded as I did. No doubt it was the dark mood I was in at the time—coupled with my anger over how my father and Molly had conspired against me. Some people simply couldn't be trusted. Most people, in fact.

"There is no case," I said, pushing my coffee cup aside. "They've found enough evidence to apprehend someone. The case is solved."

Her eyes widened. "Truly? That's wonderful. I'm just surprised." She thought for a moment. "Who did you arrest?"

My father rejoined us, sucking vigorously on one of the candies that offered him temporary relief.

"I can take no credit for the arrest," I said, avoiding her question. She could read all about Poe herself in the papers soon enough; I had no desire to discuss it. "But Captain Mulvaney has solid evidence linking the man he arrested to the murders."

"So you don't believe they have the right man?" My father's eyes lit up with interest.

"I've no reason to disagree," I replied.

"Ah," he said, touching a finger to his lips. "But not disagreeing—and actually agreeing—are two entirely different matters, are they not?"

"Not where irrefutable evidence is involved." I was in no mood to discuss my own doubts right now.

"Pshaw," he said with a jovial look. "I say, show me the evidence, and I'll show you evidence a skillful chap like me can manipulate. Even fingerprints. I've been known to fake them myself in my time."

"Yes, well, it's not like that." I turned to Molly. "What was it you wanted to tell me anyhow?"

"I guess it doesn't matter now."

It was with little regret that I thanked her for thinking of me and I assured her that the case was resolved. It was unlike me. Normally I'd have wanted her answer nonetheless—simply to complete the process and ensure I'd left no lead unexplored, no stone unturned. But tonight, I'd had enough.

After some further talk in which I reluctantly agreed to meet my father for dinner that Friday, I took my train to the small, dingy flat in Dobson, not far from the railroad tracks, that I called home.

I tiptoed up the stairs so as not to wake my landlady on the first floor, opened the door soundlessly, and collapsed onto the threadbare gold sofa that the prior tenant had not bothered to remove—and I had not bothered to replace.

This night, it looked particularly worn and shabby. A depressing place, I thought. The walls were a faded yellow rose wallpaper. A rickety rocking chair with a broken wooden slat was beside me. But the carpet—provided by my landlady herself so that downstairs she would not hear footsteps—was a nice, thick blue wool.

Though I could have afforded a nicer place, it seemed pointless to do so when my time here was limited . . . when there was no one with whom to enjoy it.

I reached over to my brown satchel and emptied its contents. There were several pages of notes that should probably be returned to Mulvaney, if only for his files. And an apple, now bruised, that I had meant to eat at lunchtime, but never had.

It was only after I tossed the limp leather bag aside that I noticed a dirty, crumpled white paper protruding from the side flap pocket. I pulled it out.

At first, I felt violated that someone had slipped it into my bag without my knowing it.

Then I took a long time to read it and thoroughly absorb its contents.

Detective Ziele,

I'm writing to you on the chance that I will see you again or find a sympathetic soul to deliver this message. You seem to be a fair-minded man who will listen to me, even though others believe I am lying.

I swear to you I am innocent. I've killed no one: I was not at the Aerial Gardens, and I've never touched those needles.

I've been framed—tricked in the worst way imaginable. On Saturday, a man stopped to ask me for directions. When I leaned down to examine his map, he covered my mouth with something to make me pass out. I can remember nothing else until the time of my arrest.

I can't survive this for much longer. I'm sure to die if you cannot help.

Timothy Poe

Poe must have placed it in my bag when he reached toward me at the precinct house earlier today. It was an act of complete desperation.

Were the contents of the letter genuine?

I wasn't sure. But after reading the letter over and over, I couldn't put it aside, its claims forgotten and ignored.

My gut told me that Timothy Poe was innocent of these murders. He was an accomplished actor who had lied to me and hidden scandalous aspects of his life. Despite that, I couldn't imagine him wining and dining these actresses as the killer had done, buying them dresses and promising to make them stars, before coldly killing them.

And now in this letter before me, Poe's words, rambling and disjointed as they were, seemed to strike a note of truth. I knew Alistair would agree. He had never felt that Poe fit the profile of this killer. The letter was just what I needed to turn my frustrated belief into the kind of action that might save the case.

After several telephone exchanges, Alistair and I made arrangements to meet downtown at the New York University offices of Dr. Vollman the next morning. I still had the film from the tattooed verse, and I agreed to have it processed and bring the photographs to the meeting for Alistair's handwriting expert to examine.

I did not bother to telephone Mulvaney, who would have dismissed Poe's letter as the posturing of a desperate, guilty man. We would be on our own.

Was I meddling in a case now best left alone? Maybe.

But, despite all evidence to the contrary, I believed what Poe had written. At worst, I would waste my efforts over the next several days while I chased a red herring. I could live with that. Besides, I was still on official leave from my job as a policeman in Dobson. And if Mulvaney had indeed imprisoned the wrong man, then I had a larger responsibility to an as-yet-unknown actress—one at risk of playing her final role.

PART
THREE

Our position is altered; the right course is
no longer what it was before.
—George Eliot, *The Mill on the Floss*

Tuesday
March 20, 1906

CHAPTER 22

Dorrey's Coffee Shop

After a night of unrelenting insomnia, I woke to a pounding headache the following morning. Dawn's first light—as well as a cup of coffee and a dose of Bromo-Seltzer—finally brought me some measure of relief. I was distinctly uncomfortable with the idea of working behind Mulvaney's back on a case he believed to be closed. We had been friends and colleagues for so long, it seemed almost a betrayal of trust—never mind that he no longer kept me within his own confidence.

To be fully at ease with my decision, I wanted to evaluate one discrepancy that continued to vex me. Specifically, it was the claim Timothy Poe had made in his letter that he had never been to the Aerial Gardens—and had never touched a hypodermic needle like those found in his flat on MacDougal Street.

Yet, Mulvaney had obtained the most solid evidence I could imagine to contradict that claim: Poe's fingerprints.

Last night my father had said that fingerprints could be faked easily enough—and today I intended to find out how.

Based on a tip from the desk clerk at the hotel where I knew my father was staying, I found him at a small coffee shop on Greenwich Avenue called Dorrey's, across the street from his hotel. It was a nondescript place with four tables and a grumpy matron servicing them.

He looked up in surprise when I came in. I noted the heavy lines on his face and dark circles under his eyes. He had not slept last night, either.

He coughed into his handkerchief. "Simon, why . . . I didn't expect to see you before our dinner on Friday."

He pushed aside a plate of half-burnt, buttered toast. He had eaten little, and I couldn't tell whether the bread was simply inedible—or whether the tuberculosis had taken its toll on his appetite.

I took the seat across from his, glancing briefly at the empty coffee mug and crumbs in front of me.

"You just missed Molly," he explained.

I pushed her leftover mug aside.

"I have a question and I need your help. Last night," I said carefully, "you told me that fingerprints can be faked. It sounded to me as though you'd even done it yourself. I need to know more."

He smiled broadly, revealing even teeth that were no longer as white and well cared for as I remembered. Then he tapped his head. "Nothing a smart man with a particular kind of education cannot master, if you get my drift."

I nodded, but said nothing. It was encouragement enough for him.

"Back in the day when I needed some extra cash, I got a job from Bully Mike—"

"No details, please." I cut him off with a quick smile and a note of warning.

"Oh, well—of course, of course." He coughed again, hard, but if there was blood I saw no sign of it.

I remained silent for a moment until his coughing fit eased, and Mrs. Dorrey finished pouring me a cup of coffee. Though the brew wasn't as strong as I normally preferred, it would do. After downing half the cup, I moved the saucer to my far left, positioning it on a small section of the tablecloth that was un-stained by some previous diner's breakfast.

My father returned his handkerchief to his pocket, then shifted his position, trying to get comfortable again. He leaned in close to me. "A couple years ago, I was commissioned, shall we say, with the task of making someone's fingerprint appear in a place it had never actually been. And your police department bought it hook, line, and sinker—though they weren't the audience I intended to fool." He paused and looked around before he said, "Private justice, you understand," in a conspiratorial whisper.

It was all I could do not to groan aloud. My father was a con artist: his skills ran along the lines of trickery and deceit, not violence. But he also practiced what I considered willful blind-ness. Always desperate for money, he scrutinized neither the hand that paid him nor the consequences that inevitably fol-lowed the "tasks" he undertook.

"Walk me through the process, then, step-by-step."

His eyes lit up. "Are you telling me that your training as a detective has taught you none of this?"

"Why would it?" I shrugged. "Until fingerprints have more value in court, there's little point in fully understanding how they can be altered or outright forged."

"You don't say. I didn't realize they were so unimportant. In fact, I learned my forgery trick from a fellow who spent time up at Sing Sing. Time in jail didn't take him out of the game, but his fingerprints did, temporarily at least. At first, because the state had his prints on file, he had to be careful. Then he learned the art of forgery and was able to return to his old ways."

I finished my coffee and ordered yet another. "You were about to tell me," I reminded him, "exactly how you forged this print."

"Ah." He laced his fingers together. "Do you read detective fiction, son? Are you familiar with Arthur Conan Doyle's story 'The Adventure of the Norwood Builder'?"

"Frankly, I'm surprised that you are," I said dryly. My father was not an educated man and had never been much of a reader. His active mind had favored other pursuits.

"Well, it interested me for reasons other than literary merit," he said between coughs. "You see, in the story, a man uses his thumb to press down upon a soft wax seal—as is typical when sealing up a legal packet. The villain in the story then takes the wax impression from that seal, moistens it with his own blood, and transfers it to a wall at the scene of a murder."

"But that's fiction. Made up."

"Is it?" He arched an eyebrow. "Don't think it hasn't been tried."

"So if you generate a mold, you can fake a fingerprint?" I asked, my tone skeptical.

"Ah." He touched a finger to his lips. "That way is often complicated. But it has inspired some of us to seek out other, more successful ways. . . ."

"Such as?"

"You can directly transfer the print without obtaining a mold. All you need is a decent surface to capture the original print, like a cup or glass," he motioned to his empty water glass, "and a little candle wax."

"Go on." For once, I actually had the sense that he knew what he was talking about.

"Well, you take something that will pick up the fingerprint and its residue, like a thin veneer of candle wax. That's what I used. The print is reversed, but that's okay. Because when you then press the wax to the final surface—the one where you want the print to appear—it flips yet again and is perfect. Of course," he smiled proudly, "very few people can do it correctly. It's a difficult skill."

"But when the police can't use it . . ."

"It still can create suspicion, no? That was all I was hired to do when I planted a fingerprint on an object its owner had never touched. Not provide definitive proof, but to create suspicion. It's a powerful emotion, son, suspicion. Once it catches hold of someone, all rational thought tends to disappear—"

I cut him off once again and thanked him for his time, promising to see him on Friday.

"One more thing." I had almost reached the door when I turned around. "Molly Hansen had something to tell me last night. What was it?"

His eyes widened. "You'll have to ask her. She never told me."

"Do you at least know why she thought her information pertained to my case?" I asked, annoyed now that he didn't know more.

He shrugged. "It was none of my business. She didn't tell me, and I'd never ask. But if you want to find her later, she lives at Madame Pinoche's, south of Washington Square Park. She should be there 'til about three o'clock."

Not for the first time, I cursed the perverse mood I'd been in last night—the odd frame of mind that had led me to ignore what she'd wanted to share.

"How long have you known Molly?" I asked, trying to sound as though his answer wouldn't be important to me.

He shrugged. "Two months? Maybe three?"

"You don't even know?" As exasperating as it was to think of, I supposed that at least it was a sign that my father's illness hadn't prevented him from keeping up with some of his old ways. "So it's nothing serious," I said, finishing lamely.

He gave me a sad smile. "You know me, son. Nothing ever is." He wrapped long, fragile fingers around his coffee mug. "She found me and decided, sick as I was, I could still show her a bit of the good life. If she wants to give me a bit of pleasure in my old age, well then . . . why not, I say."

Why not, indeed? I thought of my mother, cold in her grave. I supposed he was right. It didn't matter now.

I left and walked a few blocks east, toward the office building at New York University where I was to meet Alistair and his handwriting expert, Dr. Vollman. I kept thinking about something my father had just said about suspicion. He had been exactly right, I decided. The truth—even definitive proof of it—was not the most important thing in Poe's case. Instead, it was all those terrible, nagging, awful suspicions about Poe that had grown, become insurmountable, and now threatened to seal his fate.

CHAPTER 23

Greenwich Village

Washington Square Park buzzed with activity this morning, with throngs of people milling in all directions, vying for space with the newsboys and pushcart men who competed for the best locations from which to purvey their wares.

"Series murderer captured last night in opium den," hollered one newsboy. "Read all about it! Full story in today's *Times*."

The answering cry came from a pushcart owner. "Hot sausage on a roll! Come and get 'em while they're hot."

I walked along the park's north side, breathing hard because of the heavy, stale smoke from a terrible fire yesterday that continued to permeate the air. The building that had burned—Benedict's Undertaking, better known as the West Side Morgue—was much farther south, in the Italian section of

Greenwich Village. But it had been a significant fire, killing four firemen. And its aroma would last for days as a pungent reminder of the tragedy.

Death seemed to draw even closer as I passed Hangman's Tree, rumored to have been an execution site some hundred years ago. I quickened my steps, slowing only as I came to the marble Washington Arch, under which Fifth Avenue passed. I turned left, past stately redbrick Greek Revival row houses—no longer home to the city's most fashionable, wealthy residents, who had since moved farther uptown, but still beautifully maintained. Dr. Vollman's well-appointed offices were in the last building near the corner of University Place.

He greeted me enthusiastically when I knocked, which led me to believe he and the others had been impatiently awaiting my arrival—though I was right on time as promised.

"Professor of sociology?" I asked, noticing the brass-and-iron plaque outside his door. "Surely this isn't a university building."

I knew that New York University had largely moved its undergraduate classes uptown to the Heights campus in the Bronx, but a few classroom buildings remained, mainly by the factories that bordered the east side of the park. In short, they were nothing like the upscale row house I had just entered.

Dr. Vollman made a sound that passed for a laugh, but could just as easily have been a hacking cough. "Sociology remains my official affiliation," he said, eyes twinkling, "at least until they create a department of forensic learning. And I daresay that will not come 'til I'm long in the grave. Follow me," he added. "The others are waiting for you."

Leaning on his cane more heavily than I remembered from

our first meeting, he led me along a wide corridor of cream walls and thick gold-and-red carpet to a back room. Along the way, he explained that he had adapted the first floor of his residence for academic purposes with the university's approval. As the aging professor had found it more difficult to navigate the university's sprawling campus, his department had accommodated his physical limitations.

"Besides," he added, "they like to continue offering some courses here at the Washington Square Park campus. It's more convenient for many of our students."

He directed me into the simple spare room that he had obviously created for classroom purposes. A large chalkboard was at its rear, behind a round table designed to seat at least ten students. To the left, an oversized window offered an unobstructed view of the horse stables on Washington Mews. A plain walnut desk, polished to a high gloss, was in front of the window, facing into the room.

Alistair and Isabella were already seated at the table, but both rose automatically to greet me and exchange the usual pleasantries before our discussion turned to the business at hand.

"So you want me to look at new items—and also reassess some old material." Dr. Vollman lowered himself gingerly into a chair, taking out a silk cloth to polish his glasses.

"That's right." I put my bag on the table, first spreading out the photographs of Emmaline Billings's tattoo, which a photographer in Dobson had developed for me the night before. "We hoped you might be able to make something of these," I said as the handwriting expert inched his chair closer to me.

He grunted, holding each photograph up to the light, one by one.

"Careful," I said, for he was handling them more roughly than I would have preferred. "We'll need to turn these over to the police soon."

In fact, I'd have to turn them over the moment Mulvaney remembered to ask me for them—though in the excitement of Poe's arrest, he appeared to have forgotten about this piece of evidence. I had taken eight close-up photographs, and the three of us watched hopefully as Dr. Vollman reviewed them.

But in the end, he shook his head sadly. "I can do nothing with this. Handwriting analysis cannot interpret what has been written with a needle rather than a pen. You may be able to do something with the grammar, but I can do nothing with the writing itself."

He whistled as he pushed the pictures aside. "He's a real bastard, isn't he, to do this?" He glanced at Isabella. "Pardon my language, miss. But if Emmaline Billings was alive, the process of getting this tattoo would've been pure torture." He paused for only a beat. "Do you know whether she was?"

"We don't," I said. "Not yet."

And to find out, I'd need to contact the coroner's office directly. I was unlikely to hear further details from Mulvaney— and I ignored another pang of guilt that I was pursuing this matter behind his back.

Alistair drummed his fingers lightly against the table, which had the same glossy walnut finish as Dr. Vollman's desk. When he finally spoke, he chose his words carefully. "The man— for the evidence does suggest he is a man—that we seek here has the most unusual criminal mind I have encountered in my career."

"You've studied so many violent criminals who have done

terrible things. I don't understand why you believe this man to be unique," Isabella spoke quietly.

"Because I believe we are seeking a man whose personal charm completely masks his violent tendencies. According to their friends, at least two victims had a new man in their lives—specifically, a new beau who sent gifts and squired each victim about town."

"But plenty of actresses have admirers," I reminded him. "And there is no evidence to suggest the new gentleman each actress was seeing was the same man."

"Likewise, there's no evidence to suggest he was not," Alistair parried. He took a deep breath. "Whoever he is, he has managed to gain his victims' trust, convincing them to meet him alone at strange hours at the theater. After he came to know them and seduce them, only then did he kill them. And he did so in a manner that reveals two striking elements unique to this killer's personality: his brilliant theatricality and his cruelty."

"But his cruelty wasn't obvious until Miss Billings's murder," Isabella said, troubled. "His first two murders were . . . well, almost shockingly beautiful."

"Because he didn't mark their bodies before," Alistair said, musing, "whereas here he did."

It was the same thought that had occurred to me at the dead house. "Why would he change his behavior like this?"

Alistair leaned back in his chair, intertwining his fingers. "It's what I've been thinking about ever since you told me. And something important has occurred to me: his cruelty wasn't visibly obvious in the other murders—but it was there, all the same."

"But the act of writing on her body has to mean something additional," I persisted.

I directed my question to Alistair, but Isabella intervened to answer. "Maybe we can figure out *why* he did it by looking at *what* he wrote."

I sat up straighter. "Yes, I'd wanted to ask you about that as well." I spread the photo before us again.

Lo! 'tis a gala night
. . . its hero the Conqueror Worm

"I guessed that 'gala night' refers to the theater," I said. "He repeated the phrase in his latest letter to *The Times*."

"It may also be another strategy to frame Poe," she said, eyes dancing.

"Because?" I asked, eyebrows raised.

"These two lines are from a poem by Edgar Allan Poe called 'The Conqueror Worm,'" she replied. "It's about a play in which mimes run around aimlessly, chasing a Phantom they never capture. There is an audience of angels who can only weep— and in the end, a monstrous worm emerges to eat the mimes before the curtain falls."

"It sounds awful," I said, aghast.

She laughed, and the sound was like the pealing of bells. "It *is* awful. It suggests life is nothing but a ridiculous dance, at the end of which awaits a hideous death."

"Literally, worms eating the body?" Alistair asked.

"Yes," she agreed.

"Why in the world would he put that on her back?" I asked.

Isabella's response was slow but sure. "I believe he means to tell us that we're the angels."

"How so?" I demanded.

"Because our fate is to watch—weep—and accomplish nothing," she said simply. "And he has defiled her body, just as the Conqueror Worm will do."

We were all quiet for several moments.

"But who is he?" I said, drumming my fingers against the table. "And why is he targeting Frohman's actresses?"

"He is someone who is cunning and seductive. Remember, he entices the women to dress themselves, perhaps even rehearse a scene onstage after everyone else has gone home. He told each victim that he planned to 'make her a star.'"

I flashed once again to the image of Charles Frohman rehearsing with his Juliet at the Knickerbocker Hotel. For now, I put it out of my mind and continued to talk.

"The moment each victim realized what he really had in mind would have been a horrible, cruel betrayal. And strangulation itself—well, it's one of the more excruciatingly painful methods by which to die. So even if he managed to make each victim *appear* to have died a beautiful, peaceful death—the reality each experienced was anything but." My voice was bitter. I agreed with Alistair: this killer was among the most brutal I'd ever run across.

"So first things first," Alistair said. "We know that we are dealing with an uncommonly vicious killer. We believe him to be someone other than Timothy Poe; perhaps Dr. Vollman will now be kind enough to confirm that for us."

"Of course." Dr. Vollman had removed his spectacles, but now he put them back on as Alistair placed a copy of the Eliza Downs letter in front of him. I added the *Times* letter that had been received yesterday.

"I have the *Times* reporters, Riley and Bogarty, to thank for procuring the Downs letter," Alistair said with a grin. "They caught Captain Mulvaney in a generous mood; he agreed to lend them this letter for their breaking news feature about Poe, which hit newsstands this morning. But they intend to milk the story for all it's worth—so in exchange for another interview, they agreed to share the letter with me."

Captain Mulvaney had indeed been in a charitable mood if he had resorted to lending out evidence to reporters. Unless— and this was quite possible, I realized—the prosecutor didn't plan to charge Poe with Eliza Downs's murder. He didn't have the cooperation of the Downs family; they had objected strenu- ously to the idea of having her body exhumed. And the case against Poe for the two subsequent murders appeared airtight— more than what was needed to sentence him to the electric chair at Sing Sing. Miss Downs's death, less clear-cut, might actually hurt the prosecution's case.

"And I have some additional samples you can use for com- parison," I said. I handed him the notebook page where Poe had written his first, false address as well as the declaration of in- nocence Poe had passed to me yesterday. I had also managed to procure a receipt signed by Charles Frohman—the result of my having shamelessly bribed one of the Knickerbocker Hotel clerks.

To these, Alistair added his own find. "Another gift from the *Times* reporters," he explained as he placed down a card such as might come from a bouquet of flowers. "As you know, they spoke extensively with the friends of Annie Germaine, the sec- ond victim. One of them discovered this note among her things."

We read its three-word question, printed in a sloppy script: "Backstage at 11?"

"So you'd like me to compare these samples for consisten-
cies that may indicate the same writer. Excellent." Dr. Vollman
put on a pair of white cotton gloves.

At first I thought he did so from habit, since each writing
specimen was preserved in a wrapper. But, one by one, he temporarily removed each document from its protective cover,
walked it over to the five-foot-high window, and examined the
paper in the light. We were silent for some fifteen minutes until
at last he was done and pronounced his verdict.

"If Timothy Poe is indeed the writer of these," he said, picking up the address scrap and yesterday's letter, "then he cannot
be the same writer who penned this." He pointed to the eggshell-
blue letter found by the first murder victim.

"What did you find?" I asked, excited that he may have seen
something to confirm I was right about Poe.

His lips curved into a half smile. "I compared the way there
is a loop in the blue-letter writer's *j* and *y* to similar letters in
your writing sample by Poe. They are not alike, at all. Also, we
noted the first time we met how the blue letter begins with a
false leftward slant that shifts rightward by its closing. Poe's
writing is absent any slant, even in his long, rambling confes-
sional to you. Look here."

He pointed to the phrase *I swear to you I am innocent.*

"In such a state of agitation," Dr. Vollman continued, "he
could not camouflage his natural handwriting even if he wished
to do so. So I see—word by word, slant by slant—that you have
two very different writers at work."

He passed the letters back to us, explaining more about his
analysis of the writer's pressure. It was a relief to hear Dr. Vollman confirm what we instinctually believed. Even if this sort of

evidence wouldn't prove conclusive in a court of law, it was essential to our theory.

"And what about the Frohman signature? And the flower card?" I asked.

"Inconclusive," he said without hesitation. "You've given me two words in one sample," he gestured to Frohman's signature, "and three in the other," he nodded to the card. "There is simply not enough material for me to compare consistency of loops, pen lifts, and letter heights."

So we had ruled out one suspect, Timothy Poe. But we could not narrow our suspicions among the others. I was desperate for more.

"When we first met, you said that because of the regular cycle of pen lifts and movements you observed, you believe this killer is still in the prime of his life," I said, thinking we at least could divide our primary suspects by age range: Charles Frohman was about fifty, Leon Iseman was in his midforties, and the admirers who had pursued each of these actresses had been variously described as in their late twenties or thirties. "Can you be more specific?" I asked Dr. Vollman. "Are there any characteristics that you can decipher?"

Dr. Vollman gave each of us a severe look, as though he was offended by the question—lingering longest on me. Then he stood up, slowly and with great effort, grasping on to his cane.

He coughed, then spoke deliberately. "When I first met with you, I was careful to say I was not a graphologist. In other words, I refrain from speculating on the personality traits of any writer whose penmanship I study. I am at ease," he coughed again and thumped his chest, "working with more scientifically recognized specifics that are valuable to know in forensic-identification cases." He noted Isabella's puzzled look. "That means I tell the judge in a court of law whether a document is a forgery or not."

He circled the table, walking slowly to the chalkboard. "But when Alistair called me last night and impressed upon me the grave nature of this case . . . and when I see evidence of the evil this killer has wrought," he motioned to the photographs of the tattoo on Miss Billings's body, "I see now that, despite my misgivings, I must help you in all the ways I can."

"You never told me that you actively practiced graphology," Alistair said, looking at his colleague in a new light.

Dr. Vollman hooked his cane on the back of his chair. "I don't advertise the skills I prefer not to use. But see here. You want to know what kind of man you're dealing with? Let me help you find out."

I well remembered what he had said during our first meeting—that the field of graphology was filled with charlatans. Presumably he didn't count himself as one, but—interested as I was in his input—I remained highly skeptical.

He smiled as though he understood my skepticism when he picked up a piece of chalk. "Graphology is controversial, yes, but it has its experts and adherents, just like any other field of study. It's actually one of our oldest fields: the Chinese invented it, thousands of years ago. And the better practitioners today uphold fixed standards, particularly the 'rule of three' developed by French graphologists. That means," he explained, "that a valid interpretation of someone's writing requires three separate elements that each point to a similar meaning. One alone will not do."

"So you trust the information it yields?" I was still suspicious.

"When it's done well—then yes. Let me explain. When we were children, each one of us went to school and learned a standard method of handwriting. Here in America, certainly in New York, that is typically the Palmer method, which relies on repetitive drills. But despite the fact that we all begin with Palmer, learning the same drills, consider how we each end up with unique penmanship. Not one of us has the same writing as an adult as we were taught as a child."

We all nodded in agreement. Certainly my writing little resembled what I had learned in grade school.

He cleared his throat. "Graphology maintains that the writer's personality begins to manifest itself in the writing as he or she matures, because writing is inherently expressive. That means we can read it as surely as we can read human expressions. It functions as a symbol, just as a woman's tears signify sadness or a child's smile shows pure happiness."

"So, if I understand you," Alistair said, clarifying, "graphology assumes that our emotions of the moment—in addition to our personality traits—are manifest in our writing."

"Yes," the expert replied firmly. "To do so, graphology examines the same relevant markers that I examine in my forgery cases—the elements of size and spacing, pressure and lifts, and of course slant—but with an explanation that goes beyond simple consistency."

Dr. Vollman drew a leftward slant on the board, followed by a rightward slant. "The killer's letters always began leftward, an attempt to disguise his natural tendencies. By letter's end, he cannot help but revert to his natural tendency and slant rightward with heavier pressure. I find three indications in his writing—using the 'rule of three' that I mentioned before—that inform me that you seek a person who is unusually excitable or energetic."

He encouraged us to look at the eggshell-blue letter before us. "Generally, he has a light script. I like Detective Ziele's description of it as 'spidery.' But despite his feathery penmanship, I see characteristics indicative of aggression. Look at the way he forms his *g, p,* and *y.* There's greater pressure in these downstrokes. We also see closed ovals, which indicate that he is a private person, quite adept at keeping his own secrets." He looked at me specifically. "We also see aggression in that same characteristic."

"He has killed three victims that we know of, and a fourth may yet die as a result," I said, thinking again of the intensely private Charles Frohman. "I don't think we need a heavy downstroke to tell us this killer is aggressive."

"No? But maybe what I tell you next will help slightly more," Dr. Vollman added, unperturbed by my skepticism. "Notice how he doesn't connect his letters in quite the same way from sentence to sentence, word to word. That suggests he's a man with different, conflicting aspects to his personality. To one person, he may be a loyal friend. To another, he may be a backstabbing competitor."

"So, to put it another way," Alistair said, "the fractures in his writing suggest a splintered life."

"Yes." The handwriting expert nodded excitedly. "But he's practical-minded; I see that evidenced in the short upper reach of his *l* and *b.* Not like you, Alistair." Dr. Vollman chuckled, but the sound was another hoarse cackle. "Your long *l*s and *b*s signify your desire to reach intellectual heights." The professor sat again in the nearest chair, exhausted by his efforts. "One more thing. The man is cautious, evidenced by the wide spacing between words as well as the generally small size of his words. He knows how to keep his distance. You'll not catch him easily. Not without a fight, I'd guess."

"I'm not sure we've really learned anything that will help us to identify the killer—specifically, that is," I said, still skeptical. "The character traits you've mentioned can't even help us narrow down our list of suspects . . ." I broke off in frustration, got up, and began pacing the length of the room.

After a few moments I returned to the table and addressed the three of them. "We need to refocus on one important question. It's safe to say that if the killer is not Timothy Poe, then our killer set him up to take the fall. But why? And more importantly, who would have the means to do so?"

"Well, other than Poe, whom were you getting close to?" Alistair asked, his tone matter-of-fact.

"Charles Frohman." I went on to explain all that Isabella and I had learned from our interview with him the other night, including what was most troubling: the fact that all the victims worked for his syndicate, that he had held each of them to high standards, and each—by his own admission—had fallen short. "My only concern with Frohman is that he may not have had the means to frame Poe," I acknowledged.

"You've mentioned his associates before. He seems to have minions and political allies everywhere," Alistair responded, one eyebrow raised.

"True. And I've told you that I've come to believe that Leon Iseman merits a close look. He has as much knowledge of the theater as Frohman—and I've seen firsthand an example of his temper. But would he have had the skill to forge fingerprints, as the person who framed Poe seems to have successfully done?" I went on to tell them what I had learned from my father about the application of candle wax in copying a print—and the considerable skill it required. If Poe had been out cold for a period of time, then it would have been easy enough to get his real prints on the hypodermic needles. But transferring his thumbprint to the elevator at the Aerial Gardens would involve the kind of talent only men like my father possessed.

"If Frohman is as well connected to the political elite of this city as you say," Alistair said, his face grim, "then he—and his associates—would know how to find whatever help they might need."

He didn't have to say it. Such people always knew how to find a man with skills like my father's—and employ them, if necessary.

"Then there is our wild-card suspect," I said, "the man who seems to have courted each of these actresses before killing them. He has been described differently—and we still know next to nothing about him, despite all interviews and best efforts."

"Could Frohman or Iseman have pulled that off, without being recognized?" Alistair asked.

"If a man like Frohman courted an actress," I said, thinking aloud, "then he would have been discreet. He might have engaged help—meaning different men—which would explain why there is no consistent description of the man who brought flowers and messages to each victim."

"The same could be said of Leon Iseman," Isabella offered.

"Or, the stage-door hanger-on others have mentioned could be our killer," I said.

"The more perplexing question is, why?" Alistair continued to follow my train of thought. "Whether it is Frohman, Iseman, or a separate hanger-on who wooed each actress, there was a motivation at play. And *that* is what we can use to draw him out."

"Well," I replied soberly, "then we need to focus more on his motive."

"Go on," Alistair urged.

"It's possible the killer has now completed his goal—whatever that was—and simply plans to scapegoat Poe and be done."

"It's certainly possible." Alistair gave me a dubious look.

"But you're not convinced," I said, "and I agree with you. The problem as I see it is this: if he's done, he has accomplished nothing. Yes, he has killed three actresses in increasingly theatrical fashion. But what does that do for him?"

"Perhaps only one of the women was a specific target and the others were killed to confuse us," Isabella said.

Alistair's eyes twinkled. "Now that's a capital idea. And it makes sense, except we've no indication any one was targeted other than for reasons of opportunity."

"And the three of them are so alike, they seem virtually interchangeable," I added.

To keep our ideas straight, I began writing the various possibilities on the chalkboard as the others watched. "Charles Frohman" was front and center—but annotated with the troublesome question: "what would killing three of his own actresses accomplish?"

"In fact, their deaths have brought about just the opposite of what Frohman desires. Now at least one of his theaters is temporarily shut," Isabella said.

"True. But Frohman owns many theaters, and his pockets are deep enough to withstand the closure of just one," Alistair replied.

"He gains press coverage in all the papers," Isabella suggested again.

Dr. Vollman made a noise of agreement. "Especially now that Poe is safely imprisoned at the Tombs, there will be even more interest in Frohman's shows. But it hardly seems the sort of publicity worth killing for."

Alistair shook his head. "No. From what you've told me, Ziele, Frohman can get publicity through other, legitimate means. I just can't see it."

"Leon Iseman is temperamental, plus he possesses the right kind of knowledge," Isabella added. "We simply don't know enough about him yet."

"And if it's the backstage admirer," I said, "then that person had to have access to Poe."

I stepped back and surveyed the board. That left the case wide open. In fact, virtually any man working in Mulvaney's precinct—or anyone connected with the theater—would have known about Poe. Something was missing.

"There is one other possibility," Alastair said, appearing pleased. "It's an idea I call distraction." He leaned back in his chair, hands flexed behind his head. "He wants to misdirect us, and in the process, gain additional time for himself."

I stared at him, and felt a flash of annoyance that he looked so pleased with himself at the moment. "Distraction," I said flatly.

Isabella simply laughed. "Stop being so mysterious, Alistair, and tell us what you mean."

"If the killer is—as I strongly believe—not yet done with murder, then I have to ask myself: why frame Poe? With the next death that follows, it will be obvious to all that Poe is innocent. He'll have the perfect alibi, in fact, by virtue of being incarcerated in the Tombs. So what would be the point?" He looked at each of us.

We waited for him to explain more.

"A killer," he said, "who has consistently raised the stakes with each murder is building up to something, not walking away quietly. I believe he has something big in mind planned next. His own 'gala night.' The question remains, what?"

"It has to be a show," I said, my excitement rising as we finally seemed to make progress in our thinking. "Every killing has happened at a theater. We'd stand a chance of stopping him just by adding protection at every theater in the city."

"Yes," Alistair said indulgently, "but I think our man would be smart enough to work around that somehow. I also think he's someone who fits in at these theaters. He doesn't attract attention."

"Yet it's of critical importance for *us* to identify him—and stop him before he kills again."

"Of course," Alistair agreed. "But—especially given how adept I believe his social functioning to be—to look among Frohman's employees or Poe's neighbors or even Mulvaney's men would be like searching for the proverbial needle in a haystack. Whereas if we look to this killer's predicted behavior, we force him to show himself to us. We have no idea who he is. But we know exactly how he behaves when he kills." Alistair paused to catch his breath. "First, we have to try to hypothesize some ideas for his next move. We should find out if any new shows are opening in the next couple weeks—"

Isabella bolted straight up in her chair and interrupted him. "*Romeo and Juliet.* It's going to be *Romeo and Juliet.*"

It took a moment for me to understand what she was saying, but the moment I did, it made perfect sense.

"Of course. When Isabella and I met with Frohman night before last," I said excitedly, "he was rehearsing the role of Juliet with one of his actresses. I'm willing to bet it opens in the next few weeks."

Alistair leaned over to his briefcase and pulled out his newspaper. It took him little time to scan the arts section and find the answer. "Several shows premiere in the next two or three weeks: *It's All Your Fault* at the Savoy opens April second, a Shubert musical called *The Social Whirl* opens the ninth at the Casino, *Arms and the Man* opens the sixteenth at the Lyric, *The American Lord* opens at the Hudson on the sixteenth, and *Romeo and Juliet* premieres this Thursday night at the Lyceum."

"And how many of those are Frohman productions?"

"Only two. *The American Lord* and *Romeo and Juliet.*"

"We don't want to ignore the other productions, but based on the three prior murders, I say we focus on the two Frohman premieres."

Alistair was silent for a long moment. Then he finally agreed.

I turned to Isabella. "We have complete transcripts for each letter written by this murderer. Would you take a look at each and try to figure out if we may have missed something?"

"What exactly am I to look for?" she asked, her brown eyes pools of worry.

"I've no idea, honestly," I said. "But I'm confident that if something is there, you'll recognize it when you find it."

I stared at the board for another long moment.

"Alistair, would you be able to find out more detail about each of these Frohman premieres? It would be helpful to learn the names of those involved, particularly the actresses. And ask around to see if anyone unusual has been observing the dress rehearsals."

"Of course," Alistair replied. "But as I've repeatedly said, I believe our killer fits in at the theater." He caught my look and hastily added, "But yes—I'll ask around."

"And I need to chase down a lead that I ignored yesterday."

We had formed a plan of action—a good one, I thought. And after thanking Dr. Vollman and agreeing to meet up at Alistair's apartment that evening, we split up in the interest of efficiency.

Isabella immediately caught a cab back uptown, but Alistair and I walked through the park, headed toward the southwest corner.

"We've much to do to prepare for Thursday night's show," Alistair was saying, "and I think we ought to start by . . ."

But even as I listened to Alistair's ideas, I wanted to enjoy this moment while it lasted. We still had no idea whom we were searching for. But we had accomplished something important: we had quite possibly identified the killer's next venue.

Alistair and I soon parted ways, for his plans took him to the West Side, where he would catch the subway back uptown to the theater district.

I continued walking south, passing a saxophone player who had attracted a lunchtime crowd, playing a tune I recognized but couldn't name from a recent George M. Cohan musical. For once, I felt we were a step ahead of the killer we sought, and not the other way around. That was a feeling worth savoring, and I did so—with every step as I made my way toward Molly Hansen's boardinghouse and the information I had so stupidly chosen to ignore the night before.

CHAPTER 24
Madame Pinoche's Boardinghouse

My hunger got the better of me before I left Washington Square Park, so I decided a five-minute lunch break was in order. I bought a sausage and roll from a pushcart, as well as an apple from a nearby fruit wagon and a copy of *The Times* from the corner newsboy. Crossing the walking path, I found a vacant park bench and opened my *Times* in search of the article that Frank Riley and Jack Bogarty had certainly written by now on the theater murders. I scanned coverage on the front page, seeing stories about the fire at Benedict's Undertaking, another fire at the Columbus Circle subway station, and a father who had killed his daughter just before her wedding day. Then I found it: PREDATORY MURDERER STALKS ACTRESSES OF GREAT WHITE WAY; APPREHENDED IN OPIUM DEN.

The article, penned in language more sensational than was

typical for *The Times*, praised Alistair lavishly. Apparently, his criminological theories had been invaluable to the investigation and were almost single-handedly responsible for the killer's timely capture. Mulvaney would be incensed to read that one, all right. However Alistair had managed it, he'd certainly made friends of those reporters. I realized with some surprise that he must have grown far closer to them than I'd first imagined.

But how would they rewrite the news when Poe was proven innocent—as I believed would happen in the coming days? Their effusive praise could not help but make me concerned that Alistair was beholden to them. I would have to be careful of where his loyalties stood, should any conflict of interest arise.

I made short work of my lunch and left the park, crossing Washington Square South to enter a neighborhood of boarding-houses and hotels that catered to actors, artists, and musicians. My father had said I'd find Molly at the three-and-a-half-story redbrick building several blocks south run by Madame Pinoche. Actors and actresses, writers and artists—most were still at home at this hour of the afternoon, socializing throughout first-floor common rooms—but I was ushered into a private parlor and assured that Miss Hansen would be down shortly.

Molly was not surprised to see me. "I figured your curiosity would get the better of you," she said with a bright smile as she took a seat primly on the sofa across from me.

I sat awkwardly, legs crossed, my knees thrust tightly against a satinwood coffee table. The parlor was clearly set up for courting couples, with opposite sofas arranged in cozy fashion—though not so close as to invite any impropriety. Clearly, arrangements had been designed for the comfort of men shorter than myself.

Molly looked at me askance. "Last night you said the case was closed and my information was of no importance. Mind telling me what changed?"

"Let's just say I'd had a rough day yesterday. I'm entitled to a change of heart, no?"

"They say it's a woman's prerogative." She was almost flirtatious as she flashed another dimpled smile. "But I'll allow it."

I uncrossed my legs, attempting to stretch them. "You said you had information relating to the case. Was it about one of the more recent victims?"

"No," she said, shaking her head. "But remember how I told you the other night that Annie had met a new fellow—someone she believed would make her into a star?" She caught her breath. "Well, there's a man who's been hanging out around the stage door recently, paying a lot of attention to me and the other girls."

I simply waited, letting her continue to talk.

"Of course I've no way of knowing if he's the same person as the fellow who was courting Annie."

A fellow had been paying attention to Miss Downs and Miss Billings as well . . . but she'd know nothing of that, of course. I kept my expression poker-faced, betraying nothing.

She was saying, "Maybe it's just my knowing what happened to Annie, but this man makes me uncomfortable."

"Uncomfortable in what way?"

When she remained silent, at a loss for words, I helped her out. "Do you mean he is too familiar? Or maybe he seems to know too much about you?"

She considered it for a moment. "I suppose he is just odd— both familiar and indifferent, at the same time. He's brought me flowers after every performance—and to the other girls, too. But he doesn't seem to like any one of us, in particular. It's as though he's waiting to see which one of us will encourage him most."

"And have you—encouraged him?"

I hoped that for a moment she could forget that I was my father's son. I didn't want her to lie to me now, and I couldn't have cared less about the particulars of their relationship. For all I knew, her expectations mirrored those of my father, and he—a consummate womanizer—would think nothing of turning his own attention in a new direction.

If she lied, it wasn't in the way I expected.

"I can encourage him if you want." She thrust her chin out, then almost immediately looked away, blushing, as though she'd just realized what she'd offered. "Only if it would help your investigation," she added lamely.

"What would help me is any details you can give," I said gently, "such as his name, or his general description?"

She seemed almost surprised that my questions were so simple.

"He's a regular sort of guy: clean-cut, young, in his late twenties if I had to guess. Light brown hair that could almost be described as a dirty blond. He dresses well and is quite confident and sure of himself."

"And his name?"

She was silent for a minute. "I think I heard one of the other girls call him Daniel."

Charles Frohman had a brother named Daniel, I had learned from reading news files about the syndicate. But of course, there was no reason to believe that the suitor Molly described was using his real name.

"How does he sign the card with his flowers?"

She smirked. "'An ardent admirer.' He signs all our cards the same way."

I laughed. "He's not very discreet, then. Do you still have the card he sent you?"

A guilty expression crossed her face before she shook her head. "I tossed them all. But I can ask the other girls when I see them tonight."

"Please, when they come in. And if he's at tonight's show . . ."

She tossed her head. "Will you come tonight, to watch and see?"

"Maybe. If I can't, I'll send someone I trust."

I caught her look of disappointment. But she hadn't told me enough—at least yet—to entice me to spend time at her stage door rather than pursue more-likely leads. The odd suitor she described sounded like a starstruck, not terribly sophisticated young man, and there was nothing to indicate he was the same man who had courted and killed three other actresses. Alistair had been right: it was like looking for a needle in a haystack.

I decided to give her one more chance. "Is there anything else about this man that you remember as distinctive or unusual? Anything that makes you suspicious, other than the fact of his indiscriminate attentions?"

She bit her lip, said, "No," and I was struck that she was unsatisfied—that something was left unsaid.

Then I realized we were not alone.

My father had entered the room, dressed in his best blue suit with a silk handkerchief showing from his pocket. He at least looked the part of a man with money in his pocket and not a care in the world.

"Simon, my boy," he said with a cavalier smile. "I came to take Molly to the theater. Are you ready, love?"

She reached into her pocket, pulled out her watch, and started when she saw the time. She ran a hand anxiously through her red curls, then stood. "I'm sorry. I wasn't thinking of the time, and it's an earlier rehearsal call than usual. We have a couple of new chorus members who need a full run-through." She walked to my father and gave him a quick peck on the cheek. "I'll be just ten minutes. You're a dear to come by to remind me."

He gave her an indulgent smile. "Don't I always walk you to the theater and home again these days? Can't be too careful, given the case that Simon's investigating."

"Thank you for sharing the information you did. Every detail helps," I said, getting up with no small measure of relief, for my legs now ached from their cramped position. I pulled awkwardly to lift my satchel, which was half stuck under the sofa.

She nodded to me and was gone.

I turned to my father. "I can be reached at this number tonight, should she remember anything else." I wrote Alistair's number on a card and passed it to him.

"Simon, I—" He regarded me with sincere concern.

"Everything's fine. I'll see you at dinner on Friday."

My meeting with Molly Hansen had been brief, so I decided to catch up with Alistair in the theater district, reasoning that with so many theaters and productions to canvass, he could use some help. I canvassed the Savoy, the Lyric, and the Casino theaters, simply because I wanted to be thorough. While they were not Frohman theaters, they still had productions opening in the coming weeks—so I wanted to know about their operations and the people involved in the shows. There was no sign of Alistair; his strategy had obviously been to visit the Frohman theaters first. Perhaps, between the two of us, we'd manage to see them all today.

It was as I left the Casino that I noticed a large office on the second floor, filled with memorabilia and posters, with an executive oak-and-leather desk in the back corner. It gave me just the germ of an idea that might help. . . .

I caught the ear of one of the office staff—a gawky young man who was delivering some papers to the office in question. "Is that Mr. Shubert's office?" I asked.

"Sure is," he said with a nod. "Mr. Sam Shubert, that is. His brother's office is one more floor up. Both of them are traveling this week."

Charles Frohman, I realized, would have an office just like this one. I would double-check, but I was almost certain it was at the Empire, where Frohman's biggest hit continued to play: *Peter Pan*, starring Maude Adams.

I had formed a new plan within minutes. And it just might work—assuming, of course, that I could convince Isabella to join me for a night at the theater.

CHAPTER 25

The Dakota Building, 1 West Seventy-second Street

This time, Mrs. Mellown gave me a welcoming smile when she opened the door to apartment 8B.

"Shall I set another plate for dinner, Detective?" she asked as she took my coat and hat from me. "Maybe that will encourage the professor to eat. Whatever case you're working on has him so wound up, he won't come to the table—and his pot roast is getting cold." She made a clucking noise of disapproval.

I thanked her and accepted the invitation as she ushered me into Alistair's library. Alistair might be uninterested, but Mrs. Mellown's roast would be my only chance of a meal this evening. I still had to dress for the eight o'clock show, so there would be no time for dinner out.

"Simon!" Isabella looked up in surprise. She was seated on

Alistair's sofa, making notes on a tablet. "I didn't expect to see you this evening."

"I have two tickets to see *Peter Pan* tonight—would you come with me?" I blurted.

Isabella's eyes widened in confusion.

"Only the two of you?" Alistair raised his eyebrows. "It's a fabulous show. I've seen it twice already, and Miss Adams always outdoes herself. . . ." His thoughts seemed to drift off to some other place.

"It's for the investigation. Unfortunately, I was only able to get two tickets," I explained for Alistair's benefit. That wasn't entirely true, but I didn't want his help tonight. And at $2.50 apiece for prime third-row aisle seats, I couldn't easily afford a third ticket.

"Besides, I believe Isabella makes a far more suitable companion," I added with a smile. "I was hoping you might watch the stage door at the Garrick. Molly Hansen complained to me this afternoon that she's being pursued by a stagestruck young man. And just in case it's the same man . . ."

I didn't bother to finish. Alistair immediately understood and agreed.

"Of course, of course." Alistair chuckled. "And what sort of project are you pursuing, old chap?"

"One that involves learning more about Frohman. Come." I gestured for Alistair to follow me. "I believe Mrs. Mellown has set dinner for us. Let's talk briefly before I have to leave."

Isabella sprang into action, leaving us in short order. "I'll be back. I've got to dress."

Alistair frowned at me in disapproval. "And you certainly can't go to the theater dressed like that."

My cheap brown suit, I knew, had seen better days. Even the patch on my left-sleeve elbow was becoming threadbare.

"I was hoping to borrow an evening jacket," I said, following his cue.

"You'll find appropriate evening wear in Ted—" he caught himself, "I mean, in the guest-bedroom closet."

And he was gone before I caught even a glimpse of his expression.

But I could not imagine that he was entirely comfortable with my putting on his deceased son's suit and squiring the same son's widow to the theater. I certainly wasn't. And the fact that Teddy's clothing proved to be almost a perfect fit—suggesting that I was more or less his same build and size—did not help matters at all.

I gritted my teeth and resolved not to think of it. It was just the first of many discomfiting things I would need to do this night.

Alistair had no comment when I joined him at the dinner table some ten minutes later, and our talk immediately turned to the case. Alistair's theater visits had turned up little of interest, other than the names of all actresses in each production. After I briefed him on my progress that afternoon, Alistair made a prediction. "I'm in complete agreement with Isabella: the killer's next target will be *Romeo and Juliet*."

He waited for a moment, then looked around, suddenly distracted. "Did Mrs. Mellown not open a bottle of wine for us?" He went over to his wine cabinet and made a selection, showing it to me before he uncorked it. "I picked up this Burgundy last summer in France. It has a refined complexity that is remarkable." He poured two glasses, passing one to me to taste.

I enjoyed it—though I didn't register its "complexity," which was too sophisticated for my palate.

Now settled in with his favored Burgundy, he picked at the pot roast on the plate before him and refocused his thoughts. "All the shows—other than *Romeo and Juliet*—share a single characteristic that, I believe, disqualifies them as an appropriate setting for his next murder."

"And what characteristic is that?" I hunted through the roast in search of more vegetables.

With a pleased expression, he leaned back in his chair, his right fingers tracing the stem of his wineglass. "*It's All Your Fault* opens April second. *The Social Whirl* opens the ninth. And *Arms and the Man* premieres the sixteenth, the same date as Frohman's *The American Lord*. And I ask you—what do those dates all have in common that *Romeo and Juliet* does not?"

I played along, though I had never enjoyed Alistair's games. "They all premiere in April, *Romeo and Juliet* opens in March, and you think the killer's in a hurry," I said, tongue-in-cheek.

He gave me an approving glance. "You're learning, Ziele—though that's not exactly what I had in mind." He pushed his half-eaten dinner to the side. "Our killer may be in a hurry—or not. I've no way of knowing that." Then he edged his chair closer to the table, leaning in toward me. "But I do know he is trying to outdo himself with every murder. I think he's aiming for something big. For a grand premiere itself, not just an ordinary night. And *Romeo and Juliet* will have the most lavish premiere."

I shook my head. "I'm not saying that it doesn't make sense,

Alistair. But why has it got to be a premiere? Why not a dress rehearsal—or an ordinary performance, as he's chosen before?"

Alistair smiled. "Because of something Isabella found when she reviewed the letters. Not a message," he added hastily when he saw my reaction, "but a common refrain in each letter, up to and including the most recent one he sent to *The New York Times*. He wants to transform his victims into stars. And with each victim, he has aimed for increasingly larger audiences."

"You'll need to walk me through this one."

"Well, his initial effort was simple. He left his first blue letter by his victim, wanting his audience to understand what he'd done. But that didn't work. Eliza Downs was seen as a suicide, and the note he wrote was actually mistaken to be her own suicide letter. That must have been a disappointment," he said, putting it delicately. "Next," he took a breath, "he decided to give some advance warning of his designs. So, prior to Annie Germaine's murder, he sent a letter to *The Times*, detailing his plans, no doubt hoping the press would become interested in the case. But not only didn't they notice until it was too late—they viewed the letter as a joke and ignored it. Just as the letter by Miss Germaine's body might have been disregarded if Leon Iseman had not noticed the similarities to Miss Downs's murder and called the police."

"At last gaining him the attention he wanted."

"But not enough. We prevailed upon *The Times* to keep quiet until the case was solved. So he upped the stakes, yet again, with Miss Billings—complete with playbill ads in the lobby and a booby trap to injure whoever responded with help. He taunted us with his reference to Poe's "The Conqueror Worm." This time there was no mistaking him: he was as dramatic as he was dangerous, making clear he was someone to be reckoned with."

I raised a skeptical brow. "True. But from that, you get that he is going for a premiere show?"

When he answered, his voice reflected his conviction. "Absolutely. He keeps escalating, and it takes more to satisfy him. I don't know if you noticed in today's *Times*," he added, "but I prevailed upon our friends there to suppress any mention of Detective Marwin."

I had noticed, but had thought it was the result of luck, not of Alistair's intervention. And Alistair's leap of logic—from "the killer is escalating his behavior" to "the killer will definitely choose a premiere"—was speculative at best.

Alistair saw my hesitation and immediately tried to allay my fears. "You know, in what I do, I freely admit there's as much 'art' involved as there is 'science.' Sometimes you simply have to trust your instincts, just as you did in deciding to believe Timothy Poe's declaration of innocence."

"But I have no instinct on this," I said, spreading my hands wide.

"That's why I'm asking you to trust me."

I simply stared at him. It was a hard thing to ask—especially where Alistair was concerned. His brilliance, I trusted implicitly. But his instincts?

I'd previously found them to be lacking, at least where ethical boundaries—not criminal behavior—were concerned.

Then again, as I well knew, the hardest ethical judgment calls involved compromising one ideal in the service of another. I'd certainly done it myself, when lives were at stake.

I was still mulling over the issue when Isabella's clear voice called out to me, asking if I was ready for the theater.

She stood by the entrance to Alistair's dining room, breathtaking in a black-velvet-and-sequin evening gown with her hair done up in a more elegant fashion than I'd seen before. A small diamond heart nestled within the hollow of her throat. The effect was simple yet stunning.

I got up, stiff and suddenly awkward—and aware, with a pang of guilt, that I was not myself. Tonight I had dressed in borrowed clothes, preparing to play a role not my own.

"Enjoy yourselves," Alistair said, pouring himself another glass of wine as he gave us a look that was almost mournful. "And don't worry—I'll be at the Garrick by half past ten to observe anyone who approaches Molly Hansen."

He was not pleased to be left at home by himself, then sent to perform a thankless task. I thought briefly of including him, but I preferred that he not know my plan tonight. At least, not until I'd successfully accomplished it.

At the elevator, Isabella handed me her coat, wanting my help to put it on. I caught a whiff of her perfume—something that reminded me of springtime flowers—as I leaned briefly closer to her.

She rewarded me with a smile, but spoke briskly. "We *will* be late if you don't hurry, Simon."

And it dawned on me: of course she expected to take a cab, not the subway, dressed as she was. I felt in my pockets on the elevator down, and breathed more easily once I realized I had sufficient money not only to pay for a round-trip hansom cab but also to tip the attendant at the Dakota who would help me to find one at this time of night. Judging from the other well-dressed people in the lobby, we were obviously not the only ones heading out for a night of entertainment in the city.

Though it was only a Tuesday, there was a sellout crowd at the Empire. That wasn't entirely unexpected, since *Peter Pan* was Broadway's most popular hit. I'd been lucky to get seats at all—much less good ones—on such short notice. We sat in row C on the far-right aisle of the long auditorium. Though the space was luxurious, decorated in muted shades of red and green, it was more subdued than the other theaters I'd visited in recent weeks.

When I remarked upon it, Isabella said simply, "He wants his audience to focus upon his show and his stars, not his decor."

By "he" she meant Frohman, of course—and my stomach flipped in nervous anticipation of what I had to do that night.

We talked briefly about Frohman's stars, especially his brightest, Maude Adams, who would play Peter Pan tonight. Isabella had seen them all onstage over the years, whereas I had seen them for the first time tonight—in the lobby, where their large portraits filled virtually every inch of wall space.

It was only when the curtain rose that I whispered to her a few words of warning that I would be stepping out briefly during the first act. She looked at me in surprise, but said nothing, turning her attention to the stage—for the show had begun.

I watched. And I waited, biding my time until the Darling children's adventures with the Lost Boys were well under way, and—pressing Isabella's hand gently as a sign—I slipped out of the auditorium using the side exit I had already canvassed.

I reminded myself that in my borrowed suit—which was of a finer cut and far more luxuriant material than I'd ever worn

before—I looked the part of a wealthy gentleman with the lei-
sure to enjoy a Tuesday-evening performance. I was unlikely to
be questioned as I made my way to the fifth floor.

I made it to the third floor before I was noticed.

"Sir."

The voice came again, more insistently when my steps did
not slow. "Excuse me, sir."

Steeling myself, I turned around slowly and came face-to-
face with a young man wearing the garb of an usher. I forced a
pleasant expression, but said nothing.

"Can I direct you somewhere, sir? These are administrative
offices here only. All closed to the public."

"Yes," I said agreeably, "but they told me I would find another gentlemen's lounge up here."

"There's one on four." He frowned in disapproval. "But it's
for staff. I'll have to have a word with the boys downstairs if
they're directing you there. The main lounge is much nicer for
gentlemen like yourself."

I offered up the excuse I'd prepared in advance, making
sure I gave feeling to the lie. "Some poor fellow in the lounge
downstairs is ill, and I wanted to give him some privacy."

The young man was taken aback. "Oh, of course, sir. My
apologies. Go right on up. You'll find it just to the left once you
reach the fourth floor."

"Thank you." I forced myself to walk up the stairs with confident steps, hoping fervently that he wouldn't decide to follow
me—or, worse yet, check on the sick patron I had invented
downstairs. I watched him carefully from the corner of my eye
as I rounded the next landing, and saw that he had retreated to
a red velvet chair, where he sat and picked up a magazine. I

made sure he would not see—or hear—that I in fact continued all the way up to the fifth floor.

It was pitch dark. But no office door on the floor was closed, much less locked. So, at least I could say I was not breaking and entering—and the last I'd checked, illegal trespass was still only a misdemeanor.

Charles Frohman's office was the third one on the right. It was easy to identify, for it was the largest and most opulently furnished, decorated with extensive theater memorabilia. I closed the door behind me, turned on his desk lamp, and threw my suit jacket over it to dim its light.

I had never done anything quite like this before—and for a split second, when my right hand began to shake, I thought I would lose my nerve. Instead, I closed my eyes and imagined three women, once-vibrant actresses, now dead. That would be the fate of yet another if I failed. And while I could not envisage her—this unknown, faceless woman—I still knew what I needed to do to save her.

I wasn't quite sure what I hoped to find. I knew that I wanted more of Frohman's handwriting as well as that of Leon Iseman and any important associates; before I left, I would take a few papers that would not be missed. I suppose I also hoped I might uncover something—anything—that would connect the three murdered actresses and even point to the next target.

I discovered nothing of importance. I found receipts. I found notes assessing each syndicate actor or actress in terms of performance, potential, and professionalism. The three Ps, he called it. And, just as he'd told us last Sunday evening, each of the victims had a poor record marked by lateness and lack of preparation. Leon Iseman as well as other theater managers had issued a number of reports; unfortunately, all were type-written.

Suddenly, from the room next door, I heard a crash. A large and heavy object had fallen.

I froze in panic. Someone was there.

I dived for the wall where the lamp was plugged in, yanking the cord from its socket. Then I grabbed my jacket—which had served me well in dimming the light—and retreated under Frohman's desk.

I waited, hearing the rush of footsteps in the hallway, seeing the blaze of light as the hallway became fully illuminated.

Two men were talking.

"Which room did it come from?" I recognized the voice of the third-floor usher.

"I dunno."

I caught my breath. Was that Leon Iseman's voice?

The door to Frohman's office opened and I froze, afraid to breathe.

"Come look at this!" The usher's voice came from next door, and I heard footsteps retreating.

More lights went on, coupled with the sounds of furniture being moved.

"What in the devil! Look at this mess."

"Looks like someone shoved a whole pile of papers off that bookcase up there."

"You gotta be kidding me."

The first voice definitely belonged to Leon Iseman. I hoped fervently that they'd stay next door. But more worrisome: papers didn't fall by themselves. Had whoever pushed them seen me? It was hard to imagine otherwise.

I was so focused upon their every word and movement that I started violently—knocking my head hard into the underside of Frohman's desk—when the answer came and brushed up against me. It was a gray cat, furry and soft, purring loudly.

My relief was short-lived when I heard footsteps headed this way again. The room's overhead light flipped on.

"Say, what's Frohman been doing in here?"

They obviously had noticed the huge pile of receipts and papers I had been viewing, all of which covered Frohman's desk.

A pause. "Charlie? You around here?" Iseman's voice rang out loudly.

I petted the cat reassuringly for a split second before I pushed it out from under the desk. It dashed across the room.

"I think I see the culprit who caused all the racket," the usher said.

I held my breath.

The cat meowed loudly in protest as large hands reached down and summarily hoisted it into the air.

"Disgusting animal," Iseman said. He began to walk away.

The usher laughed heartily as he stroked the furry animal. "Where's all your fellow mousers tonight, little minx? Usually there's a passel of you around, on the hunt. Can't believe you made all that racket and mess in Mr. Landry's office by yourself." He paused for a minute, then called out after Iseman, "You want me to clean up the mess next door?"

Iseman's response was automatic. "Nah. We can leave it for the night janitor. After all, it was the cat's fault. Troublesome creatures. If we didn't need mousers . . ."

I held my breath for several minutes after they were gone, listening for all sound and light to disappear. It had been a close call. I replugged the light, restoring my jacket on top, and went back to work.

Knowing I had little time remaining until intermission, I worked even more quickly—file after file, cabinet after cabinet. The last cabinet I reached appeared to be devoted to old scripts, and as I read through them, I determined that Frohman kept hold of even the manuscripts he rejected. According to notes I found, it appeared that he kept them to check his own judgment: the small handful that had gone on to find homes with other producer-directors and found success were very clearly marked. Frohman was not easy on himself when he missed out on the opportunity to produce a hit.

I had almost given up by the time I opened the last folder, which I assumed would contain only more of the same. In fact, flipping through six—no, seven—scripts that Frohman had considered producing, I almost missed the name attached to them: Leon Iseman. Scanning through them, I saw Frohman's notes and it became clear: due to his close relationship with Iseman, he had felt compelled to read them. But reading between the lines of his comments, it was clear that he had not considered them worthy of producing—a decision that must have affected their working relationship.

Could Iseman be the killer we sought? He had submitted his most recent play a year ago. A year was a long time to plot revenge: enough time to breathe it, live it, and plan it very carefully. Of all people, Iseman knew how passionately Frohman loved the theater—and that he could destroy Frohman by striking what he cherished most.

I was so caught up in these thoughts about Iseman that I nearly missed the note attached to the front of the next script.

Its content was unremarkable, mentioning only a name, date, and address. But the writing itself—now eerily familiar—sent chills down my spine.

In fact, my body reacted first, recoiling from pure instinct. My right hand shook, and I dropped the entire folder as surely as though it had burned my flesh. And in another moment, my mind understood, for there was no mistaking the distinctive, spidery, slanting handwriting. I had seen this writing before— on the blue letters that had accompanied the first two brutal murders.

The note contained scant information: "Revisions submitted February 1905. Robert Coby, Bay Avenue, Shelter Island."

Beneath the note were several scripts that Robert Coby had submitted—and subsequently revised—for Charles Frohman. From the tenor of Frohman's commentary, it was clear that Frohman had disliked the revisions. He had rejected this script at the same time as Iseman's: exactly one year ago. And ironically— within that same pile of scripts—I saw that Leon Iseman himself had signed one of the typewritten rejection letters sent to Robert Coby.

The name wasn't familiar to me. In fact, I was confident that I had never run across it in the course of our investigation.

I sat for what seemed a long time, staring at the file cabinet before me. I'd thumbed through at least seventy-five rejected scripts . . . only to discover one note in the handwriting of a murderer, sandwiched between two rejected playwrights: Leon Iseman and Robert Coby. One of them must have written the note: but which one? The playwright Robert Coby himself—or Frohman's disappointed associate, Leon Iseman.

I examined Leon Iseman's signature on the typewritten

letter. It was like the one we had shown Dr. Vollman, only to be told it was "inconclusive." And while to my eye it looked dissimilar to the handwriting on the note, I was no expert.

I knew enough about Leon Iseman to know I disliked him. But was he a murderer?

Robert Coby was as yet a name only. I wanted to figure out who he was.

Alistair was right: the killer's identity was irrelevant if we could look to his predicted behavior to stop him. But there was no room for error in that kind of approach. Wasn't it better to know the adversary we faced?

I knew Shelter Island to be a summer retreat, sandwiched between the two forks at the east end of Long Island. It was our first substantial lead—though of course I knew it wouldn't be as simple as finding an address, showing up, and possibly identifying a violent killer.

Or would it? I supposed stranger things had happened.

From the noises below, I determined that tonight's intermission had started. I'd barely escaped discovery once, and I'd no desire to risk it again. Fearing someone would come, I returned everything to its original state. But I took with me the note and the first pages of both Leon Iseman's and Robert Coby's scripts.

I put my suit jacket back on, turned out the light, and—folding my contraband materials into my pocket—I slipped back into the hallway, sped down the stairs, and blended once more into the crowds that swarmed throughout the lobby.

Isabella was still in her seat.

"Where were you, Simon?" she asked, indignant now. "You said you had to step out briefly. But you missed the entire first act."

"I promise to tell you everything when we return to

Alistair's." I tried to smile reassuringly. "I can get your coat now, if you'd like."

She stood her ground, regarding me in amazement. "You paid five dollars to secure these seats, among the best in the house. Why would you leave before we've seen the second act—especially when you missed the first one?"

After apologizing again, I settled into my seat and determined to enjoy the remaining hour of *Peter Pan* and Isabella's company. Everything I had learned could wait until the end of the show. However curious I was about Robert Coby, I would not be going to Shelter Island at this time of night anyway.

And so I enjoyed watching Maude Adams sing and dance—in one case, literally flying up into the air and across the length of the stage, to the audience's openmouthed delight. Sinking deep into my plush velvet seat, in the darkness of the auditorium with Isabella beside me, I could—just almost—forget everything that troubled me.

With the killer we sought still at large, it was not a time for distractions. And yet, when the lights came up, and I lightly touched Isabella's arm to guide her through the crowds and into a waiting hansom cab, I realized how easy it would be to become accustomed to this sort of life.

Too easy, in fact.

Wednesday
March 21, 1906

CHAPTER 26

The Coby Residence, Bay Avenue, Shelter Island

Cold sleet fell that morning—the kind that made me wish I were anywhere other than aboard a small ferry bound for Shelter Island. It had not been an easy journey. Alistair and I had taken the first train of the day from New York, bound for the town of Greenport, Long Island. From there, we'd transferred to the ferry that now lurched across the choppy gray waters. As we crossed Greenport Bay toward the Shelter Heights dock, I gripped the railing hard, fixing my line of sight at the spit of land I saw before me. Alistair stayed under the scant shelter provided by the pilot-house, apparently preferring the captain's cigar smoke to the elements. We had prevailed upon Isabella to stay in the city, asking her to work with Dr. Vollman in examining the additional samples of handwriting I had secured last night. Their findings would supplement whatever evidence we uncovered this day.

I needed the air and the feel of the cutting rain against my face. It kept my senses alert, and though the damp caused my right arm to throb, even that sensation calmed me in a fashion. The turbulent water tossed the ferry about as though it were a child's toy, and I fought an irrational sense of panic. I'd no doubt we would make it. But I disliked ferries of all kinds.

Not for the first time in recent days, I asked myself: why was I doing this? The official investigation had gone wrong and familiar allies had deserted me. I was jeopardizing my livelihood—and possibly all common sense—to conduct what was a rogue investigation.

I wanted to believe that I was gathering evidence for Mulvaney so I could clear the name of an innocent man—before another actress's murder accomplished that goal. But was I being honest with myself? Maybe I was heeding not the call of justice but the selfish desire to prove I was right—that I had not lost the instincts and skills that had once made me one of the city's finest detectives. In any event, I now found myself traveling through uncertain waters, assuming a role that was strange to me.

As we began to dock, I entered the pilothouse and attempted to engage the ferryman in conversation. "Those of you who are year-round residents must be a tight-knit community. Do you know the Coby family on Bay Avenue?"

He didn't even turn to look at me, staying focused on the wheel of his boat.

"We're visiting them today," I added after a few moments.

This time, he turned, regarding me with suspicious eyes that mirrored the blue-and-gray expanse around us. "You boys sure about that? Ain't no Cobys on this island. Not anymore."

Alistair's reply was smooth. "I hope we were not misinformed. We were told the family of Robert Coby still lives on Bay Avenue." He paused, then added, "We need to locate Mr. Coby's family with regard to an important business matter. I'm an attorney-at-law from the city, you see."

The ferryman raised his bushy salt-and-pepper eyebrows and muttered something about city folk minding their own business.

I tried again. "But someone must be left who can help us."

He glared at me before making a curt reply. "If she even agrees to see you, Mrs. Layton will be no help."

Then, pulling his cap over his ears, he ignored our questions, and our efforts to learn more were of no avail.

As we approached the ferry landing, soaked through and chilled, we looked across the street and saw Prospect House, a majestic white hotel that seemed to stretch half a mile long beside the green expanse that was named Prospect Park, just like its Brooklyn counterpart. Alistair had explained to me earlier that the area was a popular summer resort, but I had not expected to see a building on this grand a scale.

"Let's stop in there for a moment and get something hot to warm us up. It will only take a few minutes," Alistair said.

I checked my watch and overruled him. We had spent most of the morning in transit, and whatever awaited us on Bay Avenue, I was ready to confront it without delay.

We circled Prospect Park and turned the corner onto Bay Avenue. Alistair had explained that the neighborhood we were in, known as Shelter Heights, had been designed as a planned community. In fact, during this morning's long train ride, Alistair had given me a virtual treatise on its history: how landscape architects including Frederick Law Olmsted had designed it to be a resort setting, with more than a hundred cottages laid out on scalloped roads rising to ever greater heights, many with sweeping views of the water. Each was an easy walking distance to the ferry, Prospect Park, and Union Chapel—which we soon saw, set far back from the road in a grove. Bay Avenue itself was lined on each side by rows of neatly buttoned-up, white summer cottages with steeply pitched gable roofs and elaborate wood trim on their windows, doors, and front porches.

The house at number 13 was near the end of the street, at the corner of Waverly Place. It stood slightly apart from its neighbors, much like a neglected, ugly stepsister embarrassed to draw too close. For though it shared their architectural features, its wood trim was broken and shingles were falling off, its paint was chipped and peeling, and there were multiple shattered windows on its top floor.

Our steps slowed the moment we saw it.

"Does anyone live there?" Alistair asked in disbelief.

"Hard to imagine, isn't it?" I replied. Of course I'd seen people living in even more-deplorable conditions, simply not amid what was supposed to be a luxurious resort community.

Even worse, its front veranda was filled with furniture, abandoned toys, and all manner of trash. We stared, silent, for several minutes before gathering the courage to go on—and squeezing past the piles of refuse, we made our way to the front door. I took a deep breath and sounded the knocker.

Though all was silent inside, we could make out the slight glow of a light from the back of the house.

I rapped the knocker again, more loudly this time.

We heard slow, shuffling footsteps making their way toward

the door, and instinctively I backed up—forcing Alistair to do so as well. Based on what the ferryman had told us, I expected a Mrs. Layton to answer the door. But we didn't know whether she actually would—or even if she did, what her connection to the Coby family would be.

The woman who answered our knock glared at us from behind the screen. "What do you want?" The question may have been belligerent, but her voice—quavering and timid—was not.

I made the introductions, but she seemed not to hear me. Instead, she stared into my face, and for a moment her eyes flashed with something like recognition. "Robby, is that you?"

"I'm not Robert," I said gently, "but I came to ask you about him."

Her confused brown eyes watered slightly as she stared at me with a vacant expression.

"May we come in?"

Her eyes lit up with a flash of comprehension. "Have you seen him recently?"

"We'd like your help figuring that out." I opened the wooden screen door that still separated us. "May we?" I asked again.

Again, she seemed not to have heard or comprehended—but then she finally stepped back and permitted us to enter. Arms folded, she eyed us suspiciously.

I could see her more clearly now that we were inside. Her heavyset frame was bundled in at least two shawls; they hung over a green floral dress. It was no wonder, as the house was frigid and damp.

Plip-plop. Plip-plop. The rain beat a steady rhythm as it dripped into pails placed strategically throughout the first floor, including two in the entry hall itself. I suspected the broken windows we'd observed were responsible—but the house was in such disrepair, there were no doubt many sources to blame. Water always found its own path, often far from the root of the problem. That lesson I'd learned the hard way in the Lower East Side tenement building where I'd grown up.

"Perhaps we can help you lay a fire, Mrs. Layton. Where do you keep your wood?" I asked.

Her answer was a blank stare.

"Do you have a covered porch out back?"

She continued to ignore my question, but as my coat was still on, I ventured through the kitchen to the back porch, where I found a small stockpile of wood. There was not much—but it was enough to build a fire and warm her sitting room. We could help her secure more later on.

I corralled Alistair into helping me carry in several logs and, together, we followed Mrs. Layton into her front parlor, laid the logs in the fireplace, and coaxed them into roaring flames. Only then did we settle back into uncomfortable hard-back chairs and survey the rest of the room.

It was tired and broken-down, filled to capacity with the residue of her life. The fireplace wall was lined with old newspapers, piled at least five feet high and three rows deep. When Alistair pointed out that it wasn't safe to keep newspapers like that, especially so close to the fireplace, she laughed—a full cackle that revealed a mouthful of missing teeth.

"My reviews," she said, chortling. "Well, some mine, some hers. My mother would've said old news is no news and not worth keeping around. God knows she never kept anything of ours. But I like seeing 'em."

"What kind of reviews?" I asked, wanting her to clarify.

"Theater reviews. Sure, we were actresses once. She got lots of write-ups." She looked in the direction of the window as though she were acknowledging another person—so convincingly that I actually turned my head. But of course no one was there.

"Who is she? A friend?" I asked.

But she didn't answer. She crossed her arms, then graced us with another toothless grin. And I could not help but wonder: was she a bit off in the head, or simply ignoring half of my questions?

Alistair picked up one of the yellowed papers and handed it to her.

"May we see the review in this one?"

She emitted another laugh that was almost a cackle as she opened the paper and flipped the brittle pages so vigorously that they began to disintegrate and fall to the floor right in front of her. But when she found what she wanted, she cradled its page with surprising delicacy—even as the remaining pages she held dropped to the floor.

Alistair and I both drew nearer to see what she held. The strong scent of old newspaper and smoke mingled with her own odor: musky and slightly sour. The smell of unwashed old age. Breathing through my mouth, I focused on the yellowed page she showed us. A vibrant young woman in a lacy dress twirled onstage as a young man held her one outstretched arm.

"That's her," she said. "She played Rosalind in *As You Like It*."

I scanned the article below the picture. The reviewer focused upon the production's elaborate staging, but did mention an Elaine Coby briefly. Was this the woman beside me—before marriage changed her name and age ravaged her looks? She was a "refreshing new voice" with "surprising emotional range." She was also beautiful. It was sad to think what was lost, assuming she had evolved into the woman here—alone and apparently half addled by dementia.

"The review is a glowing one; you must have been quite talented when you were young," I said.

"Not me," she said, irritated. "Didn't I just say it was *her*? I'd left the stage before she even got her first role."

"Who is she?" I hoped she would remain cognizant.

"Elaine, my sister," she said, her tone irritated. She seemed to think she'd told me half a dozen times. Her earlier reply at least answered my question about their age difference. It had to be significant, probably well over a decade—even assuming she had not aged well, which I presumed, given her current living conditions.

We returned to our seats and I asked her for clarification. "She was much younger than you?"

At first, she seemed not to hear me—but finally she nodded. "We both started out working in repertory theaters; me in the seventies, she in the eighties," she said. "I was good. Elaine was better. Once, she had a supporting role in a production with Ellen Terry."

"Ah, the fabulous Ellen Terry," Alistair said, working hard to gain Mrs. Layton's trust. "I saw her perform with Henry Irving in *King Arthur* maybe ten years ago. Her Guinevere was the finest performance I've ever seen."

"That was Elaine's dream," she said in a soft voice, "until they took it all away."

"Who?" I asked.

"Who else?" She sighed in frustration. "Charlie Frohman ended her career with a few choice words. He and his brother— they and their clerk spread lies about her. They didn't just end her stint at the Garden. They made sure she'd never work again, anywhere, just because she was with child."

Alistair explained that Mrs. Layton was apparently referring to an earlier time period, when Charles Frohman had gotten his start in the theater by working with his older brother Daniel at Madison Square Garden. Even when he'd been new to the business, Charles had been controlling of his performers and particular about their conduct—especially their moral behavior.

"What clerk?" I asked.

"Iseberg," she said with a shudder. "Horrible man. He was sweet on Elaine. But then he turned on her when she needed his help most."

"Do you mean Leon Iseman?" I mentioned his name carefully—I didn't want to presume, and yet the name was so close.

"Maybe." She spat on the floor. "Whoever he was, he was tight with Charlie."

That sounded like Leon Iseman—and it served as a powerful reminder that I shouldn't discount Frohman's longtime assistant, who was entangled with this family in a way I hadn't anticipated.

"And Elaine's child?"

"They wanted her to get rid of it. But she wouldn't." She leaned back in her chair, and a look of terrible sadness crossed her face.

"That child was Robert," I said, prodding her carefully.

But I lost her again as she retreated somewhere deep in the recesses of her memory, and her answer ignored my question. "Watching the way the Frohman brothers have treated others over the years, they'd never have given her a second chance anyway," she said.

"Were there no other options, perhaps outside of New York?"

She interrupted me. "Not for an actress with ambitions like Elaine. He destroyed her, he did," she pounded the end table beside her with vehemence, "when he took that away from her. She was forced to come here and have the child. My husband, Eddie, and I took her in. We spread the word she was recently widowed."

"And she stayed over the years, with her son?"

She nodded. "What else would she have done? Besides, we were family. Her Robert and my daughter were very close. Though they were ten years apart in age, they were as close as brother and sister."

I followed up by asking whether Robert had developed close childhood friends or, as he'd grown up, even romantic attachments. But Mrs. Layton's mind seemed to grasp the distant past far better than more-recent events, and she could tell me nothing.

"Where is your sister now? I take it she no longer lives here," I said.

"No, but she's nearby; just right over there." She lifted her arm and pointed out the window toward the bay and ferry landing.

"She lives on the mainland? In Greenport?"

Another cackle. "I mean right *in* the bay. She has, ever since the day five years ago that she went out for a short walk and never returned." She shook her head sadly. "She'd gone for a walk as usual, right about eleven o'clock. They said at the post office that she'd stopped by and mailed some letters. Then she headed toward home. But at the last minute, she went to the bay instead. A young boy saw her." She began breathing heavily, laboring under the memory of what had happened. "He thought she was collecting shells. But it turned out they were heavy rocks to put in her pockets. When she found enough, she walked right in. The boy ran for help, but it was too late. They found her three weeks later, when a fisherman on the other side of the island pulled her body out."

"I'm sorry," I said, and meant it. Was there some lack of sanity, I wondered, that affected the entire Coby family? Each generation had been touched in some way by it: Mrs. Layton maintained a precarious grip on present reality, her sister had committed suicide, and her nephew was quite possibly responsible for a series of heinous murders.

"Did Robert live here at the time?" Alistair asked.

"He was nearby, in Montauk, working odd jobs on the fishing boats."

"Where is he now, Mrs. Layton? Please think hard," I said.

She gave me an annoyed look. "I don't have to think hard. He's out on the boats. But he visits me every year, on the anniversary of her death."

"When is that?"

"Why, April first." She seemed surprised by the question—and I wasn't entirely sure it was relevant. But the anniversary would occur in a matter of days, so if we had no better luck beforehand . . . But I immediately pushed the thought out of my head. Someone's life was at stake, and this was no time to anticipate failure. We'd succeed now—simply because we had to.

We continued to talk, uneasily conversing in the front sitting room, listening to the drip of the rain leaks, smelling the dank, musty odor of the house. Alistair helped me to wrap up our conversation with Mrs. Layton quickly, passing over the details of her life on Shelter Island and Robert's upbringing. We soon came to the present: her husband was long deceased, Robert was away on the fishing boats, and her own daughter had inherited her love of the theater and gone onstage, albeit with limited success, doing traveling shows. The postcards came regularly: from Philadelphia and Boston, St. Louis and Chicago. "But I don't know where she is, either. Anywhere but New York," she said, shaking her head.

"Do you have anything of Robert's to help us to locate him? His most recent address? Even a picture?"

Mrs. Layton had no address, but she duly looked for a picture to give us. Among the newspapers, she found a dog-eared silver-and-gray photograph from Robert's childhood, and I recognized Elaine from the newspaper. She caressed a five-year-old, earnest-faced boy who must have been Robert, as well as a younger Mrs. Layton with her husband and their daughter. Mrs. Layton, I was startled to realize, had been attractive once. And though her face was half obscured by an elaborate hat with many feathers and a fishnet veil, her daughter was also obviously a beauty. They gave every appearance of being a contented family . . . and I wondered anew what had happened to upset it all. Elaine Coby's suicide must have played a large role . . . but I didn't think it alone sufficed as an explanation. Perhaps mental illness had played the largest role in destroying this family, taking hold of its members one by one. A family curse, of sorts.

"We were so happy then," she said wistfully, gazing at the photograph.

"Is there any other room in the house that Robert used?" I asked. "Perhaps he maintained a desk somewhere? Or stored his things in the basement?"

I was thinking about his plays—or anything else he might have written while living in this house. We still didn't know if he was truly the killer we sought—but his handwriting might settle the issue immediately.

She shook her head. "He took everything when he moved out. Besides, the basement's prone to get water anyway. Can't store anything there."

We thanked her for her time. When we had almost left the property, I stopped Alistair short.

"Do you see that?" I asked. "There, in the back corner," I added, pointing to a ramshackle building to the rear of the property.

"It looks deserted." Alistair and I exchanged meaningful glances.

I surveyed the manicured neighboring lot. The division between what was well kempt and what was neglected could not have been clearer. "It's on the Layton property."

With purposeful steps that belied my apprehension—even my fear—I turned back. In a few short strides, I led Alistair to the far northwest corner of the yard, where, nearly obscured by trees, vines, and overgrown shrubs, there was a wood-plank shed secured with a rusted iron padlock. There were no windows; only the small door in front. I'd have preferred to keep walking, right back to the street and the ferry landing, as for away as I could get from this godforsaken place.

But we had come too far today not to see our inquiry through, wherever it took us.

And so, with very little force, I broke open the padlock that secured the deserted shed and pushed open the door.

I didn't regret my choice the moment I entered—making my way through cobwebs into a small, enclosed space that seemed to contain the very heart of evil itself.

CHAPTER 27

The Woodshed. Bay Avenue, Shelter Island

I entered first, breaking through the cobweb mesh that blocked the door almost as if by design. It had a dirt floor beneath wood planks haphazardly laid, which was no doubt responsible for the strong damp, putrid odor that nearly overwhelmed me. Within seconds, I had stumbled into a collection of five boxes at the center of the room.

"Is everything all right?" Alistair's voice sounded worried.

"Fine," I said. "I could just use some light." Though it was a small room, no more than eight feet by ten feet wide, the dull gray skies outside permitted little natural light to illuminate the space.

"I've got a box of Lucifers, if that helps," Alistair called out, sounding very far away.

"Let me find a candle." If Robert had spent time in here, I

reasoned, he would have sometimes come in after dark—and would have needed a light. I finally found a half-burned candle in a saucer on top of a small table to my left. Alistair stepped inside with his matches and we lit it—then stood perfectly still in the flickering light, allowing our eyes to adjust to the room around us. I could hear my heartbeat pounding in anticipation. After a few minutes, we saw more clearly.

I scanned the other contents of the table. It was covered with dirt and detritus, the cast-off items of someone's life: a spool of thread, some jacks and a ball, a deck of cards, knitting needles, and countless books. The latter smelled of mold and mildew; it appeared that the shed was far from watertight. There was also a playbill and two ticket stubs dated November 30 from an 1899 production of *Cyrano de Bergerac* at the Garden Theater. I recognized the star—Richard Mansfield—but it was not a Frohman production.

"Let's start here," I said, grim-faced, pointing to the south wall, where some photographs and cards were tacked to the wall. I stepped carefully, avoiding piles of old shoes, both men's and women's.

Alistair looked nervously at the open door behind us.

"I'd rather have the air and the light," I said. "I don't think anyone will notice. It's not visible from the street."

With a deep breath, he came close to me, the wood floor groaning loudly under the strain of his step.

"Careful," I warned, as he nearly tripped over the mountain of shoes that I'd just avoided.

I held the light up to the wall, illuminating each picture one by one as best as the flickering candle would allow. And there, on the wall, was the evidence that told us we had identified our adversary: pictures of Pygmalion.

A black-and-white postcard depicted a man reaching out toward a nude woman. It looked like a reproduction of a painting, such as what vendors sold for a penny outside the Metropolitan Museum of Art. Its subtitle read PYGMALION AND GALATEA. We quickly realized that the second picture was its twin: the same figures, this time from the rear perspective.

Alistair let forth a low whistle.

"You must know these," I said.

Alistair nodded. "These postcards replicate two paintings by Jean-Léon Gérôme of the sculptor Pygmalion and his creation Galatea. Both depict the moment she comes to life. And here she is again," he said with excitement, pointing to another card tacked on the wall below, depicting the woman, the sculptor, and a baby. "I've seen this one as well. I forget the name of the painter . . . Anne something, from the early nineteenth century. She's drawing on one version of the myth that suggests Pygmalion and his statue bore a son."

I turned my attention to the space to the right of the postcards, where a phrase was painted in red, sloppy letters: "The gods make life. I can only make death."

I felt the blood drain from my face. Here, in this godforsaken place, the words seemed especially chilling—almost tantamount to an admission of murder. We had truly found our man.

Alistair had said that this killer, whom we now knew to be Robert Coby, was one of the most unusual criminals he had ever encountered. His mind, obviously filled with crazy obsessions, was not one I particularly wanted to know or understand. Yet, I understood that to catch him, I needed to do exactly that. So, taking a deep breath, I asked Alistair if he believed the phrase related to the postcards in some way.

Alistair placed the candle on a plank that jutted out from the wall, much like a shelf, and ran his fingers over the words. "I'm not sure," he finally said, "but I believe it refers yet again to Pygmalion. It may even be from the play itself."

I pulled out my notebook and pencil to write it all down.

Alistair ran his hand over his brow. "We need to imagine all this," he gestured to the walls around us, "from Robert's perspective. I believe it's safe to assume he co-opted this space because it was set apart from the main house, offering him privacy. He's used that privacy to nurture the obsession we see here." His voice grew sober. "We're in the very space where he gave birth to his fantasies."

"Fantasies he took with him to the city and made real on the stages of three different theaters," I said, picking up Alistair's train of thought.

I'd not often thought so, but today I was grateful for Alistair's companionship, even for his help. For the first time, we seemed to be allies in understanding, working toward a common goal.

"But I'm confused by how Frohman—and perhaps Leon Iseman—played a role in Robert's plans. We know Coby has an obsession with certain women—specifically, those who can fulfill his fantasies about Pygmalion and Galatea. Yet he targeted Frohman's theaters. His aunt blames Frohman and Iseman for working in concert to destroy Elaine Coby, Robert's mother. Frankly, Coby's obsession sounds exactly like what you've always told me: that fantasy plays a large role in forming criminal behavior."

"Go on," Alistair said.

"But the rest of it sounds like a standard revenge plot. I can't make sense of it, together." I gestured to the walls around us.

Alistair gave me a bemused smile. "You've said so yourself: life doesn't always follow a scientific theory. What if Robert Coby has channeled his obsession with women—specifically, dead women, Galatea figures—into the service of his hatred of Charles Frohman?"

"Allowing him to kill two birds with one stone, to use a poor analogy?"

"Exactly."

I looked again at the red-painted phrase and felt only one sensation: fear.

As though he knew what I was feeling, Alistair said, "Remember what I've told you: evil is less threatening the more we understand it."

I considered the five boxes at the center of the room. "I suppose something in those may help shed light on the question."

With no small amount of trepidation, we pushed our way to the boxes, brushing aside more cobwebs, listening to the floor squeak beneath our feet.

I bent over, using my pocketknife to open the first box, which was taped shut. I had just reached in to pull out the first item when—with a great gust of air—the door slammed shut, extinguishing the light.

We jumped—and in sheer panic, Alistair rushed for the door, throwing it open and looking out into the yard.

I was right behind him, my right hand reaching for my gun.

We split up, circling to the back of the shed, looking in and around the overgrowth of vines and shrubs that shrouded the building.

"Maybe it was the wind?" He gave me a doubtful look, because though it was a blustery day, the door had shut with amazing force.

But whatever the reason for the door closing, no one was here now. We went back inside, relit the candle, and resumed working with renewed energy. I couldn't shake the sense that this was a sinister place we were searching, and I was anxious to finish our business and be on our way.

We tackled each box, one by one, pulling out its contents to survey by the candle's flickering light. At first, there was nothing of significance: scores of notebooks filled with writing—years' worth, including plays and poems written in the spidery hand we now knew so well. But nothing resembling a diary. No photographs. No personal letters, not even from his mother. I was surprised, since most people kept something. My own flat in Dobson contained few personal possessions, but there was a box in the top of my closet that contained photographs and letters written by my mother and Hannah. The items were too painful to see yet too precious to throw away. But Robert may have kept similar items elsewhere—or even purged his life of such memories altogether.

After we finished, I checked the shed thoroughly to make sure we had missed nothing. It was then that I found the final box. It was a small trunk, really, made of sturdier material than cardboard. Far heavier than the others, it was buried in the ground, underneath a series of loose planks that I kicked out of the way.

We brought it up with some difficulty, placing it on top of the other boxes. It had a padlock on front—but it was unsophisticated, and I was easily able to pick it open with the tools I had brought.

Alistair held the candle high above its contents.

We peered inside and saw only a crumpled sheet, its floral pattern heavily stained with a dark substance.

I reached in and pulled it aside to see what it obscured. Slowly, slowly . . . until Alistair and I had a full view of what lay below.

Had we not been prepared for the worst, we might have jumped, even cried out.

"What in the devil's name . . ." Alistair swore softly.

Someone's hand—at least, the skeletal remains of it—rested in the box. The bones were small, delicate even—though of course I could not really know what they had looked like in life. On the third skeletal finger was a small diamond-and-sapphire ring. It glittered brilliantly in the candlelight.

We stared—shivering as a draft of cold air wafted in through the open door.

"Are the bones human—perhaps a girl's?" I asked, hesitating—aware that I was making an assumption based on the fact that the ring was obviously a female's, and that this victim had been killed wearing it.

Alistair paused for a moment to consider. "They're small enough. And the fact that he left the ring around her finger—or, put it there postmortem—must have some significance."

We checked the remaining contents of the box but there was nothing.

There were noises from the street, so we quickly emptied

the contents of Alistair's satchel into my own, then transplanted the skeletal hand and ring to Alistair's bag for transport. Making our way back to the ferry, we discussed the two biggest challenges now facing us: how to prove these remains were human, and how to find Robert Coby.

"I have to go to Mulvaney," I explained. "But I won't convince him that he has gotten the case wrong without solid proof."

"Surely we found enough evidence today?" Alistair looked at me in surprise.

"It's all circumstantial," I said, shaking my head. "We can't even confirm that these remains are in fact human."

"They certainly look to be," he said sharply.

"And looks can deceive," I retorted. "I won't stake my reputation on unsubstantiated evidence."

Fortunately, Alistair soon came up with a solution: he had a friend, a paleontologist at the American Museum of Natural History, who could be counted on for his discretion and knowledge.

"Are you sure?" I pressed Alistair. "After all, dinosaur bones and human ones are very different. Perhaps I should risk calling Dr. Wilcox."

He waved away my objection, saying, "My friend will be up to the task."

And so we boarded the last train to New York, sitting silently most of the trip. But the bones Alistair carried in his bag—the skeletal remains of the hand of an unknown girl—called out to me throughout the journey, refusing me rest, reminding me of justice undone.

Thursday
March 22, 1906

CHAPTER 28

The American Museum of Natural History,
Central Park West,
between Seventy-eighth and Eighty-first streets

"You entertain dark suspicions, gentlemen. My own poor skills may not be up to the task of confirming them." Professor Saul Loman pushed his glasses back up from where they had fallen to the tip of his nose.

"We'll take that chance," Alistair said, clearing his throat as he made a weak attempt at humor. "We also appreciate that no other bone expert in this city would meet us on such short notice to analyze these remains and tell us something about their owner's age, gender, and life history."

Saul chuckled. "You have high hopes, my friend."

The electric light inside flickered in response to a loud thunderclap—for a full-fledged thunderstorm was now raging outside. It was past midnight in the bowels of New York's Museum of Natural History. Alistair had managed to locate a telephone at the hotel in Greenport before we boarded our train home: he had made two telephone calls. His frantic call to Saul Loman had convinced the paleontologist to open his lab to us after-hours, when he should by all rights have been home in bed. And his call to Frank Riley had prompted the reporter to search old news files for any missing-persons cases on Shelter Island during the past decade. I had made one call myself, to an old friend in the Fifth Precinct; he had promised to run a search through police records as well as the city directory for any mention of Robert Coby.

Alistair had explained to me earlier that Saul Loman was one of the museum's elite researchers, handpicked by Henry Fairfield Osborn to help restore several impressive dinosaur-fossil discoveries. But I cared more for what Professor Loman might tell us about the bones we had found on Shelter Island. With each passing hour, Thursday night's premiere of *Romeo and Juliet* drew nearer. And I needed proof to secure Mulvaney's help.

"I realize we'd be better off with a human anthropologist," Alistair said by way of apology. "Or even someone from the coroner's office."

"So why did you call me?" The professor's voice was gruff, belying the gleam of interest that flickered in his eyes. "There are other men with far more expertise. Aleš Hrdlička at the Smithsonian specializes in human remains analysis. And George Dorsey at the Field Museum in Chicago has experience with sensational murder cases, including that one involving the sausage maker a few years ago. Either man," he said, "would provide far better help than I can offer."

My words sounded desperate, even to my own ears. "We

needed someone's help immediately. Even tomorrow morning may be too late for us."

He remained dubious, so I added, "We're actually working at the moment in an unofficial capacity."

"Ah." An even brighter glint appeared in his eyes. And I saw that he was more than a man of discretion: he actually enjoyed the prospect of participating in a secret, unofficial investigation. It excited him in ways that a more traditional inquiry did not. I should have known that a man who would meet us in the dead of night—unlocking the door to the museum where he worked— was a maverick of sorts. *Just like Alistair,* I reflected. Saul Loman would risk a great deal for any cause he supported; fortunately, based on whatever Alistair had told him, he appeared ready to support ours.

"All right then." He moved closer to the skeletal hand, which was laid out on a white sheet. Touching it gently with a small instrument that resembled a toothpick, he began his analysis.

"Well, I can tell you straight off, these bones are indeed human. You can see how they match up here." He showed us an anatomical chart—a virtual diagram of the human skeletal hand. "The finger bones here are called phalanges. Note how well each correlates to the diagram. For example, look at the thumb." He touched the relevant bone fragment with his instrument. "We can see the tip, or distal phalanx, the proximal phalanx, and the metacarpal. The bones in the palm, here," he continued to point, "are the carpals."

He opened an overstuffed manual titled *Human Anatomy* that he had pulled from his bookshelf soon after we arrived. "The bones you have, unfortunately, are not the most dispositive in yielding information about this skeleton's life history. The pelvis bone, for example, might have allowed me to tell you conclusively that these are the bones of a woman. That's because, to accommodate childbirth, the female pelvis is typically wider than that of the average male. The skull might have allowed me to estimate her age based upon the presence and condition of her teeth."

"We understand there will be limits to what you can tell us." Alistair moved closer to the table, listening to the professor with rapt attention.

"And what I tell you will not necessarily be accepted by all scientists—or even the majority of them. It may prove nothing." Quickly flipping to a section on measurements, Loman continued to talk. "Long bones provide more accurate information, but based on the measurements of the finger bones here, I believe this hand is from a female skeleton. You'll see the fingers are actually within the averages compiled by researchers for typical female phalanges."

"And of course, that would make sense given the circumstances in which we found them: wearing a ring," Alistair said.

"Can you tell us how quickly her corpse would have decomposed into these skeletal remains?" I asked.

Professor Loman shrugged. "It depends, based upon where her body was found. For example, if animals or insects had access to it, then she might have skeletonized in as little as one to two months."

"And what's the outside estimate, assuming her corpse decomposed more slowly?"

He took a breath, considered it, and said, "A conservative estimate would be around six months. More than that, her bones will not tell me. She may have lain in a forest for three months—or for three years. The fact that her hand is now a skeleton only really tells us she did not die in recent weeks." He pulled out his magnifying glass to examine the thumb. "I can see that she once broke her thumb. The small bump here," he used his toothpick to touch the area, "shows a well-healed fracture."

"How long before her death?" Alistair asked.

He shrugged. "Impossible to tell, but I suspect it was a childhood injury. It's something else that may help you with identification. Assuming, of course, that the owner of the ring and the remains are one and the same."

I thought again of the gold ring, its sapphire gem anchored on either side by two tiny diamonds. It was the kind of ring typically worn by a young lady. Of course, it was possible that Robert Coby had simply found the ring. Or that it was a family ring, taken from his mother's possessions. Yet I believed it had significance, if only because I had some idea of the man with whom we were dealing. For Robert Coby did not make insignificant choices.

CHAPTER 29

The Vandergriff Mansion, 969 Fifth Avenue

We managed to catch a couple of hours' sleep at Alistair's apartment before daybreak, waking to discover that Frank Riley had come through for us overnight. He had discovered that a beautiful young socialite named Francine Vandergriff had disappeared five years ago while summering with her family on Shelter Island. Aware that time was short, I was satisfied with the probable victim's name. But Alistair knew the Vandergriffs well—and so he prevailed upon me to visit them that morning.

"Mulvaney thinks the case is wrapped up," he reminded me. "You won't find him in his office before nine o'clock. Besides, the Vandergriffs may know of Robert Coby's current whereabouts."

That chance was reason enough to meet with Mrs. Vandergriff briefly, I decided. My friend down at the Fifth Precinct had turned up nothing on Robert Coby. "It's strange," he had said. "It's as though the man doesn't even exist."

"Will Mrs. Vandergriff even receive us at this hour?" It was not yet eight o'clock, and so early a visit seemed the height of impropriety.

Yet Alistair was no doubt right when he replied, "It concerns her only daughter. She'll see us."

And so the hansom cab whisked us through Central Park that morning to the Vandergriff residence on Millionaires' Row, as the string of mansions along Fifth Avenue was called. The Vandergriff home, a white marble masterpiece surrounded by an iron fence with an elaborate filigree pattern, was among the largest and most imposing. Yet it struck me immediately as a house in mourning.

I knew that the Vandergriffs, like Alistair, counted themselves among Mrs. Astor's Four Hundred—considered a marker of New York's social elite. I'd not often had occasion to enter the home of a society matron like Mrs. Vandergriff, and I was certain that the stiff restraint exercised by the young housemaid who admitted us was not atypical. Nor were the dour, heavy furnishings that adorned the dark-paneled room in which we sat; they were in keeping with the prevailing taste of many wealthy New York families. But the sadness that was so palpable had nothing to do with furnishings or attitudes. It permeated the very air around us.

We did not wait for long before Mrs. Vandergriff entered the room majestically. She was an imposing grande dame with high cheekbones, gray hair with silver highlights, and a haughty attitude. In one sweeping gesture, she placed her pince-nez onto her nose; it had formerly been suspended from the ivory brooch pinned to her dark purple satin dress. She then peered at Alistair with fixed attention.

"Your wife has not called upon me in months," she said, her lips curling into a disapproving frown. "Yet you disturb me at this ungodly hour of the morning."

I groaned inwardly, for this was not a promising start to our conversation.

But Alistair merely smiled, saying, "My wife has not exactly called upon me in months, either. She more or less resides abroad permanently now."

His words earned him a severe look and a tart response. "Then you might have called upon me yourself and inquired into my health. Or that of Henry—that is, Mr. Vandergriff."

Alistair's sarcastic reply was no doubt affected by his lack of sleep. "Perhaps we ought to comment on the weather. We can say it's been a particularly cold and snowy March—and then move on to more serious discussion."

I thought she would rebuke him for his rudeness, but instead I watched as her face relaxed into a half smile. "Very well, Alistair. I will concur with you on the weather—and agree to move on." She made a sound that was almost a chortle.

"Thank you for agreeing to see us at this early hour," Alistair said, introducing me and doing his best to move the conversation along. "It's been a while," he said gently, "but we are here about your daughter."

"Francine?" she said. Her voice cracked as she looked at us hopefully.

"I'm sorry. We haven't found her," Alistair said. "But in the course of investigating another young woman's disappearance, the name Robert Coby has come up. Are you acquainted with him?"

She looked at Alistair, readjusting the paisley shawl that covered her shoulders. But she said nothing.

"We have reason to believe your daughter's disappearance was connected with Robert Coby." Alistair paused for only a beat before he added, "Anything you can tell us about Robert Coby or your daughter's relationship with him may help us."

Her angry gaze fixed on him. "You slander my daughter's reputation by implying a connection where there is none. And you insult me by broaching a topic of conversation that you know to be painful."

"I mean no disrespect, Mrs. Vandergriff. And I am sorry to bring up a subject that must be difficult for you. But the connection that your family—" he paused for a split second, "particularly that your daughter—formed with Robert Coby is the best hope we have to find him quickly. And I assure you, it is urgent that we do so."

They stared at each other for several moments, a contest of wills.

Her resolve broke first. She bit her lip, and when her words came, for the first time she spoke without pretense. "Do you think finding Robert would lead us to my Francine?"

"I believe it may."

She stared ahead, her jaw working silently.

"I do not come here lightly, Mrs. Vandergriff. Don't forget—I also know what it is to lose a child." Alistair's voice was thick with emotion.

"So did Robert," she finally said. She removed her pince-nez, letting it hang once more from the ivory brooch pinned to her chest. "At least he seemed to."

"Robert?" I barely breathed the name.

She sighed. "I'll be honest. I disliked Robert Coby at first. I resented the attention he paid to my daughter. I worried for her reputation, you see: he was a most unsuitable attachment for her. And I felt my husband gave him false encouragement by taking an interest in his career. As a philanthropic gesture, my Henry—Mr. Vandergriff, that is—tried to help Robert gain a foothold in the theater business."

She was then silent for some moments, and we simply waited for her to continue speaking.

"Robert fancied himself a writer—a playwright, specifically. Mr. Vandergriff had read some of his work and felt it was quite good; as a result, he made some introductions for Robert, helping him to meet some of our city's more influential theater types." Her emphasis fell upon "theater types"—an exaggerated sniff underscoring her disapproval of them. "I don't think anything ever came of it."

"You mentioned that you eventually changed your mind about Robert. Why?" I asked.

"Because I saw that I had been wrong. I had judged him too harshly." She pursed her lips. "When Francine disappeared, that last summer on Shelter Island, Robert was absolutely marvelous," she said, her hands breaking apart in an expansive gesture. "No one could have been more supportive. He organized a search of the island. He wrote news articles about her for all the local Long Island papers, in the hopes that someone would recognize her photograph or description. He checked on us every day." She took a deep breath. "And when we had no choice but to give up and return to the city, he gave the most beautiful gift. He called it *A Prayer for Francine* and it was a collection of poems, each one an homage to our daughter in beautiful verse. Somehow, he managed to find words for those emotions that were locked deep in my heart." She placed a hand upon her chest.

"But you don't see him regularly now? You don't know where he lives?" I asked, puzzled.

"No. He's a young man with his own interests," she said with a wan smile. Then with a flash of defiance she added, "After everything I've told you about Robert, you see now why he could not have been involved in Francine's disappearance. Not after everything he did for us. Not," she emphasized the word, "in light of the beautiful poems he wrote about her."

Alistair's voice was gentle when he asked, "Might we see the book of poetry that he wrote?"

"Of course; but a few poems won't lead you to a missing man," she said, her spirit returning as she excused herself.

I glanced at my watch. We were pressed for time, I reminded Alistair.

"We've still got to show her the ring," he said. "Patience."

She returned moments later with an inlaid-ivory book caressed between her hands. She passed it to Alistair somewhat reluctantly.

"As I said, the verses are beautiful—" She broke off awkwardly.

Alistair handed the book to me, and I saw that each poem

was carefully typewritten and surrounded by elaborate illustrations, mainly floral. Mrs. Vandergriff was right: their emotional tenor was one of tender remembrance of something precious and lost, as a parent might feel for a child. Not one of them smacked of passion or romance.

She placed her hand over her heart. "He managed to put into words every feeling I had for her. My enduring affection. My grief and loss."

I looked away as she pulled a lace handkerchief from her pocket and dabbed at her eyes—for I felt I was intruding on something deeply personal.

"Thank you, Mrs. Vandergriff. Just one more thing." Alistair placed the sapphire-and-diamond ring on the coffee table that separated us from the society matron. "Is there any chance this was Francine's ring?"

She stiffened. "Where did you find it?" Her words were hoarse and broken as they came from her throat. She reached out as if to touch the ring—pulled her hand back as though afraid—and then recovered her nerve and tried again. This time she succeeded and gingerly picked up the ring, tracing her forefinger lightly over its filigree band.

"Someone on Shelter Island found it and gave it to us, knowing we planned to see you," Alistair said, twisting the facts into a half-truth.

"But where?" Her eyes were searching as she looked from me to Alistair.

"Outside the hotel." Another half-lie.

Her face collapsed in relief. "Of course. She walked on the path past the hotel all the time."

Now she clasped the ring tightly in her fingers, and brought it against her heart. "Her father and I . . . we gave it to her for her eighteenth birthday. Only a year before we lost her."

"One more question that may sound odd—but did your daughter ever break her thumb?"

"Why, yes," she said, and looked at us in amazement. "She'd just turned ten. We'd taken a sailboat out on the bay, and she wrenched her thumb playing with the mast."

Alistair and I exchanged sad glances. Of course we could tell her nothing yet—so Alistair mumbled a half-excuse that appeared to placate her for the moment, especially since she was so distracted by the finding of her daughter's ring.

I didn't feel too guilty. When bad news had waited this long, a few more days would make little difference.

I reached out for the ring. "We need to keep your daughter's ring just a little while longer, Mrs. Vandergriff. Then I promise we will return it to you."

Reluctantly, she gave it up.

Alistair picked up the ivory-inlaid book of verse, glanced at a couple of the poems once more, then handed it back to Mrs. Vandergriff. As he did, an envelope that had been tucked into the back lining fell out. As he passed that to her as well, she opened it, asking us, "Would you like to see a couple of pictures of Francine? These were taken the last Christmas we spent with her."

It was all I could do not to refuse. I was impatient to talk with Mulvaney and move on with this case. I nearly didn't look when she passed me the photographs, each featuring a smiling young lady with high cheekbones and curly dark hair. She clearly had her mother's confidence and determination: it was evident in both her posture and expression. I glanced at the last photograph quickly—it was of a group of young people clustered around a piano at a Christmas party, with a decorated evergreen visible in the background.

I pulled out my pocket watch again. It was now nearly nine o'clock in the morning. We needed to leave.

Something, however, made me give the last picture a second look.

I focused on the man in the back row who was smiling broadly. Even in black-and-white sepia, I could see that his handsome face was framed by perfectly coiffed hair and a smile that revealed even, perfect teeth. He stared at me almost as though taunting me—mocking my inability to recognize him. For it slowly registered that this was a face I already knew.

"How is this man connected with Francine and Robert?" I asked, my voice rising in excitement.

In a world-weary voice, Mrs. Vandergriff responded, "Whomever are you talking about?"

I pointed again. "Here in the back row, just behind Francine."

But Mrs. Vandergriff was distracted by her own thoughts, so she dismissed me with a look of mild frustration. "My dear," she said, "you're impossibly mixed up. How could Robert know *whom* well? You're pointing to Robert himself."

She repeated it again when we continued to stare at her blankly.

Now thoroughly flustered by our reaction, she added, "The photograph was taken right here in our ballroom, by the piano."

We glanced again at the man with the charming smile, whose book of poetry and careful attentions had so captivated this grande dame of society.

The same man who had murdered her daughter.

A man who went by a different name than Robert Coby.

He'd known our every step, for covering our investigation had been his job.

Alistair had worked with him closely. Too closely, it would seem.

It all suddenly made sense.

A frustrated playwright.

A respected theater critic for *The New York Times*.

Robert Coby.

Jack Bogarty.

One and the same.

CHAPTER 30

Central Park, Fifth Avenue and Seventy-eighth Street

There's a singular moment I wait for in every investigation when disjointed fragments of evidence magically come together and present the solution whole. Sometimes it happens because of hard work or astute thinking. But more often, it's the result of a lucky break, like the one we had just gotten from Mrs. Vandergriff.

We crossed Fifth Avenue and walked south along the edge of Central Park.

"It makes perfect sense now that we know," Alistair said, shaking his head in disbelief, "but I swear to you he gave no sign in any of my dealings with him."

"Or mine," I said dryly. "Yet you've told me before that the most diabolical killers are those who best deceive their closest friends and associates."

"His public persona utterly masks his psychotic tendencies. Unlike many killers I've interviewed, he has no social maladjustment," Alistair said. He tapped his fingers together. "Do you prefer to see Mulvaney on your own, or would you like me to accompany you downtown?"

"I'm not going to Mulvaney—not yet."

"Why in heaven's name not? A moment ago, you couldn't wait to see him." Alistair's voice filled with exasperation. "Everything we did last night and this morning was designed to help you provide Mulvaney with sufficient evidence to exonerate Poe and secure Robert Coby's—I mean Jack's—arrest." He patted the briefcase he carried, which contained the picture we had borrowed from Mrs. Vandergriff.

"With a man like Jack Bogarty, it's not enough. I see that now." I quickened my pace. "Jack is too smooth and polished. If you put him on the witness stand with insufficient evidence, he'll charm the jury into granting him an acquittal."

Alistair spread his hands wide in amazement. "How can you say that before he's even been tried? We have a lot connecting him to these crimes. It's as though you don't trust our legal system to handle the evidence you would provide them."

But my conviction only grew as I spoke. "He will argue that we've made a terrible mistake and charged the wrong man based on circumstantial evidence. I've seen it happen before, in fact— just over a week ago."

I explained to him about Lydia Snyder, who had been on trial for poisoning her husband. Despite evidence pointing undeniably in her direction, she had used her charm and personality to persuade the jury to ignore all circumstantial evidence that damned her.

"And since it was a murder case, all they needed was reasonable doubt to acquit her." Alistair understood, taking me seriously now.

"Jack Bogarty would be just like her," I said. "He's a successful theater critic who is well liked and respected. Plenty of people will believe he could never do such a thing. We won't succeed in putting this man behind bars if we can't secure the evidence that will pin him to these killings. He has sufficient personal charisma to sway any jury. And if they acquit him, he will do as he's done before: disappear into a new life with a new name. And the killings will continue."

"You're right about his behavioral pattern," Alistair said at last. "And if you truly don't trust the prosecution to build an airtight case against him based on the circumstances—"

"It's not a matter of trust. I'm saying that for some people—those like Jack Bogarty—you need something tighter than mere circumstance to bind them to their crimes. We've got to catch him in the act."

We were silent for a moment. Then Alistair said, "It sounds like you have something already in mind."

"I do. But I need a few hours to pull it together. I need you to approach Mulvaney tonight and convince him to come to *Romeo and Juliet.*"

"But why don't you—"

Ignoring the apprehension that filled his face, I said, "I'll meet you there. *Romeo and Juliet.* Bring Mulvaney half an hour after the show ends."

CHAPTER 31

The Fortune Club, 30 Pell Street

"Not as a favor," I said, pulling an envelope from my coat pocket. "What I want is a straight business arrangement."

Nick Scarpetta grunted, then ground the butt of his cigar into the ashtray beside him. He reached a thick hand toward the small black candlestick telephone on the left side of his desk and pulled it to him. "Get me Underwood 342," he said.

I waited, listening as the operator connected him.

That he would help me, I'd had no doubt. Nicky had rescued me from a tough spot on more than one occasion—in fact, probably more often than I even knew. When I was a child, he had been a familiar figure at my mother's door, overcoming her objections, returning my father's gambling losses to her in secret. "For you and the children. Make sure *he* don't see a cent of it," he'd mumble before he disappeared yet again—only to resurface during the next crisis. Just months ago, he had used his connections to help me locate Isabella before a killer took her life.

He had always kept a benevolent eye on me, never too far away, though my role as a police detective had placed some strain on our relationship. Nicky was a pivotal figure within the criminal underworld, but so far, I'd been able to maintain my friendship with him—without entangling myself in his darker dealings. But I also knew that the more I asked of him, the less likely I'd be able to maintain that separation.

That was why today I asked no favors. I approached Nicky this time as a paying customer, knowing his services did not come cheap.

The telephone connection was finally made. "This is Louie, right? I need you and Isador. My place. Fifteen minutes." It was all Nicky said before he returned the receiver to its hook. He had eventually installed a telephone out of necessity, but he never conducted business over it, quite rightly concerned about those eavesdropping. Business was done in person, from the back room of his saloon.

"Two men for one evening," he said gruffly.

I pulled several bills from the envelope. "Five hundred, right?"

He nodded and tucked the money away almost the moment I produced it.

"There's one more thing," I began delicately. "My father is back in town."

Nicky let forth a loud guffaw. "Tell me something I don't know. Took him what—two weeks?—before he was in debt at every joint downtown."

"How much does he owe you?"

"Too much." He looked at me with no small measure of concern in his drooping, baggy eyes. "Why?"

"Because I intend to repay his debt to you," I said. I lifted my chin and looked at him with a calm, steady gaze.

He opened the large humidor centered on his desk and I breathed in the pungent odor of Spanish cedar, which was so strong that it actually overpowered the scent of tobacco. He chose a cigar with care, then reached for a match and lit it in a motion that was surprisingly fluid for a man with thick stubs for fingers.

He took several puffs from the cigar before he spoke. "You got no cause to do that."

"No," I smiled ruefully, "but I intend to all the same. How much—one thousand? Or more like two?"

They were large numbers, but I never underestimated my father's misplaced faith in a pair of aces.

He leaned forward across his desk and fixed me with a firm look. "He don't deserve it. Not the way he treated you—not to mention the fine woman who was your mother."

I remained firm. "Agreed. But I'm still paying it."

Nicky smoked in silence for some moments, just thinking as he puffed perfect O rings that rose to the ceiling.

My goal was to square things all around with Nicky. I had done that in part by paying for the services of his henchmen, whose help I needed tonight. But I also needed to repay my father's debt if I was to clear all obligations. In recent months, I had lived in trepidation that Nicky would call in a favor I'd be loath to grant yet afraid to refuse. And so, in buying my father's freedom, I also secured my own.

"Fifteen hundred," he said at last.

It represented two years' salary—and many more years of saving and scrimping.

For a split second, I hesitated. *Do I really want to do this? It would be so easy to walk away. . . .*

But instead, I took a deep breath and paid it, receiving his note in return.

Then we spoke of happier topics until his men arrived. Louie and Isador, the two henchmen I'd hired to assist me, appeared more than capable of providing the brute strength I feared I would need. Louie, a tall African man with chiseled muscles, had been a boxer before Nicky offered him more profitable employment. And Isador, Nicky's distant cousin, was short, squat, and reputed to be handy with a knife.

They were all ears when I explained what I needed from them.

I met with my father afterward at The Emerald Isle—the same bar where I had first met with Molly Hansen, following Annie Germaine's murder. After I explained how I needed his help, he regarded me with somber eyes.

"I heard from Nicky this afternoon. He sent a personal message saying I'm square with him. How can that be?"

"I took care of it," I said, my voice even.

"You paid him off?"

I nodded.

"You don't have that kind of money," he said darkly. "I owed him over a thousand. Exactly what kind of deal did you make?"

I smiled at the irony of it. My father had made every kind of deal over the years with far worse than the likes of Nicky

Scarpetta. And yet he was incensed to think I might have done the same.

"I do have that kind of money, actually. I've saved up over the years." I shrugged. "You forget, I once had other goals and plans. . . ."

His mouth opened the moment it dawned on him. "It was because you meant to marry the girl, wasn't it? Now I see." He set his mouth firmly. "You shouldn't have done that, Simon. Not for me. I'm not long for this world, and there will be other women—"

"I did it for me," I said sharply. "I needed Nicky's help—or at least that of his henchmen. So do me a favor. If you've got to keep playing cards, do it somewhere else. Not at Nicky's. Not anymore."

I found it strange that he had any concerns on this matter. But the money no longer represented my future with Hannah; in fact, it never had. What it represented was security: specifically, the kind I'd never had growing up.

I'd been harsher than I'd intended. But now that I'd satisfied any obligation I had to Nicky, I didn't want further trouble from my father. I left him, still nursing his pint of Guinness, with a simple reminder.

"The Lyceum Theater. *Romeo and Juliet*. I'll need you in position with Molly right after the show ends."

CHAPTER 32

The Lyceum Theater, 149 West Forty-fifth Street

The curtain fell to rapt applause—with a standing ovation for Helen Bell's performance as Juliet.

I waited for some twenty minutes, my nerves on end, before I emerged from the crossover behind the set. The theater had emptied.

I lit a match—held it high—then blew it out.

Looking up at the catwalk, I saw Louie's answering signal that he was in position and all was quiet.

I checked on Isador in person. When I called out to him, he emerged from his hiding area behind the curtain.

"Everything's fine?"

"Good here, boss."

I gave him a quick nod. "Keep watch. I'll be back."

Turning the corner toward Helen Bell's dressing room

backstage, I paused. I had the distinct sense that I was being watched. But no one was in sight.

I was on edge, that was all.

My father answered my knock, opening the door to Miss Bell's room. "Just the man I wanted to see," he said, beaming. "Come in."

I entered the room, careful to avoid several bouquets of flowers that obstructed the entry. Tonight, the tiny space overflowed with flowers and cards sent by well-wishers.

Miss Bell sat at her dressing table, biting her lip.

"See here, I told you my son would come to make things all right."

My father smiled. Miss Bell didn't.

"I'm Detective Simon Ziele," I said, pulling a chair close to her. "My father has already explained to you that you're in danger tonight. But you've no reason to be afraid. I've asked him to take you to a safe place."

"Do you really believe Charlie means to kill me?" Her voice betrayed her fear.

Charlie—the false name he'd given her.

"I do, Miss Bell." Then I forced myself to sound confident. "But don't worry, we're going to stop him. Another actress is going to take your place. *She* will risk any danger by acting as your decoy." I turned to my father. "Is Molly ready?"

"Just next door," he said. "I'll get her."

I had asked my father—a master of disguise—to help Molly become a believable substitute for Miss Bell. But I wasn't prepared for the sight of her when she walked through the door—for Molly Hansen had been transformed into Helen Bell's identical twin. Her curls were gone, replaced by a wig that replicated Helen's straight brown locks. Her freckles-and-cream coloring, likewise, had been camouflaged by grease-paint to reproduce Helen's darker olive tones. She already had the same build as Helen's, and now she wore identical clothes. In short, she made a mirror image of the woman she intended to replace this night.

Helen's face turned a ghastly pale. "Is this necessary?" she whispered.

"I'm afraid it is," I replied.

"It's just a bit of greasepaint and a good wig," my father said with plenty of bravado.

"But Charlie will notice she's not me." Helen bit her lip.

"Hopefully not until it's too late," I said, adding wryly, "My father has always said that's the art of the con: people see only what they *expect* to see."

I exchanged glances with my father. It was time.

"Let's get you home, Miss Bell," he said.

"Can I take my things?" she asked, casting a lingering glance toward the flower bouquets that lined the room.

"Tomorrow," I said. "They'll be here, waiting. But we don't want to draw extra attention to you tonight."

After she had left, I looked down and read the note that was still on her dressing table: "Late dinner after the show? Let's celebrate.—Charlie"

The note had come, just as we had expected. I resisted the urge to take it into evidence. Everything needed to appear normal to Jack if we were to foil his plans.

"You're all set?" I asked Molly.

"Absolutely." And with a toss of her head, she took the

dressing-room chair Helen had just vacated. "And you'd best get into position. You wouldn't want him to see you here," she warned.

If she was nervous, she didn't show it. Maybe it was because of her many years of training as an actress. Still, it was brave of her to assume this role tonight—as I knew she'd done for the sake of my father. She must have loved him even more than I'd suspected. Still, I felt a pang of guilt: was it fair of me to put her in harm's way?

A flicker of doubt crossed her expression. "Are you sure he's going to come tonight?"

I tried to give her a reassuring smile. "As certain as I can be. We've looked to his past crime-scene behavior and found nothing but a consistent pattern."

"But how do you know it will be Helen Bell?"

"Because once we realized *Romeo and Juliet* was the targeted performance, we interviewed all the women cast in the play. Only Helen has been courted by a very charming suitor who has bombarded her with love poems, flowers, and dinners."

I wished her luck, then returned to the main stage. Everyone else had now left.

I emerged onstage intending to hide myself on the left side of the auditorium. But the moment I was there, I retreated into the shadows of the curtains.

Something was different.

Center front stage, I saw a blue envelope and a sapphire-blue satin sash. It swirled around a letter as if it were a serpent poised to strike.

My heart raced.

He was early.

In the theater somewhere—but where? I looked around, saw no movement. Had he seen me—or any of the others?

I glanced up, searching for Louie on the catwalk where he had been positioned. All was dark, quiet. Was he still there? I didn't dare light a match and risk betraying my whereabouts to Jack.

I checked my watch. Still nearly twenty minutes before Alistair planned to bring Mulvaney. If Jack was here already, then our timing had been wrong. They would be too late, and I'd have to hope that Mulvaney would accept the word of multiple witnesses to Jack's actions.

I moved to the left, making my way toward the curtained space where Isador was keeping watch. I had to warn him that Jack was here—assuming he didn't already know.

I stayed close to the black curtains, coming closer and closer to the backstage-door area.

Not a sound around me anywhere. Only my own accelerated breathing.

But something wasn't right.

"Isador," I whispered—first softly, then again more loudly.

"Izzy." My voice was urgent now. "Are you still there?"

I pulled back the curtain that obscured Isador's station. He was not there, I thought. I stepped to the left and nearly fell over an obstruction on the floor.

A leg.

Isador.

This hulking brute of a man was sprawled out on the floor, incapacitated.

I shook him.

No response.

I felt his neck.

No pulse.

Was he truly dead? I had no time to find out.

Now panicked, I automatically retraced my steps toward Helen's dressing room, around to the side and back through the crossover. I remembered Alistair's words: "Jack is enjoying every aspect of his handiwork. And a man who enjoys something this much will not stop—at least, not of his own accord."

He was here, and somehow he'd managed to incapacitate Isador both quickly and noiselessly. He had bested our toughest henchman, a veteran of far more dangerous fights than this should have been.

But how? Without a sound or scuffle—and when Isador had at least a two-hundred-pound advantage over Jack. It made no sense.

We'd underestimated him. If he succeeded, all would be lost.

The moment I touched the doorknob to Helen's dressing room, I heard a scuttling noise inside.

Molly!

I reached for my Smith & Wesson with my stronger, left hand while I used my right to push the door open.

Beyond the bouquets of flowers, I saw him sitting in the chair.

Not Jack Bogarty, but my father—arms and legs tied with rope, a red bandanna as a gag.

He was alone.

"Here." I rushed to untie him, placing my gun on the floor.

He thrashed wildly, grunting, eyes wide with alarm.

Confused, I paused for a moment too long.

The blow to my head came without warning.

I recoiled, for the pain was intense—and I had barely enough presence of mind to look around for my assailant.

Where is Jack?

The pain seared through my head, and I dropped to my knees from the dizziness.

Mulvaney will never make it in time. We've failed, and now our own lives are in jeopardy.

Another blow came from nowhere.

Reeling from more pain than I'd thought possible, I collapsed to the floor as the room spun wildly.

I forced my eyes to stay open. I saw the ceiling and a bouquet of red roses above me as I fought the blackness that threatened to envelop me.

Then I saw a face, one with determined eyes and a resolute expression.

She had come to help—or so I thought.

I didn't realize the danger until it was too late, and I saw the rope . . . followed by the bloodstained blade of a knife as both inched toward my neck.

A cruel laugh burst forth from the face in front of me—an image that spun around in dizzying circles. Was it my imagination?

For it was a person I'd not expected to see—no, not in this way.

Never like this.

I wanted to understand, but I couldn't make sense of it. I knew only that I had been wrong about her—else she wouldn't be grabbing my arms, binding them together.

I could think of no reason why she would help Jack Bogarty—and certainly no reason for her to betray us as cruelly as she had.

I closed my eyes as all conscious thought disappeared.

And all pain.

Only the image of Molly Hansen wielding a knife continued to linger, until the final moment when all went dark.

CHAPTER 33

The Lyceum Theater, 149 West Forty-fifth Street

I woke in a state of sheer panic. It was pitch black. I couldn't move—and I couldn't get enough air.

Intense claustrophobia took hold. And pain, for my head throbbed and my right arm was in agony.

I closed my eyes again, willing myself to breathe slowly and focus. There would be sufficient air, if only I relaxed.

The air around me was dank and close, stinking of paint.

Without opening my eyes again, I took stock of my position. Hands? Immobile, wedged behind me, tied with rope.

Legs? There was a heavy, stiff pressure on top of them. But I wriggled them—first left, then right—ascertaining that they were not tied together. Still, I couldn't move them.

What else did I smell—besides paint? Freshly sawed wood. And the unmistakable musty smell of a damp place.

I was still in the theater . . . in the only space where there would be paint . . . and wood . . . and water sometimes seeping in. *The basement* . . . where theatrical sets were designed and painted.

I tried to gain a perspective on the room. The lighting was dim, but once my eyes adjusted, I could tell that I was wedged under what appeared to be stacks of lumber. A heavy pile weighed down my legs. And another mound almost blocked my face, with some boards jutting out mere inches from my nose.

I summoned every ounce of strength in my legs to push. I had to get myself out of this predicament. But whatever weighed them down was far too heavy.

Instead, I wriggled my torso with greater success and got my face and upper body free of the lumber that towered above me.

I heard a muffled sound, causing me to wrench my head to find out its source.

My father.

He was bound and gagged in the far corner.

"Pop," I called out. My childhood name for him—one I'd not used in years.

He made a half-coughing, half-gargling sound. I wanted to help him but I could not move.

Racked with frustration, I used my hands and arms to wrest myself into a sitting position. I moved out from under the tower of lumber far enough to send it toppling with a powerful shove from my left shoulder.

A mistake—for footsteps came running.

Whose footsteps?

And from where?

I froze, berating myself for not having been more careful.

The footsteps had stopped.

Molly's face emerged from behind a forest—or, rather, the green-painted stage set that was meant to represent one. Satisfied that we were still incapacitated, she walked around the giant set and gazed down, first at me, then at my father.

She breathed in relief. "Still here, I see. But causing trouble." She nodded toward the pile of lumber that I'd toppled.

"You know Captain Mulvaney is on his way. If you help us now, I can cut you a deal."

She gave me a knowing look. "I don't need a deal. And I'm afraid your captain won't be coming, after all."

Molly had known the whole plan. And that meant that Jack had known exactly how to foil each part of it.

My father made a gurgling sound. From the light of Molly's lantern, I saw that his chin was streaked with blood. For a split second, I thought he had been hurt. But then, as he nearly choked trying to cough, I realized the blood was from his consumption.

"Good God!" I burst out. "He's going to drown in his own blood if you don't remove that gag."

A harsh laugh. "He's going to die anyway. What do I care?"

Another awful hacking noise.

At the sound, she relented, muttering, "But I'd rather not listen to it."

"Lean forward," she said to him. And before she removed the gag, she checked the knots that secured his hands and feet. Satisfied, she reached for the knot that tied the blood-soaked bandanna behind his head.

"I'm taking this off," she said, warning, "but if you so much as make a noise, I'll replace it, even tighter."

I watched my father carefully. She was close enough that he might be able to kick her.

Fight, I silently commanded.

But all he said was, "Please, it hurts. Can't you let me straighten my arms out?"

"No. Because you'll simply undo the knots that bind you."

"Molly." He paused for a moment, then simply asked, "Why?"

Ignoring him, she searched around the room until she found a crowbar.

I stared at it, wondering if she meant to use it on us—or to move some of the wood that had fallen all around the floor in a mess.

Who is she?

Then, in a flash, I realized it.

There was no resemblance, at least not in the face or build. No matter. Some families didn't look alike, and I'd never been good at discerning the finer points of family likeness anyway.

Nonetheless—and I thought it was because of a movement she made as she leaned over to pick up a plank of wood—Mrs. Layton's words sprang to mind: "Robert and my daughter were very close," she had said, "as close as brother and sister."

"Where's your cousin?" I asked.

A churlish smile. "Good job, Detective. You figured that one out."

She returned to stacking piles of lumber.

"He's upstairs? And you've been helping him all this time?"

Not one member of this family is right in the head.

"I guess he couldn't have done it without you." I affected a look of sincerity—or so I hoped. "But I can't figure out *why.* Why help him?"

She muttered something incomprehensible.

"How long has he been killing them, Molly? When did you first find out? Because it's been going on far longer than just the past few weeks."

She stared at me, saying nothing. She'd just righted the last of the planks on the table, seeming to forget that previously they had lain on top of me. I needed to keep her distracted.

"A man who can strangle a woman without leaving a single mark is practiced at this skill," Alistair had said.

"He's been doing it a long time," I said quietly. "Have you been helping him all along?"

Her eyes narrowed. "Robby has a . . . a sickness. He loves certain women so much that he ends up hurting them."

"You mean killing them," I said coldly.

"He just doesn't want them to change," she said. "That's what he always told me. It's just that sometimes he goes too far."

"So why help him?"

"I'm not *helping* him," she said in a burst of anger. "I'm *protecting* him. I make sure he doesn't get caught."

"Which ensures that even more women will die."

"They would put him in a mental hospital, if they didn't kill him," she said stubbornly, "and I won't stand for it. It's bad enough our whole family has been destroyed—" She choked on her words.

And in that moment, I thought I understood.

"You wanted to destroy Charles Frohman," I said softly. "That's why you've involved yourself to this extent."

She looked up sharply in surprise.

"You blamed him for your aunt's death," I continued.

"More than that," she said. "He owed us. *All* of us. And he never did right, not by any of us."

"I know Robert had written some plays—"

"Good plays. Plays that should have been produced, not the least because Robby was Frohman's own son."

My father collapsed into a coughing fit that sent up more blood.

"Here." She tossed a stained towel in his direction, shooting him a look of disgust as he maneuvered awkwardly, trying to reach it. Her laugh was brittle as she watched his helplessness, for his hands remained tied behind his back.

"Charles Frohman and Elaine Coby?" I'd not suspected that one, assuming it was true. Jack Bogarty's—or rather, Robert Coby's—image popped into my mind. There was no trace of resemblance I could detect.

"Absolutely. What do you think he does with all these actresses he makes into stars? It's part of the deal—one reason why he never permits them to marry or step out with anyone else. But in Aunt Elaine's case," she took a breath, "instead of doing right by her, he blacklisted her and ruined her career. Her entire life, in fact."

I wasn't about to argue. Instead, I said only, "I can see how you believe he owed better to Robert and Elaine. But you said he owed *all* of you. . . ."

"And he did owe me." Her voice was bitter. "I have Elaine's gifts. I look like her. I act like her. And I've more than her share of talent. She even wrote to him, asking him to help me out. . . ."

"And he didn't, so years later, when he rejected Robert's work as well, the two of you conspired to hurt Frohman."

"Robert was going to pursue his women no matter what."
She tossed her head. "It was my idea that he could turn his habits to a productive end. All it took was showing him a few pictures, making a suggestion or two—"

"But the women don't even look alike," I said.

"They didn't have to." She looked at me in amazement. "You don't get it, do you? Their appeal didn't lie in what they *were*. Robby was drawn to who they might *become*—with his help. All I had to do was plant the *seed*—"

"But they were innocent women, all of them. They deserved better."

"Spare me, Detective. No one's innocent. And no one ever gets what they deserve. . . ." Her words dripped with bitterness.

"By God, they were murdered! And where you had the power to stop it, you actually encouraged it."

"They served my purposes," she said coldly.

There was a noise—voices upstairs.

She turned and left us without saying another word. We listened to her footsteps thud up the wooden staircase; then a key turned in the lock at the top of the basement door.

"I'm so sorry, son," my father said with another cough. "I really bungled this one up."

"You couldn't have known," I said. Or could he? Had there been some sign that he missed? I'd no way of knowing.

The shift in weight was something I'd sensed immediately— the collapse of the first lumber tower had seemed to knock several planks off the pile that anchored my legs. I'd been lucky that she had put the fallen wood on top of the table. Now . . . yes, it moved. I pushed with all my might, and felt . . . movement.

Inch by inch, I wriggled my legs until my feet appeared . . . first just the heel, then the toes of both feet.

Stiff, and still in painful agony, I began inching my way toward him.

"What are you doing?"

"You're going to untie me."

"I can't," he whimpered. "Not with my own hands tied."

"You've no choice. And this is no time for false modesty. I know you've never met a knot you couldn't manage to untangle."

I wrested my body around until my wrists touched his own. Sitting back-to-back with him, I commanded, "Now. Try."

Minutes later, I was able to wriggle my left hand free, then my right. I rubbed them vigorously, then turned to the task of undoing the knots that restrained him.

I tugged and pulled, trying to loosen them. "Tell me what happened. You and Helen Bell had left, I thought. . . ."

"Me too," he said bitterly. "I took her out the stage door and through the alley. But he was waiting for me there, just like he knew I was coming. He had a gun, so he forced us back inside. He watched as Molly tied me up in her dressing room. I don't know where he took Helen."

"I've got a good guess," I said grimly.

I shook the rope to the floor. "There. Your arms are free."

He gingerly stretched first one, then the other, around to his front.

"Do you want me to do the one on your legs?"

"No. I'm faster."

When he removed the rope, I took it from him and shoved it into my pocket—for the simple reason that it might come in handy.

We were up the stairs in a flash, grabbing a small crowbar

and a hammer along the way. Molly had taken my Smith & Wesson from me earlier, when I was tied up, so she and Jack were armed with at least two guns and probably Isador's knife. Luckily they hadn't taken the small file that I kept in my pocket. I handed it to my father.

"I daresay you're faster with a lock."

He accepted it eagerly and made short work of the flimsy contraption that secured the basement door.

We opened it slowly, careful to make no sound.

I stopped—sniffing the air deeply.

"What's that?" I whispered.

We both inhaled, deeper this time. It was the unmistakable, acrid smell of something burning. *Fire*.

"We've got to get out of here," my father said.

I glanced at my watch.

Was there a chance Mulvaney would come, despite Molly's claim to have thwarted our plans? It didn't matter. Even if Mulvaney arrived as expected, he still wouldn't be in time to save us. Or Helen . . .

"We've got to stop Jack ourselves," I said.

He reached out and grabbed my arm. "If you go out there with no weapons and no help, you'll never make it," he whispered in a panic.

"And if I don't, then Helen will die," I said.

"They're armed," he hissed.

"I'll think of something. Look," I pointed to the backstage door, "your way is clear. I'll watch to make sure you get out okay. There's a hotel halfway down the block. Get them to call in the fire. And the police, too," I added as he scampered toward the door.

There was a flash of light from the street when he first opened the door, then the night closed around him and he was gone.

The smoke was getting thicker, so I grabbed a handkerchief to put over my mouth as I made my way through the crossover to the opposite side of the stage.

Where is Louie? Have they found him, too?

Hurrying as fast as I could, I made my way to the stage-left wing—where I stopped short. Molly stood eight feet in front of me.

Any sound right now would be fatal. I grabbed the rope and tiptoed toward her—reaching out and taking her by surprise at the last moment. She cried out and slumped into me, but I caught her arms swiftly and had them tied behind her back in no time.

"Robby!" she half screamed before I was able to cover her mouth and mute her protest.

I counted on his being otherwise occupied. Had he heard her? Maybe, but would he have cared enough to interrupt his own plans? I hoped not.

I dragged her back to Helen Bell's dressing room, where I made use of several scarves I found there. One knotted her feet tightly together, quieting her kicking. Two more formed a more permanent gag to stop her from calling out to her accomplice. And while I doubted she had my father's skill for untying a knot, I used an additional scarf to secure her to the chair.

She thrashed about wildly, which only made the knots tighter.

"The police will be here shortly," I said as I closed the door behind her—and prayed I was right.

I made my way back to the stage, knowing it was likely that I no longer had the advantage of surprise.

It was ablaze in light—a series of torches from some past production, each burning brightly, created a semicircular backdrop.

In the middle of the stage was a chaise longue covered with blankets to resemble a bed. Helen Bell sat on it, hands and feet bound with long scarves.

Stretched out at her feet lay a man. With a sharp intake of breath, I recognized Louie.

The last person who might have helped me tonight.

Helen wriggled violently to protest her restraints, but Louie lay still. Was he merely unconscious—or already dead?

Jack's back was toward me as he worked over some kind of costume, but he sensed my presence and spoke.

"Detective, we've been expecting you." He slowly turned to face me, holding a blazing torch in one hand, my own Smith & Wesson in the other.

A maniacal grin crossed his face and he made a mock bow in greeting.

"You're just in time for the grand finale."

CHAPTER 34

Onstage at the Lyceum Theater

"We're picking up at the end of act five. *Othello*, of course." He turned and kicked at Louie's limp body. "Unfortunately, we had to make a slight change in the script. Normally the African moor is the last to die, after he murders Desdemona." Jack gestured toward Helen, quaking on the makeshift bed. "But tonight, as you can see, he died first. Ah well," he said, brandishing his torch, "I've always been flexible."

He put the torch in a stand and marched across the stage toward me. "Tonight I'm the director. Who shall you play? Iago, perhaps? But I'm not sure you covet our leading lady sufficiently. Perhaps you ought to look at her to appreciate her better. She's beautiful tonight, no?"

He drew close and threw his right arm around me. His left hand still carried the gun.

I convulsed at his touch—though from fear, repulsion, or both, I did not know.

He didn't notice, but nudged me forward onstage. "I'm afraid I have you to blame for her lack of cooperation. Normally my leading ladies enjoy working with me. They are anxious to play their little roles. But tonight," he made a mock frown, "you seem to have said something to put my star in a sour mood. Perhaps now you can cheer her on, encourage her to play."

My mouth was dry when I responded. "Don't worry, Miss Bell."

Jack flopped into the chair opposite us, convulsed in laughter. "Yes, Miss Bell, no need to worry. The great detective here has it all under control."

He began twirling my Smith & Wesson, spinning it on his right forefinger.

Helen Bell whimpered in fright.

"You put together quite a fine plan, Detective. I was impressed, let me tell you."

"You've got to give this up, Jack. Or—should I call you Robert?" I cocked my head to the left. "Unless you prefer 'Charlie'?"

"Jack, of course. Name I picked myself. Jack-Be-Nimble, Jack-Be-Quick. Jack-and-the-Beanstalk. Jack and Jill went up the hill. Jack Sprat could eat no fat and his wife could eat no lean." He leaned forward and spoke in a confidential whisper. "It's a popular name, you see. All the children love it."

It was all a game to him. Only another sign that he was raving mad. How was I supposed to talk with someone like this?

More important, how was I going to retrieve my gun from him? I would have fought him then, except for the gun.

I had to buy time until my father could bring help.

I went with the first thing that popped into my head. "If Jack is such a fine name, why did you tell Miss Bell that your name was Charlie?"

"Simple logic." He sprang out of the chair and circled behind Helen Bell. "She might have told her friends all about me," he waved his hands, then leaned down low, "even told them my name. They might have remembered that she was stepping out with a theater critic from *The New York Times*. And then," he made a mock sigh, "policemen like you would have wanted to talk with me after she turned up dead."

"She doesn't have to die," I said calmly.

"What?" He staggered back as if in shock. "Of *course* she has to die. Desdemona *always* has to die. It's her fate. The great bard has decreed it."

"Helen is not Desdemona," I said, trying again. "You can end all this now. Just put down the gun and walk away."

Helen Bell began to cry, which prompted Jack to move closer to her. His long fingers stretched out and caressed her head. "Don't cry, my love. Desdemona never cries. She thinks only of her love for the man who must kill her. Who must preserve her honor . . ."

She began to shake.

Jack grabbed one of his torches and began to light an area of the stage I hadn't even realized was part of the scene.

"What I can't figure out is how you managed it all," I said, aware that I needed to keep him talking.

He turned back to me, cocked his head. "Because I am Pygmalion, Detective. I take what is unfinished, imperfect—and create beauty."

"You killed them all without leaving a single mark. The coroner has never seen anything like it," I said. "How?"

He pulled a chair toward me, sat down, folded his arms, and regarded me soberly. "It's a God-given gift." Seeing that I was taken aback, he continued. "And the ideas themselves, Detective, came from the bard. I saw how the actor strangled his victim in a production of *Othello* when I was young. It was beautiful. And later, I realized I'd been blessed with the touch. The magic touch required to take a life," he waved his hands, "and yet leave no sign."

The man was a raving lunatic.

I swallowed hard, and said only, "You nearly managed to frame another man."

He half danced across the stage toward Helen Bell. "Ever the detective, aren't you? Focused only on these mundane details. You bore me." He yawned.

He reached out to caress Helen's head once again, ignoring her trembling. "It was fortuitous, of course, when I was assigned to help Frank Riley report on the murders." He turned away, clapped his hands together once. "Ha! Poor Frank probably believes I've got the makings of a first-rate crime reporter now, with all the evidence I managed to gather and send his way."

"But even before that, you'd laid the groundwork to frame Timothy Poe."

He gave me an odd look. "Actually, I didn't even know Poe was a suspect until the professor helping you told us. It gave me an idea. You see, I don't mind telling you I was a bit nervous," he said in a confidential whisper. "After all, I was being thrust into an investigation—about me. But then it occurred to me: I'd been given a unique opportunity. All I had to do was find a better suspect and serve him up."

He circled the stage again, his voice taking on a scornful tone. "Poe was too easy, actually. Your police captain already suspected Poe because of his association with *Pygmalion*. Good fortune was looking out for me there. And then, when I followed him one day and learned his secret, why," he paused, his lips spreading into a wide grin, "I saw he was the perfect scapegoat. He would be convicted of my crimes based on his reputation alone."

"But you did more than just make use of the fact he has an African male lover. You framed him with fingerprints," I said, pushing him to keep talking. "You planted hypodermic needles in his apartment."

He looked pleased. "I don't know what I'd do without Molly. That was her idea; and she followed through and orchestrated all of it. She even figured out how to position the syringe behind Miss Billings so it would discharge its contents when someone tried to remove it."

"But she's an actress," I said, puzzled. "How did she learn to pull off something like that?"

"'My dear old papa,'" he sang out loud, laughing across the stage. Then he stopped and turned. "Do you know the song? Though in this case, it should be *your* dear papa, Detective. He taught her everything he knew."

So she had seduced my father, not the other way around. But I couldn't imagine why. . . .

As though he had read my thoughts, he said, "I've really no idea why she targeted him, except that she thought he had skills and connections she could use."

My father had mistakenly thought she wanted to bring him some happiness in his final days. It was shocking—and yet it made sense. She had ascertained the areas where her skills—and Jack's—would prove lacking. My father had suited her purposes.

Just like the women she encouraged Jack to kill.

Jack continued to ramble on, but I focused instead on how I might tackle him and retrieve my gun—without endangering Helen Bell.

If only he would come closer to me.

He leaned over and grabbed the silk scarves that lay near the blue letter onstage.

"It is time," he announced. Waving the Smith & Wesson, he indicated for me to step toward the chair.

Why doesn't anyone come to help? What is taking my father so long?

I had one final surprise that might give us a little more time.

"Maybe your leading lady would like more jewelry," I said as I pulled Francine Vandergriff's diamond-and-sapphire ring out of my pocket and held it high. The diamonds glittered brilliantly in the light of the flickering torches.

He turned, eyes widening. The instant he recognized it, he crossed the stage and seized my wrist. "Where did you get this?" he snarled.

I leveled my gaze at him. "Right where you left it."

He wrenched it from my hand, but then caressed it in his own. "My beautiful Francine," he whispered. He placed it at the midpoint of his smallest finger, and a wild grin spread over his face. "You're actually right. It's better to have such baubles to remember those we loved. No need to keep a fine artifact like this buried in the ground, literally on the hand of one who can no longer appreciate it. Now, come sit."

The man was a loose cannon. I had played my last card; the ring had momentarily distracted him, but now he appeared to have remembered his plan. I took a seat, struggling to control my fear.

"I'll stay here. But let Miss Bell go."

He took one of the scarves and let it dangle near my head. "How chivalrous of you, Detective. But I require a lady for my purposes."

"According to Molly, you want to hurt Charles Frohman. It strikes me that there are better ways than injuring innocent women who have nothing to do with him."

"Nothing? Did you say nothing?" He wheeled around and turned to face me. "They have *everything* to do with him. Whores to the success he promises. False promises leading to ruin—that was all he ever gave us. Me. My mother. Molly."

"So why not kill him? What did these women ever do to you?"

With a savage voice, Jack replied, "He ought to feel the same pain I felt watching the dreams I loved die. Because to-night, I destroy his reputation once and for all."

He turned and grabbed a large jug filled with a liquid that sloshed as he carried it close to the chaise longue. "This," he said, looking all around him, "should've been my birthright. My legacy." He splashed some of the liquid toward one of the torches. It must have contained alcohol, for it made the torch blaze hotter and higher, igniting the wood scenery behind it.

Jack fanned the flames, laughing, before turning to the next torch. He repeated the same action as before, and, with a deliberateness that chilled me, he turned and doused Helen Bell with the same liquid.

He reached for his torch.

I dove for Helen, grabbing her feet and yanking her off the chaise longue, out of his grip.

He charged toward me, pointing the Smith & Wesson directly at my head. I managed to shove Helen behind me; with feet and hands still bound, she could not move of her own accord.

"Desdemona doesn't burn," I said.

Jack stared at me, blinking in astonishment. "You're right," he finally said. He threw one arm out wide. "This shall be her funeral pyre, but first she ought to die according to script."

Come closer. Come closer.

I leaned back on the floor, pushing my back against Helen, prepared to kick him the moment he came near.

But he stepped back and leveled the gun at me. "You, on the other hand . . ."

No . . . no . . . I fought rising panic as I realized what he meant to do. I looked around wildly, but there were no good options.

If I moved, I exposed Helen to his shot.

If I stayed in position, I died.

It was hopeless either way.

The shots took forever to come—first one deafening crack, followed immediately by another. I prepared myself for the searing pain and blackness that would end it all.

Instead, Jack cried out and fell forward, hard, grasping at his side. He dropped the Smith & Wesson.

I lunged for it, grabbed it tightly.

But he wasn't down.

And in a matter of seconds, he had a second gun in hand.

Louie's gun. Of course.

I had no choice. I pushed Helen Bell to my left—hard. I winced, hearing her shriek in pain as she hit part of the wooden scenery. But at least she was out of the line of fire.

Who had shot Jack? I looked around the theater before I leveled my gun at him.

He looked back at me and laughed. "Interesting situation we got here, isn't it?" He pointed his own gun at me. "Who shoots whom first?" Another laugh. "Bang."

Then his eyes changed and I knew he would shoot now. I had to take my shot.

But a dark figure rose behind him, knocking him to the ground.

"No!" he cried out.

"No!" I echoed loudly, though the word seemed to come from somewhere else.

And a single gunshot sounded.

My father had tackled him. My father—who was supposed to have left the theater for safety. He should not have come back.

Now, he rolled over, clutching his gut, and I realized that he was badly hit.

He lay helpless and bleeding while Jack continued, out of control.

Jack reached for the jug of alcohol and spilled it around my father. Next, he began sloshing it wildly over everything. I turned my face away as the liquid landed on me, narrowly avoiding my eyes.

"Stop!" I commanded, my gun pointed directly at him. I would take the shot if he gave me no choice.

"Police!" The word came from the back of the theater.

Jack stood up, stooped in pain, but able to walk.

He was going for the torches. He meant to light up the whole place.

"I said police! Halt!" I recognized Mulvaney's voice.

But Mulvaney was too far away.

Jack laughed—a fiendish laugh as he reached out with two hands toward the nearby torches.

We were covered in the alcohol. My father, Miss Bell, and I—we would all die a fiery death unless I did something.

With a deep breath and something that might have been a prayer, I took the shot.

Then I watched him fall to his knees, just shy of the torches—and saw the dark stain spread over his chest.

He fell to the floor, but managed to heave himself backward into one of the flaming torches.

As it toppled over, igniting an explosion of fire, I dropped my gun, grabbed Helen and my father, and pulled both of them off the stage seconds before the flames would have enveloped us.

"Are you all right?" I asked him.

But the moment I looked at his ashen face—even before I noticed the gaping wound in his chest—I knew the answer was no. He'd already lost way too much blood. Jack's shot must have hit its mark.

I reached behind me and made short work of Helen Bell's restraints. "Are *you* okay?" I asked her.

She nodded mutely.

Mulvaney was at my side, and I was conscious of several officers surrounding us.

The fire was burning out of control, the heat terrific.

"Help me." I started to pull my father down the aisle, closer to the door. My right arm was throbbing in pain. There was no way I could lift him, so I continued to drag him away from the heat and the fire until two police officers took him from me, gently lifting him and carrying him out of the building.

Mulvaney was behind me, helping Miss Bell.

I gave him a weary glance. "There's a woman in the dressing room backstage, too. Someone should get her—and place her under immediate arrest."

Mulvaney's eyes were sorrowful when they met my own.

"Schneider, Arnow," he called out. "Get your men to evacuate the dressing rooms backstage. A female suspect is secure back there."

I almost mentioned the two bodies onstage, but as I looked back at the raging fire, I realized it was too late. As Jack had planned, the stage had become a funeral pyre—but not for Miss Bell. Instead, for Louie, dead by Jack's hand. And Jack himself, killed by my own.

In the street, passersby swarmed around my father and me.

"I've imagined my own death countless times," he said in large, gasping breaths. "But never like this."

I placed more pressure on his chest wound, attempting to stem the massive flow of blood. "Don't give up yet," I warned.

"It's all right, Simon." He smiled weakly. "Your mother would be proud." His breaths were ragged. "I'm going out aces-up. It was my last hand . . . and I played a good turn."

And so he had. He'd saved two lives tonight—Helen's as well as my own.

And so I held him tightly until his ragged breaths stopped

altogether, and Mulvaney's hands gently pried me away. Other men hoisted his body up onto a stretcher and into the coroner's wagon, taking him to places I would not follow.

Watching him go, I felt emptiness no longer. Instead, I was conscious of a profound sadness for what was lost—which was really the promise of everything that might have been.

Sunday
April 1, 1906

CHAPTER 35

Dobson, New York

"It's a grand sight, isn't it?" Mulvaney's voice boomed from behind me. "Spectacular, in fact."

I gazed out over the Hudson River, leaning forward against the iron railing so that the Conduit Cable Factory to our south would not obstruct my view. "You came all the way here to join me in admiring the scenery?"

"Dammit, Simon, you know I didn't." He pulled a cigarette from its tin and lit it, taking slow, deliberate puffs.

"It's hard enough to admit I was wrong . . . or to apologize, say that I'm sorry," he finally said. "It's harder still to know that I made a terrible mistake. And that my mistake caused the death of your father."

I turned to Mulvaney. His eyes were puffy circles with dark bags underneath. And it was the first time I'd seen him light a

cigarette in more than a year. "Only one person killed my father: the man who shot the gun. Jack Bogarty. Or Robert Coby.
Or whoever he was in the end."

Mulvaney nodded. "It's what we say in order to live with
ourselves: blame it on the bad guy. But it's not always true.
We make mistakes, too. And they have consequences. . . ."
His voice choked up.

"I'm not minimizing the consequences." I steadied my gaze
when I looked at him. "But in this case, it was always going to
be Jack's fault. And the fault of those who had the ability to
stop him, like Molly."

He took several rapid puffs from his cigarette, then tossed it
into the river. "I'm sorry, Simon. I should have listened to you.
Or at least heard you out."

"I expect you to remember that, next time," I said with better humor. "Let's walk." I pointed toward the dirt path that followed the river.

"Has Poe been released?" I asked after we had continued
for several minutes.

"I oversaw his release myself, Friday night. I think he's left
for Europe, already. Can't blame him." Mulvaney hung his head
low. "I feel awful about it, but there's nothing I can do. The fact
is, he'll never work here again."

"Perhaps he'll be happier. People are more tolerant on the
continent. Or so I hear," I said.

"Molly Hansen took Poe's place in the Tombs. Your professor has been by several times to talk with her," Mulvaney said.
"I think he fancies her to be his next research subject—assuming
she isn't given the death sentence after her trial."

But she wouldn't be executed—at least, not if Alistair and

his connections were helping her. I didn't mind; I had no death wish for Molly Hansen, so long as she remained in jail, unable to harm anyone else.

"So you have all the evidence you need?" I asked.

Mulvaney whistled. "You should have seen the mother-lode of evidence we found in Bogarty's apartment. The man was addicted to his journal; he wrote *everything* down. In addition to the eyewitnesses from Friday night, there's plenty to implicate Molly as well."

We continued walking, watching the ferryboats, barges, and sailboats pass up and down the river. A peaceful April afternoon.

"Was there any truth to Jack's claim that Frohman was actually his father?"

"Not that we can find," Mulvaney said. "Who knows? It's not as though Frohman would acknowledge it now, absent any proof to force his hand."

"How is Detective Marwin doing?" I asked.

"Better," Mulvaney replied. "They were eventually able to move him to a hospital; a few days ago, he went home."

He shot me a sideways look. "He's not coming back to the department, though. It means there's an open spot, if you want it." More humbly, he added, "I'd be honored to have you. And the top brass authorized a starting bonus—designed to cover what you spent on labor for hire and suffered in lost salary."

I nodded, but said nothing.

He stopped short. "Speaking of that labor, I meant to tell you first thing—one of the men helping you, Isador, is going to make a full recovery. He was knocked unconscious Friday night, not killed."

I looked at him sharply. "But I checked. He had no pulse."

Mulvaney chuckled before saying good-naturedly, "I guess miracles can happen, Ziele. Or—given the circumstances that night—maybe you just didn't give it enough time."

Either way, I was glad to hear some positive news come out of that awful night.

"There's one more thing, Ziele," Mulvaney added, his voice sober. "There's going to be an article in *The Times* tomorrow. I spoke with Ira Salzburg—and though they're slightly embarrassed, they're going to use it. It will sell them a lot of papers."

I raised an eyebrow. "What is it?"

"They're going to run a story by Jack Bogarty. Sort of an 'in his own words' feature."

"But how?" I was dumbfounded.

"He wrote the article Friday, before the premiere. It's an interview with the killer. A farce is what it is, but it'll run all the same. No one else had the inside scoop."

No one except us.

Sunday
May 13, 1906

CHAPTER 36

Six weeks later
Woodlawn Cemetery, Bronx, New York

I stood quietly under the silver linden tree at Woodlawn Cemetery, looking down upon my father's grave.

The coroner's office had taken several weeks to release his body, due to the ongoing murder investigation. But now, finally, he lay at peace in the ground.

There'd been no funeral, for who would have grieved for him but me?

Not my mother, who was in the ground herself—at a distance several plots over, for she would have objected to spending eternity by his side.

Certainly not my sister. I had finally located her in Milwaukee and sent a cable with news of his death. Her reply had been one of polite words, nothing more.

And not Molly, who was imprisoned at Auburn prison for

life, having avoided the electric chair thanks to Alistair's expert legal maneuvering. Mulvaney had been right: Alistair planned to interview her as part of his research into the criminal mind.

So it was only me.

He was out of my life—forever, this time. And I had nothing to say.

A priest who'd just finished a funeral nearby noticed, came over, and offered his help. He was a young man, lanky and awkward, no doubt fresh from the seminary.

I smiled my thanks. "But he wasn't Catholic."

"It's all right," he said, adding in a conspiratorial voice, "I know others disagree—but I believe God's mercy knows no denomination."

And so I'd accepted—feeling guilty because I had no words of my own.

My father wouldn't have cared. "Funerals are for the living," he'd always said. "The dead pay no mind."

That meant this funeral was for me, and so I let the priest's words wash over me. They were standard prayers, only half familiar to me from other funerals I'd attended.

Words only. What gave them meaning was the priest's kindness in saying them.

He came to his last prayer, intoning the words I knew to be final.

"We therefore commit his body to the ground; earth to earth, ashes to ashes, dust to dust; in the sure and certain hope of the Resurrection to eternal life."

"I'm sorry for your troubles, my friend," he said, placing a warm hand on my shoulder.

Then he was gone.

I looked down at the freshly dug earth below me, whispered a goodbye, and walked once more past the linden tree and down the hill to the cemetery entrance.

There, waiting for me next to Alistair's Ford Model B motorcar, were two figures in black. They'd respected my wish to go to the grave site alone. But Alistair and Isabella had insisted on waiting nearby. "No one should bury a father alone," they had said.

I rejoined them, noticing for the first time that Isabella held a small package—a book perhaps—in a brown paper wrapper.

"We weren't sure whether to give you this," Isabella added nervously.

"What is it?"

"A condolence card and gift from Mrs. Vandergriff," she said automatically. "It's kindly meant, but . . ." She trailed off awkwardly.

"She gave it to me when I returned her daughter's ring. She had read about your father's passing, and . . ." Alistair explained. But he likewise broke off, refusing to finish what he had wanted to say.

Shaking my head at their reticence, I took the parcel from Isabella and ripped it open.

A Prayer for Francine. A Volume of Poems and Verses, by Robert A. Coby.

"Why?" was all I could manage.

"Mrs. Vandergriff has read the papers," Alistair said, "but she remains in denial. She simply cannot accept that Robert Coby was her daughter's killer. So she has published his poetry at her own expense. I might add, it's being received with great critical acclaim. It's spawning all kinds of wild speculation about Jack Bogarty's true identity. No one believes he and Robert Coby were one and the same."

I stared in disgust at the bound book of verse in my hand. "Why not?"

He gave me a wry look. "Because no one can believe a vicious killer—a madman—could have composed verses of such beauty and style."

Jack's body had been burned beyond recognition in the fire at the Lyceum and eventually buried in Potter's Field. His aunt had refused to claim his body; she maintained that it was a case of mistaken identity, and that her nephew Robert was still alive, perhaps gone fishing on some distant trawler boat. Even though the bones of three female victims—including Francine Vandergriff—had been found in the woods adjacent to the Layton property.

"I suppose there's nothing that will convince the skeptics otherwise."

"No. What some cannot understand is that the potential for greatness—or evil—exists in all of us," he said with a shrug. "In Jack's case, he inclined to both."

Isabella's expression was distant and thoughtful. "It reminds me of the Egyptian legend of the lotus flower," she said. "Its grotesque roots thrive in muddy swampland, yet when it blooms above water once a day, it is among the most exquisite and beautiful of all plants. You would think such ugliness and loveliness couldn't coexist within the same plant—but they do."

"If you were able to read these poems without knowing their author, you'd probably enjoy them," Alistair added. "They're quite good."

"But I'll never be able to do that," I said, and meant it. I'd never be able to appreciate anything associated with a man who had done so much evil. The same man I had killed by my own hand.

I returned the book to its wrapper and handed it to Alistair. "For your research?"

He beamed. "Now there's an idea, Ziele. A capital idea."

Alistair approached the hand crank to restart his automobile. Now that it was springtime, he was enjoying driving it once again.

"So what's it to be this evening?" he called out. "Home to Dobson? Or will you join us in the city?"

I glanced at Isabella, her brown eyes hopeful as she looked up at me.

"Join us," she said softly. "It's not a time to be alone."

I gazed back toward the crest of the hill behind us, where my father lay at rest. Whatever else might be said of him, he had always been a risk taker. Always striving for something better. I liked to think that was why, after a lifetime of failings, he had chosen a hero's death.

"You know," I said, taking Isabella's hand and helping her into the automobile, "I heard there's a great new Italian place on Forty-ninth Street. Maybe we could try it."

And so we made our way south through the Bronx, past rising buildings and vacant farmland and the new factories that had sprung up near the rail lines. The Bronx, like the city, was growing rapidly—and with the planned subway expansion north, that trend was sure to continue.

We finally crossed into Manhattan. I looked out the open window, noting that my surroundings had become grimy, filled with noisy crowds on the sidewalks: men in derby hats and women in white summer dresses, all enjoying this warm spring night. And in the distance, the darkened city skyline rose into the clouds, illuminated by a vast and brilliant red sunset that cast ribbons of purple, orange, and pink throughout the evening sky.

I found myself thinking of the violence and corruption and senseless deaths that I'd encountered. I'd once wanted nothing more than to escape it all. Now, I wasn't so sure.

I looked down at Isabella beside me and thought of possibilities unexplored. There was something about the city that called to me, beckoning me despite all better judgment.

Perhaps I was my father's son, after all.

AUTHOR'S NOTE

For as long as I can remember, I've been fascinated by a particular type of murderer: the kind who writes about his crimes. He is present throughout history—from Jack the Ripper (who wrote to the newspapers) and Albert Fish (who wrote to his victim's mother) to modern examples such as BTK and the Unabomber. My villain in this book draws loosely upon yet another example: Jack Unterweger, who was convicted of murdering his first girlfriend, yet went on in prison to write a memoir that earned him great critical acclaim and secured his parole. His supporters argued that his writing was itself evidence of his reform, for surely no one who wrote so beautifully could kill so viciously. He became the toast of the Austrian literary elite, writing poetry and even a novel, but it was not enough to quell his drive to kill. Still, it diverted suspicion away from him for the better part of a decade as he continued to murder prostitutes. To learn more about him, see *Entering Hades: The Double Life of a Serial Killer* by John Leake.

A historical figure who appears in the book, Charles Frohman, was a theater magnate who wielded tremendous influence in the early twentieth century before dying aboard the *Lusitania* in World War I. In real life, he was neither a murder suspect nor the father of an illegitimate child, but he was known for his remarkable ability to develop and manage theater talent. Nevertheless, he was a controversial figure, and his detractors repeatedly argued that he created a monopoly that harmed the theater. To read more about him, see *Charles Frohman: Manager and Man* by Isaac Frederick Marcosson and Daniel Frohman.

For my understanding of how cyanide poisoning was treated at the turn of the twentieth century, no source was more helpful than Harold Schechter's *The Devil's Gentleman*.

Finally, a note on *Pygmalion*. In the decades leading up to 1906, the legend of Pygmalion was reinvented many times, culminating in W. S. Gilbert's *Pygmalion and Galatea*, which debuted on Broadway in 1883. It was this version that Timothy Poe would have performed. While modern audiences may be more familiar with George Bernard Shaw's version of *Pygmalion*, it did not premiere until 1916.